Keyflame

TALLULAH LUCY

Astral Owl Press

Astral Owl Press
Text copyright © 2020 by Tallulah Lucy van der Made

First edition, March 2020
ISBN-13: 978-0-620855341

This is a work of fiction. Names, characters, incidents and dialogues are used fictitiously. Any resemblance to actual people, living or dead, is coincidental.

Edited by: Nerine Dorman, Yolandie Horak, Laurie Janey
Typeset and cover design by: Covers by Tallulah

Produced in association with Skolion.

All applicable content warnings can be found at
www.tallulahlucy.com/keyflame

Sign up to the author's newsletter for extras
and to remain informed of future books
www.tallulahlucy.com/newsletter

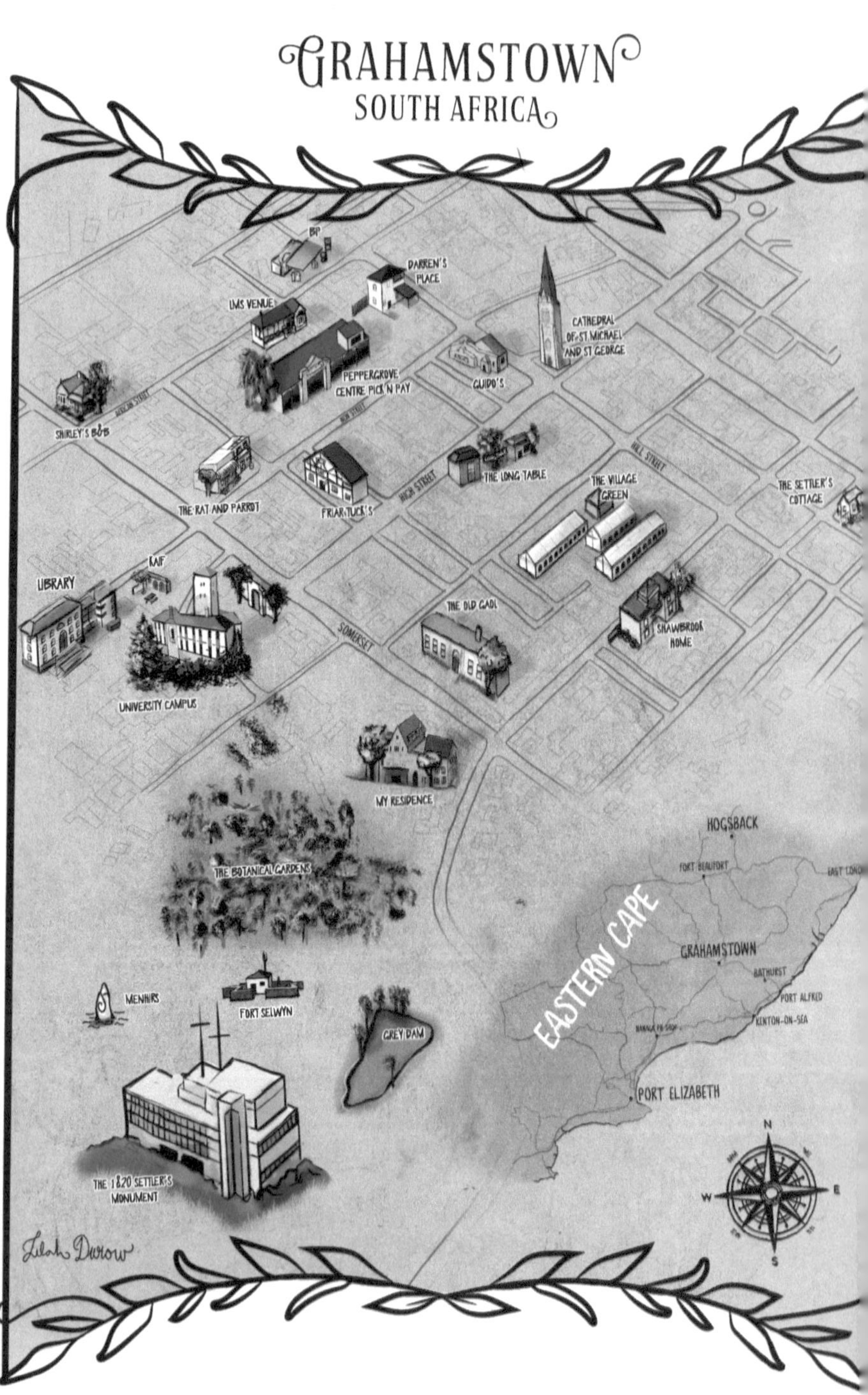

GRAHAMSTOWN
SOUTH AFRICA
BP
DARREN'S PLACE
LMS VENUE
CATHEDRAL OF ST MICHAEL AND ST GEORGE
PEPPERGROVE CENTRE PICK 'N PAY
GUIDO'S
SHIRLEY'S B&B
HILL STREET
THE LONG TABLE
THE VILLAGE GREEN
THE SETTLER'S COTTAGE
THE RAT AND PARROT
FRIAR TUCK'S
HIGH STREET
LIBRARY
KAIF
SOMERSET
THE OLD GAOL
SHAWBROOK HOME
UNIVERSITY CAMPUS
MY RESIDENCE
THE BOTANICAL GARDENS
HOGSBACK
FORT BEAUFORT
EAST LONDON
EASTERN CAPE
MENHIRS
FORT SELWYN
GREY DAM
GRAHAMSTOWN
BATHURST
PORT ALFRED
KENTON-ON-SEA
HAMLA FM SHOP
THE 1820 SETTLER'S MONUMENT
PORT ELIZABETH
N
S
E
W
Lilah Durow

For the teachers

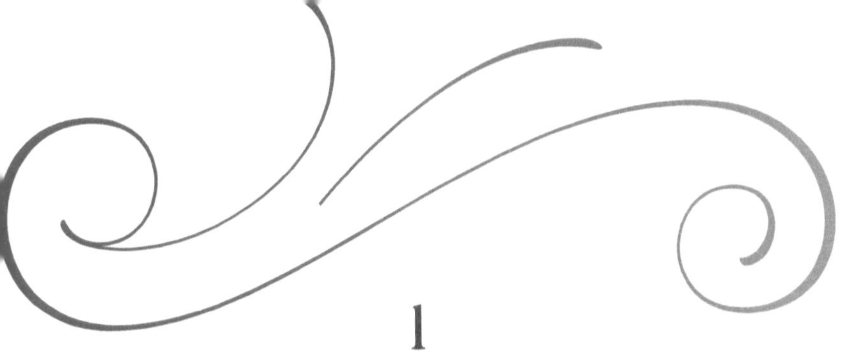

1

Two masts rise out of the mist like there's a wrecked ship in this ocean of cloud. I blink.

Dad and I have been driving for twelve hours to get to Grahamstown and I'm apparently already having visions like the scurvied sailors who first rounded the African continent. Only, my *Flying Dutchman* ghost ship is on solid land. Solid land three hours from the coast.

I blink again, but the vision does not disappear.

I need to get more sleep.

Dad taps on the windscreen. "Look, Lilah, the 1820 Settlers Monument."

Oh.

Beneath the masts, a squat face brick building emerges from the fog. The monument has featured in his stories about this place, but he never mentioned the masts.

"That's where they'll hold your graduation ceremony," he adds.

We haven't even reached my university residence yet, and he's already talking about graduation. I rest my head against the cold window and watch as my breath steams it up.

"You're going to love it here." He fills the silence, as he always does.

Of course he expects me to love it here. *He* loved it here. But I'm not like him. My father is the fearless Prosecutor Durow. Every day he faces the worst of humanity and locks them away. He's practically a superhero. Me? I'm nothing unless I have an exam paper in front of me. If my father's footsteps leave echoes that will be heard for decades to come, mine ring out as loud as bluebells. Which is to say, not at all.

"You'll be okay." Dad keeps his attention on the road. "It's beautiful. You'll see." He rattles off the names of places I know only from his tales. He always makes Grahamstown sound magical, a land of ivy-covered walls and spiral staircases, with rolling green lawns and quaint townhouses.

When I was younger, his stories enchanted me. I listened to descriptions of classes, canteen food, and midnight escapades to Grey Dam the way other kids would listen to the adventures of Robin Hood. Sometimes he'd even mention my mother. These were the only times he did. Like Guinevere or Rapunzel, my mother existed solely within his stories. Sometimes I wonder how much of his love for Grahamstown was truly for the town itself, and how much was for the fair maiden he met here.

Like most of the old myths, their story ends with a tragedy, one he will never talk about. Not even today, when we drove right past the place where it happened.

I wrench my morbid thoughts towards safer shores for both of us. "Why is the monument shaped like a ship?"

The lines around Dad's mouth pull into a frown as he realises I wasn't listening to his story at all. I tense as I wait for him to scold me for interrupting, but he doesn't. *There's a first.*

"Well, they arrived here by sea, the settlers. King George sent them off with the promise of 'farms in Africa'. Poor bastards. Didn't tell them the land was already occupied. Between famine, disease and war, it's a wonder Grahamstown is still here at all."

So much for the glittering fairy tale.

Grahamstown is now an island of a town, two hours away from the nearest city, which happens to be Port Elizabeth. That's the city where I was born, but I haven't been to this part of the country since I was a few weeks old. Home for me is Cape Town, a full day's drive away. Home has malls and cinemas and libraries.

Does Grahamstown even have a library?

My chest tightens with sudden dread.

Don't be an idiot. Of course, it has a library.

It's a university town and a cultural hub known for its annual Festival of the Arts. It will have a library for certain. Maybe even two. And museums and theatres. And anyway, I'll be home for vacation in just a couple of months.

A giant sign beside the rain-slicked road welcomes us. Below, an advert for the local supermarket boasts, "With prices so low, even the students get fed!"

I'm not ready for this.

I thought I would be. When my cousin Tammy set off to backpack through Europe last week, I confessed how desperate I was to escape from Dad's scrutiny.

He wishes to shield me from the horrors he sees in court. I can't blame him for that, but it's suffocating. I've been counting down the days until I can have a little freedom, until I can be around people my own age without having to explain my every move.

Only, now that it's finally happening, I feel ill.

We pull up outside my residence: a dull red brick building with arched windows and decorative cornices. The acceptance letter said I'd have my own room, and I'm grateful for that tiny piece of reassurance, because from the outside this looks like the sort of place where you'd find students packed in narrow bunk beds, rising at dawn to sing "It's a Hard Knock Life".

Perhaps I'm only exchanging one prison for another. The dreary sky above is hardly the most promising of welcomes.

Orientation for new students officially starts tomorrow, but the letter strongly recommended I attend a meet-and-greet tonight. Dad assured me it would be worth getting up at 4am and driving through for, but I suspect he was just excited to get to Grahamstown.

The smell of potpourri-scented wood polish hits us as we walk through a wide wooden door into the entrance hall. Rain patters against high windows, doing nothing to lift my unease. We're ushered through to a room packed with people. There are so many of them it's almost impossible to move without brushing someone's shoulder, and the air is warm and thick, like there's not enough of it.

Dad takes my elbow and guides me through the crowd towards an older woman at the other end of the room. She has brown skin and bright, cheerful eyes. She's talking to a small group of girls my age, but she stops when she sees Dad, and her hand flies to her mouth.

"Sukwini." He gives her a smile, but it's kind of tight. Which is odd because he told me that Miss Sukwini, the warden, is an old friend. Maybe he's just nervous to see her after such a long time.

Her gaze moves immediately to me, and there's an unexpected intensity there. "This must be Lilah! My-my, you're the image of your mother, aren't you?"

I wish I knew. Dad only keeps one photograph of her, so I'm not exactly the expert.

Sukwini grasps me by the shoulders and has a good, hard look. "Don't worry about a thing. We'll take care of you here."

I feel my cheeks heating under her intense scrutiny. That doesn't sound much like freedom. It sounds like I'm being passed off to another protective parent.

"You should go mingle, Lah," Dad says, but his gaze is focused on Sukwini and she nods almost imperceptibly.

Great, time to brief the new guardian on just how much of my life she should control.

I know when his suggestions are anything but, so I head into the crowd to *mingle.* As if it's that easy. As if I can just approach some stranger and strike up a conversation. I skirt the edges of the crowd, trying to find anyone who's standing alone, but all the other girls are either talking to their parents or to each other. And they're all beautiful. They're wearing trendy clothes and makeup, they're laughing and smiling, and their hair is sleek and perfect.

Here I am with wild black hair mussed by the long drive, in my baggy jersey and probably the only pair of jeans in the room that doesn't have fashionable rips. While scanning the crowd, I spot an open door a little way away. It lets in a cool breeze and invites us to spill out into a garden.

If I have to choose between rain and socialising with strangers, it's a no-brainer.

I make a strategic exit.

Clumps of dripping lavender, soaked marigolds and soft pink flowers small as butterfly wings brighten the garden's edges. Beyond that is a rolling lawn. The wet air smells like earth and floral perfume, and the rain is so light it barely tickles my skin. Through the haze of drizzle, a giant marquee dominates the green. Men on ladders are stringing up twinkling lights across the tent's entrance.

Perhaps Grahamstown is just a little bit magical after all.

I settle on a rain-damp bench, pull out my phone and thumb to the Kindle app.

Dad is none too pleased when he finds me sitting alone in the garden on my phone when I was supposed to be forging friendships that would last a lifetime. He doesn't say as much, but I'm the only child of a single parent. I can sense it in the clipped edge of his sentences, in the stiff way he moves as Miss Sukwini leads us to see my room.

The fact that I won't be sharing it is about all that can be said in its favour. It's small, dim and smells of damp.

Miss Sukwini hurries past me and opens the grey curtains above a desk on the far side. Weak light trickles in. A tree blocks most of the view of the street. I'm tensed for Dad's bluster, given his mood, but it doesn't come. He stands in the doorway nodding at each piece of furniture in turn, which doesn't take him long considering there's only a small sink, a closet, the desk, and a narrow bed. My suitcase takes up the remaining floor space.

"Well, I'll leave you to get settled, then," Dad says. "I'm going to— I think I'll go find myself a shower. See you tomorrow, Lah. You know I'm just a phone call away if you need anything."

And by anything he means if I freak out at the party and need Daddy to come rescue me. "See you tomorrow, Dad."

After he leaves with the warden, I sit down heavily on the bed.

My room. It's not quite what I pictured – there isn't even space for a bookshelf – but a small thrill runs through me because it's *mine.*

I unpack carefully, deciding on a system of sorting and then rearranging to fit the tiny cupboard. When I come to the final item in my suitcase, twilight is tinting everything blue, and it's almost time for our tour of the facilities. I might be a little late, but I want to do this first.

I withdraw the map from my case as if it's some smuggled artefact. It's not. Although, I suppose, it *was* brought here illicitly. It holds no value to anyone but me. It's not even a map of a real place. It's a drawing.

Dad could never understand why I enjoyed sketching, let alone sketching cartography of a non-existent kingdom. He encouraged me to give up this weird hobby and, as far as he knows, I did at around the same time that I gave up stuffed animals. Looking down at the map now in the strange light, it strikes me that this isn't even a very well-drawn map and that maybe my little act of rebellion is kinda pitiful.

Regardless, there's a hook above the bed and I hang the map. It matches the sombre dark wood of the room and makes it feel a tiny bit more like home.

A crowd of girls is already milling about in the common room, and Miss Sukwini is in the midst of them, answering questions I can't quite make out above the general chatter. I'm a blob of monochrome in a sea of bleach-blonde and sparkles. Tammy, who is a fan of pink and shiny, tried to convince me to bring some of her clothes so that I'd fit in. But Tammy is older than me, and different from me in almost every way. Her clothes would have been wasted sitting in that closet upstairs. Still, at this moment in time, I regret my refusal. *Smile, Lilah,* she'd coached. *Don't be so standoffish. Be approachable.* I realise my arms are folded, and my jaw is clenched. I draw a deep breath and try to relax my posture, try to force a smile.

It feels false, as if I'm a robot trying to figure out how to act human. It must be working, though, because one of the girls standing near me grins back and bounces excitedly on the balls of her feet.

Miss Sukwini introduces herself, listing facts that I already know from Dad. She's a nurse at the local hospital by day (another mark in her favour as my guardian, as far as Dad was concerned); she was born in Grahamstown, but her family now lives in the city; we mustn't hesitate to come to her if we have any problems. She takes us through the res, shows us the bathroom and the laundry room and briefs us on emergency procedure. Then we walk through the drizzle to the dining hall. It's made of brick too but adorned with large stained-glass windows and I overhear someone saying that it's a remnant of the monastery that used to occupy these grounds.

The excited girl falls into step beside me as we enter the hall. "Oh em gee, am I loving this architecture?"

Is she trying to start a conversation? If so, I wish she'd given me a better opener. I know nothing about architecture. "Uh, yes. It's nice."

She spins on the spot, her blonde hair flies about her, and her little black dress flares out. She giggles. "University!"

Again, I'm at a loss for what more to say. Luckily, she sticks out her hand. "I'm Jess."

"Lilah."

"That's a pretty name."

"Thank you."

"Where are you from?"

I hate small talk, but I'm relieved for it as we line up for our dinner trays. Jess directs the conversation effortlessly, and during our meal of warm lamb stew I learn every banal detail about her I could wish to. She's from Johannesburg, her parents want her to study accounting, but she plans to register for "something that won't bore me to death". She has brothers, but they studied elsewhere. She's attended the Arts Festival in Grahamstown before, but has never visited campus. I smile through the whole thing. I want to be friendly. I want to be liked. And it would be nice to have a friend, even if we have little in common.

On the way back to res, she wants to talk outfits for the meet-and-greet, and I am tongue-tied. I may be able to bluff my way through dinner table conversation, but when she starts talking fashion brands I am outed as a clueless nerd.

My ears are hot as I shrug and say, "I like to wear what's comfortable."

"I get it." She nods, and for a moment I think she understands. "I got this cute black dress at a thrift shop once."

Oh. She thinks it's about money. I'm not sure which is worse. I try to laugh, and make an odd grating sound instead.

"What size are you?" Jess asks.

"I, uh—" It's doubtful anything she owns will fit me; she looks as though a strong gust of wind might carry her off.

"A medium, I guess."

She startles me by reaching out and taking a clump of my hair. "Come with me. We'll sort this out."

And just like that, I'm apparently signed up for a beauty makeover. I don't know what to expect. Television show montages and movie transformations play through my mind as I follow her up to her room. It's the same size as mine but pink from top to bottom. Jess has brought her own duvet set, her own curtains and even her own fluffy rug.

"Do you have a boyfriend, Lilah?" she asks as she sweeps hangers aside in the closet.

Really? We can't talk about something that's actually interesting?

I have *never* had a boyfriend. The closest I ever came was a blind date Tammy set up for me. He spoke about World of Warcraft the whole time, and I spilled hot chocolate down my front. Needless to say, there was no second date.

I tell Jess "No", but I try to sound confident about it, as if it's a choice.

"Well, you'll have one before the end of the night." She winks at me. "I'll make it my personal mission."

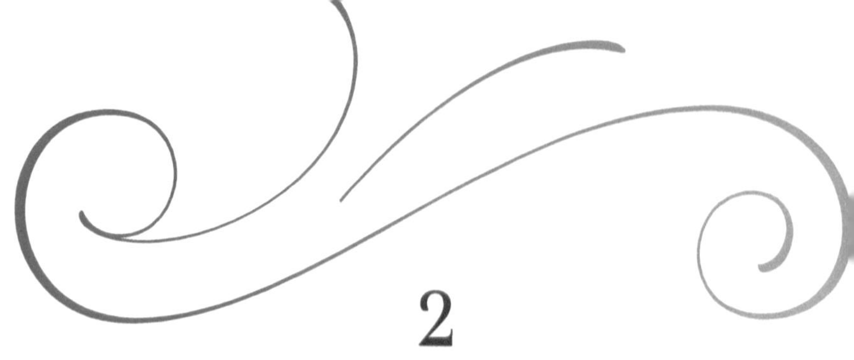

2

My eyes are itchy.

The sun has set and we're all gathered in the entrance hall, waiting to go to the party. I try to catch sight of myself in the door's reflection. Has Jess pulled off a Hollywood-style miracle? I didn't get a chance to see myself before we left her room, but I imagine I'm now a human-sized porcelain doll. She's dressed me in a white summer dress with large, black polka dots and a ribbon at the waist. She went at my hair with a ghd, so it's perfectly straight instead of its usual wavy mess. (That will last all of two seconds in the rain.)

I ball my hands to stop from scratching at my eyes, where she's fixed fake lashes. I think what she was going for was 1950s chic, but it turned out I couldn't balance in her heels, which put a damper on that plan. Jess, however, is wearing the five-inch heels you only see in the big cities. They make her tall and her black cocktail dress shimmers elegantly. If the accounting thing doesn't work out she could probably be a model.

Dad lived in one of these residences himself, and he used to tell me about the sense of calm he'd feel walking to class. I can feel that same blanket of stillness now, detectable even while the girls around me twitter and giggle. The rain has stopped, but a layer of mist has descended, making everything feel a bit dreamlike. The girls sparkle, the fairy lights twinkle, and music emanates from the big white tent where the boys from our brother res await. Warmth flickers in my chest, a remnant of the excitement I'd felt before leaving home. I can be new here, a different Lilah, one who is grown up and popular.

We gather within the tent, stand shoulder-to-shoulder as the university faculty welcome us. Then we are set free to *mingle*.

People form small groups or push past to get at the boxed wine and yellow cheese laid out for us. I scan the crowd for Jess, but she's nowhere. Around me, fellow students smile at one another, shake hands. Once more I am the oddity, standing alone in the middle of the room while everyone else is making friends.

I hover by the drinks table, even though I've never had alcohol, and technically shouldn't since I'm only seventeen. Maybe that's what's wrong with me. The age difference.

You think you're cleverer than the rest of us because your daddy pulled strings.

I didn't skip a grade because I thought I was better, I did it because *Dad* thought I was better. Pretty much the same reason I'm here now.

I reach for the wine. My hand is shaking so hard I end up spilling a good deal. It smells like vinegar, but everyone else is happily drinking. I take a tentative sip. It's disgusting. My tongue wants to shrivel up.

I'm not that much younger than them. A couple of months, maybe. How am I so different from every single person here?

I turn around to set down my glass and bump straight into one of the boys. The glass slips out of my hand. I see it almost in slow motion. As it falls, it splashes red wine all the way down his shirt.

"Watch where you're going!" he bites out, brushing at his ruined shirt.

"I'm so sorry." I stumble back in mortification and collide with someone else who curses at me.

I need to get away. Away from the beautiful, confident people.

Away from the press of strange bodies.

I don't belong here.

Before I can cause any more disruption, I turn and run.

⁓⸙⁓

I think I'm heading towards the residence and the refuge of my tiny room, but I find myself crossing a bridge I don't remember at all from the walk to the party.

My feet thunder on the wood in the too-still night. I pause. There should be music. In the tent, they were playing a cacophony of jazz and people were projecting their voices to be heard over it. My ears ring. Why can't I hear the music anymore? I whip around.

I don't know what I expected. That the tent had disappeared into the mist for a hundred years, like the mythical town of Brigadoon? But it's still there, twinkling benignly through the fog.

The silence is eerie, but I like the party far better from here. I can just make out the silhouettes of the other students, but they can't see me. The cool, damp air fills my lungs, and my rapid pulse calms.

I watch for a few more minutes, then continue along the path. I was probably just unaware of crossing the bridge earlier. Besides, I'm on campus. How lost can I possibly get?

When the path winds around a dark tennis court, I know I've discovered the answer to that question: very. There was definitely no tennis court when we walked here before, and now I've lost sight of the tent. My route has brought me between tall bushes and looming trees with limbs that look like they're waiting to snatch me.

I hug myself. What's wrong with me? I'd hoped that in an intellectual institution I might finally fit in. Yet, I'm as odd here as I was in Cape Town.

A shadow jumps ahead of me and my pulse rockets. There's a flash of light through the bushes, then a man rounds the corner, illuminating the way with his phone torch.

He stops when he sees me and gives me a polite smile. "Lost?"

He's tall, with a square face and glasses, so my immediate impression of him in the semi-darkness is that I'm talking to Clark Kent.

My fingers fist in my dress as I do my best to stand up straight and look confident.

"No, just looking around," I say.

"All right. Enjoy."

I move aside so he can pass me, and he does, but he pauses a little way away to say, "You know, it might be a better idea to explore during the day. If you continue that way, you'll end up in the Botanical Gardens."

"Oh."

"Yeah. I mean it's not particularly dangerous. Unless of course you walk straight for, uh, six hundred metres or so? Then you might fall into the dam."

"I see."

He doesn't move. "I *could* take you back to the party instead?"

"What makes you think I've come from the party?"

I can hear the grin in his voice. "Much as I'd love to call myself a brilliant detective, it's literally the only thing happening on campus tonight. And you're a little too dressed up to be sleep walking."

I smile too, despite myself. Now would be the time for a response that's both coy and charming, but my brain offers up nothing. Zip. Nada. For all those distinctions I finished school with, my brain has zero to contribute right now.

The man holds out his hand. "I'm Darren. And I'm not a creep, despite the atmosphere." He waves vaguely, encapsulating the forest and the mist. "I work for the university."

"Lilah." I take his hand. It's large and warm. "And I may be a *little* lost."

"Don't worry, this part of campus is a maze."

As we head back, Darren tells me that he's the tech on duty who was called to the rescue when the sound system crashed. Which explains why the music stopped. He doesn't really seem old enough to work for the university, and when I say so, he shrugs.

"I was a student up until recently."

"What happened?"

"I graduated."

Before I find a tactful way to ask why he's still here if he graduated, he adds, "I'm local. My parents worked for the university. Their parents worked for the university. I think their parents worked for the university too, although I can never quite recall."

"And now you're continuing the proud family tradition?"

"Something like that. Where are you from?"

I tell him about Cape Town, and he calls me a Big City Girl. He thinks I'm like Jess, and why not? I am in her clothes, wearing her makeup. I don't correct him. I can be a Big City Girl for a night.

He stops walking abruptly and I have just enough time to wonder what's wrong before he takes my wrist. "Come, City Girl. I want to show you something."

He tilts his head to the right and heads off the path into the spiky bushes. I hesitate. City Girl has been told time and time again that letting strange men guide you into dark places is not a good idea.

Then Darren smiles at me, showing perfectly straight white teeth. "Do you want to see a ghost?"

I have absolutely no desire to see a ghost, but now I'm curious. I let him pull me along until we come to a bridge, perhaps the very same one I fled over earlier. He drops my wrist and puts a finger to his lips. He creeps forward, then ducks behind one of the trees and gestures for me to join him.

This feels silly. *I* feel silly. But I follow him.

We crouch low, peeking through the branches, and as we creep forward he says, "All right, she's there. Look at the bench. Do you see the grey nun?"

A large jacaranda obscures some of the bridge, with a bench set against it. On the bench, sitting serenely, there… I blink. There appears to be an old woman. My neck prickles, and a chill rushes through me.

"She used to be a nun," Darren says. "She waits there every night."

I recall that thing about how this part of campus used to be a monastery. I can hardly breathe, but I manage to ask, "Why?"

"No one knows."

I stare at the lonely figure. It's impossible to see any details. She's merely a shadow in the fog, waiting for all eternity. Alone.

What could she possibly have done in life to deserve such an awful fate in death?

I swallow down emotion, but Darren must mistake it for fear because he laughs. He's grinning, and the expression is too happy, too easy for someone who's in the presence of something so supernatural and so sad.

"Come, I want you to meet her." He grabs my arm again and pulls me up.

What? "No, wait!"

"Don't be scared." He tugs me forward. I dig my heels into the ground, but he's strong and I stumble after him. The figure doesn't disappear as we grow nearer. If anything, it becomes more solid.

Yes, definitely *more solid*.

It's no ghost. It's no figure at all. Our proximity reveals her to be nothing but a knobbly, bulging feature of the jacaranda's trunk.

Darren is still laughing at me. My cheeks burn, but I can't stop staring at the trunk.

Am I disappointed that there was no ghost?

My lack of amusement quietens Darren.

"Sorry," he says sheepishly.

"Don't be. It was fun." That's not really what I want to say.

What I mean to say is that I appreciate him weaving the story for me and giving me this experience, even if he aimed to frighten me.

"There are real ghosts around Grahamstown, apparently," he says as we walk back to the party. "If you're here for Fest, there's a tour. The guy does it every year."

"I'll remember that." I don't say that I have no intention of staying in Grahamstown during the winter break.

The glowing tent emerges from the mist, and now I can hear people singing – the students attempting to make their own music.

Darren throws me a tortured look. "I think I'm needed."

As he hurries towards the caterwauling, Jess bounds up to me. "Lilah, where have you been?"

She looks so legitimately concerned that I can't accuse her of abandoning me. She nudges my rib and tilts her chin. "Who's the hottie?"

"He's just a… person."

"I told you we'd find you a boyfriend."

A blond-haired boy stumbles up to us waving two glasses of white wine, only he's swished them around so much that there's hardly anything left in them. Jess accepts one. "You're a doll."

The boy beams at her attention, then spots me. "Hi, I'm Mi… Michael." He blinks slowly, as if struggling to focus, and hands me the other glass.

"No thanks, I don't drink."

They both look at me as if I've lost my mind. Jess opens her mouth, but the speakers crackle and her protests are drowned out by Ed Sheeran's latest chart topper. So she takes Michael's hand and calls to me, instead, "I wonder if he can dance?"

The way he's struggling to stand steady, I doubt it. "There's only one way to find out…"

She gives an exaggerated wink – her intense eyeliner makes her look like a cartoon character – and drags him towards the tent, leaving me with the wine.

I could try it. It might taste better than the red. I swirl it around in the glass, sniff it. *Ugh. Pickle juice.*

"I wouldn't bother." Darren arrives at my side again.

I lower the glass with some relief.

"If you want real wine, you should come back to my place. I have a stack of it. I used to be part of Winesoc."

Did he just invite me home? Me? Lilah? "Wine *sock*?"

He chuckles. "The wine-tasting society. I suppose you haven't had a chance to suss out the societies yet?"

I shake my head. My heart drums in my ears.

"You do realise this party is only going downhill from here?" As if to emphasise his words, someone stumbles out of the tent behind him and rushes to one of the bushes to empty the contents of their stomach. "Offer's there, if you want?"

"Offer?" My mouth's gone dry.

"Yeah." He shifts his weight. "Decent wine. I don't live far from here."

There's heat crawling up my neck. I let myself imagine accepting his offer, what else it might lead to. But I'm Cinderella, and when this makeup comes off, I'll no longer be the interesting Big City Girl. I'll be lame ol' Lilah with her anxiety, her books and her very limited experience of the big bad world.

"Thanks for the offer..."

"I sense a 'but' coming?"

"Yeah. It's my first night in town. I think I should stay near my res. You know, in case they do a roll call or something?"

He glances at the tent. "I assure you, they won't, but I understand if you'd feel more comfortable."

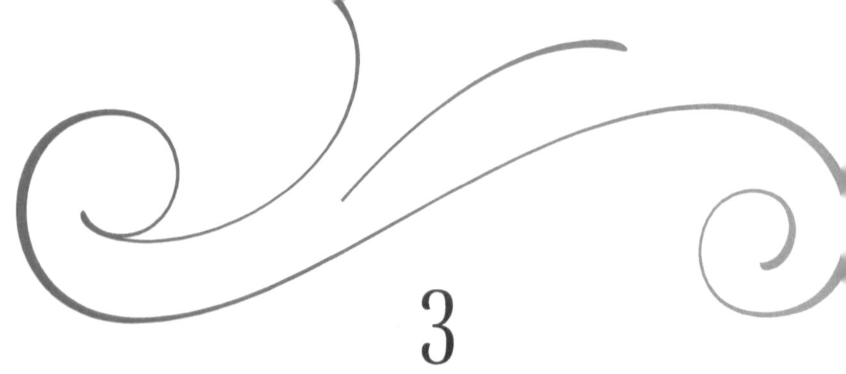

3

ape Town skies are like watercolour paintings: they're white and pink and pale baby blue. The Grahamstown sky I wake to is azure from horizon to horizon, so bright it's like someone's placed a filter over it.

The registration office buzzes with excited students and the photograph they take for my student ID card shows me with a genuine smile.

I meet Dad on campus at a cafeteria called The Kaif.

"This isn't what it used to be," he mutters, staring down at a toasted sandwich in a paper packet. "It used to be much nicer."

I think it's nice. We're sitting at a wooden table in a small bricked courtyard smattered with young acacia trees. The university buildings stretch tall and white all around us, and I can see the gigantic library just a few meters away. I'm admiring some bright yellow birds that are chirping and hopping from branch to branch above us when one flies overhead, and Dad cries out. A large dropping has landed on the shoulder of his fancy charcoal grey suit. I try desperately to suppress my laughter as he jumps up, waving his hands about in disgust.

"Oh, this is perfect! Just perfect!" He grabs a serviette and dabs at the mark, trying to get as much off as possible. He growls when his efforts prove less than effective. "Wait here. I'm going to find a bathroom."

When he's gone, I finally give in to my giggles.

"I hear it's good luck."

I turn to find a stranger at the neighbouring table smirking in amusement. He has a narrow face with angular cheekbones and honey-coloured hair that's tied back in a messy ponytail.

"Sorry?" I ask.

"Bird droppings, on your shoulder. I hear it's good luck."

"Oh."

He shrugs. "Small consolation."

His accent is unfamiliar. It's more clipped than my own, but more rounded on the vowel sounds than British. Maybe this is my first taste of the local Grahamstown accent.

"Yeah."

I doubt Dad will see it that way. He doesn't believe in luck.

The stranger gets to his feet, crumples up a paper sandwich packet and shoves it into the pocket of his long brown jacket. He nods towards the indoor section of the café. "You may want to move inside."

There are one or two tables inside, but it looks cramped. "No, I think we'll be fine. Chances of it happening again…"

"I meant because it's going to rain."

I seriously doubt that. How could rain fall from that bright blue sky? Dad's heading towards the table now with that determined march that usually means someone is going to feel very sorry for themselves soon and it won't be him.

"I think I'll take my chances out here," I tell the stranger.

"All right, but don't say I didn't warn you."

Dad starts ranting about the lack of facilities in this new Kaif before he sits down. I'm only half listening. A drop of water just landed on my hand, followed by another.

I'm still staring in wonder at it when the skies open in earnest.

The weather is erratic. Throughout the day it switches between sunshine and rain. It even storms and gets icy for about half an hour in the late afternoon.

Dad leaves as soon as the storm abates. He's fed up. So far today he's lost an expensive suit to a bird and an equally expensive pair of shoes to the rain. He's also lost his way a few times. We took a drive to find his old digs and, when we eventually did, we discovered it's now a liquor store.

"Sign of what the world's coming to," he mumbled.

I think he expected to return to his university and find everything the same. That Grahamstown *is* still here, like the Grahamstown of the 1800s is, lurking beneath moss and beneath new roads and in the people: their faces, their attitudes, their genes. But it's not the town from his stories. That place doesn't exist anymore.

After seeing him off, I return to the dim closet that is my new home and email Tammy while absently scrolling through social media feeds. Jess has posted a few pics from last night to Instagram and there's one with me. She's duck-facing at the camera so her lips look pouty and her cheekbones stand out. I look pretty bewildered, but I have to marvel at the makeup job she did on me. I *do* look like a doll, but not in a bad way. I send the pic to Tammy because I know she'll get a kick out of it.

I'm considering pulling out a pad of paper and redrawing the map that's above my bed, when someone hammers on my door. My heart is in my throat when I get up to answer. Did I forget about something important?

It's only Jess, with Michael. "We're going out. Wanna join?"

What time is it? "Aren't they serving dinner soon?"

"This isn't boarding school, Lilah. You don't have to eat that slop if you don't want to."

Going out for dinner might be nice, although I'm not sure what Grahamstown has by way of restaurants. "Uh, sure. Let me grab my things."

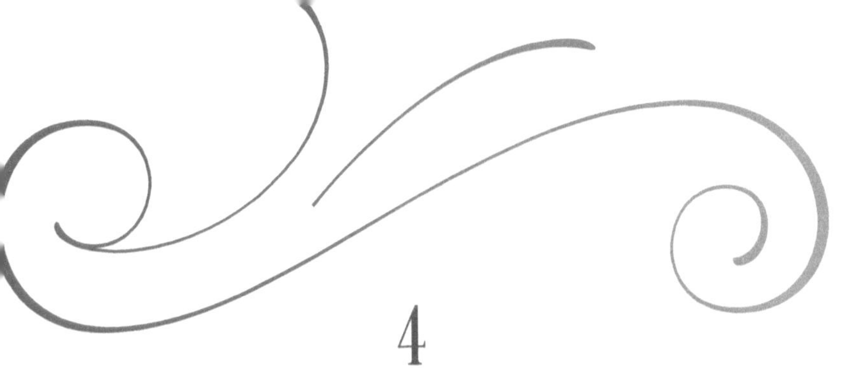

4

There's a donkey in the road.

When I was nine, I had a penpal in the States who asked me if wild animals roamed the streets of South Africa. I was so insulted I didn't reply to her. Cape Town is a bustling metropolis. On the outskirts, you may be burgled by baboons, but other than that, the only place you'll see real wild animals is on a game drive.

Except now there's a donkey meandering down the road in front of us, and Jess is squealing and pointing while Michael is snapping pics on his phone. The beast sticks its head into a garbage can, and even though Jess is cautious about approaching it, it doesn't even take notice of us when we walk past. We're far from the only people out tonight, but we're the only ones who seem to find the donkey strange. No one else so much as turns to look at it.

New Street is apparently the "happening" part of town. Michael has an older brother who went to university here, so he's our guide. He takes us past a pizzeria that already has a crowd of students milling outside, and I think we might step into the bistro opposite; it glows with inviting yellow light from beneath canopied windows. But instead, we carry on a little way down the road to a bright green building with a gilded wooden sign across the top declaring it the Rat & Parrot. Above the sign, crowds push against a balcony railing, holding glasses and bottles while shouting to each other.

Even if it weren't for that, I'd have known it was a pub the instant we stepped inside. The smell of beer and smoke hits me full in the face. The smoke is so thick I want to choke. It hangs in the air, blurring out the people who cluster around the tables. The onslaught of noise is no less repulsive. There's a game on the TV above the bar, but it might be muted for all I can hear it. Something exciting must happen as we enter, because there's a roar that rattles my eardrums. (Celebration? Despair? I can't even tell.)

It's too much for my senses. I want to get out, I want to run away again, but Jess grabs my wrist and pulls me through the press of bodies.

As soon as we're on the stairs, I can breathe again. It's slow progress, in a shambling queue of people trying to get to the second floor, but eventually we emerge at the top of the stairs, where there's a second, smaller bar. This room is less stuffy because the balcony doors are thrown open, but it's just as loud and there are no free tables.

"Jess!" I can barely make out the female voice above the ruckus. A girl rises at one of the tables and waves at us. She has dark red hair, a little black dress and bright makeup.

Jess waves back, using her whole arm, and pulls me with her through the sea of people.

The two of them embrace and exchange excited conversation I can't hear, before the girl is introduced to me as Sam, one of Jess's school friends who also decided to study in Grahamstown. There are two others at her table, a girl and a guy, and they budge up along the wooden benches to make room for us.

Before Michael has a chance to sit, Jess hands him her purse. "Would you be a darl and get us some drinks?"

He stands a little straighter as if he's going to refuse, but after a beat he says, "Sure. What do you want?"

"I'll have a vodka and Sprite."

"Lilah?" It's the first time he's used my name. I didn't even know he remembered it.

"I, um…"

"She doesn't drink," Jess says.

My stomach drops. He was there last night. If he remembers my name, he'll remember that. So it must have been for the benefit of her other friends.

"A Coke, please." My voice struggles to get out of my throat because it's so constricted with embarrassment. I have to repeat myself twice before Michael understands, and by that stage everyone at the table has definitely heard me and I catch a few raised eyebrows, and glances exchanged between them.

I look at the menu, avoid eye contact. Why is it such a big deal, anyway?

I can hardly hear the others' conversation, and what I do hear is about celebrities I'm not familiar with, or experiences they had in Joburg that I can't relate to.

By the time I've finished my Coke, it's clear no one intends to eat. Sam orders a round of shots and they toast ("To starting university!"), then Jess sends Michael off for more drinks. I don't fit in. They know it, I know it. Halfway through the second round of drinks, I'm trying to think of an excuse to leave when I catch my name over the din.

Even though no one in this town would be calling me, I follow the voice.

Darren is waving over the crowd, and he starts towards us. It takes him a while to move through the people, and that whole time I'm aware of my companions eyeing him. What would a good-looking guy like him want with a girl like me?

I'd feel more confident if I knew the answer to that question myself.

I don't wait for him to reach us. This is the excuse I needed.

Michael is now sitting on the end of the bench, fencing me in. I make a "can I get out please" gesture. He stares at me blankly.

"Can I get out?" I say aloud.

Even right next to me, he can't hear me. "What?"

"Out?" I repeat louder. "Out. Can I? Please?"

He finally gets what I'm saying when I start shifting towards him. He's drunk already. I should have realised. There's a disconnect between his mind and his limbs, and it takes a moment for him to shuffle off the bench so I can escape.

By the time I finally do, Darren is at the table, and he's looking at me with an amused expression.

He speaks but I can't hear what he says.

When I shake my head and shrug, he steps in close and leans down so that he's speaking directly into my ear. "It might have been easier to climb over."

His breath tickles my neck, and the mental image makes me giggle. I can't imagine what Jess's group would have made of that. Especially if I knocked their drinks over.

What he says next is drowned out when the room erupts into noise; someone has scored a goal or a wicket or a try. When it dies down, Darren says, "I can't even hear myself think, want to come downstairs for a bit?"

I can't imagine downstairs will be any better, but I'm emboldened by my desperate desire to be anywhere but here. I glance at Jess, worried about abandoning her, but she's moved in next to Michael and they're kissing. Definitely time for me to go.

I nod and follow Darren to the bar.

There's only one bartender and he spins a bottle with one hand and slides a glass to a customer with the other as we approach. Sweat glistens on his dark skin.

"Sibu!" Darren greets him.

"You're going to have to pour for yourself, mate," the bartender replies without looking at him.

Darren slides around the bar and reaches up for two glasses. He sets them down and gives me a smile. "You ever tried a katemba?"

Sibu chuckles. "Eish, you still drink that stuff?"

"Why do you think I'm up here? Bernie told me to piss off when I asked downstairs."

Sibu whistles and shakes his head, but he doesn't offer further comment as he continues to serve the other customers.

Darren raises his eyebrows at me. "So?"

I could tell him I don't drink, as I told the others, but I'm curious, and, well, I'm also a little worried that he'll be as put off as they were. I'm no longer doll pretty with a city sparkle to charm him. I'm just me. Boring enough as is.

Sibu laughs again at my hesitation. "Girl's got taste."

Darren pulls a bottle of wine from behind the bar. "Tell you what, you can give it a try and if you hate it, I'll finish it. Will save me another trip up here."

"Okay." That seems fair.

The wine that splashes into the glass is blood red and probably expensive. Then again, maybe not. The next thing he pours in is Coca-Cola.

"So, this here is your classic katemba, a Mozambican cocktail."

"Ay-ay-ay." Sibu shakes his head again.

The customer he's serving – an older man with a scruffy brown beard – chimes in. "Cocktail, Darren? Quit trying to impress the lady. It's an abomination. That's what it is."

"The Proteas are an abomination," he responds.

The man grimaces and mutters, "Low blow, low blow," while looking balefully up at the TV.

Darren reaches into the fridge behind him and pulls out a tall blue box that looks like a milk carton.

He winks at me. "And this is what I call localisation."

Sibu cringes. I smell pineapples as Darren fills the glasses the rest of the way up.

"You're in pineapple country now." He passes me the drink.

I have to clutch it to my chest to avoid spilling as we fight our way downstairs. It's still as loud and smoky as it was earlier. Darren can't mean to talk here? He swings open a door I didn't even see, against the wall between the stairs and the bar, and sunlight slices through the cigarette fog.

There's a garden out there: a secret garden, enclosed by high walls with a trellis dripping plants. I can hardly believe it. There are tables here too, but only three of them and they're all occupied.

"Is this the VIP area?" I ask.

"No, City Girl, you're in Grahamstown. Who would the VIPs be? Lecturers?"

I duck my chin, feeling silly, but the way he smiles at me is good-natured.

"It's the beer garden. No table service, no smoking, no TVs, open to the elements. Less appealing for the average student, which makes it perfect. Wouldn't you agree?"

Before I can answer, a dark-haired woman at one of the tables stands up. She's got a baby in a wrap snuggled against her chest. "Who's this?"

The others at the table turn to look at us. There are four of them, but they're just a blur of judgemental faces as I swallow and try to calm my racing heart.

"This is Lilah," Darren says easily. "And that is my sister, Bianca. She won our entire family's worth of charm in the genetic lottery. Isn't that right?"

The sound Bianca makes can only be described as a growl. He introduces the others. I don't catch names, but there are three men and another woman, all older than me.

Bianca excuses herself before I can sit down and one of the men – bald, with a full sleeve tattoo – leaves with her.

It's awkward sitting down with what's clearly a close-knit group of friends, but the remaining three make pleasant small talk asking about my studies and my reason for choosing Grahamstown. The girl even warns me about one of the more boring law professors and advises me to have a strong cup of coffee before his class.

They tease Darren about his katemba the way Sibu did and hold their collective breath when I finally gather the courage to try it. It's all I can do not to gag as I take the first sip. The bitter wine hits first, then the snap of sweetness from the Coke and finally the sticky acid of the pineapple. It seems to glue the dry red wine to the back of my throat. I imagine you could get a similar effect by letting a few old coins sit in water overnight.

They all laugh at what must be a very amusing expression when I swallow it down. But they're not laughing at me, they're laughing at Darren.

"Guys! I don't see what the big deal is. It's practically sangria."

But they don't appear to hear his protests.

I go get myself another cooldrink to wash it down, and when I return to the table, Darren's friends have pulled out a deck of cards and are playing poker. They offer to deal me in, but I don't even know the rules. Not that I'm willing to admit that.

Darren folds, and we spend the next hour watching them and talking. He's easy to talk to. I tell him about Dad and his most recent work as chief prosecution on the Dumi corruption case that's been in all the headlines. He doesn't really follow the news, however, and I have nothing much to add about the case as Dad makes a point of not bringing work home. We order pizza and I discover that Darren finished a degree in software engineering last year, but instead of using his degree, he works in the computer science department as a general techie. "Keeping the lights on," is how he puts it.

"Do you think you'll ever leave Grahamstown?" I ask.

"Probably. At the moment I have no reason to. I have a job, my family's here."

I imagine that after a while being a non-student in a student world begins to suck, though. Everyone around you gets younger and stupider and crazier as the years progress.

The beer garden is dark by the time the poker game ends, but fairy lights wound into the trellis above our heads twinkle and cast dappled shadows.

The winner of the game – one of the guys – gets informed that the next round of drinks is on him. He agrees, on the condition that they do shots.

Darren suggests that we go to the club across the street instead.

"Come on, one last hurrah before the start of the academic year?"

That's my cue to leave. I stand, but he snags my hand. My heart cartwheels, and I'm so glad he's not looking at me, because I'm probably scarlet. The idea gets passed around the group, but I stay quiet. Then it's decided and everyone leaves the table together.

"You coming?" Darren asks, still holding my hand.

"I should get to res…"

"You know there's no curfew, right?"

I nod and chew on my bottom lip. I'm afraid that if I tell him the truth, he'll start looking at me as if I'm a child. But the alternative is that I let him think I don't want to go with them, which isn't true. I do. The idea of clubbing is terrifying, but also thrilling. It's a new experience that Old Lilah would never have tried.

I take too long to answer. He frowns. "What is it?"

"I…" I can't find the words, so I pull out my student ID and show it to him.

It takes him a minute to see my birthday and work out what that means. I won't be permitted to enter the club because I'm not eighteen yet.

"Ah," he says. "Don't worry about that. It won't be a problem."

⁘

I'm a bundle of nerves as we stand in line outside Friar Tuck's, the local night spot. There's a heavyset bouncer at the door checking IDs. His black shirt is pulled tight over his muscles, and I shrink into myself as we draw near. But Darren greets him with a grin and a handshake and pushes me forward.

"This is Lilah. She won't be drinking. She just wants to dance."

And the big, scary bouncer lets us past without protest.

"Do you know everyone in this town?" I ask Darren.

He laughs. "Pretty much. It's a very small town."

We shuffle into the club with a crowd, and at first everything is

~28~

dark and close and loud. I thought the pub was loud, but this sound is a physical force vibrating through me, *doof doof doof doof.* Rainbow light spills from the ceiling, bounces off a disco ball to splash down onto us. Darren is painted in shades of pink and purple as he takes my arm and walks to a clear section of the dance floor. Then he's dancing with me.

I don't know what to do. I don't know how to act, how to move.

"Relax!" he shouts to me over the music.

I breathe in. The air tastes metallic. It's smoky but this is a different smoke from the bar, this is the manufactured stuff they have in theatres, and it doesn't choke my lungs the same way.

I'm intensely aware of how many people are packed in around us. Stairs lead up from the dance floor to a mezzanine bar level. People lean against the balustrade, peering down at us and I wonder if they're watching me, and if they are what they're thinking.

Darren looks at me with a soft, understanding smile. It's as if he knows exactly what I'm thinking.

He takes my hands and leans close to say into my ear, "They can't even see you through the smoke. Relax."

And I do. He's a solid, comforting presence. His grip is firm, and his body shields me from the crowds. I sway with him and we fall into a rhythm. There's something primal about the beat, something that my body knows even if my mind does not.

We grow closer as the club fills up, and we're forced into a smaller and smaller space. His hands move around my waist and my spine tingles pleasantly at the unfamiliar sensation.

I have no idea how long we dance, but it's long enough for my legs to go numb, and by that stage we're practically squeezed together. Darren smells like expensive cologne. Or maybe aftershave. I'm hardly the expert, but whatever it is it's fresh and heady. I don't want to admit that I'm getting tired. Before I have to, one of his friends finds us and says that they're leaving. Darren moves away from me, and disappointment cuts through me. He's going to leave. I'm going to go back to res and back to being my boring old self.

I don't hear what he says to his friend, but I jump when his hand slips into mine again.

"Aren't you leaving?" I ask above the music.

He smiles and says, "I'll walk you home?"

After the heat of the dance floor, I'm not prepared for the shock of cold as we step outside. Other couples are milling about, sharing cigarettes or talking. Couples. I'm walking close to Darren – close enough to touch – but I move away, at once self-conscious. Goose bumps prickle up my arms, and my breath mists in front of me. Then Darren's arm is around me and he's drawing me close. He's so very warm.

"I'd offer you my jacket, but—"

But he's not wearing one. He's wearing a plain grey shirt no thicker than my own.

"Is it always so cold at night here?" I have to force my jaw to move; my teeth want to clench against the cold. He rubs up and down my arm to warm it.

"Not always, but hey, it's Grahamstown. Weird weather is our thing."

"I thought your thing was pineapples."

"No, that's Bathurst's thing."

"Bathurst?"

"You've never been to the Giant Pineapple?"

I feel well and truly like Alice fallen down the rabbit hole. "What?"

"Roadside attraction. World famous."

"If it was world famous, I would have heard of it."

"Well I'm not sure about that. You'd never heard of a katemba, had you?"

He has a point; I'm not exactly the most worldly person.

"Word to the wise though, layers are your friend. And don't go anywhere without a raincoat."

"All right, noted. From the man who isn't wearing a jacket."

He laughs, a jolly sound as warm as his arms as he squeezes me a bit tighter.

We're not far from campus – nothing in Grahamstown is far from campus – and we soon cross onto the university grounds. It's much quieter then. The ghost of that bewitching rhythm is still humming in my ears, but otherwise everything is still. Streetlights bathe the road orange, and there's the tang of ice in the air; it tastes like dawn. What time is it? I search for the moon, because pulling out my phone seems rude.

Darren follows my gaze and misunderstands it.

"You're not used to seeing them so bright, are you?"

I don't find the moon, but I can see the entire Milky Way smeared across the sky.

In Cape Town the stars are flecks of light. This is more like a child's first encounter with glitter-glue.

"No," I breathe. What I don't say is 'there are so many of them'; what I don't voice is how small I feel right then. If I were to hold my thumb up to that sky, it would blot out a hundred million worlds.

Darren takes my hand again, and he guides me silently towards the university. We tramp over the grassy patch in front of the main administration building, cross a street, then we're back on the twisting overgrown paths where we met. Night sounds surround us – crickets, birds and the whisper of leaves. We are almost at my res and I don't want this night to end.

We come to the bridge with its not-a-ghost tree, and he tugs me onward. He's grinning now and it takes me until we're halfway across the field to realise why. For when we're standing there, where that great white tent was last night, the sky is a dome above us as crisp as the night is cold.

My knees are weak at the sight. It's us alone with the universe.

"What do you think, City Girl?"

I mumble something unintelligible, not even sure what I'm trying to say. There are no words that can adequately describe that sight. I feel like I could fall up into space.

Darren sits down on the grass and pats the ground next to him. "You're going to crick your neck like that."

I sink down beside him, still looking upward. So, I don't see him moving to wrap his arm around me again until it's there and my head is against his chest. I can hear his heartbeat. It's not as rapid as mine.

How much of my racing pulse is because of the stars, and how much is him?

Darren is charming, funny and easy to get along with. I'm not one for crushes – I was always the nerdy girl at school no one wanted, and mooning over boys seemed like an exercise in torture – but I might be developing a crush on Darren.

He's just being kind, helping the new girl feel like she fits in. There's no way someone like him is single. Even if he is, there's no way he'd want me.

Then he ducks his head and kisses me.

I'm too startled to respond. All I'm aware of is that his lips are warm and soft. The kiss is gentle, a question. It's over before my mind has accepted that it's happening.

I battle to breathe. My heart is kicking as if he'd shown me another ghost, not done something so tender.

"Sorry," he says. "It felt like one of those moments. I should have asked."

"No," I manage. "No, it's…"

His face is still close to mine. His brow is knitted with concern. There's a vague buzzing behind my ears. Do I tell him that was my first kiss? Will that just embarrass him?

My head is spinning, it's difficult to think.

It's much, much easier to simply kiss him back.

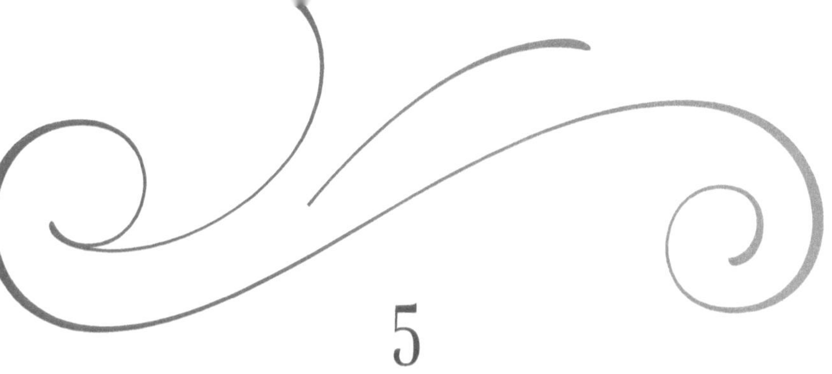

5

I find Jess in the dining hall, stirring her tea with a fork because she must have also woken up late, and they're clearly out of spoons. She has the look of someone with a bad head cold, but judging by the shots on the table when I left her I'm guessing it's less flu and more alcohol to blame.

"Saw you in Friars last night, dancing with that guy," she says, as I sit down with my tray.

The blush that heats my cheeks is incriminating. "I didn't know you were there."

"Unsurprising. You couldn't take your eyes off him."

My stomach flips. I want to tell her how we lay on the grass beneath the stars until they started to fade, alternating between staring up at them and kissing, about how warm I felt despite the night's chill, how I couldn't stop grinning when he walked me to my door and asked for my number. But I don't say anything. I want the memory to be mine, and just mine, for a time.

Jess and I spend that day and the next few going to introductory lectures. I know what I'll be majoring in – have since I was five. But the first year of the LLB degree allows for three other courses, a surprise choice I didn't know I'd get to make.

I try out Journalism, because that's what my mom majored in. Jess's boyfriend Michael is there, but he doesn't appear to notice me. When the lecturer speaks about how we'll have to interview townsfolk as part of our coursework, I know it's not for me. Sorry, Mom.

I attend some Economics lectures with Jess and decide that's even less for me. We're both drawn to Psychology. Jess follows me to English Literature and, when she sees the professor is hot, she's sold. I suspect she thinks it's going to be nothing more than a giant book club, but I don't try to dissuade her. It would be nice to have a friend to sit with.

My final elective is Politics, which Dad recommends when he phones to check in. I miss his first three calls and finally pick up while sitting on the bleachers in the university's sports hall watching Jess do try-outs for something called dance sport.

He's annoyed. "I understand that you're busy, but you know I worry."

I'm sure he's already spoken to Miss Sukwini a few times, but I choose the path of least resistance and apologise. I *have* been busy. While the days have showcased our academic choices, the nights have been packed with club and society exhibitions and Jess has dragged me to almost every one.

So far, the only one I've tried myself is archery, because I guess it seemed romantic. I now have a nasty bruise on my arm to show for it. I briefly considered signing up with the wine society so I could at least offer Darren an educated opinion on his katembas. But I don't like wine, and joining a society over a boy seems a little much.

There's a pleasant bubbly feeling in my chest when I think of Darren. I haven't seen him since *that* night. but we text a lot. He loves emojis. The way he scatters them liberally through his otherwise short messages makes him seem like an over-excited puppy. It's hardly Hemingway, but it's endearing.

I realise that I'm daydreaming and return my attention to Dad who's now warmed to the topic of my academic future. I let him go through the merits of each of the possible courses in my ear while a woman in a purple flared dress twirls in front of the prospective club members below, demonstrating the kind of dance they might one day do competitively. Her choker and smile sparkle, but what she's trying to pass off as glamour seems gaudy in the bright hall. A man in a tux joins her and music erupts as he pulls her close.

I remember Darren's body against mine in Friars and my stomach flips again.

When Dad finally ends the call, I write Darren a text that I have to read three times before I'm brave enough to hit send. "I'm at the sports hall, want to meet up?"

Jess is waving for me to come down when my phone beeps with the reply. "Sorry, can't tonight frowny-face frowny-face sorry-hands. Maybe tomorrow?"

But the next night, he's working. And the night after that I need to get to bed early before my first lectures, and I don't bother asking.

⸎

Jess gets a nasty shock when we walk into the dim English lecture theatre. The person standing up front is not the hot guy from before, but an old woman with a walking stick who talks at us for twenty minutes about iambic pentameter. I should be taking notes, but I'm watching Jess's face as the reality of what she's signed up for slowly dawns. By the time we're handed the reading list, I think she might pass out.

I get a taste of what she went through when I go to my first politics lecture that afternoon. Jess would appreciate the lecturer – he's Italian and he wears a loose white blouse that makes him look more like a dancer than a teacher. But the introduction to types of city state and government sends my mind reeling, and I'm too focused on my page, scribbling down everything he says, to pay much attention to how he looks.

A flash of brown in the corner of my eye is the only warning I get before someone slides into the seat beside me. *Urgh!* I purposefully waited until the lecture theatre was almost full so I could pick a place where I didn't have to sit next to anyone. This person has not only arrived late but has disrupted my focus and now nothing the lecturer is talking about makes any sense.

The intruder chuckles.

I look up with a glare I usually reserve for people who talk loudly in libraries.

It's the guy from the Kaif, and the thing that's amused him is my page. He's inspecting my writing, mouth quirked. He catches the full force of my glare, but if anything, it amuses him further.

"Yes?" I hiss.

"You really don't have to write *everything* down," he says.

He's brought a small journal that makes my school-issue notepad seem extremely childish. On the front, in a messy scrawl, is his name: Kalin.

I scowl. "Thanks for the advice, Kalin, but I think comprehensive notes might come in handy around exam time."

My voice is low, but the boy in front of us turns to look at me. I sink down a little in my seat. Kalin does likewise, so that he's level with me. "*Kay-lin,*" He corrects my pronunciation. "If you try to write everything down, you'll miss half of what he says."

"*You* missed the first fifteen minutes of what he said," I point out in a whisper.

"Ten. And this is the first lecture. I promise we won't be quizzed on it."

His attitude grates. He knows nothing about me, or my academic record. What gives him the right to act so superior? I yank my notepad closer and prop it up against the desk, pointedly turned away from him. I resume my note-taking.

⚶

I see Kalin a few times over the next couple of days. He's easy to spot with his long hair and that brown coat, so he's easy to avoid.

I learn a lot that week. First, that I should have spent some time at the gym before enrolling here because Grahamstown is hilly and the lectures are sometimes ten minutes apart on opposite sides of campus. My thighs and calves ache when I eventually stumble into the dining hall each night. Second, that the meals in the dining hall are nothing like what's described on the intranet menu. I overhear someone calling the "steak" donkey meat and decide that I'll probably order takeout on Tuesdays from then on. And third, that Darren was right about the weather. Jess and I get caught in the rain twice between lectures on Wednesday and her perfectly straight blonde hair fuzzes out like the fur of a frightened cat.

When I see her late that night in the common room, in her pyjamas, poring over a poetry book with her hair piled in a messy bun, I take pity on her.

"Still prepping for the tut?" I ask as I sit beside her.

She lets out a long sigh without looking up.

Tutorials – or 'tuts' – have been one of the easiest parts of university for me to adjust to so far. They're similar to the extra lessons Dad made me take when I was little, only it's a requirement for everyone to attend. Each tut group is only nine or ten students and is led by either a lecturer or a postgrad. We have a poetry analysis due for our English Literature tut tomorrow.

"I just don't understand." Jess buries her head in her hands. "I don't know that I'm cut out for this uni thing. Where's the partying? Where's the fun?"

I'm not sure what to tell her. The fact that she'd have to study can't be *that* much of a surprise?

"It's only the first week," I say eventually. "It will get easier from here."

I take the book and pencil from her gently. I'm not good at partying – in truth it's a relief that there aren't as many parties as the movies imply. I'm not good at comforting, either. I imagine someone else might hug her and tell her she's beautiful or something, but that doesn't come naturally to me. There are many things that I'm not good at. But I'm good at *this*.

"You go to bed, I'll do it."

She stares at me. "Really?"

"Yeah. I've already done mine, so it will only take a minute. Get some sleep. Things will seem brighter in the morning." I offer her a smile.

I think she's going to argue, but her exhaustion must get the better of her because she throws her arms around me, nearly knocking the book from my grasp. "Aww Lilah! You're the best."

The common room is empty this late, and there are worse ways to spend a night than curled up with a book as rain patters against the window.

⸎

When I first discovered that Jess and I were assigned to different tuts, I was disappointed. Now I'm relieved because we're asked to read out our assignments. If we'd had the same tutor, they would have known one person did the work. As it is, I stutter and stumble through my analysis with my face burning, while the other eight people watch me.

When the mousy-haired tutor smiles and tells me I've done a good job, I want to die a little. I discovered years ago that the best way to get by as a nerd is to sit down and shut up. I ready myself for the resentful glares from the others – praise begets jealousy, after all. But none come. In fact, the next girl to present builds off my argument and the next also agrees with everything I've said. I flush with something different then. Maybe I *do* belong.

I manage to hold onto that fantasy until I encounter *Law*. My major. My life's purpose. The first lecture is even more confusing than politics, and of course Kalin is there. He doesn't sit next to me, but when I arrive at the tut on Friday, he's the only person in the room and he's staring blankly out the window with his arms folded. My heart leaps all the way up to my throat. Is he the tutor?

"You may as well sit," he says without moving his attention

from the window.

I swallow. I'm too hot from rushing across campus. My legs are shaky. I consider waiting outside in the cool corridor and maybe gathering my wits before everyone else arrives. But he looks at me and raises his eyebrows in question. I'm standing in the doorway like an idiot. Like I'm frightened of him. I don't want him to think that, so I do as he suggested and find myself a seat.

"Ms van Zyl will be a minute," he says. "The tutor."

"You're friends?" If he is local, as I first guessed, he probably knows a few of the lecturers the way Darren knew the people at the bar. It's a tiny town, after all.

His mouth twitches. "Early. She was here when I arrived."

"Timekeeping not a strong suit?"

"No, I suppose it isn't."

We sit in awkward silence for what feels like ages but is probably only a few seconds. It's a beautiful day outside, with one of those Grahamstown blue skies. Through the window behind Kalin I can see the tops of trees, a corner of the bright white library building that I still haven't had a chance to explore. But I can't focus on any of it.

When I was about six, Dad took me to the science centre to see an exhibit about space. There was this man giving a presentation on gravity using marbles and a stretched piece of Lycra. The fabric was space-time, he said, and we watched the marbles journey across it without interruption until he placed some weights near the middle. The weights represented stars, I guess. Or black holes. And as soon as they sank into the fabric, they changed the trajectory of the marbles completely.

Kalin reminds me of those weights. He pulls my attention.

"I don't think I ever got your name," he says, and I jerk. At my startled response, he gives me one of his half-smile-smirks. "Although I might have. I feel like we've met before, but I can't quite place you."

"Uh, Lilah. And yes. At the Kaif. My father..." I gesture to my collar and his eyes light with recognition.

He chuckles. "Right."

I should leave it at that, but I can't quite. I've spent too much of my life being forgotten to let it slide. "And you told me I was taking too many notes in Politics."

As he opens his mouth to respond, a middle-aged woman swoops in, arms laden with files, apologising for making us wait.

The tutorial is excruciating. The room is too hot, even when I shrug out of my in-case-it-rains coat, and I find it difficult to concentrate. Everyone else seems to have a better grasp of the subject than I do, and my mind keeps drifting. Birds are hopping between the branches of that tree outside. Is the weather this nice wherever Tammy is? I worry about what the tandoori chicken described on the dinner menu will taste like. I think about Darren and how he hasn't texted me since last night. He was being flirty, and I didn't know how to respond. Did I say something wrong? What does it mean that I haven't seen him since he kissed me?

When I do tune in, it's usually because Kalin is being annoying. He argues with the tutor, but he does it in a calm, even tone so that it seems polite. He's extending this torture unnecessarily, and I want to kick him. He should be thankful I can't reach him across the room.

With a jolt, I realise he's currently talking about my father's case.

They were discussing the South African constitution. Now they seem to be debating whether the tenet of "innocent until proven guilty" should apply to politicians, and Kalin has picked the Dumi case as an example.

"A cabinet member accused of human trafficking. Witnesses came forward and have now mysteriously disappeared or taken plea deals. You can't argue it's ethical to let him go knowing the power he has and the number of people who may be hurt."

The rest of the class erupts into fevered debate. I want to melt into my seat. Does the tutor know my full name? Will she realise the connection?

"Letting him go is undermining the very idea of justice," Kalin insists. "You can argue it is the law, but you can*not* argue that it is ethical."

The tutor holds up a hand for silence. She addresses Kalin directly. "It is ethical to treat everyone fairly, and if there is no proof—"

"Yes, but not everyone has the means to pay off the prosecution."

It's like the air is sucked out of me. My blood pumps cold, there's roaring in my ears. My annoyance turns to pure hatred. How dare he. How dare he imply that about my father.

"There is no evidence of that," I say, each word deliberate, because if I'm not careful, I'm going to lose it in front of everyone.

I don't know if it's the ice in my voice that draws all the eyes in the room, or that this is the first time I've said anything. I don't care. I can feel my pulse in my throat.

Kalin seems as immune to my tone as he was to my glare in Politics. "There's no evidence, full stop," he says. "There *was* evidence, people came forward. Where did they go?"

"And your answer is that he's bribed the very people trying to put him behind bars?"

"He has the means. Someone who has as much money as Dumi, as much power, can pull strings. You think someone capable of human trafficking is not capable of paying off the prosecution? Any prosecutor actually doing his job would have seen—"

He stops mid-sentence. He's still looking at me. Everyone else is quiet, waiting on the end of his sentence.

Something indefinable flickers in his gaze. When he finally speaks again, his voice is much softer. "*I* should have seen. Lilah. Lilah Durow."

He's put the pieces together, matched the man with the bird

excrement on his suit with the villain he was accusing. Now the room's focus is back on me. The tutor gives me a sympathetic look.

I can almost feel the tide of realisation washing across the tut. Whatever they didn't gather from his words, they've gathered from her look or from the colour that's flooded into my face.

Ms van Zyl clears her throat. "Well I think that's enough discussion for today. Please answer the questions on page five for next week."

I rush out as soon as I can, still shoving my books into my bag. I hear footsteps echoing down the hall after me.

"Lilah, wait!"

He catches up with me on the stairs where I have to slow down because I'm afraid I'll slip on the smooth tiles and break my neck.

"Addie Shahid."

"What?"

I'm a little pleased to see he's out of breath. He runs a hand through his hair. "Addie Shahid. Chief witness. She's the one who went to the media initially. Then, all of a sudden, she's taking a plea deal? Seems strange. Your father's a good prosecutor. I saw what he did on the Spear case a few years ago. It's not like him to miss evidence like—"

I round on him. "Is this your way of apologising?"

He shakes his head. Students hurry past us on the way to lectures or labs, and my shoulder gets jostled, knocking my notebook from my bag. He bends to pick it up.

"I'm not apologising, I'm explaining why I said what I did. It wasn't personal."

He tries to pass me the notebook, but I don't take it.

"You said what you said because you're an arrogant know-it-all who was enjoying the limelight." The words come almost of their own accord. I don't think I've ever been as rude, or as direct in my life.

Kalin stares at me, and I have no idea what he's thinking. I brush past him before I find out, leaving him holding the book.

6

I'm still seething that afternoon, standing in Grahamstown's only bookshop.

I've been hiding between the stacks under the guise of looking for my set works, but I'll probably grab them on Kindle. My room doesn't really have space for piles of textbooks. The smell of paper is comforting, though, and the books absorb the sound of the traffic outside. I feel like I'm back in the school library, taking refuge from the popular girls who'd tease me about how pale and strange I was. Familiar friends sit on these shelves, many boasting new jackets in the latest styles. I say hello and silently apologise to the few that are now wearing movie poster covers. No book deserves that.

When I come to the journals, I remember Kalin bending to pick up my notebook and scowl. I don't want to think about him, or about anything he said.

I suppose I will need something new to write in. I select a hardbound A5 with a plain black cover that has both lined and unlined pages. I'm on my way to the front to finally pay when a man with freckles and a bright green shirt approaches me.

"Come to the show tonight?" He thrusts a pink piece of paper at me and offers a blinding smile.

"Ah—" is all I get to say before he's turned away to go harass another customer.

The slip of paper is a flier for a band, hand-drawn and

photocopied. The text at the bottom gives an address and a date. There's a stamp on the corner saying, "LMS: join the Live Music Society today. R20 for a year's membership."

Jess is waiting for me outside res with a guy I haven't met. He has long, black hair and leans against the wall typing into his phone.

She waves frantically when she spots me. "Lilah! Lilah! Help!"

My heart lurches. "What is it?"

"Othello."

She pulls out a battered copy of Shakespeare. "Philip doesn't understand it."

"Philip?"

The guy glances up from the phone. "'Sup."

Star Trek's Spock would raise an eyebrow, Darren would send a confused emoji. I clear my throat and repeat the question: "*Philip?*".

Jess takes my arm and tugs me around a corner out of his earshot. "He said he can't go out after his show tonight because he needs to work on an essay about Othello."

That sounds like an excuse of the 'I've got to wash my hair' variety to me.

"It's Friday. Can't he work on it tomorrow?"

"I don't know!" Her voice pitches. "That's what he said, okay?"

"Okay. And you want him to go out tonight, because…?"

"Because have you seen him?!"

"What about Michael?"

"What *about* Michael? He's annoying. Clingy. Philip is in second year. He's the lead singer of a band."

I can't quite suppress the groan. "I don't want to be involved in this."

"You're not! Don't worry about Michael. I'll let him down easy. Just help me out with the homework bit? Please? You know

Shakespeare, don't you?"

I do, but I consider lying. Helping her is one thing, but helping the guy she has the hots for… is another thing entirely.

"I'm not sure about this. It doesn't seem right."

"Please, Lilah."

"Jess…" *You don't even know this guy. He's using you.* The type is unfortunately all too familiar to me. 'You can sit with us if you let us see your answers.' My throat closes before I can get any of that out because I don't want to risk ruining this new friendship. Instead of saying what I'm thinking, I let out an empty breath. Then, "How long is the essay?"

She jumps up and down and squeals as if I've already agreed.

It's a wonder that Philip is willing to trust a first-year with his homework, but I suppose academic success isn't a top priority for someone who's the lead singer of a college band. Luckily for him, we studied Othello in high school, so I'm familiar with the material. Also, luckily for him, I'm a loser who has nothing better to do on a Friday night. I don't agree to write the essay, but I agree to at least give him an outline that he can beef up tomorrow.

Jess isn't at dinner (little wonder), so I have some one-on-one time with my social media feeds. Tammy has posted pics of her trip. She's all tanned and all smiles, but she hasn't responded to my email, so a Skype catch-up later is probably out of the question. Darren still hasn't messaged.

Looks like it's just me and the Bard tonight.

I settle on my little bed and make a start. I've written the first sentence three times when I eventually dial Dad. I can't stop thinking about what Kalin said.

There's no subtle way to bring up the rumour, and once I have Dad's confident, steady voice on the line I feel ashamed for even considering it. If I mention it, he'll think I'm entertaining it. Which I'm not, would never. My dad's a superhero who puts away bad guys. I fill him in on the other, less interesting details of my day and end the call.

I try to work on the essay again, but it's impossible to focus. Still nothing from Darren. Still nothing from Tammy.

I end up writing the first two paragraphs in full, because writing them is easier than trying to explain how to write them. I pull out the new journal to write them neatly. It has inviting cream paper that will be a pleasure to doodle on. I have half a mind to draw something, just to calm my thoughts. The pink flier falls into my lap.

The man on the flier is screaming into a microphone, but he may as well be screaming at me. *What are you doing, Lilah? What happened to the new you? A week ago, you were dancing in a club and now you're in your room doing homework on a Friday night.*

Not even my own homework.

I've heard of walls pressing in before, but now I fully understand the expression. My room seems to shrink even smaller. In the dim light from my lamp it's nothing but a tiny dark box. I need to get out.

⁂

I walk up New Street alone, but I'm not really alone. Students are everywhere, some already drunk. I pass a trio linked arm-in-arm, singing at the tops of their voices. I feel a niggle of guilt for not finishing Philip's outline, but I can always do that later. For now, I can breathe again. The crisp air is so very good, and the freedom is even better. The night is rich with things to see and do and try for the first time.

I hear the Live Music Society show from a block away and that's when the doubts beat their way to the surface. Am I really going to walk in there alone? I shove down my anxiety, because I want so badly to be normal, like all these other students, to be able to have a good time out on the town regardless of who I'm with.

The venue is an old, rambling house on the same street as Dad's digs-cum-liquor-store. Loads of people are hanging around outside; some of them are typical musos with black clothes and funky hair, but there's a spectrum of everyone else between that and whatever I am in my jeans and hoodie. The event is clearly a popular one.

Inside the house is as dark as the club was. The only illumination is a blue wash over the bar on my right, and the flash of lights from a doorway ahead. The stage must be through there, but this room is also packed. People stand in groups, somehow managing to talk over the music, or press against the bar. I hug myself. *Well, New Lilah, now what?*

There are too many people. My limbs feel like a random jumble of awkward parts, and I can't get them to move.

"Hey!"

I'm almost bowled over by an enthusiastic hug from a complete stranger. It's a woman. She smells like hair dye and she's wearing a strappy top despite the cold outside. As she pulls away, some of the beer she's holding sloshes onto me.

"Leila isn't it?" she asks. It's almost my name. How does she know it?

I stare at her while she takes a swig of her drink. She has dark red hair that is perhaps vaguely familiar, but I've met so many people recently I can't guess where I know her from.

"Lilah," I say. When she doesn't say anything more, I add. "Like the colour, but without the c."

If she hears me, she gives no indication. She pats my arm with far too much familiarity. "Are you looking for Jess? She's through there with that guy."

Jess! And at once I recognise the girl – Sam, Jess's school friend from the Rat & Parrot.

I give her a smile, but she's already turning away to greet someone else.

It makes perfect sense that Jess would be here with Philip. His band is probably playing.

I shoulder through the crowd towards the stage, feeling much lighter, and much braver.

If he asks about the outline, I'll just say it's done, and I'll finish it when I get home. No big deal.

Noise pounds against me as I step into the other room. It's claustrophobic and reeks of alcohol and smoke. A band occupies a stage on the far side of the room. It's barely big enough for the three members and the guy on the guitar is standing squeezed up against the guy on the drums while the third screams into the mic, just like on the poster.

Some people right at the front are dancing – although from where I am it looks more like violent jumping – but the majority are standing, listening.

The first I see of Jess is her blonde hair. She's lip-locked with someone, who I know immediately isn't Philip because his hair is short. I think it must be Michael, but even in the flashing lights from the stage, I know the hair isn't the right colour.

Then I see the glasses.

My stomach turns to ice. The roaring in my ears drowns out even this deafening music.

I must be wrong. I must be mistaken.

I stand there long enough to know for certain I'm not.

She's kissing Darren. 'That guy' is Darren.

Someone jostles me, tells me to get out of the way, I'm blocking the entrance. I back numbly out of the room.

Each beat of my heart slams painfully into my chest, my face burns with shame. How could I think I was anything special to him after one night? I'm not pretty like Jess is; I don't have her magnetic personality. Why wouldn't he prefer her?

The tide of people has pushed me to the bar.

"What can I get you, lovey?" the barman asks.

My hands are shaking so hard when I open my purse that I nearly drop it. I need *something*, but I don't know what.

Dad's liquor cabinet is the first thing that comes to mind. I see the labels.

"Uh… Glenfiddich?" *Please don't ask for my ID.*

His eyes go wide, then he cracks a smile. "Afraid the best I can offer you is this."

He holds up a bottle of Jack Daniels.

I nod and he pours.

Sometimes Dad drinks whiskey after a particularly hard case. I've seen him sitting alone in his office nursing a glass when he's tired of showing a brave face. I asked him why once, and he said it helps keep the feelings at bay.

That's what I need. Something, anything, to make my body feel less like it's caving in on itself.

"Straight?" The barman asks.

I almost say yes, but I'm not quite that brave. I know the stuff must be strong. "With Coke?"

The drink is bitter, but it's not as unpleasant as the katemba.

It's a little bit like liquorice, if that liquorice was on fire. It burns my throat, but it makes my cheeks tingle. I drink the first glass like medicine, with the same determination I use to get through a dose of cough mixture.

The second glass isn't as bad.

❦

It's cold. It's so cold. My head is spinning, and my stomach is also spinning, but in the other direction. My face is numb, and I can't stop shivering.

"Okay, just breathe," a low voice says in my ear, and I feel a warm hand on my back. "There you go. Better now?"

I'm on the curb. The roar of the party is somewhere behind me. I've possibly just thrown up, but my mouth is numb so I'm not sure. I suck in the cold air and try to remember where I am and how I got here.

"Just breathe."

My forehead is on my knees, my hair is a curtain around my face. I can't see who's speaking.

When I lift my head, the world swirls and tilts.

"Oh no," I hear myself say.

Kalin is beside me. It's his hand that's on my back.

I fall forward again. "Go away."

"If I go away, how will you get home?"

"I'll walk," I say with confidence that is entirely false.

"All right then." He shifts away, and I immediately miss his warmth. I hear him stand. "Can I help you up, at least?"

I don't want to get up, I don't want to move. It's difficult to breathe, like I'm trying to pull in air around a boulder that's lodged itself where my lungs should be.

I can see Kalin's boots beneath my hair. They're ugly black combat boots. He's waiting for my answer.

"I'm fine."

He doesn't move.

I still don't want to get up, but I need to prove to him that I can so he'll leave me alone. I manage to get my feet under me, manage to stand. Then my knees give in.

He catches me. He's so warm, and he smells nice. Like camphor and old library books.

"Right, you're fine."

"Are you laughing at me?" My tongue struggles to form the words.

"No, no of course not."

I plant my feet firmly and pull away from him. "I *am* fine."

He doesn't quite let go of me. He's still got a hand under my elbow, as if he expects me to topple over at any moment. I can see the old house behind him now, though, and can hear the dull beat of the music. I remember where I am.

And then I remember what I saw.

The alcohol was supposed to put a wall between me and my

feelings, but the memory crashes into me. The ache is so intense, I can't even think. It spreads outwards from my stomach, up through my chest, along my limbs. I'm imploding, and there's nothing I can do to stop it.

My neck is rubber and my head falls forward again, this time onto Kalin's chest, and I don't even care. I want tonight to not have happened; I want to be sitting in my room reading Othello.

Kalin stands steady. The last thing I want is for him to see me cry but I can feel the hot pinpricks of tears.

"All right," he says softly. "Let's get you home, come on."

His chest moves, and I think he's going to push me away, but then warmth covers my back. He's draped his big brown coat across my shoulders. He slips an arm around my waist and starts guiding me down the street. We move slowly, because I'm still struggling to balance.

"Why are you being nice?" I ask.

"Why shouldn't I be nice?"

The streetlights glitter; it's like I'm looking at the world through wet glass.

"Because… I called you names."

"You called me on my crap."

A group of raucous students passes us, whooping and laughing. It's surreal that they can sound so happy while I'm so miserable. My tears are close to the surface again, and I have to stop to brush them away.

"Hey…" Kalin's noticed I'm crying. I want to sink into the ground and disappear.

"It's so stupid. I'm so stupid. *This* is so stupid."

He sighs. "You wanted to be normal. Part of being a normal student is being stupid."

I look up at him. His eyes are a rich amber. Is he a mind reader? Did he peer into me and read my thoughts? How else could he know that?

"Don't look so shocked." He smiles. "This *is* the third time we're having this conversation."

My stomach leaps. I have no memory of anything between that second glass and the curb.

"It is? What else did I say?"

We start walking again. "To be fair, the first time you weren't particularly coherent. But the second time I got the gist of it. Someone called Darren, your best friend… Othello? I'm still not sure how that comes into it unless you intend to murder him for his infidelity."

Nausea swells in a wave that I think has little to do with the alcohol. "It's hardly infidelity. Has to be a fidelity first for that. All we had was stars and emojis. I thought he wanted more. My mistake. My fault. Was stupid to think he was interested in me."

Kalin is silent long enough for me to wonder if I've said all this before too. Then he says, "I'm sure he *is* interested in you. He's just interested in everyone else too."

Maybe he intended the words to be comforting, but they aren't. I have this sudden image of Darren beneath the stars with Jess and I lurch to the side to empty the contents of my stomach.

7

I'm steadier on my feet after that little detour into the bushes. Kalin doesn't have to hold me, but he walks close enough to grab me if I fall. I didn't throw up *on* him, so that's something.

"Totalitarianism," I mutter as we turn into New Street.

"What?" Kalin looks at me as if I've now well and truly gone off the deep end.

"I can say it. If you're drunk, you can't. It's a test."

"Ah." He doesn't sound convinced.

New Street is still busy at whatever hour this is, but most of the students are on the right-hand side of the road where all the night spots are. We cross over to the other side, which is practically empty and there's more space to walk.

"Touch your nose," Kalin says.

"Huh?"

"It's a test. Close your eyes, hold out your arm, touch your nose."

"That's too easy."

"And saying totalitarianism is where the bar is set, is it?"

I stop walking and hold out my arm dramatically. It's surprisingly difficult to keep it steady. With great gusto I touch my nose. And miss. My finger lands on my cheek.

Kalin's lips are pursed as if he's trying not to laugh at me. He takes my hand and moves it slightly to the left so that my forefinger presses against the tip of my nose.

"There." His voice is low. It makes me think of the wind.

He's staring at me, his hand still around mine. He's close enough that I see an odd look in his eyes, a slight furrow of his brow, almost as if he's confused.

Then his expression clears and he drops my hand and turns away. "Wait here. Don't move."

I stand like an idiot with my finger on my nose for a good few moments, watching him dash across the road and jog down the other side, before I realise he probably meant that I shouldn't wander off.

There's a cloud of smoke in front of the Rat & Parrot and Kalin disappears into it. When he emerges, he's holding what look like two hotdogs – one in each hand. He hurries back to me and I feel bad when I notice he's wearing a threadbare brown shirt while I'm cosy in his jacket. But when he hands me the bun, all thoughts of the cold disappear. It's a boerewors roll, laden with dripping onion rings and fried tomato. I start to salivate.

"This should help sober you up," he says, as I bite into it.

I swear it's the most amazing thing I've ever tasted. It's juicy and salty and satisfying in a way I can't remember food ever being before. I think I even moan.

Kalin smiles, and we sit on the steps of the darkened bistro, because walking and eating at the same time is quite beyond me right now.

The smell of the cooking drifts towards us. It's the scent of summer, of braais outdoors surrounded by friends and family. I miss Tammy. I miss Dad. I even miss Uncle Clay, Tammy's father, who I've never liked. He's my dad's brother, but he's like the mirror universe version of him: also a lawyer, but slimy with greasy hair and an attitude to match.

The hollowness in my chest reopens, a black hole of homesickness and rejection pulling me in.

We're supposed to sign boys in, but Kalin ignores the guest log as he guides me through the entrance hall of my res. Even though my stomach has stopped roiling, I still can't seem to walk straight. The claustrophobic corridors are too hot after the night air, and too quiet after the LMS show and vibrant New Street. My ears ring.

I thank Kalin for the escort when we arrive at my door, and he leans against the opposite wall watching me struggle with the lock for a few minutes before he takes pity on me and opens the door for me.

He invites himself in, and I probably should be more nervous considering my city girl upbringing, but I see my bed and its siren song is stronger than any concern. I fall face first onto it.

It's not quite soft enough to absorb my impact. "Ow."

Paper rustles near my head.

"Ah, and here we have the Othello connection," Kalin says.

I vaguely remember leaving the essay on my pillow, but it's difficult to be worried about that because the room's started spinning.

The papers rustle again. "This is a second-year student number." He must have noticed it scrawled across the top of the page.

"Philip's," I provide.

"And Philip would be?"

"That's what I said."

"So, you're working on an essay for someone you don't know, who's a year above you, and you've been here, what? A week?"

"Shuddup." I know I'm a gullible fool; I don't need him rubbing it in. Certainly not while I'm like this.

He sighs, but he drops the subject. "You can't sleep like that."

"You're so bossy."

"Some would say I'm an arrogant know-it-all."

"Go away."

He laughs. It's not an unpleasant sound. Then he's pulling my shoulder, turning me onto my back and I'm decidedly less impressed.

"Leave me alone!"

"I'll leave you when I'm certain you're not going to drown in your own sick."

That's why he's here? A fresh wave of shame flushes over me, and I wriggle away from him. "I'm not. I'm fine now."

"You said you were fine an hour ago."

Has it really been that long? How slowly did we walk?

"That was an hour ago. Now I can touch my nose. See."

I demonstrate for him. This time I don't miss, but my eyes are also open, so it's probably cheating. He's still hovering over me, and my heart gives a loud thump when I realise what this might look like from the outside. Like sleeping beauty and her prince charming. Except I'm not a beauty, especially not now, and he's certainly not charming.

"Very good," he says in the most patronising way possible. "Now roll onto your side."

"Want me to play dead while I'm at it?"

"Preferably not."

I do as he instructs, mostly so he'll leave me alone and I can sleep. He seems satisfied because he wanders over to my desk and sits there instead of hovering.

"You're not technically allowed to be here," I tell him. I can only imagine Dad's reaction if Miss Sukwini discovers Kalin in my room.

"You're not technically allowed to write other people's essays for them. I suppose we're both rule breakers."

"Hah-hah." I close my eyes. The dark is lovely. It feels like my body is seeping into the thin mattress. I want to sleep for a week.

"What's with the map?" Kalin asks.

I cringe inwardly. Maybe outwardly too. *Have I not suffered enough humiliation for one night?* "Nothing."

"The Mist Woods?" His voice is closer, and I imagine him squinting up at my careful labels. "The Dark Frontier?

Where is this?"

"Nowhere. It's made up."

"Is it from a book?"

I recall the *Game of Thrones* map Tammy used to have up in her room. I could lie and say it's from a hit movie or TV show, but I lack the brainpower to be convincing if he asks for details.

"An evil sorcerer rules over the Kingdom of Night. Didn't used to be called that. No one remembers its original name though, 'cause that's what *he* calls it. The people try fight him and sometimes they push back the frontier, but he's too powerful. He's got spies everywhere, from the Bitter Sea to the shores of Bright. And he controls the only trading port. You can see it there. I tried to draw it."

Either my rambling has devolved into nonsense, or Kalin is struck speechless by my weirdness. Either way, he doesn't respond, and I'm finally able to sleep.

I jerk awake to loud banging on my door. It sounds like it's *inside my head.* The light from the window stabs my eyes, and my mouth is so dry it feels like my tongue might crumble away if I try to move it. Everything hurts. My head, my heart, my stomach, and even the muscles in my legs. I somehow manage to stumble to the door and open it a crack.

"What?"

There's a dark-haired man there, and it takes my addled brain a beat to realise it's Philip.

"My essay?" he has the gall to ask.

I snatch up the papers from the desk where Kalin left them and shove them into his hands. He makes a goldfish face, but I don't wait for him to find words. I slam the door and crawl back into bed.

I miss both breakfast and lunch, curled up and stuck between restless sleep and torturous consciousness. My phone beeps with several messages I don't have the courage to check. When Jess comes to my door, knocking and calling for me, I can't bear to answer. How do I handle this? What is the mature thing to do? Confront her and accuse her of stealing my not-boyfriend? Have her throw in my face how naïve I was? She'll no doubt discard me as easily as she discarded Michael. I shouldn't want her friendship now, but I do, and I hate myself a little for it.

When I can no longer see the shadow of the tree outside against my door and I can hear the birds settling in to roost for the night, I finally text her and tell her I've come down with the flu. It doesn't feel that far from the truth.

There's a message from Darren waiting. "Bunch of us going down to Grey Dam tomoz. You keen?"

I don't reply.

8

There's a sheen over campus when I head to class on Monday morning. It rained all of Sunday and water still clings to leaves and gathers on the uneven pavement. I stomp through puddles, breaking up reflected pieces of bright blue sky.

I spent a long time feeling sorry for myself this weekend and have now concluded that I'm not going to confront Jess about Friday. I'm going to pretend it never happened. That way, at least I have someone to sit with during English and Psych. That way at least I'm spared the indignity of being told how pathetic I am.

Jess is waiting for me at the Kaif. She has a Chelsea bun in her mouth and is holding two cups of coffee.

"Mmm mmm mmm!" she waves one of the cups at me, and I take it. She removes the bun. "I didn't know what to get you, so I got you a flat white. You do do dairy, right? You're not vegan or something?"

"I'm not vegan," I confirm.

Unbidden, the memory of the boerewors roll comes back to me, and my heart leaps. I'm going to have to see Kalin in just over an hour, and I have no idea what to say to him.

"How are you feeling?" Jess asks.

Right, I'm supposed to be sick. I sniff and clear my throat. "Fine now. I suppose it was just one of those twenty-four-hour head colds."

She nods and sips her coffee. We walk up the ramp towards the library. English is just across the way, and I don't know how to fill the silence before the lecture starts.

"I… I hope Philip wasn't too upset I didn't manage to finish his essay?" I venture.

Jess rolls her eyes. "Screw Philip."

"I thought that was the point?"

She giggles into her cup.

Now would be the perfect time to ask what happened that night, but the pain in my chest makes me look away.

The library is a tall, two-tone building of red brick and eggshell stucco. Foot traffic trickles through its large glass entrance, even this early. A few students have settled in front of it, reading and talking. It looks like one of those university recruitment posters where everyone's holding papers and laughing in the sunshine. To the left of the entrance is a group of Journalism students. The one is holding a camera; another has a boom.

"Did you hear about the missing first years?" Jess asks.

I'm grateful for something to talk about that isn't Friday night. "No?"

"Yeah apparently three girls from Drostdy Hall disappeared during o-week." Orientation week. "They didn't return to res. Everyone thought they were having naps but apparently they're still missing."

"Naps?"

"Oh Lilah, you're so innocent – oh shoot." She hisses.

I think she's spilled her coffee, but she's backing behind a pot plant. I follow her gaze.

Michael has just come out of the library and he joins the Journalism students. He's smiling, until he spots me, and his expression instantly sours.

"So… how did that go?" I ask Jess, who's now pressed so flat against the wall that she might be trying to sink into it.

"It went okay. Is he looking at me? Please say he hasn't seen me?"

"He's glaring right at you." Right at *us*. I give a small wave.

"Don't do that!" Jess squeaks.

I feel a sense of kinship with him. "Seems they'll be a while. You might have to stay there until the lecture starts."

⁓

I almost skip Politics because I am that desperate to avoid Kalin, but the subject is already so confusing, I don't dare risk it.

I wait until the lecture's about to start before I slip in and find a seat in the back row. Huddled in my jacket, with my head down, I make careful notes in my new journal. It's a more elegant solution than a pot plant, but only barely.

When the professor calls an end to the lecture and the rest of the students start filing out, I look up to find Kalin at the end of my row. My insides squirm. Is turning and running out the theatre's other entrance an option? Somehow I don't think that would ease the embarrassment crawling up my spine.

I stand aside for the others in the row to get out. Then, when I can't avoid it any longer, I approach him. Before I can say anything, Kalin plops my notebook down on the desk.

"Thought you might miss this."

I was prepared for something snide about Friday night. I'm momentarily thrown.

Before I can find words, he says, "I owe you an apology."

"You owe *me* an apology?"

"You probably won't believe me, but I didn't immediately know who your father was. I don't own a television."

"Television?"

"I know of him – his name, a few photographs from newspapers. He looked vaguely familiar when I saw him with you, but I made the connection too late."

That's what he wants to speak about? I change mental tracks, try to follow what he's saying. It's not much of an apology. He's

⁓61⁓

apologising for not recognising Dad, not for what he said about him.

I nearly call him on it, but the theatre has cleared out, and the next class will arrive soon. Besides…

"Look, I can't really be upset with you, can I? You, on Friday, I…"

I'm tripping over my words and he's looking at me like he's laughing on the inside.

"Thank you," I manage.

The corner of his mouth lifts. "First time drinking?"

I fold my arms, pleading with my cheeks to remain cool. "No."

It's not really a lie. I did try that katemba and the wine at the meet and greet.

His expression clouds. "You should learn your alcohol tolerance. It's dangerous to—"

Oh, spare me. I don't wait for him to finish his admonishment. I grab the book and shove it into my bag. "I need to go."

He catches my arm as I try to pass him. "Wait."

"I already have a lecture scheduled for next period. If you visit the dean's office I'm sure they'd be happy to add you to my timetable. Until then, I'm afraid I have to decline."

"No lecture then. Some unsolicited advice." He's still holding my arm, and he speaks in that low, soft voice. "Being normal is overrated. Don't give up who you are in trying to be like the rest of them."

"Wisdom from the great sage, Kalin?"

"Wisdom from someone who's different."

The lecture doors swing open, and he drops my arm as the first students for the next period come in.

For the next few weeks, I concentrate on what I'm good at: studying. There's more than enough work to keep me busy. We don't have exams during the first term, so the faculties make up for it with essays and assignments. The library becomes a second home. It's so vast that if I climb all the way to the top floor and go to the desk right at the back of the stacks, no one disturbs me. The best part is, it's open until ten-thirty at night. I can sit entirely alone, listening to music on my phone, for ages. During those hours, I don't think about Darren – who gave up texting me when my replies became short and emoji-less; I don't think about Jess; I don't think about not fitting in, or about Dad's case. All I think about is my work and, when that's done, I read for leisure or draw little pictures on the blank pages in my notebook.

I'm walking home from the library late one night, when fog rolls in. At first, it's pleasant in the way that heavy snow is from afar. There's no one else around and everything is twinkly and magical. But soon it's difficult to see the road ahead of me, and then it's difficult to see my hand in front of my face.

The fog becomes so dense it's like a white sheet covering me, or like being in a blank space between realities. There is no sound, no smell, nothing but the wet prickle and the icy taste as I breathe it in. I try feel my way forward. I'm not so far from res, but every step seems treacherous. Eventually I give up and stand still, waiting for it to lift.

Floaters dance across my vision, like I've been staring into the sun. It's impossible to tell whether it's my mind playing tricks on me or if there's really something there, moving just ahead of me. The pounding of my heart fills my head. Is this what happened to those missing girls Jess mentioned?

Grahamstown is hungry, and this is how she feeds.

No, stop it. My overactive imagination is has reported for duty. And even as I know that, even as I'm trying to convince myself that I'm standing alone on a pavement in the middle of campus, I think I see a pair of shadowy figures moving towards me. Their shapes are strange, as if they're wearing long jackets with hoods; as if they're wearing cloaks.

Raincoats, I scold myself.

Then one of them holds up a light and I could swear it's a lantern.

A phone. They're holding up their phone to try see and it only looks like a lantern because of the corona. And it doesn't mean anything that the light from their torch is orange, because there are so many models of phone I don't know about. Why wouldn't one have an orange flash?

"Great Ones!" a male voice exclaims behind me.

I whip around. The owner of the voice is standing quite near to me, but all I can make out is his fuzzy outline.

"Do my eyes deceive me? It is you, is it not?" He moves forward, shuffling like someone of advanced age. He's not wearing a raincoat. He's wearing what look to be silk pyjamas. *What the heck?*

I back away. "Sorry, I think you have the wrong person."

"They said you were gone." He continues towards me. "I refused to believe it. The fates would not allow it. I knew you lived." I step back again, and my foot goes down further than I expect. I stumble, flail, and hit the rough tar of the road with a yelp. I expect to see the man shambling towards me still, like the undead. But there is only dove-grey mist and somehow that's worse. Then footsteps come pounding down the pavement from the other direction. The fog must be lifting, because I see that it's a woman and she comes into focus as she draws near.

"Are you hurt?" she calls.

She must be one of the figures I saw with the torch. I dust the bits of gravel from my palms. "No, I'm fine."

She offers me a hand and helps me up. She's in a fitted leather jacket and jeans – no raincoat, no hood. Now that her features are clear, I realise I know her. She's Bianca, Darren's unsociable sister.

Please don't recognise me.

"It's Lilah, right?"

I nod. Hopefully she didn't see me cringe in the gloom. *Please don't mention your brother, please don't ask me about him.*

Instead, she frowns. "The fog is dangerous when it's like that. You're lucky you didn't wander into oncoming traffic."

"I was going to wait but—" I'm about to point out the confused old man, except now I can see quite far and there's nobody there. Am I going insane? "I suppose I got freaked out."

She follows my gaze down the road. "Understandable. You're still new here, right?"

"If you're going to tell me about the Grey Nun, Darren already got me with that one."

She smiles. "I wasn't, but that's funny. I'm going to ask him about that. You all right to get to your res or wherever?"

"Yes. Thanks." What I don't say, because I don't want her to think less of me, is that I'm terrified that the old man will reappear the instant she leaves. I watch her as she sticks her hands in her pockets and continues up the hill; I watch her until she's out of sight.

The old man does not reappear.

ᛞᚠᛖᛊ

I don't return to the library at night. I make up other excuses, but deep down I know it's because I'm rattled. The next time I get caught in the rain, which is only a few days later, I run the whole way to res, convinced that if I stop for long enough I'll see the old man's shambling form coming after me.

Studying at res has a few benefits. For one, I can cram until I drop. For another… actually, no, that's the only one. Res is stuffy, and the walls are thin. I hear absolutely everything from the surrounding rooms: excited talking, doors slamming, arguments, and even, much to my displeasure, bed springs creaking. My desk is cramped and looks out onto traffic, which brings its own irritating noises and distractions. I'm trying my best to get into study mode the night before our final English test of the term, when Jess shows up at my door.

"I need a BP run."

She's completely dishevelled. Her hair looks like it's trying to decide whether it wants to be straight or wavy. She's wearing slippers, but also a baggy jersey and bedazzled jeans.

I gawk at her. Does she want help studying? What new slang is this?

"I saw your light was on," she says. "Come with me? I don't want to walk alone."

"Walk?"

"To BP."

I finally realise what she's talking about. BP is the petrol station on the other side of town that has a 24-hour convenience store.

"I'm studying."

"Yeah, so am I. But you know what goes best with studying? Chocolate."

Difficult to argue with that logic, especially since my neighbour just got home. With her boyfriend.

It's been a while since I've spent time alone with Jess. She does most of the talking as we cut down Somerset, the street that dissects Grahamstown into campus and off-campus. It's a warm, clear night, and her hair flashes yellow under the bright streetlights as she regales me with tales from the soap opera that is her life. I don't mind. It's easier to laugh politely at her stories than to try think of things we have in common to talk about.

But as we hit New Street, she asks, "Where have you been? I've hardly seen you in weeks."

I almost tell her the truth, but I picture her rocking up at my quiet refuge with coffee and updates on which guys she's interested in, and I bite my tongue. She sees my hesitation and immediately starts laughing.

"You have a boyfriend, don't you?"

It feels like a kick in the ribs, which surprises me because I should be over it by now. "No."

She doesn't believe me.

She wants to know details, and she nags me all the way up New Street.

It says a lot about the general academic pressure on campus that the Rat is empty enough for me to hear music as we pass it. Two guys at the boerewors stand make conversation with the cook.

"Come on, Ma Pam, I'm good for it."

She's a big African lady and she gives him a glare that could wither stone. Apparently boerie rolls are not available on credit.

The smell is just as good as it was that cursed night, but now I'm sober, the dripping onion rings don't look quite as appetising.

Around the block, we pass the small Pick n Pay centre, all dark and quiet. I only realise as we reach the end of the road that the BP is on the next street – the same street where the Live Music Society event was.

Jess is entertaining herself by guessing what sort of guy I'd be interested in, and some of her suggestions are ridiculous enough that I laugh. But as we near the rambling house, it's increasingly difficult to draw even the guise of good humour up from within. I tread over the pavement where Kalin comforted me, and the memory is raw and cold.

I try not to look at the building, but I can't drag my eyes from it, and the words come from my mouth almost unbidden. "You *know* what kind of guy I like."

Jess falls silent. The temperature drops. My heart hammers. Why did I say that? I'm walking headfirst into the one conversation I don't want to have. If she asks me what I mean, what will I say?

But she doesn't ask. She looks at the house, then at me, and I know she knows what I saw. Jess sometimes plays dumb, but she isn't. She wouldn't be at university studying economics if she was.

Her brow furrows. Her gaze drops to her feet, but she doesn't say anything, just keeps walking. And I walk along beside her.

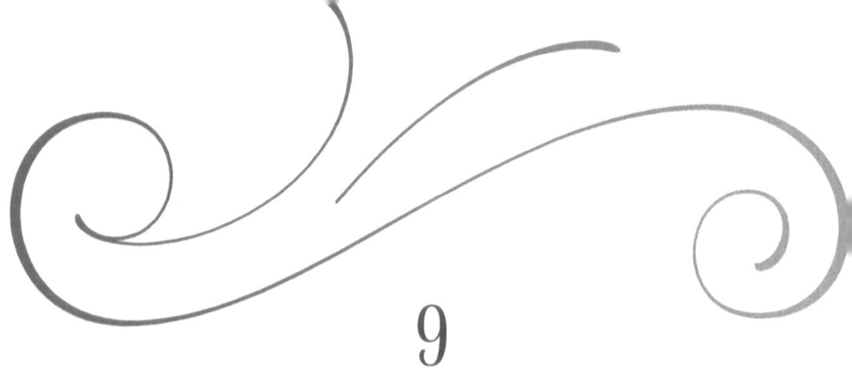

9

Jess recovers as we step beneath the harsh fluorescents of the convenience store. It's better stocked than similar shops back home, with aisles of cereal and non-perishables, and a fridge packed with ready meals. This must be how students survive living off-campus.

A pair of guys near the tills looks at us as we enter. The first is muscled and wearing a white vest, with a lei of plastic flowers around his neck. He's handsome, but I don't like the way his eyes trail Jess as she makes a beeline for the chocolate. His friend is leaning against the counter, jeans hanging low enough for the top of his underwear to be visible. He's attempting to stir a takeaway coffee, but the spoon keeps missing the cup, and when he finally manages to get it in, he drops it and swears. He's clearly drunk.

I duck behind the shelves before they notice me looking. I'm trying to decide between praline or hazelnut, and Jess is reading the label of a pack of Jelly Tots, when a high-pitched female voice yells, "Hey, *jou bliksem*!" up front.

I'm not very good at Afrikaans but I understand that. *Hey, you bastard.*

I peer around a promo stack of Lay's. A petite, tawny-skinned woman confronts the guy with the coffee cup. They're both unsteady on their feet, and the dark stain on the front of her white T-shirt tells the rest of the story. The coffee guy rises to his full height – at least a head taller than her – and leers down at her. I don't like his expression one bit. He's looking at her like she's the tasty snack he came in here for. Was spilling his drink on her even an accident?

His muscly friend swaggers forward. She turns to him and blinks slowly, as if struggling to focus.

"Hey baby," he says. "Let us make that up to you."

The woman's my age, maybe a little older, with black hair pulled into a neat bun – certainly not a baby. She sways where she's standing and mutters something in Afrikaans under her breath. He closes the distance between them, wraps an arm around her waist and ducks to speak into her ear. All I can hear is the end of it. "Out of that shirt."

She doesn't react, she's gone rigid, still staring at him with that distant look. He smiles and starts guiding her towards the door. I see him wink at his friend. My heart kicks.

I'm moving before I even know what I'm doing. "Wait!"

Mr Muscle turns to me. The girl is hugged to his side, so she moves with him, but there is nothing in her expression to indicate she even sees me.

Is that what I was like when Kalin found me? There's still a gap in my memory, and I have to swallow down revulsion at what might have happened had he not been there.

There's no one here now for this girl. Just me. "She's my friend. I'll walk her home."

She doesn't argue, and that is all the confirmation I need that I'm making the right decision. I march forward and take her arm, trying to channel Dad. I even shoot Muscles a glare, though my ears are roaring and hot with embarrassment.

His eyes narrow as if he's going to argue, but then he shrugs and tilts his head towards the door. His friend follows him out, and I'm almost tempted to give his trousers a tug because it would be nice to see him humiliated as they fall all the way down. But I've used up my quota of courage for the night. Maybe the year.

The girl undulates again. "*Ek gat kots.*"

I'm not sure what she means. "Where do you live?" I ask.

She shakes her head and surges forward, out the door with her hand over her mouth. I dash after her, ignoring Jess calling me.

The girl falls to her knees at the edge of the road and hurls into the gutter. I wish I didn't know exactly how she feels.

When Jess catches up to us, the girl is rubbing her face, but she looks no more alert.

"Where do you live?" I ask her again.

"You don't really plan to walk her home, do you?" Jess interjects. "Why can't we just call her an Uber?"

"You know we're in Grahamstown, right?" I'm pretty sure Uber's not interested in towns in the middle of nowhere.

She pulls out her phone. She might be trying to call an Uber anyway.

"We can't just leave her here."

"Can't we? I mean she clearly got here by herself."

I don't dignify that with a response. "Can you stand?" I ask the girl.

She nods.

"I'm Lilah," I say as I help her up. "This is Jess. Your name is?"

There's a long pause, then she manages, "Lani."

She takes a step and wobbles. I grab at her, but before I can get ahold of her, her knees slam into the pavement. She flings out a hand a moment before her face does the same. Then she whimpers and rolls onto her side, cradling the hand to her chest. She must have hurt it.

"Help me get her up."

Jess has her mouth agape and I have to snap her name before she answers. Between the two of us, we manage to get Lani upright with one arm across my shoulders, and one across Jess's, but when I take hold of her wrist Lani shrieks and struggles. It's definitely hurt, possibly quite badly. Could it be broken?

"Where are we going?" Jess asks.

In my mind there's only one clear option. "Sukwini's a nurse.

And she deals with drunk students all the time. She'll know what to do."

We're a slow six-legged animal meandering towards res, but we eventually get there. On the way, Lani doesn't sober up. If anything, she gets drunker, and heavier. My shoulders are aching and my arms trembling by the time we arrive at Sukwini's door.

The warden's accommodation is on the ground floor of res, behind the staircase and along a dim, wood-panelled corridor. I hesitate before knocking. It's late. Sukwini's probably asleep. I know she said that we could come to her with any problems, and this really is a problem. But Lani isn't one of her wards, so she might be angry. Then Lani's head nods forward and Jess groans and reaches around her to pound on the door.

Sukwini answers in a blue dressing gown. She takes in the scene and ushers us in.

"Tell me, what happened?"

The door opens into a sitting room. We struggle to manoeuvre Lani past a small bookcase while I tell Sukwini everything. The room is cozy. The sofa and armchairs are covered with woven quilts and scattered with colourful throw cushions, and the wall is lined with photographs and paintings. Sukwini gestures towards a large orange armchair.

As we ease Lani into it, she seems to melt, like her bones have turned to liquid. Her eyes are narrow slits beneath long dark eyelashes. Sukwini kneels in front of her, to examine her and ask her questions. Jess and I step back.

When Sukwini takes Lani's hand, she cries out in pain again. The wrist has swollen. My stomach clenches. *I should have been quicker to catch her.*

"Can you girls please make us some tea?" Sukwini asks.

"Yes of course." I'm happy to have something to do.

Jess and I duck into the tiny kitchen.

We find bright mugs on a shelf over the electric kettle, and tea and sugar in a cupboard. The kitchen smells like herbs and sunlight. Only when I go looking for the milk do I realise I didn't even ask Sukwini how she wanted her tea.

I leave Jess filling the kettle to go find out.

"Miss Su..." the words die on my lips. She's holding Lani's wrist in her hand and Lani's skin is *glowing*.

Sukwini looks up and I blink.

Trick of the light. Sukwini's wearing a watch, the light must've glinted off the face. She has a roll of bandages in her other hand. "Yes my dear?"

"Tea. Uh, how do you like your tea?"

When Jess and I return with the tea tray, Lani's wrist is bandaged up, but she's holding it in her lap rather than clutched against her body. Sukwini must have given her a painkiller.

"We have called Lani's brother and he is coming to fetch her," Sukwini says, sitting back to accept her tea.

We drink in silence. Lani even manages to lift the mug to her lips with her injured hand, but it trembles and Sukwini takes the cup from her to help her sip from it. Lani says something in Afrikaans that I don't understand. Her voice is bleary, as if she's half-asleep.

Sukwini responds, then says to me, "She's still a little out of it. You girls did the right thing bringing her here. It seems someone might have spiked her drink."

Jess and I exchange a look.

"Shouldn't she go to the police?" I ask.

"Oh, most certainly. But for now, I believe the best thing is for her to go home and get some rest. I will call a meeting tomorrow to make sure you all know to be extra careful out in town."

It's an uncomfortable thought that quiet little Grahamstown might not be all that safe after all. I hope she doesn't tell Dad.

Jess and I wait outside with Lani for her brother. She's still unsteady on her feet, so we sit with her on the front steps.

A long silver car with thrumming bass pulls up and the driver's side window rolls down. A wiry man who has the same dark skin and eyes as Lani leans out the window and calls, "Lani! *Wat maak jy?" What are you doing?*

I stand, "You're her brother?"

"That's right." He scans the length of me.

To my surprise, Jess stands too. "Some guys at the BP drugged her and tried to take her home. But you're welcome or whatever."

The brother raises a pair of fine eyebrows that disappear into his hair.

Lani rubs her face. "I feel like crap."

I did not expect her to speak English. She struggles to her feet. Jess helps her.

"I went to get smokes. I don't remember after… *Ek dink*… I think someone spilled coffee on me."

He whistles and climbs out of the car to help her. "Ay, the boss isn't going to like that stain. Come, we'll put it in some Jik overnight."

He wraps an arm around her, and she leans into him.

As we watch them drive off, Jess says, "I still want chocolate."

It may be my imagination, but Jess seems to avoid me after that night. I guess she might feel awkward after our non-conversation outside the music venue. Either that, or she's annoyed at me about coming between her and her chocolate fix, and she's being particularly passive aggressive about it.

A week before the end of term, I'm sitting reading alone at the Kaif when a shadow falls across my book. I look up to find Kalin standing there.

"Is this all you ever do?" he asks.

Even though I've seen him in our Law tuts, we haven't spoken since that time in Politics. I raise my eyebrows at him. "Excuse me?"

He sits down on the bench next to me and starts reading my notebook, like he did that first day of lectures.

"Kalin!" I snap.

He looks up.

"Can I help you?"

There's a flicker of a smile. I don't know what I've done to amuse him. "Is this all your work, or are you doing another favour for a stranger?"

Really? "What's your problem?"

"No problem. It's only, whenever I see you, you've got your head down studying. There's more to being a student than that, you know."

"This from the man who told me to be myself."

"You took my words to heart? I'm touched." He produces a folded brochure from somewhere and passes it to me with a flick of his wrist.

"What's that?"

"SciFest. It's happening up at the monument this week."

I take the brochure. It has a starscape on the front, and above it in big bold letters the words: SciFest Africa: South Africa's National Science Festival. I page through it. It seems there will be lectures and workshops on everything from Antarctic adventures to virtual reality.

"Come with me," Kalin says.

My stomach jumps. "What?"

He laughs. "You should see your face. I'm not asking you to dinner. This isn't romantic, I promise."

Of course it wouldn't be. That would be absurd. I focus on the brochure, so I don't have to meet his eyes. "Why? Don't you have friends who can go with you?"

I cringe inwardly. I'm being mean to hide my own embarrassment, and even though he annoys me, I don't want to be that person.

If he's upset at all though, it doesn't come through in his voice. "I thought you might like a break from the books. This one in particular." He extracts the copy of *Great Expectations* from my hand.

"Hey!" I protest as he closes it without marking the page.

"Don't try tell me it's the first time you've read it, I won't believe you."

"You have some nerve."

"I'm known for it. So, what do you say?"

"You're not exactly endearing yourself to me right now."

He leans forward, bringing himself closer. I catch a whiff of herbs before he tucks his hair behind his ear. "You're lonely."

"You're annoying."

"Maybe," he says with a shrug. "Maybe I'm lonely too."

I study his expression. His easy confidence hasn't faltered; there's no trace of self-pity in his gaze. It's a statement of fact.

And it is little wonder that he struggles to make friends if the way he acts around me is any indication of his usual strategy, but I don't want to say that. "Is there a particular lecture you're interested in?"

"No. Your choice."

"I'll have to look at the brochure."

He reaches for one of my pencils and, before I can stop him, he opens *Great Expectations* and writes in it.

"What are you doing!"

I snatch it back, and he laughs at me again. "My number. Give me a call tonight and let me know. And don't worry, I didn't press hard."

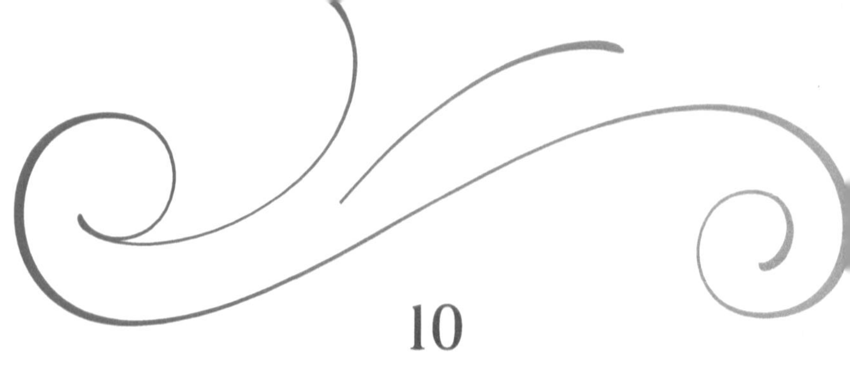

10

rahamstown has been sweltering for days, and even the hardy plants along the footpath up to the monument have wilted. The soil beneath my feet looks grey and as thirsty as I feel.

The sun beats down on my neck. I'm seriously tempted to give up and go back to res, but, as I discovered last night when I found his phone number buried in the middle of chapter 10, Kalin only has a landline. There'd be no way to get hold of him until long after I'd stood him up. Who doesn't have a mobile phone in this day and age?

When at last I reach the top of the hill, panting and sweating, I'm surprised by the size of that squat building beneath the masts. It stretches up at least three storeys into the clear sky, with a centre part that's even taller. It reminds me a bit of those buildings kids make in Lego or Minecraft: all big squares stacked together with no discernible purpose. In this case I guess it's something to do with ships and probably designed by someone famous. (Someone famous with a fondness for straight lines and authoritarian brown).

To my right, an ancient stone wall encircles a cluster of small white buildings. A plaque declares this "Fort Selwyn" and I catch a glimpse of an old canon half buried under a pile of laughing children.

The fort is not the only thing of interest occupying the patches of yellowing lawn between the parked cars. Another group of kids is skipping around a standing stone. A cluster of tourists is posing for pics by a statue of a man with a hammer.

And there's Kalin, waiting for me in front of the entrance.

He smiles when he sees me. It's a real, proper smile that lights up his face and makes his eyes crinkle. Maybe he really didn't expect me to show.

He's not wearing his usual coat in this heat. Instead, he's opted for a faded blue golf shirt that looks like it might have belonged to his grandfather – not that I'm one to judge fashion.

"You look like you're melting," he says as I approach.

"I think I am." I have a sudden image of myself glowing with sweat with a face as pink as my t-shirt. Far from attractive.

"You should have asked for a lift."

I didn't even consider that he might have a car. Kalin's age is difficult to place. He could be eighteen, I suppose, since he's taking first year courses. But now that I think of it, he does seem older. It's something about his eyes, and the fact that he has actual stubble, and… and I'm staring. I look away quickly. "I probably need the exercise. According to *some*, all I ever do is study."

"And would these 'some' be mistaken?" His voice is older too. Or is it the way he speaks?

We join the ticket line.

"I'll have you know I have a very interesting life," I say.

"Oh?"

"I attend lectures by some of the top professors in the country."

He snorts. "If the brochures are to be believed."

"And I fight bravely through Grahamstown weather." I mean its sudden changes but I think of the fog as I say it.

Kalin only nods sagely.

"Sometimes I even eat dining hall meat."

"That is adventurous indeed," Kalin agrees.

The line moves forward quickly, and soon we're in the blissfully cool reception area. We lapse into silence. I wouldn't exactly call it uncomfortable, except that I wish I could find something interesting to say, and every moment that I don't, that I stare at the wiry carpet beneath our feet or the 1970s wood panelling of the ticket booth, I grow increasingly frustrated with myself.

"I like your drawings," Kalin says out of nowhere.

"My what?"

"Your sketches. Your notebook was full of them."

My stomach jumps like I've just gone over a speedbump on a bicycle. "You looked through my notebook?" I try to remember what I doodled there. Did I write anything other than lecture notes?

Kalin is saved from answering because we've reached the front. He hands over money for both of our tickets before I can stop him, which makes telling him off for the notebook thing a little difficult.

I bite my tongue as we enter the building proper, and all at once there's air and sun and noise. Light bounces in from giant windows to our left and stone stairs are carved into the floor before us, forming a sort of amphitheatre packed with people. At their base is a gigantic wooden artwork that reaches up three storeys. I mistake it for a scaffold at first, then I realise it's supposed to be a representation of the Union Jack. Wood-panelled balconies poke from mezzanine levels on either side of it, and they're flanked by huge artworks in earthy pigments. There's so much to look at. And there are so many people. Those who aren't sitting on the stairs are standing talking while children weave between their legs, or are walking around and laughing and pointing and taking selfies and shaking hands and nodding and clustering together to discuss the programme and—

Kalin touches my elbow to get my attention. "I believe there's a café down there where we can get something cool to drink." He nods towards the stairs.

I swallow. It's busier than I thought it would be, but Kalin's presence is an anchor. As I follow him downstairs, I feel less like I'm drowning in the sea of noise and people.

The "café" turns out to be no more than a counter with a scattering of tables. I order a Coke and, once again, Kalin pays.

We find a quiet table pressed right up against the wall, furthest from the crowds.

"You promised this wasn't romantic," I tease. "You know, if you keep paying for things, you might give a lady ideas."

I expect him to laugh. Instead, he frowns deeply. "Lilah, I can't get involved with anyone."

My stomach gives an unpleasant jerk. "I wasn't being serious."

"All right. I just want to be clear about that."

Awkward. I hold up my hands. "I hear you. I was joking."

"Okay." He opens his drink and I focus hard on a nearby window. Who says I'd want to get involved with him anyway? Arrogant much? What, he walks me home one night and now suddenly I'm in love with him? I breathe in through my nose. My skin crawls from rejection even though I didn't ask for anything.

The view is all trees and rooftops in blocks that I don't yet know well enough to recognise. The town looks dusty and dry.

"Lilah?" Kalin has that same stricken expression he had after our argument in that first tut. "It's not you. I have some things going on and I just can't get involved with—"

"Kalin, drop it. It's not like I said I was interested in you, is it?"

"No," he agrees. And even though I feel a flutter of guilt at my bluntness, he seems to relax. "I considered it polite to pay since I invited you here. But if you like, you can pay for lunch? After the lecture on forensic pathology?"

I cringe. "Why did we choose to go to the CSI stuff before lunch?"

"*You* chose to go to the CSI stuff. I don't even know what CSI is."

Right, no TV. "It's a show about a team of crime-scene investigators," I explain. And I've never been a huge fan of the show – Dad loves pointing out all the inaccuracies while we watch – but I'm thankful to have something to talk about. Kalin nods along as I describe the concept and even smiles when I detail a few of the episodes I liked. Although, when we get up to leave, I can't help but think that he got one more lecture than he bargained for today.

In order to reach the first talk on our agenda, which is off the second mezzanine, we have to wade through an area labelled the SciFest Activity Zone. It's like walking across a casino floor with all the sounds and lights, except the patrons are much smaller and a decade or two younger. Also, the machines aren't taking money. Well, except for that one that's meant to simulate a black hole. As we pass, a little boy flicks a 50c piece in and watches it roll round and round in ever-tighter circles until it disappears down the middle. Next to him, a girl spins a giant globe filled with glitter that is supposed to illustrate the earth's currents.

There are so many displays, far more than I recall from when I visited the science centre in Cape Town as a kid: a Lego pinball machine, a robot dog doing tricks, a case with mirrors and lasers, and something loud that bangs and whistles that I can't see over the group of children gathered around it. Groups of children gather around nearly everything and a few times we have to squeeze between clusters of them

"Thank the Greats for air conditioning," Kalin mutters.

"The Greats?" He can't mean the likes of Leonardo Da Vinci and Van Gogh, although that would certainly be a unique religion.

"Your deity of choice." He turns sideways to pass between two popular displays.

Maybe it's a local thing.

ʊʄʊ

Every single part of SciFest is more interesting than even my most fascinating Law lecture. We see how NASA recolours images sent from deep space and hear about how technology is being used to protect endangered wildlife. The forensic pathology talk doesn't put us off our lunch in the end, and we eat hot dogs while walking through a hall filled with school projects themed around saving the environment.

I'm watching a fifth-grader's water filtration system fail, when a voice behind me says, "City Girl!"

I turn, and there's Darren. My heart lurches.

"Ah, hi." I try to sound casual, and probably fail as badly as the filter behind me that's now making a pathetic bubbling, choking noise.

"How are you? I haven't seen you in ages." Darren is, of course, completely unruffled. His smile should be on TV selling toothpaste, because that's how perfect it looks. He's here with the barman, Sibu, and another friend I haven't met who wanders off ahead. Sibu nods to me in greeting, and I'm surprised he even remembers me.

"Good. I'm good," I say.

Darren glances at Kalin. His smile falters just a little.

"Kalin, this is Darren," I stumble through the introduction, and they shake hands. Darren introduces Kalin to Sibu, but he watches me the whole time.

"What have you been up to?" he asks.

"Studying. You know how it is."

"You going to the city for vac, I guess?"

"Yeah."

His gaze flicks to Kalin again, then he ventures, "We should hang out again some time. Maybe when you get back?"

"Sure," I say, because really what else can I say right there in the middle of a crowded hall?

"It, uh, was great seeing you again." As he says this, I notice Sibu is trying not to laugh. At me, or at Darren? Either way, it makes me uncomfortable.

"It was good seeing you too. I'll message next term to see when you're free, or something?"

I want to kick myself as they carry onwards, because I don't like lying, but I'm pretty sure I just did.

Kalin sighs as if he's thinking the same thing as me. "You should confront him."

I can't remember exactly what I said to Kalin about Darren. "He didn't do anything wrong."

"You've certainly changed your tune." His voice is stiff.

"I was upset that night, but it was my fault. I obviously misunderstood what was happening between us. Maybe he just wants to be friends." Friends who kiss in the moonlight.

Kalin growls but offers no further comment.

After lunch, we go into the biggest auditorium for a talk called Theories of the Multiverse.

Kalin doesn't ask where I want to sit, because by now he knows that I prefer to sit near the front. He leads the way and we take our seats. As the hall fills up around us, I have a good look at it: plush and grand. This must be where the graduation ceremonies happen. Is this where my father graduated? My mother? Was SciFest a thing then? Did they attend together?

The lights dim and the speaker strides onto the stage.

It's Darren's sister, Bianca.

That must be what he is doing here – he must have come to support her. I would never have imagined that she was an academic, let alone a scientist. I definitely wouldn't have guessed she was a professor. She's not in the leather jacket now, of course. She's wearing a tailored pants suit and raspberry lipstick. A slide comes up on the stage with her name and the title of the talk and she scans the crowd. Her eyes land on me. Her pleasant smile disappears, and she glares. I flush cold before I realise her gaze isn't fixed on me at all, but on Kalin, who is now sitting ramrod straight, looking right back at her. His hands are clutching the armrests so tightly his knuckles have gone white. I once saw two street cats in the prelude to a fight, and it looked just like this.

Bianca turns away and smiles sweetly again. As she starts the lecture, I murmur to Kalin, "Friend of yours?"

"No. Quite the opposite."

Well yes, I gathered that. He must be too shaken for sarcasm. "Your ex?" I guess.

He looks at me sharply. "No." As if that's the most ridiculous thing he's ever heard.

I sink a little in my seat. Kalin rests his elbow on his knee and becomes intent on what Bianca is saying.

Her talk focuses on the discovery of a "cold spot" in our scans of space where our universe may have collided with another when it was born, representing the first possible proof of a parallel universe. She's a good orator. She speaks about the Mandela Effect – where some people claim to have clear memories of things that don't exist in our history, like Nelson Mandela dying on Robben Island. She gets a few laughs when she gives the example of her baby brother incorrectly remembering being their parents' favourite. I possibly laugh a bit too hard at that one. Even as I do, I recall Darren's smile faltering when he saw who I was with at lunch. Maybe it was nothing to do with me. Maybe it was to do with Kalin and Bianca's history?

She ends the lecture on the disquieting note that our entire world may be a computer simulation and she shows a few "glitch in the Matrix" memes of things too unlikely to be normal: three girls sitting on a train with the exact same hairstyle and hat, seemingly unaware of each other; two strangers on a plane who are complete doppelgängers; two black cats sitting in the exact same position. She throws one last look at Kalin when she asks the audience if they have questions, as if she expects him to raise his hand. But he doesn't.

Kalin offers me a lift back to res, and on the way to the car I ask, "Academic rival?"

"Who?"

"Bianca. Is that why she hates you?"

He bursts out laughing, and I'm left even more confused than I was before.

Kalin's car is a white Ford sedan with a big silver grille, a long bonnet and beige vinyl seats that make me think it may be older than I am. It bears a CF number plate, which I recognise as a Grahamstown registration.

"So you're local?" I ask.

"Mmhmm," he confirms. "For now."

"Oh, you have big plans then?" The car smells like old foam and baked carpet. I was hoping for aircon, but Kalin cranks open a window as we draw out of the parking lot.

Kalin appears to consider my question carefully before answering. "There's no need for small talk. What did you think of the lecture?"

My shoulders tense. "I didn't mean to annoy you."

"I'm not annoyed. I apologise if I gave you that impression."

His tone is oddly formal, a strange contrast to the easy conversation of the past few hours. Perhaps he's still unsettled by his run-in with Bianca. I shift in my seat, wishing now that I'd decided to walk. It's late afternoon, the sun is low, and my own company is far more predictable.

"Now you're annoyed." He glances at me. "I don't have big plans, no. I meant only that I'm not originally from here. I've lived here for a few years now, however, and it suits me well."

Still that odd formal tone. "'Suits me well?' Greats, you sound like Dickens."

My use of his curse has the desired effect. His mouth twitches into an uneasy smile. "You are fond of Dickens, are you not?"

I can't decide if he's mocking me, or if he's implying that he wants me to be fond of him. Maybe it's an awkward way of saying that he wants to be friends?

"I enjoyed the lecture," I answer his earlier question. "I enjoyed all of them. It was a good day. Thank you."

His smile becomes full. "You're welcome."

He turns into Somerset Street, and we're drawing up to my res when he says, "I'm not particularly good at this."

"This?"

"People. I tend to keep to myself a lot, so I don't always know what to say and how to act. I'm sorry if my comment about your sketches was inappropriate earlier."

I study his face. What made him think of that now? "The comment wasn't inappropriate," I say carefully. "Looking through my notebook might have been."

I have this mental image of him poring over my notes and smirking at every spelling mistake. What was he hoping to find there?

He's parked the car, but he still has his hands on the wheel while he stares at them as if deep in thought. "These things you draw, are they all from your fantasy kingdom?"

My stomach twists as I recall him looking at the map above my bed. I knew that would come back to haunt me. I just didn't think he'd look so serious when he asked.

"I know I'm weird," I say.

He doesn't comment. He's still looking at his hands, perfectly still and waiting for my answer.

I sigh. "Do you have brothers and sisters, Kalin?"

"No."

"So maybe you understand then, what it's like. All that time on my own as a kid... I started making up things. And some things stuck. That kingdom was one of them. I don't even remember when I came up with it. It's... I don't know. Habit, I suppose? I used to retreat there when I was bored or scared and try to work out the details of the landscape, or the names of villagers and their relations to each other." I've never told anyone this, and it makes me feel surprisingly vulnerable. There's more I want to say, but I can't quite bring myself to because I'm aware of how strange this must all sound.

He finally looks at me. "And you still retreat there now?"

"Less often since I learned how to read." I manage a small smile, although I'm not sure how convincing it is. He returns it and nods in understanding. But the real answer is yes, and I think he knows that. I think that my notebook showed him that perfectly clearly with all the little thumbnail maps and sketches of castles and buildings and lord knows what else that I can't even recall.

"My father doesn't approve of my fancies – that's what he calls them," I admit. "I probably should have grown out of them years ago."

"I hear JRR Tolkien had similar 'fancies'. I wouldn't be so quick to dismiss them."

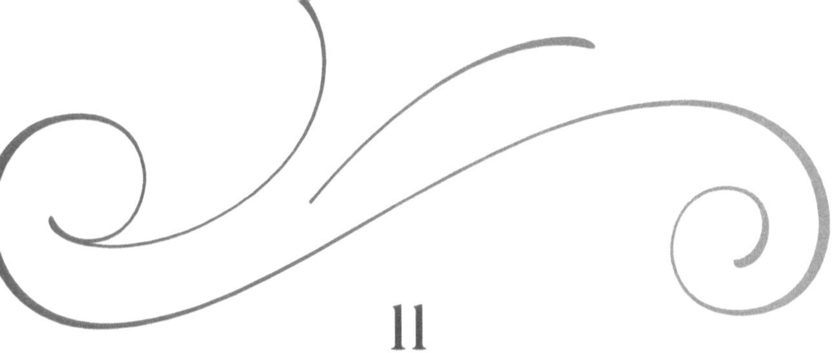

11

rahamstown must have a general shortage of accommodation, because we have to pack up our rooms before we leave for vacation. The university is renting them out to businesspeople coming to town for a conference.

I scrub my identity from my tiny room. Once everything that I'm not taking with me sits in cardboard boxes for storage, the room doesn't feel like mine at all.

I take a shuttle, heaving with fellow students, to the airport in Port Elizabeth. It's possibly the loudest three hours of my life. When we reach the city, I crane my neck to try see out the window, but only catch glimpses of brown buildings and wind-battered trees. The airport itself is tiny compared to the one in Cape Town. There's a sweet shop, a travel agent and not much else. I spend more time waiting to board than I actually do in the air.

When I finally land in Cape Town, I look for Dad at arrivals, but instead find a stranger with a sign for Lilah Durow, who explains that Dad got called to a meeting and sent a taxi to get me instead. I smile and pretend I'm not disappointed. I've been picked up from school by taxi cabs enough times. It's not like it's out of the ordinary. Except… well, except I never stayed at school for two months.

Although it's as if absolutely no time has passed in Cape Town. It could even be the very same day that I left. The temperature is the same, the sky is the same delicate baby blue and wisps of cloud are trying their best to obscure Table Mountain.

Whole seasons can pass in the Mother City with no apparent change. Winter has rain, summer is hot enough that we can pack away the electric blankets, but there are seldom extremes, and most of the time the seasons blur together. Even the trees generally stay the same shade of indelible green.

As we drive into Camp's Bay, I watch the tourists under their bright umbrellas outside the quaint cafes, the palms on the promenade jerking their fronds as the coastal wind whips at them. I look up at the mountains and breathe in the sea air. *Home.* Exactly as I left it.

We pull up to the house and it, too, is exactly as I left it. It's a narrow three-storey with white siding and chrome fixtures. The front gate rolls open as I approach and I look up into the security camera and wave, hoping it's Dad who opened for me.

Instead, I meet Phindi – Dad's most recent housekeeper – at the front door.

"Your father said he will be home by seven. Are you hungry?"

I assure her that I had lunch on the plane and head up to my room with my suitcase.

The familiar smell rushes at me. Warm wood, soft carpet, the ghost of some incense that Tammy gave me years ago. There are still books on the bedside table that I changed my mind about packing.

The space feels too large, too light. It's right at the top of the house with bleached walls and a sloped wooden roof.

Sunlight streams in through a skylight and from the large bay window that's been my reading spot since I can remember. When I sit there now and look down into the immaculate garden, I'm hit with an odd mix of emotions. Nostalgia and something else that I can't quite place. A similar feeling to when I was standing outside res that first day in Grahamstown, when the garden and the lights and all the happy smiling people belonged to one world, and I belonged to another.

Dad doesn't return home that night. He calls the house phone to tell Phindi he'll be late and to serve me dinner before she leaves. She makes a chicken casserole, but I only eat long after dark, when I'm certain Dad will be pulling another all-nighter at the office. It's not unusual for me to sit alone at the dinner table with a book in my hand while eating. It just seems unusual, and unnaturally quiet, after two months of the university dining hall.

It's a strange sensation when I crawl into my old bed, put my head down on my old pillow and listen to the distant roar and crash of the ocean that always used to lull me to sleep. It's strange because it doesn't feel comforting. It doesn't even feel familiar.

Nothing's changed here, so the thing that is wrong and out of place must be me.

ᏝᎬᏝᏖ

"Happy Birthday Lah," Dad greets me at the foot of the stairs with two helium balloons and a slice of cake the next morning.

I rub my eyes, equally relieved that he's home and that he remembered it's my birthday. I've had to remind him before, and it's always super awkward. I'd already decided that if he forgot I'd just pretend I forgot too, even though it's a big one.

"Now don't you go getting up to mischief just because you're officially an adult," he teases over breakfast.

I give him a significant look. He knows me better than that. "You mean like staying up after midnight, right?"

"That's it precisely." He seems to be in a cheerful mood. He even steals a forkful of my cake. "You realise what else this means?"

I raise my eyebrows expectantly.

He picks up his car keys and jangles them in front of me. I groan. I had one driving lesson last year after I turned seventeen – old enough for a learner's permit – and it was so terrifying I've had no desire to get behind the wheel since.

"Lessons. I've already asked around for driving schools in Grahamstown."

Before I have a chance to respond, he stands and grabs his coat.

"You're leaving?" I haven't even finished my cake yet.

He bends to give me a peck on the cheek. "I'll be back before dinner tonight. I promise. I'll take you out to that place in Sea Point that you like so much."

"For sushi?"

"You still like sushi, don't you?"

"*I* do." He, however, never has. He catches my emphasis and flashes me a smile.

"I'll make do. You're the birthday girl."

The day passes without much fanfare, although I do get a message from Tammy – the first in months – which simply wishes me a great day with a balloon emoji.

That night, Dad is true to his word and takes us out for sushi. He presents me with a gift that's perfectly wrapped in gold paper. Definitely not his own handiwork. I can still remember what my presents looked like when he used to wrap them himself: as if they'd rolled around in sticky tape before going through the wash. Gross as they were, I kinda miss the personal touch.

He watches me as I carefully peel the paper off, and he smiles ear to ear at my expression when I see he's gotten me the latest iPhone.

"I don't need this. I don't even know what most of the features are," I say. I know how much these things cost.

He takes my hand and squeezes it. "It's a big birthday, Lah. I wanted you to have something special. Plus, I expect video calls."

The evening passes too quickly. Time alone with him has been rare for years, but after the months away it's even more precious. I tell him about SciFest, but I make it sound like a group of us went. I tell him about Jess and let him think that we're still best friends. I can see in his face how happy he is that his awkward little girl has finally managed to fit in. He's even more delighted when I tell him how good my marks are.

"Yes, Nabelo told me you've been spending a lot of time in the library."

Miss Sukwini. How does she even know that? I've hardly seen her. I knew he was getting reports from her, but it's pretty disturbing that she was keeping tabs on me even when I wasn't in res.

After that night, I don't really see Dad much. He's at work during the day, and often misses dinner. The house is empty aside from Phindi and me. While she seems nice enough, I don't really know her, and we have little to talk about. In the end, I decide to stay out of her way.

It's just a short walk from our house to the promenade and March is always the best time to go to the beach. The South Easter wind still brushes the shoreline, churning up white horses, but it's not the gale force it is at other times of the year, that sandblasts your skin or pulls your hair into your eyes. I hide from the crowds at the far end of the beach, beneath a wide-brimmed sun hat with my nose in a book. There are worse ways to spend a vacation than on warm white sand, listening to kids splashing through rock pools.

I come home on the first Friday of vac to find a bunch of cars outside the house. Has Dad invited people over? My pulse tumbles at the thought of having to be social.

Then I see the black, orange and yellow markings on the car nearest to me and my heart stops completely. The logo on the cars shows the spread-winged emblem of South Africa's crime investigation unit, the Hawks. I start to run. My beach bag slams against my legs. I see Uncle Clay first.

He's dressed in a suit that probably costs more than my year's tuition and his hair is slicked back. I can smell his cologne as I come up to him. He raises a hand as if to stop me running right past him. "Lilah, sweetheart. Hold your horses."

People are crowded around the house, and it's impossible to tell who's supposed to be there and who's just curious.

"Where's Dad?" I demand.

"Now there's just been a bit of confusion…"

"Where's Dad!"

Clay nods at the Hawk car and I see Dad then, in the back, with his head bowed.

I try go to him, but Clay catches my arm. "Hold on, you just wait here with me."

Wait? For what? "What's going on?"

Tears prick at my eyes, and Clay reaches into a pocket for a handkerchief, which he offers me. I don't accept.

"Answer me!"

His eyebrows shoot up. I've never talked back to him, let alone raised my voice. He clears his throat and puts the handkerchief away. "The Hawks have a warrant to search the house in connection with the Dumi case."

"Why?" Blood roars in my ears. Everything Kalin said comes back to me.

Before Clay can answer, the front door opens, and three policemen come out of our house. One has Dad's laptop, and the others are carrying boxes, which must contain stuff they think might be evidence. It's surreal, a nightmare.

A camera clicks behind me and Uncle Clay growls. "Ah, the press. Just what we need."

He drops my arm and rushes forward, presumably to intercept the cops.

I head straight for the car. I need to speak to Dad.

I bang on the window to get his attention. As he looks at me, his face falls. He must be guilty. If he wasn't, he'd be angry, he'd be fighting, he'd be yelling about his innocence through the glass. But now he just looks sad.

I'm pulled away, and my first thought is that the police have me too. I live in the same house; they think I'm complicit. But it's Clay.

The Hawks climb into their car, and Clay holds me back as they pull away.

ℒ

The house is a mess. The Hawks tipped out drawers and emptied cupboards. Phindi is gone – dismissed by Dad perhaps, or she has run because who wants to work for a criminal? Now I'm inside, and Clay has left, I can finally cry, and I find I'm unable to. My chest is too tight. I'm shivering, but not crying.

I don't know what to do. Our Law lectures never covered what the procedure is after a raid. Will Dad be thrown into a holding cell until Monday? Will he be granted bail? Clay didn't tell me anything. Once he made sure I was safe inside, away from the press, he chased after the Hawks.

I'm alone. I've spent most of my life in solitude, but it never felt like this.

I stand in the entrance hall for a good few minutes, trying to wrap my head around what's happened. Dad can't be guilty; he can't be helping a trafficker. He just can't.

And Kalin's words keep echoing in my mind.

Kalin! Kalin will know what the procedures are. He's such a know-it-all, maybe he'll know what I should do.

I run up the stairs, nearly slipping on some papers strewn across the landing, and fall to my knees beside my suitcase. Please tell me I— Yes! I packed *Great Expectations*. I search for his number. I can't remember if I erased it yet.

It's still there. Before I can think better of it, I dial.

I struggle to breathe as it rings once, twice. On the third ring I'm going to hang up. Then he answers.

I can't make myself speak. My tongue is thick.

"Hello?" he repeats.

I close my eyes. *Say something. Get your wits together and say*

93

"Kalin." His name is all I manage, and my voice sounds so soft and weak. I fall mute again, because this is humiliating enough without my own voice betraying me.

"Lilah?"

Get a grip. I try to find my normal speaking voice to ask the questions I need to, as if they're no more than academic in nature.

"Lilah? What's happened? What's wrong?"

"Kalin… uh, I just… I wanted to find out what the procedure is after the Hawks raid a place?" Now I have him on the line, it seems so stupid. Like something I could have googled. "I mean, in South African law. All I know comes from CSI and shows like that, which is American and probably over-dramatised, and they never really show that part anyway. I mean they usually cut to a few hours later, days sometimes." I don't know how to stop babbling. "I'm sorry, you were the first person who came to mind who might know."

"What happened?" Kalin asks again, calm and steady.

"You can guess what happened." On the last word, my voice goes shrill. I'm losing control. My hands are shaking. "Please don't gloat," I whisper, holding my phone with both hands so I don't drop it. "Just tell me what to do."

"You're alone?"

I swallow. "Yes."

Because why else would I be calling him of all people?

"Have you spoken to your father's legal team?"

He says 'team' as if it's a certainty. Surely with Dad's status, it should be? Where are all his fancy lawyer friends?

"My uncle went with him. He didn't tell me anything."

"What's your address?"

I don't understand the reason for the question. Maybe he's trying to work out what prison Dad's been taken to. I give it to him.

"I'm leaving now. I'll be there in about ten hours."

"Kalin, wait, you don't have to—"

The line goes dead. I stare at my phone, trying to think what I might have said that led him to believe I was asking him to drive all the way here. It's ridiculous. Why would he do that?

I still don't know what to do with myself, so I clean. I pack away the contents of the house, I sweep and I scrub. And as I tidy, I worry that I'm doing the wrong thing. Surely I should be racing off to the courthouse to protest my father's innocence? Surely I should be searching for my own clues that will prove the Hawks are wrong? Surely there must be *something* I can do for him?

At about 10:30pm the phone rings in Dad's office. I jump and hit my head on the bookshelf I'm trying to sort.

"Lilah, sweetheart. Here's the deal," Clay says, without preamble, when I answer. "It's a no go on bail. Nature of the case."

"What?" Ice floods my veins.

"Don't get into a panic now. I assure you we did everything we could. They granted him an emergency after-hours bail application; you understand?"

My heartbeat surges and my mind spins so fast I struggle to follow. I play with the telephone cord, the receiver hot against my ear. "You've already had the bail hearing?"

"That's right," he says slowly, as if I'm eight and not eighteen. "I don't know how much you know about this case he's been working on, but it's very sensitive. *Very* sensitive. And the thing is, see the thing is…" I hear him fumbling for a smoke. "They seem to think he's at the centre of this whole Dumi business."

"But he's not!" I protest. There is no *way* he could be. He's not that sort of person.

"Well you and I know that, sweetheart, but they're concerned that he'll destroy evidence or otherwise undermine the objectives of the justice system."

This is Clay's fault. I pull at my hair. He's an awful attorney. It's one of those things we all know but no one says. Dad has friends who could do a better job. Where are they?

And it strikes me that they probably don't want to defend him. Just in case he's guilty.

"We'll appeal of course, sweetheart," Clay says between puffs. "But, fact of the matter is, well, hey, you wanna come stay here for a bit?"

No, I don't want to be anywhere near Clay. I certainly don't want to be alone with him in that big house in Constantia. He and Aunt Rosa split three years ago, and now Tammy's off backpacking, it would just be us.

"It's all right. A friend is coming to fetch me," I say.

It's only a small fib, because I know right then that I'm going to ask Kalin to take me back to Grahamstown with him. I'd rather be anywhere but here.

I start to tidy again. I tidy until I feel hollow instead of angry. At 3am, I'm done scrubbing the floors and I start vacuuming Dad's study. At 5am, when the birds in the garden alert me to the dawn, my head is aching, so I make myself a cup of coffee, but it goes to sand on my tongue like a curse.

At 6am an ancient Ford rolls into the driveway.

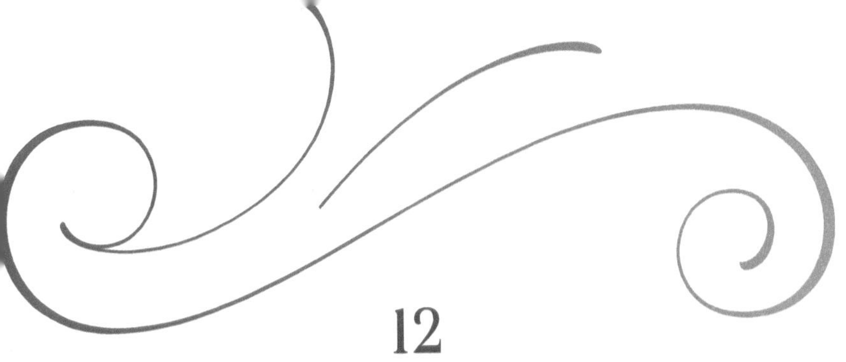

12

Kalin is on my doorstep in a peasant shirt and old jeans. His hair looks like it was in a ponytail, but staged a revolution half way down the N2 and is now a partly free and partly a bird's nest. He looks as bad as I feel.

I stare at him for much longer than is polite. I can't believe he's here, that he actually drove that far just for me.

"Would you like some coffee?" I ask eventually.

"Yes, that would be very welcome."

As I guide him inside, I notice him tilt his head to look upstairs as if he expects someone else might be lurking up there.

"It's smaller than I thought," he says.

"Huh?"

"The house. Thought you'd live somewhere larger."

"You clearly haven't seen Cape Town property prices." We enter the kitchen, which is sparkling and smells like lemons thanks to my 4am mopping frenzy. "This close to the beach? This *is* big."

"I see."

"And it's not like we need a lot of space, it being just the two of us." My voice cracks, despite how desperately I'm trying to be unaffected. I stare at the counter. "Kalin, why are you here?"

He sits on one of the stools. "How much do you know about Dumi?"

"What everybody else does."

"Right. So you know what he's accused of."

"Yeah."

Kalin says nothing, as if he's already made his point.

My sluggish, sleep-starved, mind takes a while to work out what he means. "You think I'm going to get kidnapped and sold into slavery?"

"I think that if your father is guilty—"

"He's not," I protest. "I know what you think, but he's not."

"*If* he is, and Dumi learns that he's in custody, he's going to want leverage to ensure your father doesn't tell on him."

I swallow down the urge to laugh. This isn't the movies, and what he's saying sounds like the plot of a Liam Neeson film. Yet, the Hawks were here. My father is in prison. I would have thought those things equally impossible just yesterday. I shudder.

Kalin leans forward. "I apologise. I didn't mean to alarm you further. This must be difficult enough."

"So you came here to protect me?"

"To fetch you, if you'll permit me to. I'll take you to Grahamstown."

I look up at him. He has no way of knowing I was going to ask just that. It's so kind, and so unexpected, especially considering my reaction when he first predicted this. I don't know what to say.

I turn away before Kalin can see how hard I'm fighting to hold back tears. "I— I'd better go pack. The pods are in the top drawer."

As I hit the stairs, he calls after me, "pods?", but I leave him to figure it out.

He must manage, because when I come down a few minutes later, dragging my hastily packed suitcase, I find him in the lounge with a mug in his hands. He's staring up at the framed picture of Mom and Dad on their graduation day with such intensity he doesn't appear to notice when I come in.

At least that's what I think until he asks, "Your mother?"

"That's right."

"What's that necklace she's wearing?"

I'm so used to seeing the picture I hardly notice it anymore. I have to squint to see the gold piece of jewellery against her black robe. "I'm the wrong person to ask. My dad's the one who could answer you."

I tear up again, but I manage to keep it together.

Kalin's brow furrows. What could possibly have him so perplexed about the image? Dad – who Kalin's familiar with – is in the black undergraduate robe with the purple sash of Law. He has his arm around Mom, who looks a lot like me, but she's got larger eyes, a tan and hair in perfect dark brown waves. She's wearing the red sash of Journalism. They both look young and happy, and it hurts me to see this now, at a time like this.

"Can we go?" I ask.

Kalin snaps out of his reverie and says, "Yes, of course."

"Sorry, you can finish your coffee. I don't mean to rush you. Do you want to have a nap?" I follow him as he marches into the entrance hall and picks up my suitcase for me.

"No, we should get on the road before the press arrive."

⁓⁓⁓

The scenery slides by like I'm watching it on a screen rather than through the open window of Kalin's car. There's the sea, deep blue and sparkling in the sunshine, there's an old house with intricate wrought iron balconies, there's the shipyard that marks the exit from the city, then there's Table Mountain behind us looking like a postcard in the pink light of early morning. None of it feels real.

I tilt my head slightly out of the window so that the wind beats against my cheeks and wails in my ears, bringing me out of my reverie. Kalin switches on the radio. It buzzes static until he pushes a tape – a *tape*! – into the player. I don't recognise the music. It's British folk rock, I think. Guitar and piano, then drums, then lyrics that are difficult to make out but seem to be simultaneously about falling in love and fighting The Man.

It's gone into the fifth or sixth track when Kalin asks, "What happened to your mother?"

"She died. Car accident." I always answer this question in the same blunt way, before adding, "I did too."

He looks at me sharply. They always do, as if they expect to find me suddenly transformed into a ghost or a zombie.

"I was a few days old. She was going to the store to get groceries while Dad was at work, and I was in the front seat in my baby chair. Another car skipped a red light and rammed straight into us. She died instantly, I think. When they took me out of the car, I wasn't breathing, but they managed to resuscitate me at the scene."

"I'm sorry." Kalin sounds genuinely contrite.

"I don't even remember her," I assure him. "As I said, I was a few days old. After that, Dad sold the house – this was when we lived in Port Elizabeth – and got rid of all her things and moved us to Cape Town, where he went on to be the…"

I was going to say something like hero of the people, as if what happened to my mother was nothing but a sad origin story. But I can't say that now, not with certainty.

"Anyway, that's my life's story."

"Do you want breakfast?" Kalin asks.

I don't. This numb sleep-deprived body is above all physical needs, it seems. But I'm aware that I haven't eaten since lunchtime yesterday, so it's probably a good idea.

A few minutes later, we roll into an Engen 1 Stop with a Wimpy diner. Trees dot the road beside the petrol pumps. The parking lot overlooks a vineyard picked clean by a recent harvest. It's a weird counterpoint to the bright blue and red metal of the signage, the blinding white of the building.

Kalin fills up the car and I try to pay for the petrol, but he stops me. "Save your money for now."

And I realise that the money I have is thanks to the allowance that Dad's been giving me. A spike of panic stabs through me, and

I look away while Kalin talks to the petrol attendant. I don't want him to see me crack.

What am I going to do with no money?

Inside the diner, we both order coffee and I choose the smallest breakfast on the menu, which Kalin then upsizes when we place our orders.

I don't have much of an appetite, but I make a valiant effort to at least get through my scrambled eggs.

"A question for you," Kalin says at length.

I look up at him.

"Why did you call me last night?"

My heart beats a little faster, and there's no reason it should, because my motive was honest. It's not like I wanted to hear his steady voice. I wasn't reaching out for comfort. I prod at my breakfast. "You know law things."

"I see."

I tell him exactly what happened, including how no one gave me much information, and the fact that bail was denied. My voice wavers only a little. I manage to deliver most of the story in a flat, disinterested tone, as if I'm presenting a theoretical problem for his consideration. "Clay said they'd appeal but I'm not sure when."

"Hmm," Kalin says. Which is not at all helpful.

He finishes his food, and I think that 'hmm' might be the summation of his comments on the matter. Then he says, "Lilah, I know this isn't what you want to hear, but he might be safest where he is."

"He's a prosecutor, Kalin." I don't even want to think about the implications of that. "If he's sent to Pollsmoor…"

Pollsmoor is the maximum-security prison nearest to home, and it's known for being particularly brutal. Some of South Africa's most dangerous criminals are held there. People Dad put away. I let out a little involuntary whimper.

Kalin holds up his hands as if trying to calm a horse that's about to bolt. "Precisely. He's a prosecutor, so he knows the system. If he wanted bail, he would have known how to argue for it. Likewise, he'll know how to avoid Pollsmoor. The important thing is that prisons have guards. And those guards will know he's a target, and possibly an important witness. They'll keep him safer than he could keep himself if out on bail."

"Like witness protection?" I ask, thinking about how just over a week ago I was explaining the plot of CSI to him, and now he's explaining the plot of my own life to me.

His mouth quirks a little at my question. My ears are hot. I'm studying law and I should know this stuff.

"He may very well turn witness, but I imagine he'll hold off on that unless they can guarantee your safety. Did you tell anyone where you were going?"

"I told my Uncle Clay a friend was picking me up. I didn't say where I… I don't know where I'm going."

It strikes me suddenly that res isn't an option. There's some businesswoman staying in my room. I have no money for a hotel.

Kalin taps the side of his cup, and I feel another 'hmm' coming on, as if he hasn't thought that far either.

"I used to be a bad person," he says.

"Okay?"

"Let me explain, or at least try to explain, myself a little." He looks up, as if asking my permission to continue.

"Kalin, maybe it's sleep deprivation, but you're not making much sense right now."

He nods, taps on his cup some more. "Long ago, I did some terrible things. I was… terrible. I used people, I hurt people. I'm trying to make amends. In little ways. When I can. A part of me thinks… a large part of me thinks that I'll never be able to. But I am trying." He takes a deep breath. "When you asked why I'm here, that's the real answer. I was able to come get you, take you away from that – from the press, maybe from Dumi's thugs – so I did. So, when I say this now, understand where it's coming from. I have a home, and you are welcome to stay there with me. If you need somewhere to stay."

I don't get invited to be a house guest on the regular, but that's certainly the most roundabout way of doing it I've ever heard.

"You make it sound like I'm a convenient opportunity for atonement." I remember his steady grip and the boerewors roll. "That's exactly what I am. What I was that night at the LMS party, what I was sitting alone at the Kaif. I'm an ongoing pity project."

"No," he says, without looking at me.

"Do you have a points system?" It feels good to lash out at *something*. "Ding, take the lonely girl to the festival, that's ten redemption points. Ding, walk the drunk girl home, that's fifteen because she almost threw up on your shoes. Ding—"

He stands and I jerk back.

"I'm going to use the restroom."

My heart is still in my throat as he walks away. *What are you doing, Lilah? He drove halfway across the country for you and this is how you behave?*

I make another attempt at my breakfast, but if it was difficult to get food down before, now it's nearly impossible.

I don't look up when his chair moves again. He asks for the bill, and we sit in silence, with me trying to find the courage to apologise and accept his offer of a place to stay, and him… I don't know. It feels like he's watching me.

"I didn't walk you home to earn *points*," he says eventually. "I wasn't going to leave you at that bar in the middle of a group of hungry-eyed men."

My head snaps up so fast my neck twinges. *Hungry-eyed?* He must have misread the situation. No one would be hungry for me.

"They were trying to talk to you, flirting with you, and you were in no condition to respond. I worried for your safety if I left you there."

"I'm sorr—"

"As for the science festival… I know loneliness. I'd seen the way you sequestered yourself in the library, how you were always sitting on your own. If you want to call it pity, then by all means do, but I certainly didn't invite you in hopes of earning points. I invited you because loneliness is the worst feeling in the world. Unlike me, however, you don't deserve it."

Now I can't drag my gaze away from him. His eyes are large and sorrowful, his cheeks seem almost hollow and with the stubble on his chin and the dark marks under his lower lids, he looks like a prisoner on death row. If not for that look, I may have called what he said over dramatic, but all I see is sincerity, perhaps the deepest sincerity he's ever shown me.

"I'm sorry, I didn't mean what I said."

He nods as if he expected that but doesn't quite believe it. "My home isn't very large, but you're welcome to it."

I know hardly anything about Kalin, and I can't even imagine what kind of place he lives in. My lips are suddenly dry. "I'd appreciate that."

⤎⤏

Evening is falling when we drive past the monument on its lone hill. The golden light of the sinking sun catches the windows, so that the building seems to be glowing. My impression of Grahamstown now could not be more different from my first. Everything is brushed with that warm light – the street, the trees, the houses. It really does feel like I'm being welcomed back, even though I was gone less than a week.

Kalin skirts the edge of campus, and I spot some people in suits outside my res, before he continues straight into a part of town where I've never been. The buildings are older here, and when I comment on that Kalin informs me that this is in fact the oldest part of the town.

"You see the plaque there below that window?"

I nod as the little square of metal catches the light.

National monument. Old Settler's Cottage.

It's kinda cool, and kinda creepy. More creepy when he slows down and turns into the driveway beside that very house. "You live in a national monument?"

"Rent is cheap. It's trouble to renovate. Luckily, I'm not fussy."

"You're not worried about ghosts?"

He laughs as he climbs out of the car to open the big, black gate blocking our way. If my imagination couldn't handle some fog, I'm not sure I want to know what it might come up with in this place. I picture waking in the middle of the night to find the ghost of some old settler – in a cloak, with a lantern – staring down at me and saying "Great Ones! What are you doing here?" Of course, Kalin would live somewhere old and creepy. It follows the trend, doesn't it? Old clothing, old car, old phone. Old house.

"You do have electricity?" I ask as he gets back into the car.

He smiles. "I have electricity. I'm not quite that backward."

He parks in the shade of a giant jacaranda tree. It's lost all its purple blossoms now, but it must be quite a sight in spring. An old stone wall blocks the view of the house. If he lives in an ancient hovel, that would explain why he invited me in such a circuitous way. Maybe he's embarrassed by it.

I take my case out of the trunk before he has a chance to, and he leads me to a narrow gate, which he shoulders open.

Then we're standing in the Secret Garden.

It's really a little courtyard, but it's so overgrown that it looks like a garden. At its centre is an old well with a tree growing out of it. Ivy twists up its trunk, clinging onto its rough bark. The courtyard must have once been cobbled, but now grass and weeds have pushed up between the stones, and the outside border is a tangled mess of flowers and shrubs.

The cottage at the end of this courtyard is whitewashed with a green wooden door and a pair of rectangular windows at about eye level. As Kalin approaches it, something moves in the bushes beside him and I jolt.

A big orange-and-white cat lands at his feet and meows up at him indignantly. It winds itself between his legs as he tries to unlock the door.

He nudges it gently with his boot. "Back off, Fatso. You're going to trip me."

"You named your cat Fatso?"

"He's not my cat."

The door swings open, and Fatso races in ahead of us, his bushy tail straight up. Kalin sighs, and we follow him in.

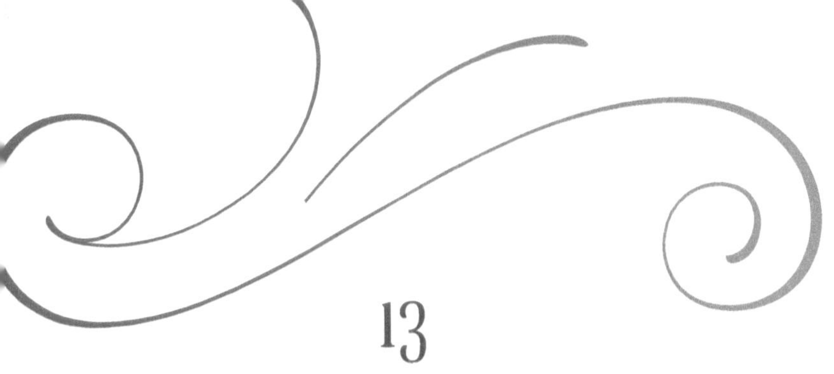

13

I'm in a small kitchen with a yellow linoleum floor. It's just wide enough for Kalin and me to stand abreast between the counter – which Fatso leaps up onto – and the fridge against the opposite wall. The sink is filled with dishes, the small table in the corner is laden with takeaway boxes, and the lacy curtains over the windows could do with a dust. But the space itself is far homier than I would have expected from Kalin.

Fatso meows again.

"Drop the act," Kalin says, and he says it so seriously that, at first, I think he's speaking to me.

Fatso's tail flicks from side to side. "Meow," he says, pointedly.

Kalin turns his full attention on the feline. He puts his hands on his hips and stares him down.

"Meow," Fatso says.

"I know you've already eaten. You can't tell me you're starving just because I wasn't here."

Fatso flops down and shows us his fluffy white belly.

Kalin sighs. "If you want food, you probably shouldn't be advertising how very well fed you are." But he opens the fridge and pulls out a milk carton.

Seeing this, Fatso hops down off the counter and returns to trying to trip Kalin while he finds a saucer in the cluttered sink, rinses it and pours out a little milk. His Ginger Highness purrs his approval loudly when Kalin sets down this offering, then promptly forgets about us as he digs in.

"So, he's not your cat?"

"No."

"He seems to think otherwise."

"He's a con artist. I shouldn't give in, but sometimes it's the only way to get peace."

We stare at Fatso for a minute before Kalin says, "You must be tired," and brushes past me to open a door to my left. He tugs a chain dangling from the ceiling and an old light flickers on to reveal a bedroom that looks like it belongs in a cosy bed and breakfast.

The wooden floor is half-hidden under a faded rug, a crocheted quilt is draped over the bed, and the bedside light is shaded by a lacy lampshade that looks like it's made from pieces of doily.

"Are you sure you live here?" I ask, because I can't see Kalin in any of this.

He smiles. "Settle in. I'll be in the study if you need me."

I don't have to ask where the study is, because only one other door leads off the kitchen.

Left to my own devices, I take a closer look around the room. The bed's been hastily made and there's white and orange hair at the foot of it. When I open the big freestanding closet to hang up my clothes, I find Kalin's brown jacket and a range of shirts. I close it quickly. This isn't a guest room. This is Kalin's room. Is he giving me his bed? Or does he intend for us to share it? Both options are equally unsettling.

In the en-suite bathroom Kalin's razor sits on the sink, his hairbrush by the mirror, but there are no personal mementos or pictures. I discover some fresh towels in a cupboard under the sink and decide to take a shower before unpacking.

Despite my fears about the ancient house's plumbing (or lack thereof), the water is hot, and I stand under it for ages, until I glow bright pink, trying to let go of the tension in my muscles. After the drive, I feel like a deck chair that's been folded up so long its joints have rusted. But most of the tension, I know, won't be alleviated no matter how long I stand here. I wish I'd said something to Dad about Kalin's accusations before it came to this. I know with more certainty than I've ever known anything, that he's not willingly contributing to modern slavery. But I can't get the image of his face yesterday out of my head. He's guilty of something, but what?

I switch off that line of thought with the water. If I let it, my mind will continue in those circles for eternity. Kalin's right, Dad knows the system well enough to protect himself. There is nothing I can do but wait. Wait for more information to come out. Wait 'til I can speak to him.

I rub my hair dry and pad through to the bedroom to dig in my suitcase for my pyjamas.

The door opens.

I'm in the middle of the room in nothing but a towel, and Kalin's in the doorway gaping at me, carrying a pile of old books.

My arms fly to my chest to make sure the towel is properly secured. I flush cold then burning hot. "I… uh, shower." All I'm capable of is caveman speak.

Kalin is still staring, but suddenly seems to realise so and drops his gaze to a spot on the floor.

"Books." He clears his throat. "I thought you might like to read. To take your mind off… I'll go."

He sets the books down on a chair by the door, and leaves me alone with my rapid heartbeat.

As if this situation needed more awkwardness.

He's seen me drunk, he's seen me sweating, he's seen sleep-starved and on the verge of tears. So why not add half-naked to the list? If I ever cared how I looked to him, that ship has long sailed. And I absolutely don't care. Still, the gym-class jeers ring fresh in my ears as I look down at my pale legs.

My head is pounding from lack of sleep, and it's this more than anything that pushes me to search my luggage for those PJs.

I want to crawl beneath that ugly quilt and lose myself to unconsciousness, but I still need to clarify just where I – where *we* – will be sleeping. Besides, I should thank him for the books.

They're beautiful. He probably hasn't heard about the invention of the Kindle, but in this case it's truly the thought that counts. The books are old (which shouldn't surprise me), old enough to maybe even be first edition. A few are leather-bound; a couple are in embossed cloth. They smell musty, like the library. There's a copy of *A Christmas Carol* that has illustrations, and the rest are all unfamiliar, but probably as carefully selected. I definitely need to thank him.

I check myself in the mirror first, though. This pair of PJs is particularly conservative – long-sleeved and navy, with buttons down the front of the shirt. I usually don't bother with the top two, but now I'm sure to do them up.

When I peek around the study door, I discover every aspect of Kalin that's absent from the rest of the house crammed into a few square metres. The left side of the room is taken up with overflowing bookshelves. Directly in front of me there's an old fireplace, and a settee so burdened with books and papers I can hardly see its cracked leather upholstery. A countertop runs beneath the courtyard window, on which a cabinet of tiny drawers and several boxes sit, piled higgledy-piggledy atop one another. The room is lit only by a dim overhead light – like the bedroom – so it's difficult to make out details, but I spot an old pendulum clock and a vintage globe on one of the shelves.

Kalin pauses in the act of pacing across the room, wearing the same expression as when he caught me in the towel.

"I'm not naked," I say, hoping to ease the tension.

"So I see."

Fatso comes running at me from some dark recess of the study and rubs himself against my legs as if we're already best friends. I stand paralysed because I've never had a cat before, and I'm not sure what to do with one.

"Sorry, he's a pest." Kalin comes and scoops him up. "Do you need something? I didn't think as far as dinner, I'm afraid. There isn't much here, but I can order in?"

I shake my head. We stopped at a farm stall earlier with the most amazing chicken pies, and I'm still full after that. "I wanted to thank you for the books."

"Oh, you're welcome." Kalin scratches Fatso's head absently. The cat leans into the touch and purrs. "I, uh, have something else for you."

He sets Fatso down on the counter and starts digging through the stack of boxes.

Something else? "I really don't need anything else," I protest. I also don't *want* anything else. He's done so much for me already.

Kalin pays me no mind and continues rummaging. So, I just stay there gazing into the chaos. Among the clutter on the counter are a number of miniature racks draped with… I don't even know. There's a crystal dangling from a black ribbon, bits of shattered geode fastened to a chord, a pewter pendant shaped like a bird's skull.

"So, uh, what is all this?" I ask.

"My workshop."

"Workshop?"

"I make jewellery. You know, to pay those bothersome bills? Ah!" He finds what he's looking for and straightens.

"You make jewellery?" I repeat.

"Well, make, repair, design… You're looking at me as if I just announced I have a third arm."

I blink. "Sorry. It's just unexpected."

He smirks at that. "I'm curious to hear what you did expect?"

"I don't know…" I don't want to say 'something more masculine', because that's a pretty old-fashioned way of thinking.

"I thought you were an academic, I guess. You know, the job that *pays you* to be a know-it-all."

"Ah, there's your mistake: thinking academia pays."

He holds out his hand to me, uncurling his fingers to reveal a silver pendant attached to a chain. It looks Celtic, an X shape connected with intricate knots, forming a circle. I search Kalin's face for meaning.

"It's not exactly gold, but…"

And I click. "My mother's necklace?"

"I thought, at a time like this, you might like it."

A time like this. This day when I feel so disconnected from my father, from who I thought he was. The books were sweet, this is next level.

"How do you even have that?"

He shrugs. "It's not an unpopular design. I think I have a brass one somewhere too."

He undoes the clasp and takes a step closer.

"Kalin, I can't. You've been so kind already. I can't possibly accept something else."

"Yes, you can." He holds it up to my throat. "It's not particularly valuable and, besides, it's broken."

It doesn't look broken, but he doesn't wait for me to say more. He reaches around my neck, and his fingers brush my skin as he fastens the chain. His light touch sends a pulse through me that I have to put down to exhaustion and a craving for comfort. In that moment I'm very aware of how close he is.

"Broken?" I'm as paralysed as I was when Fatso was winding around my feet.

"It's meant to have a gem of some sort in the centre. I didn't see what gem your mother had, unfortunately, or I could add it."

I shake my head. "Kalin, it's too much." I reach up to undo the clasp, but he halts me, with a hand over mine.

"How about this. You can pay me back for the necklace, and the board and whatever else—"

"And the twenty-four hours on the road, but I don't have money—"

"I didn't say with money." He eyes his cluttered workspace. "The Arts Fest is coming up, and I have a lot of stock to prepare, but I'm also working on something. An... academic project. I could use the help. With the stock."

"Of course." I want more than anything to be useful, and to have something to focus on besides Dad. "But I don't know the first thing about jewellery."

"I'll teach you. And you can keep this, and whatever else might take your fancy, in exchange. Deal?"

I trace a finger over the pendant. It is very pretty, and it is kind of nice to have this vague connection to my mother. I don't have anything of hers, and this is the closest I'm likely to get. "All right. But I don't want anything else."

"Fair enough." He offers a gentle smile that indicates he understands my reluctance. "Thank you."

We stand like that for an awkward minute, him too close and me grappling with how I feel about that, before he steps away. "I'm sure you're tired."

He said that in the kitchen too. Is it a polite way of saying he wants me to leave him in peace to continue pacing? "Where should I sleep?"

"Take the bed."

"Kalin, you drove through last night to rescue me. I think you should take the bed."

"I'm fine in here." He nods towards the settee.

"That doesn't seem—"

"Lilah, I'm fine. I'll see you in the morning."

All right then. I say goodnight and Fatso follows me out.

Flames flicker in a grate. I smell wood smoke. I hear people talking in low, frightened voices.

The room is lit by the fire and a few candles dripping wax onto empty tables. It's a tavern, but there are very few people here, and they're all wearing cloaks that hide their faces.

"This is a mistake," someone hisses. "We should not gather in one place. If we are discovered—"

The door on the far side of the room slams open. Snow, wind, ice, cold. The candles sputter out. Some of the cloaked people draw weapons and stand ready to face the intruder, while a few scuttle back against the wall in fear. Silhouetted in the doorway is an imposing figure – black against the white of a blizzard outside.

I hear a whispered name. Overlord.

And I know now where I am. I'm in my kingdom. The people holding this clandestine meeting are rebels, plotting against the evil sorcerer who rules this land. If that really is him, if he's found them, they're all dead.

The figure moves into the room and casts a spell towards the door. It closes itself. There's an intake of breath next to me. The man who thought this was all a bad idea in the first place looks like he's about to faint.

Now within the ring of firelight, the figure lowers its hood.

"At ease." It's a beautiful woman with dark brown hair that tumbles past her shoulders in messy waves. She has a scar on her cheek, but otherwise her skin is flawless. Did I invent her? She's only vaguely familiar.

"Lady Nuadha," the frightened man breathes.

Her dark eyes snap to him. "Do not call me that, Sloane."

"My Lady? I meant it in deference. You are of the line of—"

"Enough. My blood means nothing if it's spilled across the Overlord's floor." She unshoulders a pack that made up the bulk of her silhouette. I can't stop staring at her. She's wearing leathers that are intricately woven with countless straps and buckles under a fur-lined cloak, somehow managing to look both feminine and incredibly badass.

"Alayna." An old man shuffles from the cluster of cloaked figures. "It is good to see you. We were afraid you hadn't made it across."

"I almost didn't."

I notice then that she's cradling her left hand to her chest.

"Let me look at that, child." The old man reaches for her, but she steps away.

"We have more important things to discuss." With her right hand, she digs in the pack and draws out a roll of parchment. When she flattens it out on the table, I see it's a map. It's my map, the one I have above my bed.

She points to the edge of the Mist Wood. "This is where I was stopped."

"That's very far south."

"It is not in accordance with our predictions," one of the other cloaked figures says.

"No, it is not." She bites the edge of her thumb, and the group shuffles apart a few steps, circling around the map. I notice some of them have dropped their hoods now too.

"Does this mean he knows of our plans?" Sloane asks.

Alayna shrugs. "Probably. It was only a matter of time. He is no fool."

There's a thick silence, as if everyone is holding their breath.

"Might his army be searching for the orbs?" someone asks.

"His spies! What if he knows everything we have discovered?" a woman with a high-pitched voice asks.

"It is possible." Alayna is calm and cool. "It is also possible that he knows where they are already, but he believes that no one has the power to use them against him. He is arrogant. That has always been his weakness."

"Always?" Sloane asks. "You seem to know much about our enemy."

Alayna turns her dark eyes on him, "We cannot hope to defeat him without understanding him."

"You ask us to take many risks on faith—"

"If you do not wish to risk yourself, you should leave the resistance."

He shifts uncomfortably. Then he says, "We shall defeat him or die trying."

This mantra is taken up by the group. Alayna strides to the fireplace, where she retrieves a shard of burned wood. She flips the map over and scribbles on the back of it with the charcoal, then takes a dagger from her side and cuts the parchment into seven separate strips.

"May I have your coin purse, Sloane?"

The man fidgets, before offering it to her with clear reluctance. Slowly, while everyone watches her, she rolls up the strips and sticks them into the bag.

"This is the plan," she says as she works. "I have written the names of the orbs. We will draw one at random. We will split into teams of two. Each of us will use our knowledge and contacts to locate just one orb. None of us will know where the others are, or who is after which orb. It is safer. This way, if any of us are captured, we have limited knowledge. One year from today we shall meet and bring the orbs together."

"Where?" Sloane asks.

"A place across the sea. A place of power. We will take him as far from his fortress as possible, away from all his support."

"Take him? How will we take him?"

"I will lure him."

14

$\mathcal{M}$y ringtone wakes me. My fingers close around my phone before I'm even fully conscious.

"Dad?"

But it's not him. It's Darren.

"Lilah? I just saw the news. Are you okay?"

I rub my eyes and sit up, dislodging Fatso, who was asleep on my feet. "Um yeah. Yeah, I'm fine." Or as fine as can be expected.

"Where are you?"

I'm in Kalin's home, in Kalin's bed. I don't know what time it is, but sunlight is streaming through the window.

"I'm back in Grahamstown."

"You are? Do you have somewhere to stay?"

I'm still trying to wrap my head around the fact that Darren thought to call. His concern is surprising. "Yeah."

"Because my folks run a B&B, I'm sure you could stay there if you need somewhere. Do you want me to ask them? I'll ask them. I'll call back soon."

He ends the call, and I stare at my phone, which tells me it's 9am and also that I have about a thousand notifications (or at least enough to take up my entire screen). Everyone I've ever known has messaged me to find out what's going on. I don't want to deal with that. I don't want to deal with any of it.

I consider rolling over and going back to sleep. There was a mission in my dream, something I had to do… That's right, the

Overlord. My made-up kingdom. Orbs? It's already starting to fade. Fatso climbs onto my lap and massages my knee with his paws.

I scratch his ear. "Are you hungry?"

"Meow."

"Me too."

We go to find Kalin, but he's not in the bright kitchen or in his cluttered study. A note pinned to the front door says he'll be back later, but with no details of when that might be or where he's gone. The fridge is empty except for the carton of milk and some condiments that look as ancient as everything else Kalin owns. The cupboards are equally bare. Well, this explains the collection of takeout boxes.

Is starving himself part of that self-imposed purgatory he was talking about yesterday, or is this laziness? *Long ago, I did some terrible things*, he said. What kind of terrible things? Should I be more concerned about living under his roof?

My stomach grumbles. Fatso and I stare at each other. "I should go get some groceries. It's the least I can do."

Fatso is silent on the matter.

"Of course, there is a chance I could be kidnapped." *Kidnapped.* The thought still seems completely ludicrous. "Or ambushed by the media. I wonder what they're saying." No TV here, and I'm willing to bet no Wi-Fi. I need to buy mobile data too.

I'm not brave enough to go to the busy Pick n Pay centre, but I'm pretty sure I can find my way to the BP from here.

In the end, I don a hoodie that at least makes me feel more invisible, then leave a note for Kalin telling him exactly what I'm doing and to call me when he gets back if I haven't returned. I put down my mobile number in case he doesn't have it.

When I leave the Settler's Cottage, I'm satisfied with myself for getting out into the world rather than curling up into a useless ball of despair.

That's before I see the first headline.

A little way down the road, a poster for the Sunday paper is strapped up on a lamp post: DUMI PROSECUTOR ON PAYROLL. They didn't even have the courtesy to use a question mark.

At the BP, there's a stack of newspapers right at the front, and my father's face gazes at me from both the weekly and the daily. One is a close-up of him in court looking angry, and one is a picture of him being arrested outside our house. I pick them up and retreat to one of the quiet aisles. A wave of nausea rolls through me as I scan the pages.

Addie Shahid, the chief witness, is dead. Her body was found Thursday morning. The perp was careless and left evidence which led to his arrest that night. By Friday, he'd "sung like a canary". There's a lot of waffle in both articles from the police congratulating each other on a job well done, but the key takeaway is that this guy, this murderer, pointed the finger at Dad. And instead of saying anything in his defence, Clay is quoted as stating some variation of "no comment," leaving the journalists and various experts to speculate how deep Dad's involvement goes.

How alone Dad must feel now, how worried about me.

My phone rings again and I jump.

"Lilah? It's Darren."

I forgot he said he'd call again.

"Listen, we're having a braai at my place. You wanna come along? Take your mind off stuff?"

I really don't. I'm not comfortable with strangers at the best of times. "Thanks, but I don't think I can deal with facing people after, well, you know."

"It won't be an interrogation. Promise. I'll set a rule, no mentioning your dad. And it's a small thing anyway. Just a few of us. Come get a good meal. You can meet the fam. I'll pick you up, where are you?"

I'm relieved that I don't have to say I'm at Kalin's after the way Darren looked at him at SciFest. I'm still reluctant, but lack the energy to argue. Besides, what else am I going to do with the rest of my day? Obsess over what I'm *not* doing for Dad? I tell him I'm at the BP.

I have time to pick up some supplies before Darren rolls up in a shiny white Honda Civic.

My heart jerks when he smiles and waves at me. It's not a pleasant sensation. I feel exposed, like he knows my deepest shame, even though logically I have nothing to be ashamed of.

He keeps his word and doesn't mention Dad as I climb in next to him with my grocery bags, or as we drive. He keeps up a steady string of small talk about the weather, and the vac. His brightness makes me even more uncomfortable, because I know it's false.

We pull up at a gated complex and the security guard waves him in.

"You don't have to do this." I've been fidgeting with the grocery bag so much that one of the handles has broken.

"Don't be silly. I'm sure you could do with some company."

I tie a knot in the handle. I shouldn't have bought stuff. It's only going to make walking into the braai even more awkward. And I don't even know what I look like. What's my hair doing? It was under a hood; it's probably a bird's nest.

Darren's apartment is on the ground floor of a duplex. It's picket-fence perfect – white and clean with a pot plant by the front door and a shaded parking spot.

"Hey, we're back!" he calls from the cool tiled entrance hall, and a chorus of voices answer. I'm glad that I got the groceries after all, because now I can enter bearing Doritos and orange juice, rather than being empty-handed and destitute.

Sibu is on the tan sofa playing Xbox and he smiles and waves. An older woman with cropped grey hair and pearls hurries towards us with her arms out. "You must be Lilah!"

"Mom…" Darren cautions.

"I'm not going to say anything," she assures him, before returning her attention to me. "How do you do? I'm Shirley. Are those for us? Oh, you didn't need to bring anything." She whisks the chips and juice away. "Can I get you something?"

"Mom, don't fuss. She's fine."

"I'm not fussing, I'm being polite."

"Mom!" another voice shouts from out of sight. "Where's the potato peeler?"

Shirley gives me a pained look before turning and calling back, "It's in the drawer."

"No, it's not."

"Yes, it is." I don't hear the rest of what she mutters as she goes to follow up on this conundrum. I'm almost certain that the other voice belonged to Bianca, and that's confirmed when the man with the tattoos who I saw her with before comes into the lounge, carrying the baby.

"What's the score— Oh, I thought you had the game on." He peers at the screen over Sibu's shoulder as if he hasn't noticed us.

"Frank, you remember Lilah?" Darren says.

"Oh, yeah, hi." He waves but returns his attention to the screen almost immediately. Sibu is playing a football game, and I suppose that's a pretty close second to watching a real game. The baby seems just as entertained by the bright colours as its father.

So, when Darren said "fam" he really meant "family". This is a family gathering, and here I am, that girl he kissed the one time. And here he is, taking my packets from me and guiding me to the couch like a real friend rather than the guy I had the hots for in my first week here.

"What can I get you?" he asks once I'm seated. He flashes me that same bright smile as before. "There's Coke, beer… I promised you wine, didn't I?"

"Coke's fine."

Darren disappears, and I finally have a chance to look around.

The lounge is small, but a sliding door into a grassy yard gives it the illusion of space. Outside, a bald man in khaki shorts tends a Weber, and I suppose that must be Darren's dad. A corridor to the left of the TV leads to the rest of the house. Everything's in muted tones. Is this Darren's place or his parents'? Or both? Does he still live with his folks?

"Hey, you wanna play?" Sibu asks. "There's another controller."

I shake my head. I'll do a good enough job of humiliating myself without trying to figure out what all those buttons do. With a sports game no less. He and Frank chat about the game and the personalities that the little figures on screen are supposed to represent, then they discuss Frank's fantasy football league and I tune out.

"Lilah?" I start at my name. Darren's back and he's handing me my drink.

Shirley comes around the other side of the sofa. "Oh, come now, put off the TV. You boys are going to bore the poor girl to tears!"

"No, really, I'm fine." I try to protest, but Sibu obligingly switches off the game. At once the room seems full of people. Bianca's come in too, and she takes the baby from Frank, and Darren's dad comes in to make introductions and fetch the boerewors. Momentary chaos reigns as everyone finds places to sit, and when they do, I feel as if they're all staring at me, even though they're talking to each other.

"Where are you staying, dear?" Shirley asks after a few minutes of chatter.

"Uh, with a friend." I don't want to mention Kalin's name while Bianca is in the room. She's directly behind Shirley's armchair, feeding the baby a bottle.

Shirley's attention remains fixed on me. I feel pressed to say more. "He, uh, he's a local as well, so didn't need to go home for the vac." As if that wasn't all obvious information.

Apparently it wasn't, though, because something in that

explanation makes Darren click. "It's not that Kalin guy?"

Darren's next to me, so I don't know if he sees me flinch. Bianca looks up sharply, and Shirley's brow gathers.

My stomach twists. "Yeah." Because what else can I say, really?

"You've got space at the B&B don't you, Mom?" Darren asks, and I just want to sink into my seat and disappear because the only thing worse than her taking pity on me is Darren asking her to take pity on me.

"It's okay," I say quickly.

"Well yes, absolutely." Shirley's brow is still furrowed.

I can't pay for a room at a B&B, and I definitely don't want to take charity. It's bad enough that I'm indebted to Kalin. "Thank you, but I'm fine there. It's only for a few days anyway. My res is paid until the end of the year, so I'll be fine."

Darren's dad comes in asking where he can find the rest of the meat.

When conversation resumes, we move onto other topics. I discover that Shirley used to work in the Linguistics department of the university and that she has a doctorate in Celtic language. She tells me all about her thesis, and it probably bores everyone else in the room as much as the video game bored me, but I find it fascinating.

"Potatoes should be done," Bianca announces abruptly. She hands the sleepy baby to her mother. "Lilah, would you mind helping me for a minute?"

I jump up, grateful for the opportunity to be useful. This follows a script I know. Man make fire, woman make salad. Pretty standard South African braai stuff.

The kitchen is compact and stark compared to Kalin's. Bianca doesn't speak as she goes to the stove and takes off the pot.

"I enjoyed your talk. At SciFest," I say to try break the ice.

"Have you heard of the Formicoxenus ant?" she asks.

I don't think I can even pronounce that. "Uh, no. I don't think so." I slide further into the room, watching her drain the potatoes.

"It's a clever little thing. It takes on the aspects of other ants so it can invade their nests. Seems harmless at first, until it's too late."

My skin prickles. "Is this another story about parallel universes?" But I know it's not.

She meets my gaze. "Careful who you trust, that's all I'm saying."

"You're saying Kalin is a Formi— Forma—" I give up. "Dangerous ant?"

She snorts in what might be genuine amusement at my inability to say the scientific name. "Do you know how to make potato salad?"

"Yes."

"Great. You do that, I'll do the greens." She sets the colander of boiled potatoes on the counter next to me and goes over to the fridge to pull out the various ingredients we'll need.

"What happened between you and Kalin?" I ask.

"It's a long story."

And I want to know that story, but neither of them seem willing to tell it.

"He said he used to be a bad person."

"Did he now?"

"And that you weren't involved, uh, romantically."

She snorts again. "Are you?"

"What?"

"Involved romantically?"

Heat rushes up my neck to my cheeks. "No."

"You should keep it that way." She pulls some bowls down from a shelf and hands me one. "In fact, the more you minimise your contact with him, the better."

She breaks a head of lettuce as if for emphasis.

Making salad beside Bianca is what Jess would call "awkward AF" and I'm super relieved when we're done and can take the bowls outside.

The others are now standing around the braai with their drinks, and there's an uncomfortable silence when I arrive. I just know they were talking about me. Shirley is overly nice again, and she insists that I be the first to dish up. I blush through the whole thing.

When everyone's got their food, Darren sidles up to me and says in a low voice, "Want to go eat inside?"

Yes. Yes, I definitely do.

He must have seen my discomfort. He leads me through the lounge, past the kitchen, into the room at the end of the corridor and I only realise when I enter that this is a bedroom.

It's *his* bedroom.

Unlike Kalin's room, this one is filled with things that represent its occupant. There's a shelf of figurines, a couple of trophies, and a poster of Spider-man on the door. The double bed has a masculine grey cover, and an old Guitar Hero controller stands in the corner.

He smiles at me. "There. Nice and quiet."

The room even smells like him: the fresh, heady aroma that takes me instantly back to that night under the stars. My heart beats a little faster.

"I thought this might have been your parents' place."

"Because Dad's the braai master?"

"That. And the potato peeler thing."

"Potato peeler?"

"Bianca asked your mom where it was."

He laughs and holds up his hands defensively. "Calm down, Sherlock. I'm a bachelor. How many potatoes do you think I peel?"

Probably more than Kalin does.

Darren sits on the bed with his paper plate balanced on his knees. "We try do this every Sunday. Take turns hosting. It keeps the family close."

I sit beside him, with a decent distance between us. "Sunday lunch, South African style."

"Yeah. That's a good way to put it."

As we dig into our food – wors, lamb chops, salad and fresh white rolls – I imagine what it might be like having this kind of family. It's what I always wanted as a kid. The familiar chaos, the fussing mother, the—

Darren takes my hand and my heart stops. My jaw stops too, mid chew. He doesn't look at me, he looks at my palm where he traces the lines like a fortune teller.

"What happened, City Girl?"

I swallow and nearly choke. "What do you mean?" I know what he means.

"I thought we had something."

I can't deal with this right now. My chest goes tight and the room is at once too quiet, hanging on words that refuse to come to my mind. All I can think about is his touch as he trails a finger up to my wrist. He looks up at me.

I want this, don't I? I should be happy about this. New Lilah, the girl he met on the overgrown path and kissed beneath the stars, would. She'd kiss him now, take comfort in his warm presence, let him make her forget about Dumi and Dad and all of it. Let the past be.

But I extract my hand from his. "Do we have to talk about this now?"

"I wasn't aware it was a conversation."

I've offended him. Or hurt him. It's hard to get a read. His face is now closed off, his gaze hard.

I turn away from it. "I've just been—"

"Studying?"

That's what I said at SciFest. It's not like it's a lie. "Yes."

"With Kalin?"

Annoyance flares inside me. First Bianca, now him? It's not really an unfair question considering I'm living with the guy, but the breath I let out is hot with frustration because who is Darren to act jealous after what he did?

"What if I was?" I challenge. "What's your problem with him? What's between him and your sister?"

Darren raises a hand as if to say 'hold on', clearly startled by my vehemence. "I was only asking. And I don't know what Bianca's beef is with him. I was as surprised by that as you."

"Well, he's been nothing but kind to me."

"Okay."

"He drove all the way to Cape Town because he thought I might be in danger. He's given me a place to stay, he invited me to SciFest because he thought I looked lonely, he—"

"You don't think he might have an ulterior motive for all that?" Darren interrupts.

My pulse thrums now. How can he talk about ulterior motives when he brought me to this room, possibly this house, to have this discussion now? Why is he springing this on me when I'm at my most vulnerable?

"He walked me home the night of the LMS party," I say with deliberation so Darren can't mistake my emphasis. "Because I was heartbroken and drunk."

"The LMS..." He frowns. "Why were you heartbroken?"

The night is clearly not etched into his memory as it is in mine. Maybe he kisses girls all the time. Maybe it's his average Friday night. Sunday's for quality family time, Saturday's for Xbox and katembas, Friday's for kissing strange girls.

"I saw you with Jess." There. It's out.

Understanding dawns. His eyes go a little larger. "Jess? The blonde?"

He doesn't even remember her name?

"Lilah, I didn't know you were there."

"If you had, you would have been on your best behaviour?"

"That's not what I mean. You should have come to me; you should have said something."

I can't imagine even New Lilah having the guts to march up to him and demand an explanation while he was liplocked with Jess.

"Lilah, it wasn't what it looked like. She was trying to make some guy jealous. It didn't mean anything. It was just an act."

Some guy, huh? No prizes for guessing who. It seems we were both used for Philip's benefit that night.

Darren runs a hand through his hair.

I stare at my knees. I'm still angry but I'm also deflated because there's nowhere to focus that anger. And there's something coiling in the pit of my stomach because he probably was just being nice this whole time, and I went off at him and thought the worst of him. "I should go. Thanks for—"

"You don't have to go."

"I think I do." I stand. "I'm not thinking straight right now. There's a lot going on. It's been a really weird few days."

He stands too. "Let me drive you."

I have this cartoonish image of Dumi's thugs hiding in the bushes waiting for me, and I know it probably would be wise to accept, but I can't bear the thought of another awkward car ride with Darren now.

He frets when I refuse the offer like he's a puppy whose tail just got trod on. Seeing him contrite isn't as satisfying as I might have thought. At the door, after fetching my groceries and saying bye to his family, I thank him again.

I say, "Maybe when all this calms down..." What? We can snuggle on the lawn? We can exchange memes?

Darren gives me a thin-lipped smile of understanding. "I'll see you around, City Girl. You just give me a call if you need anything, or if you change your mind about your, uh, living arrangement."

"If Kalin transforms into the psycho your sister seems to think he is, I'll be sure to let you know."

"Yeah. For your sake, I hope that doesn't happen."

I hope so too.

⸙

I'm almost home when I get a call from Kalin.

"Where are you?" he asks, by way of greeting.

"Not in the back of an unmarked van. Don't worry."

"That's not an answer."

I pause mid stride, taken aback by his tone.

"Lilah?" he prompts.

"If you want me to check my GPS coordinates, I'm going to have to put you on hold."

He lets out a huff of air. "A general vicinity would suffice."

"I'm like a block away. I'll be there soon." I end the call. So, about that psycho thing, huh?

Kalin is pacing in the kitchen when I open the door and he stops to glare at me.

"I wasn't aware I was under house arrest," I say.

"You shouldn't go wandering around right now."

I dump the bag on the counter. "I went to get food. If you plan to keep pets, you should keep something edible in the cupboard."

"I told you, he's not my—"

"I didn't mean Fatso."

Kalin fixes his eyes on me, and I try to glare back with as much ferocity. Then he sighs and pinches the bridge of his nose. "Sorry. I was just… concerned."

"I was careful." *Kind of.* "And anyway, I wasn't alone." *For most of it.* "A friend picked me up."

"A friend?" He's probably wondering why, if I have a friend in town, he's the one who's looking after me.

I start unpacking groceries. I got some cereal, eggs, crackers, a few treat pouches for Fatso and some mixed nuts that were more expensive than I thought they would be, but at least kind of healthy. "Darren," I admit, without looking at Kalin. Before he has a chance to lecture me, I add, "His family was having a braai and he invited me."

"His family?"

I sigh. "Yes, your nemesis was there. Yes, she tried to warn me about how terrible you are. No, I didn't take them up on their offer to rescue me from you."

"Rescue?" He sounds pretty concerned.

"They offered me a room at their B&B." Maybe it was wrong of me to deny that offer. I've basically kicked Kalin out of his bed. I glance at him over my shoulder. "I can accept if it's more convenient for you?"

He's standing in the middle of the kitchen, completely tense, and his lips have gone pale.

"Kalin?"

"No," he says. "No. Please stay here."

15

Alayna kneels beside a body. His face is covered with a blanket, but I know that it's the old man. Her pain spears through me as if the body were my father's.

"This isn't your fault," someone says behind her.

She rises slowly. She's in a small room and it looks like the Hawks have been there because everything is on the floor. Except, whoever was here hasn't merely emptied drawers and shelves, they've smashed things. There's broken crockery, a toppled bookcase, food emptied out of containers.

Alayna draws a deep breath and turns to look at the one who spoke. I recognise the weathered face of Sloane – the man who was so terrified in my last dream.

"I could have done more to protect him," Alayna says. "I should have—"

"The Overlord grows stronger every moment. You could have done nothing."

Sloane steps closer and takes her shoulders. "Do you not see now how foolish this plan is? It is clear that he knows what we seek. He will try to stop us."

"Let go of me, Sloane."

"See sense, my lady. There is no way you are going to be able to gather the orbs before he—"

"Let go!"

He flies back from her, skidding in the mess on the floor.

She advances after him. "It is you who clings to legends of power, who insists on reminding me of my birthright. Do not tell me that he is too powerful. I have known him longer than any who live. When I first came into my magic, he was there. When the mad king burned my village, he was there. When they dragged me to the castle dungeons to be raised in darkness because of my precious, dangerous, blood, it was his face that I saw in my dreams. It was always going to be him and me. Do not tell me I cannot defeat him. I was born to defeat him."

Sloane shrinks from her, but she doesn't strike at him. Instead, she stalks out past him.

"My lady, wait!"

She turns in the doorway

"Allow me to accompany you at least?"

Her gaze falls on the covered body. It would be foolish to continue the hunt for her orb alone. I feel her revulsion at the/thought of travelling alongside this insipid man. But she nods. Any advantage against the Overlord.

I open my eyes and find one of Kalin's old books still in my hand. The last thing I remember is having a bowl of cereal and retreating into the bedroom at about five. I guess I'm still playing catch-up with sleep.

I roll onto my back and blink up at the ceiling. I had a similar dream last night. Alayna with my map. How bizarre that I should dream about that kingdom two nights in a row? Maybe it's my subconscious's way of dealing with Dad being behind bars.

I can hear Kalin rattling around in the kitchen. He spent the whole of yesterday afternoon and evening holed up in his study. When I went in to ask him if he needed help, I found him on the settee balancing three separate books on his lap and scowling. After that I just let him be.

Now he curses and there's a mighty crash. Something shatters. I shoot out of bed, with my heart in my throat, and as I am throwing the door open I think that if the noise was at all Dumirelated it would probably be a better strategy to keep quiet and hide.

But there are no thugs in the kitchen, only Kalin kneeling over a broken bowl slick with egg, and Fatso watching him with a twitching tail. Something sizzles on the small stove and there's the vague smell of burning.

"I realised I haven't been a very good host," Kalin says without looking up at me. "I sought to rectify that, but Fatso had other ideas."

I drop to my knees opposite him. "Here, let me help."

Kalin hops up and rushes to the stove as I gather shards of ceramic.

"I believe he was after the egg," he says. "Scrambled, right?"

"Uh, yes. Or however."

"At the diner, you asked for scrambled." He cracks some eggs into the pan. I'm surprised he remembers that.

"You really don't have to do this. What I said yesterday about the food—"

"Was fair. Besides, I intend to put you to work today." His top lip twitches.

We eat breakfast at the table, and I try to act like I don't notice that I'm balancing my plate on a pizza box. The burning smell was the toast, which is, um, "well done". He doesn't have a toaster and must have gone to the effort of doing that on the stove, so I don't say anything. Everything else is delicious: eggs, bacon, cherry tomatoes and tea.

Then he takes me into the workshop to demonstrate what he needs from me. There isn't anywhere to sit, so I hop up onto the counter, which is covered in deep green vinyl like the one in the kitchen.

I'm usually a quick study, but it takes me a while to get the hang of using pliers to finish off necklaces. Kalin makes it look so easy. His fingers are delicate and long, like a pianist's, and they're perfectly suited to such fiddly work. I, on the other hand, tumbled out of the womb missing whatever part of the brain is used for fine motor control.

He instructs me to "open the jump ring" with the pliers, which I try to do, but the little silver hoop literally jumps right out from between the metal jaws and bounces along the floor. Fatso chases after it. After my third attempt and another reminder of "roll your wrist, twist don't pull!" from Kalin, I sigh.

"Maybe I should find another job, waitressing or something."

Kalin takes my hand and guides me in the aforementioned rolling wrist motion. "That's not a bad idea."

My heart skips because it *is* a bad idea, it's a *terrible* idea. Crowds, talking to strangers, and trying to balance plates on my arm? It's like a list of things I'm bad at, all piled into one.

"Something the matter?" Kalin asks.

I wet my lips and reach for another jump ring. "No."

He steps back. "I didn't mean now, of course. When we're certain you're safe."

He turns away quickly and scratches through one of his boxes. He thinks I'm worried about Dumi. I don't correct him.

Since jump rings prove too great a challenge, he sets me to work tying knots in the ends of cord and crimping "tips" over these knots. The tips are little metal findings, made up of two hollow halves of a sphere. The knot goes in the middle, and I may not be adept at plier manipulation, but even I get the hang of squeezing the tips shut over the knot. This creates a little silver bobble to which the offending jump rings attach.

Once Kalin's satisfied I'm not going to hurt myself, he goes back to his books.

If Kalin has an aesthetic, I'd call it occult-cum-Lord-of-the-Rings. There are a ton of semi-precious stone crystals, a bunch of clay runes, and the occasional more interesting metal pendants like the one he gave me, in a variety of Celtic knots, or cast in the shape of bones or bird skulls or the crescent moon, some inlaid with gems. Most of the necklaces I finish off are on plain leather cord, but a few are fancier. Like the multithreaded choker of blue glass beads with an opal at its centre. The stone is mounted in silver filigree and shimmers pearlescent rainbows in the light.

Fatso is intently interested in what I'm doing and becomes more interested the more I try to shoo him.

"Your name shouldn't be Fatso, it should be Trouble or Pest," I tell him.

Kalin doesn't look up from his book. "Maybe it is."

He's sitting cross-legged on the settee with a large tome spread open on his lap. His hair is tied back in a messy bun, and a few tendrils escape to brush his collar. Right then I can picture him working with silver and moonstone. Maybe over a forge.

Fatso nudges my hand and rubs his cheek against the pliers.

"You don't know his real name?"

"I don't even know his real home. I suspect he may belong to the old woman behind us. She has several other cats. There was possibly some disagreement over territory." Kalin turns a page and rests his chin on his hand. I'm not sure whether he wants to continue talking.

"We should name you something better," I tell Fatso, softly.

"What would you suggest?" Kalin flips another page.

I frown at the cat. "Mr Pumblechook." The pompous glutton from *Great Expectations*.

Kalin laughs. "Surely he's not quite that bad?"

"*You* call him Fatso!"

"I mean it fondly."

I scratch behind Fatso's ear.

"Wopsle," Kalin suggests. Another character from *Great Expectations*. A wannabe actor with no talent. I tilt my head and examine Fatso, but that name doesn't fit either.

"Gatsby," I suggest.

"Hmm." Kalin turns another page. "Because he enjoys the fine things in life?"

"Because it's also a food." At least it is in Cape Town. It's our claim-to-fame street food, a roll with hot chips and other sundry toppings, often baloney. I'm not sure Kalin's ever heard of it though, because he shrugs.

"Finch," Kalin suggests. At my questioning look, he adds. "Because irony. Also, Harper Lee."

"Greebo." Has Kalin only read the classics, or is any literary name fair game?

His mouth twitches. "Pratchett? I like that one. But I seem to recall Greebo was grey. Bustopher Jones."

What follows is about half an hour of us dredging up whatever cat names we can think of from literature. It starts to feel like it isn't about Fatso at all – although he's happy to curl up on my lap while we debate it – but a challenge. The most pretentious kind of challenge; we're comparing references, getting increasingly obscure, testing each other's book knowledge.

I must be the biggest nerd in all existence, because this little game makes me warmer on the inside and happier than I've felt in days.

I eventually catch Kalin out with Crookshanks, which he insists I'm making up. He hasn't read *Harry Potter,* of all things.

But names are funny. They tend to stick. And despite our many ideas, when Kalin dishes up a treat pouch for our orange friend that night, he calls for Fatso.

✼

We order pizza for dinner, and while we eat, I give Kalin a rundown of *Harry Potter* and why it's worth his time. I get as far as describing Hogwarts when my phone rings. It's in the middle of the table, and it makes all the boxes vibrate as it flashes "private number". We stare at it for two rings. I snatch it up.

Before I can get through a greeting, an automated voice asks if I'd like to accept a call from Pollsmoor. I can't breathe; it's like there's a boulder on my chest.

"Lilah… It's so good to hear your voice." Dad sounds tinny and far away. There's a lot of noise in the background.

"Dad!" I have a million questions but can't decide which is the most important. "What happened? What's going on?"

"Everything's going to be fine, Lah."

"You're in Pollsmoor? Are you okay?" I fear the answer, but I need to know.

"Yes. Don't worry about me."

I stand because I can't bear sitting. "Of course I'm worried about you!"

"I'm fine. I'm being transferred on Thursday—"

"Transferred where?"

"Lilah, listen to me. I need to know that you're okay. Clay said you're staying with a friend?"

I nod and swallow, looking at Kalin. "Yes. I'm okay. I'm surrounded by friends and… and I got a job, so money's fine. You don't have to worry about me, just worry about getting out of there and—"

"A job?"

"Waitressing."

Kalin raises his eyebrows. I pull at the loose threads on the edge of my sleeve. I'll say anything to put Dad's mind at ease. If I thought it would bring him comfort, and that there was any chance he'd believe it, I'd declare I'd won the lottery.

There's a pause on the line and I suddenly think that maybe he's worried about me doing such a public job. "Am I in danger? Is Dumi going to…" Kidnap me? Sell me?

"Dumi's not going to do anything to you," he says firmly.

"…because a friend said I might…"

"No. You're not in danger. I promise. I wouldn't, couldn't let that happen. This mess, it has nothing to do with you, you understand?" His voice gets clearer and I picture him clutching the receiver right to his mouth.

"I understand."

"Listen, I don't have much time. Your res is paid up until the end of the year. Nabelo will take care of you. She's a good friend, and you can trust her."

I had no idea he and Miss Sukwini were quite that close. Maybe he's exaggerating to comfort me, the way I was to reassure him.

"And Lah? They're going to say a lot of things about me in the press. A lot of it won't be true."

"What *is* true? They said you're on his payroll, and that the chief witness is—"

"I can't talk about the case now. I need you to be brave. I need you to promise me you'll trust Nabelo, even if she asks you to do things that don't seem to make sense."

My head is buzzing. "What?"

"Trust Nabelo, and remember that no matter what else happens before we next speak, I love you, pumpkin. *That* is true."

I'm struck dumb – both by the emotion in his voice, and his use of that old pet name. Someone shouts something in the background.

"I've gotta go. I love you," he says. My phone beeps, and the line goes dead. I stand with the phone still pressed to my ear. My father's never been one for grandiose declarations of affection. Things must be really bad, even worse than I thought.

"I love you too," I whisper.

16

The phone call from Dad at least gave me closure on one point: I don't have to worry about would-be kidnappers jumping out of any bushes. At least, that's if I choose to believe him. Which I do.

Early the next morning, I get up and get dressed and even braid my hair, so I look neat and tidy. I meet Kalin in the kitchen. He's got a slice of toast in his mouth and is carrying a plate with another slice on it.

"Mmm mm?" He gestures to the plate.

"No, thank you. I'm going out."

"Mmm?"

"You heard what I said to Dad, I'm a waitress now."

I wish I felt half as confident as I manage to make myself sound as I leave Kalin in the kitchen. I seem to be getting better at projecting confidence though, so that's something.

It's a beautiful Grahamstown day, like someone's turned the saturation on the world way up. The sky is that vivid blue; the secret garden is a crisp green. *I can do this.*

I shed my tears quietly last night. I gave myself a pep talk in the mirror when I woke: you're a strong, confident woman. You're eighteen. In olden days you'd have three kids by now. Yes, your father is in prison, but he's alive and he says he's fine. Also, you lied to him, but it won't stay a lie if you go and make it true.

I've managed a lot of things I thought I couldn't during the past few months. Maybe this is who New Lilah is. Maybe she's not a City Girl. But maybe she's a sister doing it for herself. Maybe I can even be a sassy waitress. I won't know until I've tried!

Well, that thought lasts until the third restaurant. The problem with New Lilah is that she has no experience and no credentials. And this is a student town full of students who want student jobs and who have been waitressing since they were legally allowed to.

The managers all tell me the same thing. It's too quiet now during vac. Come back during Fest. Maybe get a year's experience under your belt first.

I work my way up New Street. The French Bistro isn't hiring, the Rat has no openings, the manager of the sports bar actually laughs at me. I even try the club thinking I could be a bartender, but they're not interested in someone who knows nothing about alcohol. I make my last attempt at the Spur – the one chain restaurant I know for certain takes on waitresses without experience. Not in Grahamstown.

The sun is scorching by the time I reach the end of the street. My throat is parched. I trudge back to Kalin's, defeated.

My positive attitude turns progressively sour. I'm tired of being helpless. I'm itching to *do* something.

When I get to the house, Kalin's out again. I pace the kitchen, flexing my fingers. Dad's voice keeps playing in my head over and over again. *I need to do something!* My gaze keeps being drawn to the takeout boxes. The damn takeout boxes. What are they even doing there? How hard is it to take them out to the trash?

In a fit of pique, I gather them up and march outside with them, dumping them into the big black bin on the curb with a lot more violence than they likely deserve. It feels good. It feels like a spring uncoiling, like the weight that's been sitting on my chest being forcibly pushed aside.

I return to the kitchen where I start scrubbing. I begin with the dishes, and when I run out of dishes, I scrub the counter. When I run out of counter, I find a mop and I clean the floor. When that's done, and Kalin's still not back, I eye his study. I hesitate for only a moment before storming in there and taking out all my pent-up rage and helplessness on his clutter.

I dust the shelves, sweep the floor. I move the piles of books off the settee and consider sorting them into the bookcase. But I picture what I'd do to someone who messed with my books while I was studying, and I pile them up instead. As I do so, one flips open. It's old. Older than the books he gave me to read. It looks almost like one of Leonardo da Vinci's sketchbooks. There are diagrams – circles, pentacles, strange symbols – and handwritten notes beside them.

What in the world is Kalin studying?

I try to make out what the notes say, but they're not in English. Maybe he's working with the Linguistics department, like Darren's mom. Maybe *that's* where Bianca knows him from. I close the book and continue with my mission.

The counter is next. I dare not attack his complicated storage systems, but I clear a good deal of the mess into neat little piles so I can scrub the vinyl. Then I notice how dusty the windows are and fetch a cloth.

I'm kneeling on the counter, scrubbing at the final windowpane when Kalin comes into the garden. He pauses as he notices me. He's carrying a messenger bag over his shoulder, which he slowly unslings. He doesn't look happy.

I have a few minutes to mentally prepare myself before he enters the study. I watch him take in the bookshelves, the floor, the settee then finally me.

"So, waitressing went well I see."

I slip down from the counter. He goes to his books and shuffles through them. I'm very glad I decided not to tidy them away.

I fiddle with my hair, which is coming loose from its braid now.

"No one wanted me. Turns out you need experience."

He picks up the old book with the strange drawings in it and flips through it. My stomach tightens. Did I drop a bookmark or something? The silence between us is thick and incredibly uncomfortable.

"What are you studying?" I ask.

He scans one of the pages. "What do *you* think I'm studying?"

It's hard to tell if he's being guarded or testing me.

"You're well-read, collect old books – old *things* in general. Linguistics? Ancient languages?"

He doesn't look up, but his mouth moves into a tight smile. "Exactly right, well done."

He snaps the book shut and his smile broadens as his eyes meet mine. "I'm going to visit a friend this afternoon. Perhaps you'd like to come with?"

Maybe I'm making progress, because the first thought that rushes into my head isn't *Eep strange people*, but *Wait, Kalin has friends?*

At my hesitation, he looks around the study again. "I'm a little concerned what might happen if I leave you here."

"This place *needed* a clean."

"I don't deny that." He focuses on me again, staring as if I'm some script to be translated. I shift from foot to foot.

While we're on the subject I may as well test my other theory. "Is that how you know Bianca? Through her mother? She said she studied Old Gaelic."

"You really won't let that go, will you? All right, yes."

"So, Bianca's not the academic rival, her mother is?"

He shakes his head. "What exactly did she tell you?"

"Nothing flattering."

"I can take it."

I weigh up the possible consequences of telling him the truth. If he really did have ulterior motives, that would be bad. But I don't know what those motives could be. I have nothing to offer him. He even specifically told me, in no uncertain terms, he can't get romantically involved with anyone. So that's seduction out.

"She said you're good at pretending to be nice."

"But that I'm evil on the inside?"

"She didn't use those words."

He leans against the bookshelf and folds his arms. "You remember what I told you at the diner, don't you?"

That he used to be a bad person. He seems awfully casual about Bianca considering his physical reaction to her the other day. I scan his body for that tension now, but his pose is completely relaxed.

"She seems a bit dramatic. I mean if this is just about a thesis or research or something."

"This *is* your first year in academia."

That's another thing I've been wondering. "And what year is it for you?"

Then he stiffens. Tension radiates through his body, every muscle going stiff even as he makes no visible move except swallowing. His gaze darts to the little antique clock. "We can pick this up later. My friend's expecting me at three."

Well, that's weird. How can that, of all questions, possibly be upsetting? Is post-doctorate PTSD a thing?

⸙

I get fidgety in the car, trying to imagine what Kalin's friend might be like and what they might make of me. But I don't have long to worry. This is Grahamstown, and everything's super close. After merely five minutes, we roll up outside what looks to be a big white mansion peeking out from behind a cluster of trees.

Kalin buzzes in at an electric gate, and I read the sign on the wall: Shawbrook Home.

Well, everything else Kalin likes is old, why not his friends too?

A lady in a bright turquoise jacket rises from behind a desk when we enter. "Kalin, I was starting to think you weren't coming this week."

"Sorry we're late. Is George still available?"

The woman beams. "Of course he is. You know how he looks forward to your visits."

Kalin signs in, then leads the way deeper into the building. He pauses outside a glass double door and whispers, "My friend suffers from dementia. He may say… strange things. Pay him no mind."

I nod and chew on my bottom lip as we go through the door. It opens to a common room with a high ceiling and beige carpet, filled with elderly people engaged in a variety of activities.

An old man seated at a chess board by the window stands and waves at us. He's dressed in a maroon cardigan and grey slacks. What remains of his white hair is combed back neatly. He has an open, friendly face.

When we're close enough, he seizes Kalin's hand in his. "I've been practising!" Then he notices me. "Who is this then, a young lady?"

"George, this is Lilah. Lilah's boarding with me for the moment."

"It is a pleasure to meet you then, Miss Lilah." He winks.

Kalin fetches a chair from beside the window for me, then takes his own seat opposite George. The board is already set up, with Kalin as the white side. Without preamble, he moves a knight.

"Always the same opening move," George notes. "He's a man of habit." He pushes a pawn forward two squares.

Kalin doesn't comment. He moves his other knight.

"Years and years we've played, and it's always the same thing."

"And I still win."

"Occasionally."

Kalin snorts.

"How do you know each other?" I ask.

"Oh, we lectured together back in the day." George moves another pawn. "Do you still lecture? I forget."

Lectured? Why is Kalin sitting in my tuts if he's been a lecturer? Is this the dementia?

"No." Kalin is playing an aggressive game. It's almost like he's in a hurry to get this over with. "I'm studying at the moment."

George lets air out between his lips. "What do you have left to study, Kallen?" He says Kalin's name differently to how I do: kah-len instead of kay-lin. Kalin doesn't correct him. It's clearly a mispronunciation that he's accustomed to.

"Lilah and I take Law together."

"Oh?" George's eyes twinkle. I never knew my grandparents, but he's what I would have imagined. He quizzes me about my interest in law, while half-heartedly moving the chess pieces. It seems neither he nor Kalin are particularly invested in the game. I steer clear of mentioning Dad, and instead stammer about a number of other noble reasons one might want to take Law. Kalin's wearing his little half-smile, and I don't know if he's amused at my struggle, or if he really is getting some enjoyment from playing chess.

"Lilah's actually majoring in English Literature," he says.

"No I—"

But before I can correct him, George's face lights up. "Now there's a subject I'm familiar with! What books have they given you this year?"

George becomes animated as we discuss books, and it doesn't take much to work out what he used to lecture. At the back of my mind I'm thinking of Kalin's study, and our cat-naming game, and how it makes sense that he might have once taught English.

Suddenly George stops talking and focuses on the board. I look at Kalin. Is something wrong? Has George suddenly forgotten where he is? But Kalin is grinning.

"You bastard," George says.

Kalin's expression doesn't falter.

"You brought a pretty girl here to distract me."

"I brought the pretty girl here to distract *her*. The rest

is your doing."

Did Kalin just call me pretty? And what does he mean by 'distract me'? From Dad, from my failure to get a job, or from my questions?

George's hand hovers over one of his bishops. Then he changes his mind and moves a rook.

Kalin shakes his head as if George has fallen neatly into his trap. He moves his knight again. "Check."

"Bastard," George repeats, quickly shifting his king to safety. To me he adds, "He's a knave, I hope you know what you're getting yourself into."

When we eventually leave the old age home, after Kalin has defeated George in both the original game and the rematch, I'm deep in thought.

We're almost home when Kalin comments, "You're quiet."

"I'm always quiet."

"Not around me."

My heart gives a little jump at that. Is it true? I never noticed.

"Something's on your mind," Kalin says.

"How long ago did you lecture with George?"

He pulls into the driveway beside the cottage. "You're full of questions today." And he climbs out without answering.

I follow him. "You asked me what's on my mind. That's what's on my mind. You said before that you've only been in Grahamstown a few years."

"Is that what I said?"

Evasive. But that's not what's really bothering me. "How old are you?"

"Twenty-three." He busies himself unlocking the door.

He's quite a bit older than me, but not as much as I thought he might be. "You're twenty-three, and you've already been a lecturer?"

"Perhaps I'm smart." He strides into the house, heading straight for his study.

"Being enigmatic isn't as charming as you think," I call after him.

"I wasn't going for charming. I was going for private!" he calls back, and that's the end of that.

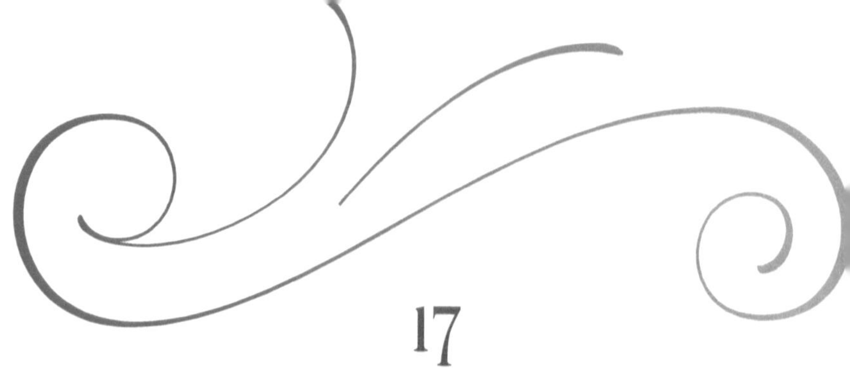

17

In the days that follow, I learn precious little else about Kalin. I learn that he likes gherkins on his pizza, and that he talks to Fatso when he thinks no one's listening. Mostly about groceries. Once, I think, about me. (But it wasn't anything interesting, just about the sleeping arrangement and how Fatso was getting overly attached. I was getting pretty attached to the orange pest myself.)

Kalin doesn't talk about himself at all. Not when we're working on jewellery, not when we're cooking or washing dishes, or at the Pick n Pay. He likes to talk about books, sometimes about philosophy, and sometimes about places he's travelled. I can never pinpoint a timeframe for these adventures, and he gets cagey whenever I ask about anything from his past. I suppose I can understand if he's really ashamed of who he used to be. I begin to suspect that there must be some tragedy there too, and I stop trying to pry.

From what little I can work out, I imagine Kalin's story to be something like this: Young savant, orphaned or at odds with his parents, takes academia by storm. Studies multiple degrees. Lectures, travels. Becomes an arrogant asshole. Has disagreement with Shirley that her daughter still resents. Tragedy strikes as a result of his ego. He decides to atone. And now he plays chess with lonely old men, rescues damsels, helps at a soup kitchen (which explains why he's so often late for class), and haunts the community billboard to see if there are any other quests of virtue he can pick up.

The night before I move back into res, I find myself surprisingly reluctant to pack. I put it off until after midnight, when I run out of things to clean in the kitchen. Kalin's busy in the study, but when I see the pile of old books by my bedside, I figure that's reason enough to disturb him.

He's asleep. He's sitting kinda upright, with the book full of symbols open on his lap and a notepad beside him. His mouth is open, and he's snoring softly. He'll probably be glad to sleep in his bed again. I watch him longer than I have any reason to, but the books get heavy, and I eventually put them down then cover him in the brown blanket that's draped over the back of the settee.

As I tuck it around him, he grabs my wrist. I freeze. He's still unconscious – eyes closed, mouth open, breathing steady – but he mumbles something that sounds like, "Anna".

A girl's name. I study his features. Is this the tragedy? Is this why he gave me that lecture about romance? There was a girl. Of course there was a girl. Maybe I should ask Darren about the name. Maybe he'll know the story. Maybe it's wrong of me to want to know it so badly.

When I fall asleep that night, I'm running through the first and last names of every person I've met in Grahamstown, starting with English lecturers, but I draw a blank.

Returning to res isn't as awkward as I feared. I built it up in my head that everyone would know who my father was and would care. In reality, no one so much as looks at me. They're too involved in their own reunions and unpacking. Kalin sees me to my room, but there are too many people crowded into the narrow corridor for us to say any kind of comfortable goodbye.

"Thanks again, for everything," I say, pressed against my door as my neighbour's boyfriend shuffles past carrying her suitcases.

Kalin, who's shoved up against the opposite wall says, "I'm glad I could help."

He hovers there a moment longer, as if he wants to say more. Then simply tilts his head indicating he's going to leave. "See you around."

By "around", I assume he means in Politics tomorrow. I smile and wave him off.

Inside my cramped room, I find a note that's been slipped under the door. The handwriting is too elegant to belong to Jess. It's cursive and swoopy.

Lilah, please pop round for tea when you get in.

— Nabelo.

I knock on Sukwini's door and there's no response. I wait a few minutes then try again. Still nothing. I'm about to leave when I hear heels clicking hurriedly along the corridor behind me. Miss Sukwini rounds the corner in a navy blue and white nurse's uniform, and she smiles when she sees me.

"Lilah, I'm so glad we didn't miss each other. I got called to the hospital."

She scratches in a black leather handbag and pulls out the key to her front door. "I was so sorry to hear about what happened with your father."

I don't really know what to say. Me too? "I got your note."

"Of course. Please come in. Make yourself at home. I'll put on the kettle."

Now the sitting room is bright and warm. Sunlight streams in from a large window that looks out onto the front parking lot.

Sukwini slips off her heels. "You don't mind, do you? They're terribly uncomfortable."

I assure her that I don't. I don't wear heels if I have the choice either.

She disappears into the kitchen and I examine the paintings and photos on the wall. I've paused at one of her and an older man when she returns with the tea tray.

"That's my father. He was a general in the SANDF."

The National Defence Force. He's wearing a military uniform and grinning at the camera. His eyes are crinkled at the corners. She's young. About sixteen? Holding some sort of certificate to her chest.

"He was so proud. I was the first in my family to matriculate. He wanted to but ended up in MK instead."

"MK?" I can't keep the surprise from my voice. uMkhonto we Sizwe was the guerrilla force that worked to end Apartheid. I always pictured them as hardened fighters trained in sabotage and explosives, not as old men with crinkly eyes.

Miss Sukwini tilts her head to the sofa. "Yes, MK. So I have some experience in what you are feeling now."

She sets the tray down on a coffee table and sits. I join her. "What *am* I feeling now?"

"No doubt you are questioning the man you know. I was your age during the TRC hearings, when the truth of what my father was involved in came to light. It was a difficult thing, to reconcile the violent actions with the father who had shown me nothing but love."

It isn't the same though. "Your father was fighting against oppression. Mine, if what they're saying is true…"

I can't get the words out. I can't say 'he's a slaver' or 'he's corrupt to his core' or any of my worst fears.

Miss Sukwini hands me a cup. It's a deep blue pottery mug. "No, but the conclusion is the same. People are not as simple as good or evil. Your father is still the man you knew, no matter what the outcome of this case may be."

I sip the tea and Miss Sukwini watches me.

Eventually the silence grows too oppressive. I clear my throat. "I didn't realise you and my father were such good friends."

She inclines her head. "I imagine he doesn't speak of those days often."

"Oh, he speaks about university all the time. I've been hearing about this place as long as I can remember."

"I didn't mean the place, my dear." She sips her own tea.

I catch her meaning with a jolt. "You mean my mother."

She nods again.

"You knew her?"

"She was a lot like you."

"How?" I'm desperate for more information about her, more desperate than I realised.

Miss Sukwini studies my face. She doesn't know me all that well. Perhaps she was just saying that because it seemed like the kind of thing I'd want to hear and now she can't think of anything.

"She was a warm person. A trusting person," she says at length. "Which is uncommon in a journalist."

I knew she wanted to be a journalist because I know the colours she wore at graduation. "Sounds like the opposite to Dad."

Her lips curve, but it's a sad expression. "Yes. Your father was the serious one. Always had his nose in a book. She coaxed him out of his shell."

"I can't picture him being in a shell."

"It's quite true, but once she took a liking to him, he started to transform."

"How did they meet?" I set down my tea, because I want to focus all my attention on what she says.

"I introduced them." Again, the sad smile. "But we should not speak of the past. I asked you here to talk of the future."

Are you kidding? She brought her up. "Please. You were right, he doesn't talk about her. At all. I don't know anything."

My desperation must be apparent in my voice, because she gives me a pitying look. "Your mother was an orphan, but there was a trust fund in her name that allowed her to come here. She was raised by friends of her parents, and my mother worked for the family."

I blink at her. "You knew her from childhood?"

She nods again. "You could say we grew up together."

My heart beats unevenly. I'm hungry for more, but I don't know where to start asking. My tongue trips over stupid questions like what her favourite colour was, and my throat closes on stupider questions like whether they went to school together, because I remember just in time that during Apartheid, they would not have been permitted to. Did she have 'silly fancies' like I did? Did she enjoy reading books? Eventually what I stammer out is, "Do you have any photos of her?"

Miss Sukwini's delicate brow knits, and I feel the need to clarify such a bizarre request. "My father only keeps the one. Of graduation."

Her head jerks back a little as if I've given her a shock.

"I know it sounds strange, it's not that he wants to forget her. It just hurts too much to look at her. He didn't keep any of her things either."

Miss Sukwini rises gracefully and straightens her skirt. Her expression is still troubled. "Well, I can see if I have anything. Tell me, which photograph is that? A little one, in a book?"

Maybe she's thinking of a specific photo that has sentimental value. "Uh, no. It's quite large, framed."

"I see."

She kneels by the bookshelf and pulls out a leather-bound book, reads the title, then shoves it back in and pulls out another, which she flips through. It's a photo album. I see several faded photographs, some in black and white like the one with her father, but she's flipping through the pages too fast for me to make out details. Eventually she stops and passes me the book without saying anything.

It's heavy, but I don't care because my mother's smiling up at me. She's maybe nine, sitting on a swing in a puffy floral dress, next to another little girl who must be Miss Sukwini. Mom's glowing with that same warmth as in the graduation photo, and with the same sleek brown hair. But here I can see she has dimples. I tear up. I've never seen my mother as a child before.

"I wanted to tell you that I am here, should you need anything," Miss Sukwini says, rising. "I would like it if we could be friends."

Is it ungrateful of me to wonder why this offer is only coming now? I've been in her res for months. She's had so much opportunity to share this history with me, but I've hardly seen her at all. I swallow down that uncharitable thought and nod.

Dad said I should trust her, so I will.

18

$\mathcal{J}$ess is completely oblivious.

She shows up at my door before dinner with a tan and a million stories about her vac and the boys she hooked up with. It's surprisingly nice to take my mind off my own problems. Instead of going to the dining hall, she insists we go get burgers in her new car.

"I told my parents that I kept getting rained on and ruined so many shoes with all this mud that they simply had to agree to let me have a car. It's second hand of course. I'm not spoilt."

It's second hand, but it's a new-style Mini, and those don't come cheap. A pink Mini, which means that it probably got a custom paint job. It looks like a Barbie car.

After a few false starts and some grating gears, she proudly drives us down to New Street, where we circle the block for about fifteen minutes trying to find a parking place that doesn't involve parallel parking. She talks all the while. My mind keeps drifting. Is Kalin going to have takeout again tonight? Will Fatso be looking for me?

Eventually we end up at the French bistro. I lose my appetite when I see the prices on the menu. Jess wants to go big to celebrate being back. I can't find it in me to tell her about my financial predicament now or, more specifically, I can't find a way to tell her that won't completely ruin the evening. Nothing spoils the mood quite like, "by the way, my father's in jail."

The cheapest thing on the menu is the 'soup of the day' so I order that and a glass of water. But then we go to the Rat, where Jess orders the first round of drinks, and even though I only have a Coke, politeness insists that I buy the second round – where she orders a cocktail.

When we eventually get back to res, and I'm finally alone in my room, I sink to the floor in the little space between my bed and the door with my head in my hands. *Stupid, stupid, stupid.*

By my calculations I only have about a hundred bucks left to my name, and I spent more than that in one night. How did I go so long without realising what things cost?

I consider asking Clay for money. But I told Dad I was fine. If I confess my predicament to Clay, Dad will find out.

No, I'm going to have to get a job. I'm going to have to go back to those restaurants and beg them. Or something.

ↄ๏๛

Jess's ex, Michael, is waiting for us outside English the next day.

"Lilah! I'm writing a story on your dad for the student paper. Do you have time for a quick interview?" He ignores Jess completely.

She rolls her eyes. "Go away, Michael."

"Who are you again?" he asks her.

"Funny."

"Why don't you go find some muso to make out with and let me speak to Lilah?"

I try to slip past them before he says anything more about Dad, but he steps into my way. "Wait. Please. First-years never get the front cover. I told them I knew you. If you'd just give me a few words?"

The front page? My blood goes cold at the thought of my life being broadcast across campus like that.

"Sorry, no." I'm desperate to get inside before he draws any more attention, or clues Jess in. I could have gotten away with it coming out halfway through dinner, but this is the worst way for her to hear about it.

"Just five minutes?"

"I'd rather not," I say between clenched teeth, hoping Jess is too self-absorbed to question that.

He shakes his head. "You know, I can understand Jess being a bitch, but I wouldn't expect it from you."

"Hey!" But I don't get to say more. He turns and stalks into the lecture theatre.

Jess whistles under her breath. "What the hell did I see in him?"

"Wine. You saw wine, in his hand." I'm not feeling particularly generous about him after that display.

She throws her head back and laughs loudly enough that we get odd looks.

Kalin isn't in Politics. I keep waiting for him to sneak in late, but he doesn't. I try not to worry. Things would be a lot easier if he had a mobile I could text, but if he's stuck in studying mode, I don't want to disturb him by calling the landline. And anyway, George made it sound like taking classes was more of a hobby for him than a necessity. He's probably just working on that project of his with the book and the symbols.

The afternoon crawls by. This morning I was all psyched up to go find a job again, but by the time I walk out of Psychology, I'm exhausted. I check my reflection in the public bathroom, and through the graffiti I look pale and tired. I had bad dreams last night, but I don't quite remember them. All I recall is a cliff face, a cave, an underground river, and Miss Sukwini arguing with someone.

"Nothing ventured, nothing gained," I tell myself.

This time I start in High Street. I visit a boutique hotel, a cocktail bar and, because it can't hurt, the bookstore. I don't know if my pitch is getting better or worse.

My bag digs into my shoulder, and I want to be sitting in a restaurant drinking something cool rather than begging them for jobs.

That night, after I've helped Jess with her English homework, I pour the contents of my purse out on the bed. I count my money and I count my blessings. I'm in res, which means meals are paid for until the end of the year. Many students don't have that. And after the end of the year… after… I swallow down the bitter taste at the back of my throat. I don't have answers about After, and I feel panicky whenever I think about After. None of this felt as real or as pressing when I was living with Kalin, but I guess I was just distracted. I know he'll help me if I'm desperate, and Miss Sukwini offered to as well, but neither of them have the resources to pay my way for me. Kalin makes jewellery for a living, and Miss Sukwini already works two jobs. I'd be a terrible burden if I were to rely on either of them. Which means I have to rely on myself.

Kalin's not in Law the next morning, and he misses Politics again.

Maybe he's ill? Or he's studying. Maybe I should check up on him? Or I should leave him be.

I buy a sandwich at the Kaif because there isn't time to go across campus between Politics and Psych for lunch. That's a third of my remaining money gone. *Irresponsible.* I can't focus on my book, and in the end, I just go and wait outside the lecture theatre.

It's already after five when we're let out and the first restaurant I try, right at the end of High Street, is too busy prepping for dinner service to even talk to me. I try a hotel – are bellhops a thing here? Apparently not, by the confused way the lady at the front desk looks at me.

This is hopeless. I'm not qualified for anything. I wouldn't even make a good waitress. What am I even doing? My chest is tight and sore, and my legs are heavy. I sink down onto a tree stump that's at the side of the road and try not to cry.

Get a grip. You're lucky. You have so much in your life. You're fine. Stop being a baby.

There are lots of people walking along this road, and it's bustling with end of day traffic – as much as it can be called traffic here. I don't want any of them to see me cry.

Get a grip!

I stare at the cars and try to distract myself from my emotional turmoil. One of them turns into a parking lot across from me. There's a greengrocer there that I never noticed before. And next to it, a faded wooden sign hangs over a darkened doorway: Guido's.

That sounds like the name of a restaurant.

I already know what the result will be, but I repeat my little mantra. "Nothing ventured, nothing gained," and heave myself to my feet. What's the worst that can happen?

Guido's is an intimate little Italian place that smells of varnish and pizza. It's got some booths at the front, some tables at the back, and a grumpy looking manager at the desk working out something in a logbook.

"We're not open for dinner yet," he says when I peek in.

"Sorry. I…"

He peers up at me with ice-blue eyes lined with stress. "No hawkers."

I take a deep breath and try to find my courage. It's retreated to somewhere in my shoes. "Actually, I'm looking for a job."

"Try again before Fest."

It's an answer I've heard many times before, but this time I press. "Please, I'll do anything. Dishes?"

"We already have a dishwasher, lovey."

"Oh." I step back, the door starts to close.

Someone at the other side of the dim restaurant shouts, "Wait!"

I hold the door. A slight woman with tawny skin and her hair up in a neat ballet bun comes to the desk. She's examining my face, and at first I don't recognise her. Then I remember. The girl from BP. Lani.

"She's my friend. I'll vouch for her," she says.

The manager chews on his inner cheek.

"*Komaan*, Harrold, we must train her now to be ready for Fest. *En ons moet mos 'n* replacement *vir* Julie *kry*."

He reaches behind him and grabs a paper menu, which he shoves at me. "Fine. Learn this. Come back tomorrow at four." To Lani, he adds, "And you are training her. I don't have time for this."

I accept the menu quickly, so he doesn't see my hand shaking. I can't quite believe what just happened. "I'm hired?" I ask.

He sizes me up. "Learn the menu. If you survive the shift tomorrow, we'll talk."

Studying, I can do. That night I colour code the menu and make cue cards and get Jess to quiz me on descriptions and prices.

"I still don't know why you want to do this," she says, lying on her stomach on her pink bed and kicking her legs in the air. "It's going to take so much time. You can get a job when you're old."

I just shrug. "It seems like fun."

"You have a strange idea of fun. Escargots."

"Snails in garlic sauce." I screw up my face, trying to picture the yellow highlighted bit on the menu. "R29.90?"

"R49.90. And you forgot the homemade bread."

I manage to convince Jess to quiz me for another hour, and again while we're waiting to go into English the next day.

19

$\mathcal{L}$ ani is in the parking lot having a smoke when I arrive for my first waitressing shift. I skipped Politics to make sure I'd be on time, and I'm a bit early.

"Thought Harrold might have scared you off." She stubs out her cigarette.

"No. I'm very grateful for the job. Thank you."

Lani smiles. "*Ag, moenie worry nie.* Us girls have to look out for each other, isn't that right?"

She gestures inside. The place is empty, no sign of the manager.

"I studied the menu," I tell her.

"How's your handwriting?" she asks.

"It's fine. I think."

"Good." She leads me through a swing door at the back of the place into the kitchens. She introduces me to the staff – there are four of them: a pizza guy, a chef, a sous chef and the dishwasher – then hands me a notepad. "You write the orders on here."

And thus begins my whirlwind lesson in waitressing. I'm given a uniform, an apron and a quick briefing about table numbers and section rotations. I get the booths tonight because it's my first night. There's so much to keep in mind that I'm completely flustered by the time the other wait staff arrives and stand no chance of remembering their names. No one asks me about the menu, but Lani makes me write down the specials of the day and repeat them back to her.

Then the first tables are being seated and Harrold is calling out orders in the kitchen and a front of house girl in a tailored suit is making harried gestures at me and I'm waitressing. I'm really waitressing.

Lani's brother mans the bar and they keep up a steady string of banter in Afrikaans that I can only half understand. I almost drop the main course over my first table's laps but recover just in time.

There's a steady stream of customers for such a dingy place. None of them are students. They all look like they've been coming here since George used to lecture and Mom and Miss Sukwini were running around in her backyard.

I make my first mistake on my third table when I write down medium steak instead of medium rare and it gets sent back. I expect Harrold to fire me on the spot, but he just calls for the chef to make another one. My next mistake is a bit worse. I place an order for a Greek salad instead of a Greek pizza. Lani is in the kitchen when Harrold yells at me, and she laughs so hard I think she'll split her sides. My face is burning when I have to go back to the table to explain and can hardly get the words out to my horrified customers. I must have failed my test, for sure.

At the end of the night, Lani explains the clean-up procedure, and I help her fill the sauce bottles. When Harrold hands out the night's tips, he gives me mine in a little envelope without comment, and I don't know what that means. Is this severance pay? I'm too embarrassed to ask.

Then, just as I'm about to leave with the other wait staff, he says, "Weekly meetings are on Thursdays at nine. You're studying at the university?"

"Um, yes sir."

He raises an eyebrow at the sir, and I know it's a mistake. Lani giggles again.

"Right, well, you'll have lectures during the lunch shifts I imagine, but you need to pick up one weekend lunch shift each week, non-negotiable. Otherwise, at least three night shifts Sunday through Thursday. Is that doable?"

"Yes. Yes absolutely."

"We pay three percent plus tips. No contracts."

"Okay." I don't even know what that means. "That's fine with me."

"Good. See you tomorrow."

And that's that. I have a job.

There's a spring in my step as I walk through the dark Grahamstown streets, and it's only when I start drawing closer to campus that I remember the night with the mist and quicken my pace.

***

I'm so relieved to have a job that I pick up both weekend day shifts that week. The Saturday is busy – there's a kid's party and a meeting of the ladies' bowling club – but the Sunday is rainy and dead quiet.

I listen to the two other waiters talking about their night at the Rat while I watch the rain flood out of the gutter, turning the parking lot into a glassy lake of ankle-deep water. I'm thinking about Kalin and the fact that he hasn't been in class all week. And that he missed our Law tut, which will get him into trouble with the faculty. If he even cares.

Maybe I should go visit him? Check up on him? But what if I was disturbing him? He must be super busy with his project if he can't even come to class. Or… or I've done something to annoy him, and now he's avoiding me. I run over small things he did or said, and in the murky light of that gloomy Sunday, they all seem to be subtle clues that he couldn't wait to be rid of me. *I wasn't going for charming; I was going for private.*

The "percentage plus tips" thing is clever on the restaurant's part. It means that if they make nothing, they don't have to pay us. That day I trudge back to res with a whole R10 in my soggy little envelope.

But then on Tuesday night, of all nights, I bring home R400 because it was someone's birthday, and they were particularly generous with tipping. Every shift is a gamble, and it's kind of fun. No one ever tests my menu knowledge, but it helps me feel less like I want to throw up when I get given a new table.

By Wednesday morning, the late nights are starting to take their toll. I miss breakfast in the dining hall, and I'm still groggy by the time I make it down to the Kaif to grab coffee before English. I must look awful, because people keep staring at me.

I fiddle with my hair while I wait in line to pay, trying to straighten it out before I encounter Jess. Then I see the paper.

There's a stack of the Campus Press by the till. Dad's picture is on the front. It already feels like there's a bowling ball in my stomach before I even scan the headline: "Durow falsified degree".

My insides turn to ice. The subhead claims that he never studied here. I don't have to read the byline to know who wrote this, but there's his name: Michael.

My vision narrows to a point. I don't need the coffee now; adrenaline throbs through me. I snatch up a copy and slam the money down on the counter. I'm pure rage as I stalk across the library quad to the English lecture theatre where I know, *I know*, I'll find him waiting, looking all smug.

He's chatting to some of his journalism friends, but I push through them. "What is this?" I wave the paper under his nose. "Who do you think you are?"

He has the gall to look shocked. One of his friends makes an "Oooooh" noise.

Michael holds up his hands defensively. "I *did* ask you for an interview."

"And when I wouldn't give it to you, you turned to defamation?" My voice is loud enough to make others in the quad stop and look at us, but I don't care.

"It's not defamation if it's true."

"It's not true!"

"Have you even read the article?" He steps forward, and my expression must falter because he shakes his head. "Thought not. I got proof. Derek Durow was never even registered here. When you said no to the interview, I started digging. My brother works at the records office. I just wanted to look at his file, see if there were any interesting facts. But there was no file. He didn't graduate here. He probably bought his degree online."

I want to slap him. My heart slams so hard it hurts, and everyone within a mile radius is staring at me.

"Your brother made a mistake." I say, but my voice falters. "He didn't look hard enough."

Michael laughs at that.

High heels click across the stone behind us and my gut sinks down to my feet an instant before Jess's shrill voice demands, "What the hell is going on? Your dad's in prison?"

"Maybe he's not really her dad." Michael is enjoying the spotlight. "Maybe your whole life is a lie."

I want to respond, but I can't get air into my lungs. They're refusing to work, and I'm hyper aware of all the faces watching, staring, judging.

"Why didn't you tell me?" Jess asks, but her voice fades out of focus.

Michael steps closer still. "Or maybe you're in on it, Durow. Maybe that's why you wouldn't let me interview you. Maybe you know your father's true identity and—"

Someone hits him. It's not me.

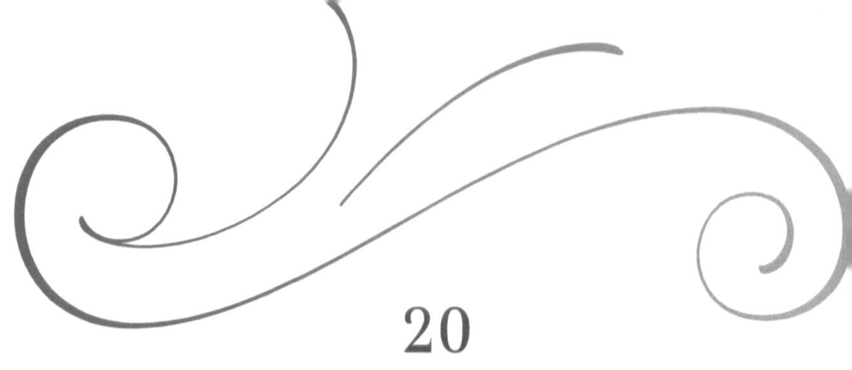

20

The gathered crowd roars. Kalin didn't hit Michael in the face, but on the shoulder. A shove more than a punch. But it came out of nowhere, and so suddenly, that Michael stumbles backwards and the crowd isn't sure exactly what happened, just that something exciting is going down.

Kalin places himself between Michael and me. He's drawn up to his full height and, in his combat boots and brown jacket, he looks intimidating as heck. "That's enough."

Michael rubs at his shoulder. "What the hell, dude?"

Kalin doesn't deign to answer. He turns to me. "Breakfast?"

I nod dumbly as he takes my arm and pulls me through the gathered students. I hear my name whispered. I still can't breathe. Kalin marches past the Kaif, down onto the road, across the admin building lawn and into town.

My chest starts to open as we reach High Street. Less chance of people knowing who I am there, more folks going about their day as if everything is ordinary. Kalin's still holding my arm when he guides me into the cocktail bar, which happens to be the first open doorway.

We sit at the counter. The man behind it seems surprised to see customers in this early. "…two mimosas?"

Kalin waves off the suggestion. "Coke, and coffee if you have."

"We don't serve coffee, sir."

"Two Cokes then."

This seems to be the most perplexing request, because the man slips behind a beaded curtain. We're left alone in the small bar that looks like it used to be someone's entrance hall. I stare at the polished wooden floor and run my thumb across my palm. None of this feels real. It feels less real than those weird dreams about the kingdom.

"When's your next shift?" Kalin's voice is deep and soft.

I look up at his face. "You know about the job?" It was the piece of news I'd been most looking forward to telling him when I saw him again.

"Yes, congratulations."

"How? And how did you— You showed up at the exact right time just now."

The man returns with our Cokes and gives us another funny look. They're in tall glasses with curly straws and he's popped a slice of lemon on the lip to add extra glamour. Kalin thanks him in a way that indicates he should leave us.

When he's ducked behind the curtain again, Kalin stares into his drink and stirs it. I'm about to ask what's on his mind when he says, "I had to come find you when I saw the paper."

My heart gives a little squeeze. I almost tell him that I missed him.

His amber eyes fix on me. "You didn't answer my question, about your next shift?"

"Oh. I… The weekly meeting's tomorrow."

He nods and returns his attention to his Coke.

"You didn't answer mine about how you knew about the job."

"This is Grahamstown. Everyone knows everything that happens."

"Honestly, though?"

"Honestly, I saw you going into Guido's the other night in uniform." He pushes the glass aside. "I'm going away for a few days. Research trip. I figure you'll want to get out of town until this dies down. Come with me?"

This request is delivered to the counter in one breath, the sentences running into each other. The question is so at odds with his body language that I don't know what to make of it.

"If this is just another good deed thing, I'll be okay. Thank you for hitting him, though."

"I didn't hit him. I pushed him."

"Well, that. If you hadn't, I would have."

His mouth quirks, but he's still looking at the counter. "I would have liked to see that."

Silence hangs between us, and I don't understand it. We didn't part on bad terms. My insecurities come rushing in, but even while they're telling me that I annoyed him, that I invaded his privacy too much, that he'd rather be anywhere than on a trip with me, I can't deny the fact that he's here and that he came to campus to find me. So why won't he look at me? What happened?

"It's not," he says at length.

"Not what?"

"Atonement points," he echoes the term I used at the diner. "I'm not inviting you with me out of pity. Story like that will probably be picked up by the other papers."

"It won't because it's shoddy journalism. It's not true."

"Perhaps. Or maybe they like the sound of it and they run it anyway. We can leave after your meeting, return Monday."

"No." Harrold was adamant about those weekend shifts. "It's only my second week, I can't miss both Saturday and Sunday. Thank you, though."

"I could return Saturday."

"I don't want you to miss—"

"I don't mind."

Silence again. I'm not sure what I want. I want Michael to have not written the story. What did I ever do to him, anyway? Is this some weird way of trying to get back at Jess?

Kalin sips his drink, I stare at mine. "Why would the university not have a record of my dad?" There must be an explanation, but I can't think of one. "Was there like a fire or something? Maybe?"

The look of pity that I get from Kalin then makes me feel a little sick.

"You believe it's true, don't you? You've always suspected he was no good. You don't even know him and—"

"You don't really know him either."

My muscles tighten.

"It seems I don't know anybody," I say coolly, and I look right into his eyes as I say it. Then I get up calmly and push in my stool. I want to deliver an equally cold goodbye, but I know my welling emotion is not going to let me. I turn for the door instead. He grabs my arm.

"Wait. Sorry. I didn't mean that. Have some Coke, you're shaking."

I didn't even realise I was, but it must be an outer reflection of the war that's going on in my chest. "He told me so many stories about Grahamstown. He met my mother here."

"Not everyone in the town is a student. Maybe he was a local."

"Why would he lie to me?"

"There are a number of reasons people lie. Not all of them are bad."

"I'm struggling to think of one good one."

"Maybe… well, maybe it was about supporting his family. You. After your mother…"

I shake my head. "You saw the photograph of them at graduation. That's proof, isn't it? He did graduate here."

"Or he wanted to make people think he did."

"I wish I could talk to him."

Kalin surprises me by reaching out and patting my hand. He's not really one for physical contact unless he's trying to guide me (or half carry me home drunk). It's a clumsy gesture, one that I'm not sure he's ever tried before.

He fists his hand as he draws it away, like he's just done something forbidden. "Have you spoken to your uncle recently?"

I shake my head. Kalin was in the study with me the last time I spoke to Clay, when Clay explained that Dad is only allowed calls very occasionally, and he currently has to use them to speak to his legal team.

"You should probably warn your uncle about the paper. He can get a statement ready."

I should have thought of that. He'll freak. "I'll send him a pic of the article."

Kalin nods. Then he nudges my Coke closer to me. "Drink up. I'll walk you back to campus if you like."

"In case you need to push anyone?"

He offers a flicker of a smile, but no answer.

The drink is sweet and cold, and somehow it does help to steady my nerves. While I sip through the fancy straw, my mind keeps going to Kalin's offer. I haven't given an answer yet, and he hasn't pressed me. Perhaps it was uncharitable for me to assume he was asking out of pity, but he's been acting weird – he's still acting weird.

"Where is this research trip of yours?"

"Have you heard of Hogsback?"

"No… That doesn't sound like a real place."

A muscle twitches in his cheek. It's like he's fighting his sense of humour with everything in him. "It was rumoured to be the inspiration for Mirkwood."

"Mirkwood, like in The Hobbit?"

"The same. Although Tolkien was three years old when he lived in the area, so I very much doubt the veracity of the tale. It's a forest in the Amathole mountains. I was planning to camp for a few days. You might enjoy the scenery. Things to sketch, places to read and not a newspaper for miles."

I guess he has come to know me quite well in the past few weeks. "I've never been camping before."

"All the more reason to come."

I don't want to face Jess, I don't want to see Michael again, and

I don't want to be followed by stares and gossip. Running away does sound appealing, even if it means I'll miss class. "What about Law? Our tut on Friday?"

"Sick note."

"But I'm not sick."

He snorts softly. Right, everyone other than me pulls sickies all the time.

"You really don't mind leaving early? And I won't disturb your research?"

"Not at all." He looks pensive. "If anything…" I wait for him to finish the thought, but he doesn't.

"If anything?"

"If anything, the company will be nice."

That afternoon, I wait outside Miss Sukwini's door for hours. It's a hot day, but the corridor beneath the res is cool, and the silence gives me a chance to get my thoughts in order. It's after six when I hear her heels clicking down the corridor and stand from where I've been sitting against the wall.

She freezes when she sees me, a silhouette in the fading light, and I can't make out her expression.

When she eventually moves forward her steps are slow and measured. "I imagined I might find you here."

"You saw the article?"

She nods as she unlocks the door.

"You need to tell them it's not true. You need to call the paper and make them print a retraction. You have to—"

"Come inside, my dear. Let me put on the kettle."

I follow her into the sitting room. "You studied with him, so you know it's not true. You probably have photographs with him, don't you?"

"No, I do not."

Her tone throws me. I can't understand why she isn't as angry about this as I am. "He's your friend; you introduced him to my mother."

Miss Sukwini's heels click over the terracotta tiles in the tiny kitchen. She fills the kettle and flicks it on, without saying anything. She looks tired. Maybe something happened at the hospital. Maybe I shouldn't have ambushed her.

She scrubs her face with her hands as the kettle roars and gurgles. "It was wrong of him to keep that picture."

What? My heart thuds. I want to say I don't know what she's talking about, but there's nothing she could mean except the graduation picture. The one I mentioned before. The one she was so shocked by.

"Why?" is what I stammer out.

"Lilah, my dear, I need to tell you something now that I was hoping – *we* were hoping – we would never need to. This turn of events is unfortunate."

My gut tumbles, and I'm regretting coming here. The kettle is too darn loud. "Tell me something?"

"Before I say anything, you must promise to me that you will not tell anybody. Not even your closest friends."

"I promise." My voice kicks up an octave.

She removes the kettle from the element, and I think she's doing that to shut it up. Then she pours in more cold water and sets it on again.

It's like in a spy movie. She's intentionally creating noise so we can't be overheard. That more than anything sets my pulse racing. It's drumming loud enough in my ears to compete with the kettle.

"At this stage, I cannot provide details, so please do not ask. But I believe it is unfair to leave you in the dark given the news that came out today." She pulls two blue mugs down from the shelf, and she stares at them in the same way that Kalin was staring at his Coke earlier. "Derek Durow is not your father's real name."

"What!" Now I'm sure I must be dreaming. I don't know that

I've ever heard something so ridiculous. I shake my head. "No. I have other family. Uncle Clay, my cousin Tammy, they'd know if he—"

"I'm sure that they consider you family, my dear. They have seen you grow up and have no doubt been involved in your life…"

"You're saying Clay's not really my uncle?"

This is crazy. She's crazy.

"Clay is your father's business partner. Someone who assisted him when he most needed it."

"No." I refuse to believe this.

"Tell me, did you not wonder why your father might choose Clay Durow to defend him when there are far more qualified, far more successful candidates?"

I did wonder, but I thought that maybe the more qualified and successful candidates wanted nothing to do with him. "Clay knows the truth?"

She inclines her head.

Clay never responded to my message about the article. I knew he'd be panicking, but I didn't imagine it was quite this bad. I ask the question she's probably expecting, and dreading. "Why? Why would he build a life on a fake name?"

"To protect you, my dear."

"Protect me from what?" My immediate thought is witness protection. "Is this to do with Dumi?"

She shakes her head. "Not that, but it is important for the time being that this remains our secret."

"But—"

The kettle clicks off and she shakes her head. "Let's have some tea."

"I don't want tea, I want answers!" I reach for the kettle to flick it on again, but she catches my hand and stops me.

"This will all resolve itself in time, my dear. For now, I ask that you are patient."

It's only after I leave her flat and am lying in my room staring up at my map that I realise how flawed the witness protection explanation is. If there were gangsters or something after him and his family, why would he come back to Grahamstown? Why didn't he take us overseas, far away from here?

Kalin was right when he said I didn't know Dad at all. I don't even know his name.

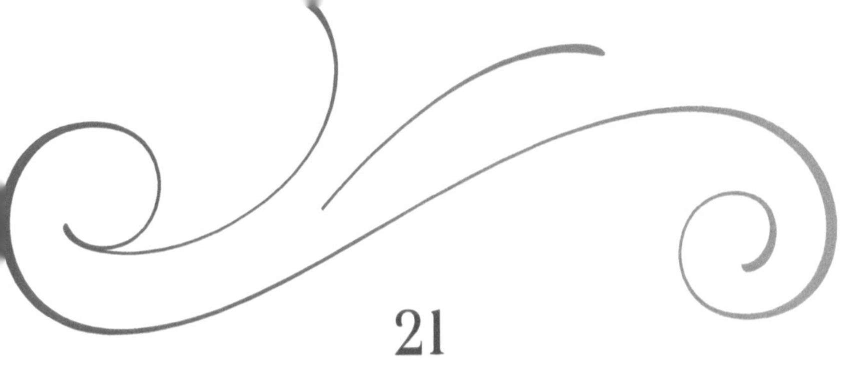

21

"You seem distracted." Kalin takes his eyes off the winding mountain road for a second to check my expression.

"It's nothing." I was thinking about whether it's possible Dad is an undercover Hawk agent and Miss Sukwini is his partner. And maybe they set up the whole Dumi thing to trap him, and it's been years in the works. I like that idea quite a lot. It also means that he wasn't involved in human trafficking, and he's still a superhero fighting bad guys. The fact that it doesn't fit with what I know of the Dumi case, or the charges against Dad, is minor. I probably just don't know enough details.

Missing class still niggles at me, but as we drive, my worry melts away. Water from the recent rains trickles down the side of the mountain in tiny waterfalls, and the grassland on our right transitions to a tangled forest. I can see how that rumour about the Mirkwood started; it's easy to imagine elves and orcs watching the road, and magic spells being cast in a green glade nearby.

We draw into the forest village of Hogsback, and Kalin pulls up outside a pub proudly advertising warm beer.

"Stretch your legs, I'll only be a minute." Kalin takes a bag out of the trunk. At my questioning look he says, "Stock."

Now his elven designs make sense. I'd bet the pretty necklace with the moonstone is in that bag. He ducks into the curio shop next to the pub. I get out as well. My legs creak like an old woman's. I've only been sitting for two hours, but it feels like much longer. The air smells fresh and earthy. There are a few other shops between the trees where I could browse. A café, a bakery, a hardware store… but nothing particularly interesting, and I end up wandering into the curio shop too.

It's airy, with whitewashed walls, a high roof and bare rafters. Kalin's by the till with his necklaces spread out on a leather mat. A curly-haired woman in a tie-dyed dress is talking to him while writing in an invoice book.

"Rose quartz is always an option," she tells him with a wink.

"Not that sort of gift."

"Right, well, maybe tell me a little about the girl?"

A sharp jolt to my midriff. *Girl? What girl?* Is that why Kalin has been distant? He's broken his no-romance rule and doesn't know how to tell me? Is that who Anna is? I consider backing out of the store.

"Lilah," Kalin says.

I jump. He still has his back to me, but he must have heard me enter the shop.

"Come here a minute?"

The woman's face brightens. "Oh, is this her?"

"This is her. What do you recommend?"

He was talking about *me*? The woman comes out from behind the desk and looks me up and down.

"I— I didn't mean to interrupt," I stammer.

She walks around me, then holds out a hand to touch my shoulder. "Do you mind?"

I shake my head. I have no idea what's going on. The woman closes her eyes. Her hand hovers near my skin, but she doesn't touch me. "Tangerine aura. Creative, intelligent, detail-oriented, prone to perfectionism."

Kalin quirks an eyebrow.

She drifts back to the desk and her skirt swishes about her ankles. "The tiger's eye would enhance the masculine energy, build confidence, help her to ground herself."

"I see."

"But then smoky quartz might protect her from negative energy, including her own thoughts."

"That sounds like a contender." Kalin tilts his head, gesturing that I should join them.

When I'm at his side, he says softly, "I want to fix your necklace. Recall I mentioned the missing stone?" There's a little basket of crystals at his elbow. "Dahlia is a reiki master. I thought her advice would be invaluable."

I don't know what reiki is, but I find it hard to imagine that the intellectual Kalin could believe in crystal energies. Maybe he's just humouring her, building rapport with a client.

"You don't have to fix it," I say, in an equally quiet voice. "I like it as it is." In fact, I haven't taken it off since he gave it to me, but I don't say that.

Dahlia nudges the basket towards me. "What do you feel drawn to, darling?"

The smoky quartz must be the one that looks like mist. I know tiger's eye from the tourist traps in Cape Town. It's a local semi-precious stone like amber velvet shot through with gold. Neither of them really appeals to me. If I was to be entirely honest, the soft pink crystal they were talking about when I came in, rose quartz, is the nicest. But her wink and his comment about it remove it from consideration.

"Go on," Kalin prompts.

"Um…" The second prettiest is the pale lavender amethyst, but I'm not sure if they want me to pick something based on how pretty it is. What do they mean by 'drawn to'? I'm all too aware of them both observing me with intensity, like this is some test. I don't want to choose the wrong one.

"Do you have any jet?" Kalin asks.

Dahlia's eyes go round. "She hasn't attracted the attention of the evil eye?"

He gives Dahlia an easy smile. "I thought it might be good for that pesky negative energy you mentioned, but you're the expert."

Dahlia rummages under the desk and emerges with a plastic bag full of gemstones. So much for the bohemian mystique. She shakes it around and digs out a pitch-black stone. It isn't as pretty as some of the others, but it looks quite sophisticated.

I remember something suddenly. "Dad wears jet."

"Oh?" Kalin asks.

I touch my wrist. "His watch. It's got a jet face."

"Jet is also a colour."

I resist the urge to roll my eyes, but only because he's buying me a gift. "I know that. It's made from jet. I'm certain of it."

"Well then it sounds like we have a winner?"

There is something poetic about the idea of combining the material from Dad's watch with mom's necklace. I nod and try not to think too hard about where that watch might be sitting now.

⁂

Kalin sets up our camp with practised ease. All I can do is watch, and try to stay out of the way. We drove halfway up a mountain, then walked at least 500 metres through the forest to get to this otherwise deserted campsite. It's clear that Kalin knows this place, and that, unlike me, he's gone camping a lot.

"Is it safe up here?" I ask as he eases a tent-pole into the ground.

"You're aware we don't get bears and wolves in South Africa?"

Yes, Mr Condescending. "I meant muggers."

He grunts. "Right, yes. We do get those." He shoves another pole into the ground. "I've never so much as seen another person in this part of the forest, but I wouldn't advise you go far. It's easy to get lost."

I pull my phone out of my pocket. "Not with this."

"Best of luck getting signal."

Right. That might be an issue.

"You may as well turn it off and leave it with the rest of

your things."

I hesitate, but I suppose that's what this whole trip is about – getting away. And that includes switching off my phone.

"So, it's true what they say about your generation then," Kalin comments.

"Oh?"

He taps his forehead. "Chip up here, controlled by that device. Best take care not to walk too far from it. Your head might explode."

"You really are an old man."

He shrugs.

"Technically we're part of the same generation, you know?"

"Sticks and stones."

I tuck the phone into my bag and, after checking one more time that there's nothing I can do to help, set off with a book. I find some semblance of a path and follow it between thick trunks and over trickling streams. A canopy stretches overhead with tiny dots of light filtering through. I don't lose my way, but I lose myself in the surroundings. There is no time here, nor distance, only one breathtaking sight after another. When my calves start to ache, I settle down to read a while in a patch of sunlight.

I've been to the Tokai forest near home on school trips, but there the trees grow wide apart, and we would collect armfuls of pinecones to throw at each other. This is far more wild. The trees are packed close and their long branches intertwine so it's impossible to tell which belongs to which tree. I keep getting distracted from my book by fluttering birds up in the branches, or the sound of a waterfall in the distance.

When I eventually follow the path back down to our camp, I find it empty.

Was I gone long enough for Kalin to launch a search and rescue? Then I see the note scribbled in the sand by my tent – 'Gone fishing', with an arrow pointing into the trees.

He drew another arrow a few metres from camp, but when I

come across it I can already hear the roaring of the water and I head towards the sound. The trees open, and there's Kalin, with his back to me, on the bank of a sparkling pool, holding a fishing rod. He's shirtless and the muscles of his shoulders are clearly defined. I clear my throat.

"How was your walk?" he asks as I step up beside him.

"Good. This place is beautiful." The pool he's found is even more idyllic than the forest. It's golden from sediment and fed by two waterfalls – a large thunderous one directly ahead of us, and a smaller one that trickles gently to my left. The water slides off a shelf and beneath that I can see the tops of trees – an ocean of green stretching all the way to a small mountain on the horizon.

"That's the hog's back," Kalin says, noticing my gaze. "It's the name of that sort of geological formation."

"I see."

Silver flickers in the water nearby.

"Ah-ha!" The afternoon light plays off Kalin's form as he reels in the line like crazy.

He seemed the lanky slender type beneath his jacket and old man clothes. He's not overly muscular, but he's more sculpted than I would have guessed. There's a chain around his neck, and a pendant that flashes with his movement, bouncing against his bare chest.

I feel strangely embarrassed watching him like this and focus on the view instead.

"I hope you eat fish?" he asks.

When I look back at him, he's removing a glistening trout from the line.

"Um…" The fish stares at me. "I've never had it this fresh before," I say diplomatically.

"Pity." He baits the hook again. "Come, give it a try."

"Oh, I—" He hands the rod to me before I can decline.

"This is the spinning reel." He points to a metal contraption on the rod. "You hold it between your fingers like so."

I let Kalin move my hand to the correct position.

"Then you open the bail. This metal part here. And you hold the line with your forefinger."

"This is a lot to remember."

"You're smart."

He steps away. Then his arms are around me.

I smell herbs. His sun-warmed skin presses against my upper arms and my brain blanks. I'm not paying attention at all as he explains how to cast, as he guides me.

"You need to actually let the line go," he says in my ear and I can hear his smile.

I swallow. "Right."

He casts with me again, and I move my forefinger off the line at the proper time. The bobber sails above us and plops into the water.

"Good. Now you close the bail."

I fumble to do that as he moves away again, leaving my skin cold and my pulse soaring.

What just happened?

The current moves the bobber across the water, and it's not long before the first fish bites, but it gets away before I can reel it in. The second manages to snap the line. Kalin insists that wasn't a fish at all, but a rock or piece of driftwood that I tried to reel in. But the third time, when the line goes taut, the tug is so strong that I end up sliding down the bank before Kalin rushes to help me. When the monster eventually emerges on the hook, it's a lot smaller than I thought it would be and Kalin chuckles when he carries it off to join its unfortunate friend.

I look down so I don't have to see what happens to them.

The mud from the bank is caked along the bottom of my jeans, and sludge is splattered all the way up to my knees. "Yuck. I hope this comes out in the wash."

"I hope you brought an alternative?"

"Of course." It may be my first time camping, but I'm not

an idiot.

"Good," Kalin says, much closer than I expect.

And that's the only warning I get before he shoves me, and I'm sent flailing, face-first, into the water.

It's icy cold. My lungs constrict. But it's thankfully not too deep and, once I find my feet, I push up to the surface, filled with righteous fury.

"What the heck was that?"

Kalin's in the water too now – he must have dived in after pushing me. He's laughing and I'm annoyed, but I'm also aware of how beautiful he looks, with his hair wet and loose and with that full smile.

Oh no. No, Lilah, you're not going there.

He must mistake my inner battle for pique, because his expression sobers. He paddles closer and reaches out to gently remove a piece of river reed from my hair. My heart ricochets in my chest.

"Sorry." He studies my face.

I take the opportunity to dunk him.

I swim away but my clothing is too heavy, and he catches up easily.

He grabs my middle. I kick out at him, squealing as I try to escape before he pulls me under again.

He slips to the side, avoiding my legs. "You think you can beat me at this, do you?"

I have just enough time to take a lungful of air before I'm pushed below the surface.

But he's made one fatal error: he's left my arms free.

I yank his legs towards me, and he flies backwards.

"I grew up on the coast," I gasp as we both break the surface again. "I can definitely beat you at this." I don't confess that all my past experience has been with bullies who probably really would have drowned me if given the chance.

Kalin holds up his hands in surrender. "Truce, then?"

I slip off my soaked shoe and throw it at him. He ducks but gets caught by the cascade of water pouring out of it. He's grinning.

I lob the other one at him too for good measure, and he catches it and tosses them both to shore.

"Anything else you'd like to throw at me?"

He doesn't mean – he can't mean – that I begin stripping. Because that would be flirting, and this is Kalin. But I wouldn't have expected Kalin to frolic in a forest pool either. It's difficult to believe this is the same person who was so stiff beside me yesterday.

He flops onto his back, as if my silence settles the matter, and floats towards the centre of the pool with lazy strokes. The water is like a mirror reflecting the forest around us. Kalin's hair fans out around him.

I'm breathless and it has nothing to do with being dunked underwater.

"I thought you were here to do research?" I ask.

"Mmm." He keeps his eyes closed.

He's clearly not in the mood for conversation. I tilt my chin up to look at the sky, and the branches that shade the pool. The rushing water fills my senses. I breathe deeply, trying to commit all of this to memory, including the unfamiliar buzz in my veins that I don't want to examine too closely.

To my surprise, it's Kalin who eventually breaks the silence. "So, tell me about this job of yours?"

I do. I tell him about Lani and how we met, and about Harrold and how intimidating he is, and how he didn't fire me for the Greek salad thing. I wait for Kalin to laugh at my mix up, but he just smiles.

"How's Fatso?" I ask.

"He misses you. He keeps walking into rooms expecting you to be there."

"Oh. I suppose he liked the extra attention."

Kalin gazes up at the trees with a wistful expression. "I suppose he did."

We float quietly a while, absorbing the peace of the forest. I'm aware of him near me, how his hair twists in the water, how his face changes as his muscles relax. I want to touch him. I want…

I bite hard on my inner cheek to interrupt my thoughts.

What's wrong with me?

The temperature drops as the sun sinks below the treeline, and when we trudge up the bank, I have to clench my jaw to stop my teeth knocking together. All the muscles along my spine go rigid with cold.

Kalin's clothes are, of course, in a neat dry pile under a tree. He whisks his coat from the bundle and wraps it around me. It's warm from the sun, but it's not quite enough to stop me shivering.

"Sorry." He rubs up and down my arms. "I failed to consider this."

His face is close to mine, and he's radiating heat. I can't look at him because if I do, I'm afraid I'll snuggle into him.

He tilts up my chin. His eyes are filled with concern. "Are you angry?"

It's not anger that's pumping through me. The feeling is kind of like that first glass of whiskey. It burns in my chest, warms my stomach, makes me a bit queasy. Is this because I saw him shirtless? Is it as primal as that?

Or have I felt this way for a while now and just refused to admit it? That time he snatched my wrist in his sleep and smiled at another woman. That moment he pushed Michael. The night alone in the mess the Hawks left, when something made me call him.

"Just cold," I say.

I'm not sure he believes me, but he wraps an arm around my shoulders as we walk back to camp and assures me I'll defrost once I'm in front of the fire.

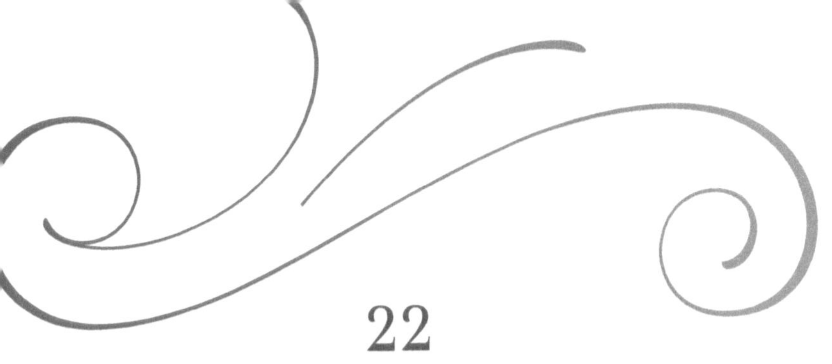

22

$\mathcal{E}$verything is different.

Kalin puts on his tattered golf shirt and ugly combat boots, and still my stomach is in knots. I can't help but admire the way he builds the fire and gets the kindling to take first try, and how the firelight paints his features. It makes his cheekbones more prominent, lends colour to his skin. His hair curls as it dries, like mine does, but his hangs in tendrils of dull gold, while I'm sure mine looks more like a frizzy mane.

Kalin is different.

And I hold on to that thought like a life raft. These feelings I'm having are for the person he is out here; for this impish, wild man who buys me gemstones and laughs so freely. When we go back to Grahamstown everything will return to normal. He'll be closed off and enigmatic and… kind, selfless, well-read.

No, *arrogant*. He'll be arrogant and pretentious and stiff. I try to remember how I felt about him when we first met, but it's difficult to be angry at past Kalin's comments about my father when he turned out to be right.

"I'm really sorry," Kalin says. Almost as if he's read my mind. It takes me a beat to realise he must be talking about throwing me into the water.

He's been preparing our dinner while I've been having my crisis, and I guess he thinks I'm silently stewing.

"I'm not angry," I assure him.

"Still, I forgot myself earlier and I owe you an apology for that."

"Forgot yourself?"

"I don't know what came over me." He shakes his head, turns the fish, which is frying in a metal saucepan.

I shift a little closer. "Kalin, you're allowed to be playful sometimes. I promise I'm not upset."

He gives me a strange look. The shadows play about his eyes. "Perhaps you should be."

"I don't understand."

He shakes his head again. "Never mind."

"Don't do that. You're doing that thing." If we were in the Settler's Cottage, he'd have gotten up and stalked into his study. On impulse, I reach out to pat his arm. His coat is too big for me and covers my hand, so my gesture of comfort is even more awkward than his at the cocktail bar.

He ducks his chin and avoids my gaze.

"This is about your past, isn't it? What, you're not allowed to play? Not allowed to feel joy?"

He presses his eyes shut, and I can tell I'm right.

"Can I ask you something?"

"You may ask. Although I do not promise to answer."

"These... good deeds of yours. How will you know when you've done enough?"

He prods the fish. "I wasn't aware there was an upper limit on good deeds a person should do."

"You know what I mean. I mean your atonement points. When will you have enough points to allow yourself to be happy?"

He scowls as if he's swallowed something bitter, and doesn't answer. My throat tightens. The fish sizzles. Birds call to each other as they roost above our heads. He removes the pan from the heat and gently shifts the fish onto plastic plates.

"Who's Anna?"

His head snaps up. "What?"

"You said it in your sleep the other night."

He frowns. "When were you watching me sleep?"

"I wasn't *watching* you. I happened to pass by while you were asleep."

Kalin hands me my dinner, busies himself with sorting out plastic cutlery. I think he's going to avoid this question, the way he's avoided all others about his past, but then he says, "Anna was a childhood friend."

"What happened?"

Again, he hesitates. "My parents died."

"Oh." The wind rustles through the leaves. I don't know what to say.

"And then we grew apart."

The warmth of the fire does nothing to ease the chill that travels through me at the despair in his voice. "I'm sorry, I didn't mean… I know you don't like talking about…"

He shrugs. There's something unguarded about the movement. He seems younger. A lonely boy who doesn't like caring about people and doesn't know how to make friends. "I regret a lot of what I said to her the last time we saw each other. I wish I could tell her that."

"Why can't you?"

He meets my gaze and there's so much pain in his eyes that I suck in air at the force of it.

I focus on my feet. "Sorry."

"There is truth in what Bianca told you. You shouldn't get attached to me."

It's a little late for that. He has no idea how hard I'm fighting the urge to hug him, to comfort him, to tell him I'm here, and I'm not going anywhere. But I hold myself still. He was very clear about where he stood on the subject. *I can't get involved with anyone.*

"I'm not attached." I force lightness into my voice. "I'm just a stray who you feed. Like Fatso." I raise a forkful of trout to underscore the statement.

The stars are even brighter than they were in Grahamstown, sparkling above our little clearing. While we eat, I ask Kalin about more comfortable topics, like fishing techniques, and I curl up in his jacket with my head on my arms and listen to him talk about bait and wind position until I drift to sleep.

I am Alayna and she is holding a golden orb. It has the weight of a soap bubble, but the warmth of a living, breathing thing. It throbs, and the static of its magic raises the hair on her arms.

"So that's it, then?" Sloane asks.

He's still panting and sweating from the last trial they had to complete. He looks just as wary as he did that night at the inn, but even he can't deny the wisdom of her plan now.

"Yes. The Keyflame." She's tired too. Her bones are tired. A gash on her leg demands attention, but she wants to laugh with joy.

Finally, after months of searching and fighting. Finally, a way to defeat her enemy. But no time to pause now. Now they must move south, must try to reach the rendezvous.

When they exit the dark labyrinth, Sloane hangs back.

He's looking at his feet, and she thinks at first that it's the sun. It's already low in the sky, but bright compared to where they've been for days.

"It…" he starts. "I did not expect we would make it this far."

Sloane, always so emotional. "It does feel surreal. But come, we must move forward."

In the forest, under a canopy of green, their horses are gone. Instead, a cloaked figure waits.

Alayna brings her hands up to cast, but she's too slow. The figure lifts its arms, and everything goes dark.

She wakes in a cave. Her hands are tied behind her back and her limbs are numb. Poison. No doubt to temper her magic so she cannot challenge her captor. Even her tongue is heavy.

The cloaked figure stands at the mouth of the cave, haloed by bright sunlight.

"You dare to challenge me?" he asks in a low, gravelly voice.

For the first time, fear floods through her. If it was some underling, she knows she could beat them. But it's him. He's come for her himself.

"You can do what you wish to me. There are others. You will fail."

"Ah, but can the others be trusted?" He casts bright scarlet magic into the depths of the cave. Someone screams.

She manages to turn her head towards the sound. Sloane is pinned to the cave wall. The red magic ghosts over his skin and he twists against it as if it is fire.

"Let him go! Stop!"

But the Overlord does not stop, and Sloane's face contorts in torment. His eyes bulge, his skin is pulled back.

"I am the one responsible. Torture me!"

Sloane falls from the wall and hits the floor with a crack. He doubles over, gasping for breath.

"I would not be so quick to defend this friend of yours," the Overlord says. "He is a traitor."

Alayna does not respond. Cold claws up her back. Sloane's words repeat in her mind.

The Overlord moves towards her. "Once I discovered what you were so busily researching, I set out to find one of these orbs for myself. And who should I come upon in that hidden tomb, trying to complete the required rituals, but two of your minions. I killed the one, but the other offered me a deal. He said if I spared his life, he would lead me to you. He even suggested that I wait until after you retrieved the Keyflame so as to capture it too."

It feels like fingers of ice being driven into her heart, into my heart. Sloane, who has travelled by her side for months, all the while leading her to her doom.

His body curls inwards as the Overlord hurls another spell at him.

"Let him go," Alayna says. It is not Sloane's fault that he is weak.

The Overlord doesn't speak for a long moment. Then he draws a breath. "He betrayed you, Anna. You wouldn't see him punished?"

I shoot awake. It's morning. The fire's dead, and I'm alone.

My pulse is racing. Stupid dreams. Stupid subconscious. This is what I get for building such an elaborate fantasy world. How many times did I plot out campaigns against the evil sorcerer as a kid? How many times did I imagine exchanges just like that one? Now my brain clearly doesn't know how to process difficult situations other than through this dumb story. I brush my frizzy hair away from my face.

"Kalin?" I call tentatively.

No answer. I clamber to my feet. My muscles protest. My back is especially unimpressed with waking up on hard-packed earth. As I stretch, I spot a bright wrapper lying beside me.

It's a Nature Valley granola bar, with a note in Kalin's untidy writing. "Good morning. Doing research. Have fun."

It's probably a good thing that he's gone off by himself. I need to get my head straight.

I set off in a different direction from yesterday, this time with my journal under my arm. I open it to one of the creamy blank pages. There's a lot to draw out here in the middle of nowhere, and nobody to judge me for filling a page with different kinds of rocks, and trying to detail all the types of trees I hike past. I start to construct a map of the forest: the little streams, the leafy paths, the jutting stones and fallen logs. I lose all sense of time but I'm vaguely aware that I'm journeying higher.

Then the forest opens in front of me, with no warning at all, and I'm standing on the edge of a precipice. My stomach swings at the sudden vertigo and I stumble backwards a few steps. Once my heart doesn't feel like it's going to leap right up out of my throat, I tip-toe forward again, slowly this time, to peek over the edge.

I'm a long, long way up. A blanket of green stretches below me. The tall firs look like no more than Christmas trees. A river winds between them, and I'm about to take out my pencil to add it to my map when I spot a figure in the middle of it, on a little island barely large enough to keep them dry. It's so surprising to see another person that I squint at them for a good while. It looks like they're holding a walking stick, and they're dragging it around them in a circular motion, as if they're drawing patterns on the edge of the water. Marking levels, maybe? There's no brown coat – I was still wearing that when I woke up – and that's probably why it takes me so long to realise it's Kalin. What is he doing? The river starts to rise around him. I blink. Trick of the light, maybe?

No. I can see the change against his legs. The water was lapping at his feet, but now it's rising past his ankles, now past his knees. Now he lifts his arms and the water seems to rise with them. It's like watching a wave swell, the crest form. Except this is happening all around *him*, and when it breaks it will break over him.

Now it's so high that I can't even see him.

I don't understand what's happening, but I understand that when the wave breaks, Kalin's going to drown.

I run.

I know I'm too far from him to help. There's no possible way that I can reach him in time. But I throw myself forward. I jump over tree roots and slide down the steep paths, and my chest burns, and my legs go numb, but I drive myself onward, down the mountain, down to the river, down to where I saw him. I run blindly. I'm too slow. I'm too—

I break through the trees and the river is ahead of me.

Kalin turns to look at me. He's standing on his little island. He's not even wet.

I collapse to my knees. My calves vibrate with strain, and the air I pull into my lungs stings.

"Lilah?" Kalin rushes to my side, drops down beside me. "Lilah, what happened?"

"The water... it was... I don't..." I pant out the words and I doubt he can hear them, let alone make sense of them.

He presses a hand to my cheek. "Did someone attack you in the forest?"

"No. You. The water."

Only now it's completely serene. What the hell? I know what saw, but when I look into Kalin's worried face, I struggle to find a way to describe it that won't make him immediately check me into a mental hospital.

"Let's get you back to camp," he says, and he helps me up.

Kalin insists that I sit inside my tent, out of the sun, while he makes us lunch. I'm tired from my run, but I don't feel like I have heatstroke.

I turn to a new page in my sketchbook and start drawing. Logically there can't be many explanations for what just happened. One, I'm losing my mind. Stress has driven me bonkers. That happens, right? Two… well, two is that I really saw what I saw. And if I did, what caused it? Is this like that day with the mist, when there was an old man and then he was gone? I swallow. I think I prefer the first option. Then there's option three. Option three is that Kalin was really, somehow, commanding the water, which is absurd. But as my hand moves over the page, that's exactly what I find myself sketching. Kalin in wizard robes making the water rise.

I drop my pencil when he pushes aside my tent flap and crawls in with a tray. Beans, eggs and burnt toast. It smells pretty good. Even the toast.

"Do you want to tell me what happened?" he asks as he places the tray beside me.

He's tied his hair back and he's wearing a loose-fitting white shirt.

I bite my lip. "What were you doing on the river?"

"Research. I left you a note—"

"No, I know. I mean what kind of research? You can't be studying old languages out here."

"Not languages, no."

"Then what?"

His expression clouds before he answers, "Customs."

"Customs to do with water?"

"What happened, Lilah?"

I focus on my knees. "I saw... It sounds ridiculous." I'm not even sure I want to confess to him, but I'm desperate for an explanation other than the terrifying ones I came up with. "I saw the water rising around you and I thought... I thought you were going to drown and there was no way I could get to you in time and—"

He grabs my hand. "Lilah, it's all right. I'm here. I'm fine."

My heart clip-clop-thuds as if it's just fallen down a flight of stairs. His hand is warm and mine fits perfectly in it, like it belongs there. So much for getting my head straight.

"I was splashing the water about quite a bit," Kalin says. "Perhaps that's what you saw?"

I *know* that's not what I saw.

His thumb brushes across my knuckles. "The Celts used to honour water spirits as life givers. They believed water linked our world with the Otherworld – what you'd call the spirit realm. Very little is known of the druidic rituals they'd perform. I discovered an old translation and was trying to figure out the components, see whether they made sense in action."

The book with the symbols.

"Maybe you did summon a water spirit?" I suggest. As absurd as that sounds, it's the most comforting of all the explanations so far.

"Or maybe the sun got to you?"

I scowl.

"What's this?" He lets go of my hand to reach for my book.

I try to snatch it away. "Nothing, just doodles."

But he grabs it and holds it up to the light. His eyes narrow as he examines my drawing of the wizard and the water. "Quite impressive for doodles."

He flips backwards, past my map, and rocks, and lecture notes. Then he pauses again. "Your kingdom?"

It's a drawing from the last dream I had, the one before this morning's. I was trying to remember the journey Sloane and Alayna took. There are figures in cloaks, some landmarks. Kalin flips back further. He pauses at a picture of Alayna – one where I struggled to get her armour quite right. "You're talented."

My heart starts skipping again. Well, in for a penny… He might as well know the full extent of my delusions. "I've been having dreams. I suppose it's some weird coping mechanism or something. Dreams of the kingdom. A story. It all sort of links together. Although I think I forget most of the dreams before I wake up."

"When did the dreams start?"

"After Dad…"

"I see." He closes the book and hands it to me.

"You think I've lost it, don't you?"

"No, I don't think that. I think maybe…" He hesitates. "I think that dreams often tell us things that we should pay attention to."

Our second night in Hogsback isn't as cold as the first. Kalin points out the constellations and tells me stories: of Orion the great hunter who is being chased by Scorpio across the sky, of fair Andromeda who was sacrificed by her family and saved by Perseus. I confess that I've never read The Iliad, and he laughs and remarks that of course I haven't, I'm only eighteen.

The comment rankles me more than it should. Our age difference is a gulf between us that I don't want to think about – not while he's smiling up at the stars like that, not with the memory of him holding my hand so fresh in my mind.

Later, I toss and turn in my tent. Every time I close my eyes, I see the Overlord. Once I even see him commanding water to rise.

We don't talk much on the drive to Grahamstown. Kalin's stiffness is back, and the man who played in a forest pool has disappeared as surely as the rising river did yesterday.

I stare out the window and try not to be disappointed. I predicted this. It's a good thing. I know from books how soul-destroying unrequited love can be, and I have no desire to experience it myself. Let cool, arrogant Kalin douse the little torch I've started carrying for him.

When he draws up outside my res, he doesn't turn off the engine immediately. He rests his hands on the steering wheel and his jaw works. "You're at the restaurant tomorrow?"

It's the first thing he's said in over an hour – the last was "bless you" after I sneezed.

"Yeah." Because of our trip, I have to pull a double shift. Hopefully the tips are better than last Sunday.

"Monday?"

"No. Tuesday and Wednesday."

He nods. "You should bring the necklace after class on Monday."

This distant Kalin still wants to add the jet? I almost insist he doesn't have to, again, but bite my tongue. Because if I don't see him then, when will I get to see him?

That night I picture everyone in the dining room turning to look at me when I go for dinner, or ducking close to gossip. But in reality no one even seems to notice me. I suppose Kalin was right about going away for a few days. Grahamstown has moved on to the next juicy thing.

I don't see Jess, and when I go to her room later to apologise and explain about Dad, she refuses to open her door even though I can hear her moving about inside.

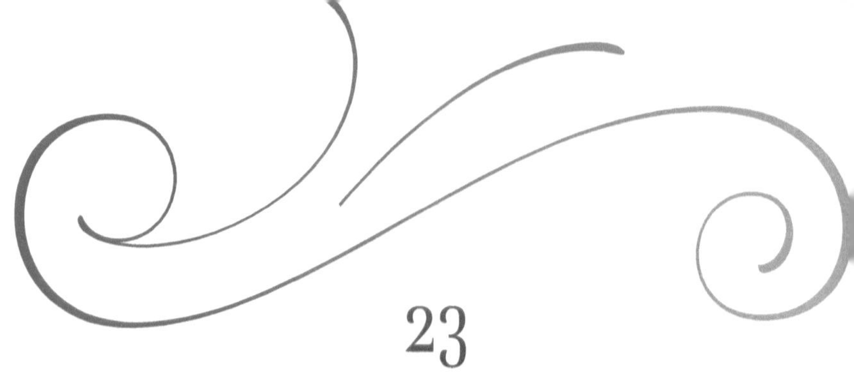

23

Fatso is waiting by the front gate when I get to the Settler's Cottage on Monday.

He meows a greeting, and I meow back at him before I see Kalin leaning against the wall with his arms folded. His mouth quirks, but he doesn't comment.

He's barefoot, in faded tracksuit bottoms and a grey T-shirt, with his hair scraped up in a manbun again. He looks like he just rolled out of bed. There should be absolutely nothing attractive about him. Yet my heart still beats a little faster as I follow him through the bright, tangled garden.

The kitchen is filled with sunlight and smells like microwaved pizza. Fatso winds between my legs until I bend to scratch his ear.

Kalin heads straight to the study. "Here. I've cut down the stone, it should fit."

I pause just inside the door. It looks like he's emptied out the whole bookshelf and piled it up on the settee. Papers and books have spilled to the floor. The air is stale. He holds out his hand for the necklace.

"How long have you been living in this room?" I ask as I pass it to him.

He laughs softly. "I've been busy."

"Your research on the river led to a revelation?"

His gaze locks with mine. "Of sorts."

There's something significant in the look that I can't grasp, but

~196~

my nearest guess is, "You've figured out how to summon spirits?"

"Hilarious. Sit down. This will only take a minute."

I wasn't actually joking.

There is literally nowhere to sit, so I stand and watch him dig for his soldering iron in the mess, plug it in and set to work on the necklace. I'm a little worried that adding the stone will make it heavy. I'm so used to it that my neck feels naked without it now.

"How was work?" Kalin asks.

"It was fine. A bit quiet. I got a big table last night, though."

"Good. I've been meaning to ask you something. I know your waitressing takes priority, and I can't pay you much, but, well, there are eight weeks until Fest."

His jewellery. "I did say I'd help you."

"Yes, but that was before Guido's. I won't hold you to it if you feel you'll be overextending yourself." He turns and holds out the necklace to me. "There, good as new."

I know immediately that jet was the right choice. The black in the centre of that Celtic knot looks so beautiful, so elegant. It's like something Alayna would wear.

"Do you like it?" Kalin asks.

"It's probably the nicest thing I've ever owned."

"Oh, I very much doubt that." He smiles. "But I'm glad you approve of the design."

He goes to pack his soldering iron away. "As I said, I can't pay very much for your assistance. But perhaps I can offer an alternative to the adventures of res food?"

He's offering to make me dinner. My stomach flutters even though I've eaten with him so many times before.

"I'd like that," I say. Is it obvious how much I'd like that?

His brow creases. Yes, it's too obvious. *Lilah, what's wrong with you?*

In tenth grade I had a crush on my English teacher. He was young and enthusiastic, and I was desperate to impress him. It mortifies me now. He probably joked with his friends about this silly schoolgirl who looked at him with hearts in her eyes. This is the same thing all over again. I should probably backtrack, tell him I'm worried about how my studies will suffer if I'm working two jobs. But I don't. Maybe working closely with him will remind me how arrogant and annoying he is.

That doesn't happen either.

For weeks I balance my studies and waitressing with visits to Kalin. I perch on the counter and attach clasps to his creations, while he works beside me. We talk, he smiles, the little cottage starts to feel like my real home. More than my res room, more than even the house in Cape Town.

Every time I visit, I find him waiting for me outside with Fatso at his feet, even when the weather starts to grow cold. And after dinner he always drives me to res to make sure I'm safe. Sometimes he comes to class – I suppose even Kalin needs a break from work now and then – and we sit together, and he teases me about my comprehensive notes.

It's during the second week of this routine that I manage to corner Jess after English one day.

"Will you at least give me the chance to explain?"

She's already changed to her winter wardrobe – knitted pink hat and gloves. Her gaze darts past me, as if she's trying to think of an excuse to flee. Then she sighs and shrugs. "Fine."

"Look, I didn't tell you about my dad because I—"

Then she does see something over my shoulder and her outlined eyes widen. I turn around, Kalin is standing there in his brown coat with his books under his arm. He's got his hair tied back neatly and he's even shaved. "Please, don't let me interrupt. It's not urgent."

"Uh…" I gesture between them. "Jess, Kalin. Kalin, Jess."

He takes her hand. "Ah, so *this* is Jess. A pleasure."

Jess raises her eyebrows, but Kalin is already looking back at me. "I just wanted to let you know I'll be home late tonight.

There's a thing at the Drama department."

My heart skitters at his turn of phrase. *Home.* "Drama department?"

"A rehearsal, I think. They've invited the oldies to attend."

"Oldies?"

He gives me his half-smile. "George wants to go. I said I'd take him. It's a matinee though so I should be back around six?"

"Six."

"Floccinaucinihilipilification."

"What?"

"Since you're repeating everything I say, I thought I'd try that one." He *winks*.

My insides flip-flop, and I duck my chin so he doesn't see the heart eyes. "What does that even mean?"

"The act of deciding something is worthless."

"So, what I'm doing to that word right now?"

He chuckles. "See you later."

Jess's eyes are still massive as we watch him walk away. "You *do* have a boyfriend. I knew it!"

"He's not a boyfriend."

"As if. *I'll be home at six? See you later?*"

"I'm helping him with a project."

She makes a sceptical sound and shakes her head. "Why did you even want to talk to me if you're just going to keep hiding things?"

"I'm not hiding things."

"Lilah, that cute little convo was the single nerdiest thing I've ever witnessed. I know I'm not clever like you, but I'm not stupid. You found someone just as big a nerd as you. You know how rare that is?"

Should I be insulted? She doesn't seem to mean it maliciously. "I know."

"So?"

If I'm going to confess my stupid feelings out loud, make them real like that, I don't want it to be to Jess. She thinks of boyfriends as accessories, and love as titillating gossip. But I know I'm on delicate ground. If I don't want our friendship to disintegrate, I have to open up. "So… *he* isn't interested."

"That's a load of crap."

"Jess…"

She puts her hands on her hips and makes her voice deep. "Hello, I'm Mister Nerdy Flirter. I use big words so Lilah will think I'm smart."

"That's not what he was doing."

"Like hell. He was looking at you like you were the last Gucci bag on a Black Friday sale."

I can't help but laugh at the mental image that evokes. I don't think Kalin would even know what Gucci is. "He definitely wasn't."

"Like a shot of espresso after three all-nighters."

That is easier to picture, but I still disagree. "He said he's not interested."

Jess frowns. "Like exactly how did he say that? Are you sure he wasn't playing hard to get?"

"Certain." I reach for the memory of his exact words. "I can't get involved with anyone. I just want to be clear about that. I have things going on."

"What does he have going on?"

I shrug. "Some research thing I think."

"Hah! Called it. Massive nerd. Doesn't change anything though. He's in lurve with you." She giggles. This is the exact sort of thing that I didn't want. She's reading too much into it and, worse, she's giving me a tiny sliver of false hope.

My confession does achieve one thing though. It melts the ice between us. She drops the subject and starts telling me about her own boy drama, and the next day, when we have English together again, she waits outside the lecture theatre with two cups of coffee.

I catch myself watching Kalin's reactions after that, reading into them when I shouldn't. Sometimes when I'm washing dishes after dinner, or when I'm fighting with a jump ring, I'll look up at him and find him staring. Not like Jess at a Gucci bag, or a sleep-deprived student at the coffee pot, but with a soft expression that makes me think of swimming in a mountain river.

One night, a moth gets trapped in my hair in a desperate attempt to escape Fatso's paws. When Kalin frees it, his hand lingers in my hair a moment after the moth is gone. Another night, he sees the label of my shirt sticking out and tucks it in for me. His fingers trail across my skin before he seems to remember himself and snatches his hand back.

During those weeks I also visit Miss Sukwini a few times. Partly because I'm hoping to glean more information about my parents, but also because she's a way to feel close to them.

Like Dad, she loves to talk about Grahamstown. I find myself trading his stories and sometimes she'll laugh and clap her hands. "I remember that day," she'll say, and I hope she'll add details, but she never does. Nor does she ever call him anything but Derek or "your father". She must be aware of my motives though, because during the third visit she digs out that old album where she found the picture of my mother and gives it to me to borrow.

"Lilah, you must promise me that you will not allow anyone else to look through this book," she says first. She reminds me of my father in that moment. I'm not sure if she means (as he would) that she's concerned about someone wrecking it, or if this is to do with the secret identity thing.

"I promise," I assure her.

I find two more images of Mom and Sukwini in the book, but I check through it about five times to make sure that's all there is. One is of them playing together in the garden, and I can't really see her face. The second one is more interesting. She's a little older than in the swing pic, maybe ten or twelve. Both girls are wearing pretty, flared dresses like they're dressed up for church or something. The interesting part is what's hanging around Mom's neck. It's the celtic knot pendant – the same one that's in the graduation photo. I hold Kalin's up to it. She doesn't seem to have a stone inlaid in hers, but it's difficult to tell from the picture. Maybe it was an heirloom and that's why she had it when she was so young? I wish Dad had kept it.

As exams draw nearer and the books pile up around my tiny room, I have to accept it's time to return the album. I don't have space for it and don't want to risk it getting damaged by heavy Law files.

The night I go to give it back, I hear raised voices from within Miss Sukwini's rooms as I approach.

The door hangs ajar, but the voices are muffled. My pulse hums. Even though it's unlikely, my overactive imagination immediately suggests that *this* could be the person she hid her voice from with the sound of the kettle. It's a low male voice, but that's about all I can tell without creeping closer.

Well, the door is open.

I let my curiosity carry me carefully up to the doorway, then I see the man and my heart stops entirely.

I know him. I know him very well.

"…nothing's changed," Kalin says.

"Everything has changed, Kallen." Miss Sukwini pronounces his name the same way George does. She draws a breath to say more, but he cuts her off.

"I'm telling you it hasn't. I'm merely helping—"

"Helping the way you help all your strays? Tell me this is no different from any other poor, destitute creature you've brought to me in the time we've known each other, Kallen. Look into my eyes and tell me that."

He does not look into her eyes. He looks at the floor. "I will do exactly what I promised."

"You can't do it." It's unclear whether she means meeting her gaze or whatever the promise was.

Now he glares at her. "You think I'm not ready for it? After all these years? I'm not going to back out now just because—"

He notices me.

I'm not cut out to be a spy. I didn't even try to hide. I've just been frozen in the doorway since I recognised his face.

At Kalin's sudden pause, Miss Sukwini turns. "Lilah." With barely a moment's hesitation she sweeps towards me, her mustard skirt dancing around her feet. "Come in, come in. Would you like some tea?"

She's so casual, as if she was expecting me and I hadn't just barged in in the middle of a confrontation. Kalin and I are not quite so skilled. We stare at each other. He must be trying to work out what I heard. Miss Sukwini takes the album from me.

She heads into the kitchen and calls over her shoulder, "Kallen, will you be staying for another cup?"

Friendly, as if they weren't just arguing.

He shakes his head. "No, I must be going." He searches my face before he says in a lower voice, "See you tomorrow?"

I nod and he leaves without bothering to say goodbye to Miss Sukwini.

I'm still standing in place when she comes in with the tea tray. "Did you find anything in the album?"

"How do you know Kalin?"

"This is Grahamstown, my dear. Everybody knows everybody. But let's not worry about that now. Come, tell me what you found, and perhaps I can remember a story to go with it."

I was going to show her Kalin's necklace, but now I'm reluctant to. My heart is still pounding. What was that argument about? It couldn't be about Kalin's big project – the old manuscript – it didn't sound academic at all. What else is he involved in?

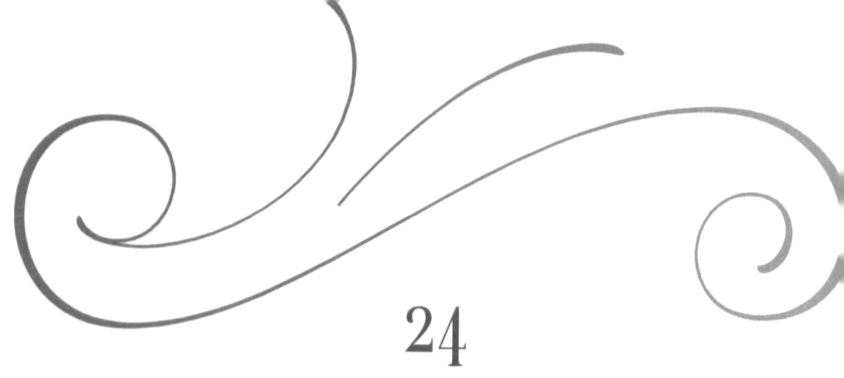

24

$\mathcal{K}$alin must know the question's coming. I'm on the counter, and he's working quietly beside me. Rain patters down in the garden and the air smells like damp earth.

We've exchanged the usual pleasantries, but there's a tension in Kalin's shoulders and I recognise that strained look on his face from the cocktail bar. I need to broach the subject sooner or later. May as well be now.

"So, you know my warden?"

"Nabelo Sukwini, yes."

"You never mentioned that before."

He reaches across me for a roll of wire on my other side. "This is a small town. You can probably assume I know most people."

He's not going to make this easy. "What were you arguing about?"

"My thesis." He answers quickly. He's had time to prepare for this interrogation.

"Miss Sukwini is a nurse. Why would she be interested in a thesis on Celtic language and rituals?"

"She's more than just a nurse."

More? In what way? "What creature did you bring to her?"

He looks up at me.

"You said you were trying to help."

I want to tell him about how I, too, brought Sukwini an injured person to help. I want to tell him about the strange glow I saw on Lani's wrist. *Tell me what you're involved in. I'll believe you, whatever it is.*

But Kalin says, dismissively, "Don't worry about it, Lilah."

I suppress a growl of annoyance. "What's changed? She said everything changed."

"Why does this concern you so much?"

The rain beats on the glass behind me. "Because my father's last instruction to me was to trust her." Because maybe whatever Kalin's involved in is the same thing that Sukwini's involved in, that Dad's involved in. Maybe it's the reason he stared at Mom's portrait so long, the reason he suspected Dad from the start. Maybe it explains everything about my life that I don't understand. "'Trust her even if she asks you to do things that don't seem to make sense', that's what he said."

"You *can* trust her," Kalin sets down the pendant he's working on. "She cares about your wellbeing. We both do."

"Both? You make it sound like you discussed me."

"Maybe we did."

My annoyance flares. "Can you stop being cryptic for once? When did you discuss me? Why?"

"On more than one occasion, if you must know."

"Why?"

"Don't be obtuse. What happened to your father is hardly a secret." He's getting annoyed too. He's stopped working, but he's still focused on the counter rather than on me.

"So you, what? Have secret meetings about what I'm up to?" Another piece clicks into place. "This is how she knew about how much time I was spending at the library!" Which she reported back to Dad. "This is how you knew about Guido's! Who else is in your spy network?"

"You're overreacting."

"Am I? No one tells me anything. My whole life is a lie – not even a lie, it's a tangled mess of people feeding me half-truths and hiding things from me." The words come from deep inside, from all the buried fears I've shoved down since that day the Hawks arrested Dad. They're bitter with truth.

"Is it honestly such a wonder that your friends watch out for you?" he asks.

"Apparently I don't have friends. I have babysitters."

"That's not true."

"You think I'm a child." Another fear I've carried too long. "Did you give Sukwini a call before inviting me to stay here too? Is it all right if Lilah spends the night, I promise I'll have her back in time for ter—"

"You're wrong."

He moves so fast I have no time to anticipate what he's going to do before his lips are on mine.

Warmth shoots into my belly and washes through me, instantly dousing the burning rage. He tastes like saltwater and his kiss is hard, almost painful.

Then he withdraws, shock written on his face, as if I was the one to suddenly kiss him.

I open my mouth to say something, but words die. There are no words. Kalin kissed me. Kalin *kissed* me.

He looks away, clenches his jaw.

My pulse beats louder than the rain outside. I wish he'd speak. I'm afraid he'll speak. I reach up to touch his cheek. My movement feels too slow, too mechanical. His gaze returns to mine and there's that soft, wistful, expression. There's a look that says *I can't get involved with anyone. But right now, I want to.* He trails his knuckles down the side of my face. His eyes drink me in.

My lips tingle. He draws nearer, hesitates, hovers an inch from me. I can feel his breath, his body heat.

I close the distance for him.

The moment our lips touch again, all Kalin's resistance breaks, like a dam wall. He crushes me to him. His hand slides to the nape of my neck, tangling in my hair. I grip his shoulders as his tongue slips between my teeth. My senses are filled with him. Camphor and library books, hard muscle, rough stubble, and his deep, deep kiss.

He kisses me like he's starving, like he'll die if he lets me go. Waves of heat radiate through my body and across my skin. I've never wanted anything as badly as I want this, as I want him.

He slips a hand beneath my shirt and his warm palm travels up my spine, leaving a trail of goose bumps. His mouth leaves mine to drag across my jaw, down my neck, to my collarbone.

Then he pauses again, half-buried in my hair, breathing raggedly. The hand that was on my back, slips down to the counter.

"I think you should go home," he says.

That's the very last thing I want to do. "Why?" I'm out of breath.

Kalin jerks away from me. "I told you, I can't get involved." He runs his fingers through his hair. His eyes are scrunched closed. "Least of all with you."

A shard of ice, straight into my core. "Least of all with me?"

He turns and paces across the study. "I shouldn't have let it get this far. Nabelo was right."

"Right? Right about what?"

Then I realise. There's only one possible answer. I'm the stray. The destitute creature. I'm what changed. "What did you promise to do to me?"

He whirls and glares at me, glares in such a way that I am, for the first time, a little frightened of his intensity. "I didn't promise to do anything to you."

I slip off the counter, heart slamming even faster than when he was kissing me. "What did you promise?"

He doesn't answer, and so many possibilities fly around my head. Something he's waited years for. Something that I might change. Something that prevents him getting involved romantically. "Is it dangerous? Are you in danger?"

"Go home, Lilah."

Where is home? Res, under Sukwini's watch? Clearly not here. "Why won't you give me a straight answer?"

"Take the umbrella."

"Kalin!" My heart is splintering. "Why won't you trust me?"

"This isn't *about* you."

"You make it sound like it is!"

"Will you just leave already!"

The words slam into my stomach, knocking the air from my lungs. He drops his head into his hands, deflated.

I wasn't built for this sort of emotional whiplash. I'm too soft. And if I stand there arguing with him much longer, he'll see just how soft I really am.

I manage to keep my voice steady as I ask, "Should I come back tomorrow?" Like we planned.

"I don't think that's a good idea." He says from beneath his hair. "I think it's probably best if you don't. Come back."

He's cutting me loose, setting me adrift without my anchor – which is him, which is this place. I shake my head and walk numbly to the door. As I push it open, I hear my name. Soft, strangled.

"Lilah."

I turn back to him.

"You didn't do anything wrong. None of this is your fault. It's all on me."

Yet I'm the one being punished. I swallow and leave without responding.

25

$\mathcal{L}$ ove is a terrible thing.

I can't think. My mind, which I've always been able to rely on even when I can't rely on anything else, is caught in a loop. I keep going back to the kiss. I keep seeing the look in Kalin's eyes, feeling his fingers against my spine, hearing his words echoing back at me. *Will you just leave already!* I'm so angry. I'm so disappointed.

I should be studying Law. My first exam is coming up. Instead, I sit in the corner of my tiny room reading Hamlet.

("I did love you once," Hamlet says.
"Indeed, my lord, you made me believe so," Ophelia replies.)

When I finally build up the courage to visit Miss Sukwini to ask about Kalin's project and his promise, she refuses to tell me anything.

"You should take this subject up with him, my dear. It is not my place to offer commentary."

I want to scream.

The only time my mind is quiet is when I'm working at Guido's – when the tables are full, and the call bell is ringing, and Harrold is shouting orders. I can focus on balancing plates without dropping them, on which of my tables needs drinks, on trying to work out how much I've earned each night. I pick up extra shifts. I become the go-to substitute when someone's too sick (or hungover) to work.

I get to know the regulars well enough to greet them by name and guess at their orders. They're always impressed when I say, "The usual, sir?"

I get to know the other staff too. Lani takes me under her wing. I gradually reveal my story to her, and she starts calling me Cinderella – Cindy for short. The privileged daddy's girl who now has to scrub tables and fill sauce bottles with the rest of them.

Her brother, whose name I discover is Chad, says, "*Nee, sy's mos* like that one with the blue dress. Goes through the town singing?" He preens and waves his arms about. "With the book. You know the one, hey?"

"Belle," I supply. "*Beauty and the Beast.*"

He makes pistol fingers at me. "Yes!"

But Cindy is the name that sticks. And I don't actually mind. In fact, it's pretty apt. When I walk through Guido's doors, I leave Lilah and all her troubles behind and become Cindy. I smile and laugh with my tables, I trade banter with the other staff. I don't think about Dad and I don't wonder about Kalin. And when pumpkin time comes, when I walk to res through the cold, quiet streets, I'm too exhausted to think about anything but bed.

About a week after my fight with Kalin, Lani pulls me aside during shift. "We're going out afterwards. You gonna come?"

I stop myself from asking *Where? Until when?* I pull on my Cindy smile. "Sure."

I learn that the Guido's staff usually go out after work, and this is kind of my official welcome into the group. That first night we go to Friars. Only a few months have passed since that time with Darren, but so much has changed. Lani shows me some dance moves and the rhythm of the bass becomes cathartic rather than alarming. Like the buzz of the restaurant, it drives all thought from my mind. I just *am*.

We don't always go to Friars. It's a discussion that usually takes place over the entire course of the evening shift. Chad keeps a tally of everyone's thoughts – as all the waiters have to visit the bar – and he passes messages, hosts debates and eventually is the one to decide the night's itinerary. Lilah would never set foot in half the places we visit, but Cindy is hungry for new experiences and anything that keeps her mind quiet. We go to the sports bar, a shebeen, and even the dodgy casino at the top of High Street. Lani leans close to me while they're checking our IDs at the door. "Watch your drinks in here."

This must be where it happened, where her drink was spiked the night we met. I nod and understanding passes between us.

At all these places I find myself looking for Kalin, even though the thought of him standing at a bar in some dive is ridiculous. I know I won't see him, but I see plenty of people who look just similar enough to make my breath catch. Whenever I let down my mental guard, I wonder what he's doing, how his mysterious project is going, if he's okay.

One day when we're the last two left cleaning the restaurant, Lani gets this sparkle in her eye.

"Can you keep a secret, Cindy?"

The kitchen is dark aside from the one light right by the door where we are. I nod, but a little tendril of dread snakes down my spine. I'm not sure my life needs *more* secrets.

She leads me to one of the giant walk-in fridges and my pulse drums. The secret could be anything – a crush, a pregnancy, even a *dead body*. What else would someone hide in one of the fridges?

I'm blinded by the bright lights that flicker on as she yanks the door open.

No bodies. Just stacks of Tupperware and a few cardboard boxes filled with produce. Lani gets down on her knees and pulls one of the cardboard boxes out from the bottom shelf. It's got a kitchen towel over it, which she gently peels aside to reveal… cupcakes.

Three rows of unfrosted sponge cake in bright paper cups.

I don't understand. "You have a secret sweet tooth?"

She shakes her head. "A secret side hustle." Carefully, she lifts the box. "Bring the other one?"

I take the second box from the shelf and follow her out of the fridge.

"You can't tell the others, hey? They'll laugh and probably tell Harrold. Even *my broer*. I love him but *jis* he's a gossip."

I've picked up as much about Chad myself. "Just what is it I'm not telling them?"

Lani sets the cupcakes out on the stainless-steel counter and switches on the workspace light. "This is what I want to do with my life. I want to have a bakery one day. These are for my cousin's baby shower tomorrow. I made them before shift. Worked a double so I'd have access to the kitchen. Sneaky, hey? You won't tell?"

I shake my head. It seems like a big risk. I'm in awe of her dedication.

"You can go if you like. I just need to do the frosting. I'm okay to lock up."

"Or I could help you?"

She looks up from her line of cupcakes and gives me a big, bright, smile. "The dancefloor might miss you, Cindy."

In a life that's full of hidden motives and unpredictable people, this feels like something real. Something genuine. She'll probably never understand what it means to me, but I try to communicate it with my answering smile. "I'm sure it will survive."

The week before exams we have a break from class to study. I'm tempted to take advantage of the time off to work extra shifts at Guido's, but my grades have been slipping. Especially Law.

If Dad were around, he'd lecture me and demand I take extra

lessons. But I've only been able to speak to him on the phone a few times, and the last thing he wants to talk about is my grades. Am I safe? Am I happy? That's what concerns him.

He won't tell me anything about the case, but he tells me about Drakenstein Correctional Centre, the low-security prison where he's been transferred. He tells me he has a view of the winelands from his cell, and that the whole experience reminds him of boarding school. (I know enough about South African prisons to know he's severely downplaying it, but I hold onto his words all the same.)

Our calls are likely recorded, so I don't ask him, "Which boarding school is that exactly? And by the way, what's your real name?" Which is what *I* really want to talk about. For now, it's enough to know he's okay.

Still, even though his actual voice isn't present, I hear it in my mind. I've never failed anything in my life, and I definitely don't want to fail my major.

So, I return to my desk in that quiet corner of the library. Sometimes I even convince Jess to join me. She is sorely disappointed when she discovers that this is not, in fact, an invitation to an extended gossip session. I show her how to colour code her notes and summarise them onto cue cards, and eventually she seems to get the hang of it.

The student council hands out free donuts on the steps every afternoon in an attempt to coax reluctant students inside, and I sit in the sunshine with a book while I eat mine. But I don't end up reading, because I'm always watching the crowds. I see almost every other student I know, but I don't see Kalin.

That Saturday when I get to work, Harrold glares at me from his spot at the front desk. Before I can ask what I've done wrong he says, "There was a man looking for you just now."

My heart flutters. I only know of one man who might come looking for me.

I keep my voice level. "Oh. Did he leave a message?"

"No. I'm not your secretary. I'd appreciate it if you pass *that* message to all of your friends and family. They shouldn't come visit you here. It's your place of work."

The week's cheese delivery must be late again to put him in such a bad mood. "I'll tell them. Sorry."

As I walk away, I'm anxious to call Kalin and find out what he wanted, but my shift ends after midnight so I don't. And by the next morning, I can't bring myself to dial the number. What if I'm wrong, and it wasn't him after all? So, in the end, I don't call. I just hope he'll come back.

A few days later, I return from the library, and something clinks against my door when I push it open. There's a note lying there, with a key taped to it.

My pulse quickens when I see the handwriting. It's a letter from Kalin. I unfold it hurriedly and read it without even moving fully into my room.

Lilah,

I need to go away for a while. I realise I am in no position to ask a favour of you, but it occurred to me that you might require somewhere to stay over the vac. So, regardless of anything else in this note, my home is open to you for that purpose.

As to the favour. I have booked and paid for a stall on the Village Green during Fest. The stock is ready, due in no small part to your assistance. Thank you. However, I will not be here to sell it. If you are willing – and only if you are willing – I have left everything in the study with further instructions. I propose a 50/50 split of the profits, but ultimately I will bow to you on that front. You may take whatever wages you deem fair.

I stare at those scratched out letters a while, puzzling over what he was going to say. But what he does say is: *Regards, Kalin.*

Stiff and formal as the rest of the letter. No indication of when he plans to return. Nothing about the kiss. I wish I'd been at Guido's when he'd come by, or I'd made that call, so I could have asked him where he's going and why.

I trace my finger over my name in his elegant writing. I can tend his stall. I've never done anything like that before, but how different from waitressing can it be? I don't want to picture all his beautiful jewellery, all our hard work, just sitting there and never getting sold. No matter how annoyed I am with him.

Will he be back before the end of the year? I don't want to think about the possibility that I might not see him again, that I might go back to Cape Town before he returns here.

I fall asleep thinking about the cottage, and Fatso, and Kalin in the middle of a forest somewhere doing his mysterious research.

shackles, chained to the ground.

The door opens. The guard who brings her meals is not alone tonight. Instead, the Overlord sweeps in ahead of him. He's still wearing his cloak, as if he's recently returned from travelling, and the hood is up, obscuring his face. The muscles along her spine go stiff. She's been expecting retribution.

"It's broken, you know," he informs her, as if they'd just been speaking, but she hasn't seen him in weeks. "Commander Connor's nose. Generally, when I send my interrogators, they're not the ones who return with the injuries."

"Perhaps you should train them better."

A snort comes from the shadows where the Overlord's face should be. "He would have killed you had I not ordered otherwise."

She keeps her back to the wall, but she tilts her chin. "Am I supposed to thank you?"

"You're supposed to cooperate." He turns in place, and gestures towards the bed. "Have I not been a good host? Have I not seen to it that you are warm, comfortable, fed? This is even your old room, is it not?"

Alayna laughs, but entirely without mirth. "You need better intelligence, Overlord."

"The princess tower for a princess." He spits the title, both times.

She eyes him warily. "Is this truly where you think King Madailein would put his bastard sorceress?"

The Overlord doesn't speak; his only movement is the flexing of a pale fist that sticks out beneath one of his draping sleeves.

She takes a hesitant step towards him. "Ember, it's not too late—"

But he lifts a hand and she slams against the wall. The air whooshes from her lungs. She's halfway to raising her hand to cast a defensive spell before she remembers she has no power. He stole her power the way she intended to steal his. It sits somewhere in this castle, locked in the Keyflame. Unless he's already destroyed it. She tries to draw air. No, he won't have destroyed the orb. It's too useful. As long as he has her magic locked away, she has motivation to behave.

It's the Overlord who closes the distance between them now. "Do not use that name. And do not expect pity from me. You did not see their corpses. You did not crawl through the smouldering ruins of our village trying to tell who was who. I knew Mother by the triquetra around her neck. I can only assume Father's body was the one beside hers. But do you know whose burnt remains I spent the red hours of that dark morn searching for? Not theirs, no. It should have been theirs, but I had a friend, you see, and I thought the soldiers must have surely come for her, with her special gift. They must have discovered her, because I was certain they had not discovered me. They must have done unspeakable things to her before razing the town. But no trace of her remained."

Alayna swallows. "You're angry at me for not dying with them?"

"Anger? That's what you think this is? Rage? You haven't seen me rage, Alayna."

Back then he had called her Anna, and before the tragedy, before the soldiers came for her, they'd run about the forest together, experimenting with their forbidden power. He had been cautious, hesitant to use his magic for fear of being caught. She'd convinced him. She was the one who had encouraged the Overlord to explore the limits of his ability.

"I did not lead the soldiers to the village," she tells him.

"No. That much I know." He pulls away. "My intelligence is not quite as poor as you believe. Madailein had been searching for you since your unfortunate birth. He just so happened to find you hiding in our village."

Alayna's own memories of that day surface. The soldiers using a famished slave with ability to sniff out her magic. Being locked in the cottage with her Nan. The sword slashing. Nan throwing herself in front of the blade. "Don't kill her, she's of the blood".

"I didn't know I was his. I wasn't told."

The Overlord's magic presses her against the wall again, cutting off her air.

"You think it matters to me now? No. The only thing that matters

to me now is that it never *happens again. Aren't you the one who once told me, magic is a part of who we are, magic ties us to the old world? Too long we denied our nature and we reverted to savagery. I will see all of that reversed. I will restore order. But first, I need names.*"

He lets her breathe, and she chokes and heaves, holding the wall for support.

"*You will come around to my way of thinking Alayna.*" He looms over her. "*I know it must be difficult for you, spending so many years under the influence of the mad king. You can no longer conceive of a world where magic is not seen as evil and wrong. It is neither of those things.*"

"*No. But you are both of those things.*"

26

The smell of fresh grass mingles with the rich spices from the Hare Krishna stall on my right, and my nose itches. I resist the urge to scratch it while the old lady in front of me examines Kalin's wares.

I was warned about the flood of people who would arrive in town as soon as the annual Arts Festival began, but I had no idea how they'd change the entire feel of the place. Overnight, Grahamstown is no longer a sleepy colonial village, but a thriving bohemia. Campus is pasted with bright posters, and every building that hasn't become a theatre, offers either bed or board for the travelling troupes of actors, artists and audiences.

Even though I live here now, most of the people who've visited my stall are more familiar with Grahamstown than I am. They've told me about the coldest winters, they've told me about the biggest shows, they've told me about the days before I was born. They know Grahamstown intimately, but in multi-coloured snippets, like posts on an Instagram feed that's only updated for two weeks every July.

My latest customer has just informed me that no Fest can quite live up to the one of 1989. She's looking for a gift for her new daughter-in-law. Something that will ensure grandchildren.

I put on my Cindy smile while surreptitiously Googling fertility charms under the table. My search displays a picture of carnelian agates. *Yes!*

"Does your daughter-in-law like orange?"

She purses her lips while I slip around the table to show her the necklace I have in mind. It's made of big, round, flame-coloured beads, knotted with Ghanaian brass.

"Oh, that's very pretty!" She reaches to feel the beads, and I notice a movement over her shoulder.

Darren is at the entrance to my stall. He waves at me.

"Do you have something a bit more subtle?" the woman asks.

"Uh," I glance at my phone. I don't recognise any of the other charms. But one of the necklaces hanging near the orange one catches my eye. "There's the tree of life?"

It's a beautiful piece – a tree charm with green aventurine chips and clear glass beads.

"Oh, yes. Yes. This is more her taste, I think. What does the tree of life mean?"

Crap. "Uh, it dates back to old Norse and…" She looks at me expectantly, but my mind's gone blank.

"And they believed it connected the nine realms." Darren sweeps in. "In the mythos it represents the renewal of life after the apocalypse."

The woman taps her lip, considering this, while I shoot Darren a grateful look.

"Well, I don't know about all that," she says, "but I like the way it looks. Sold!"

Darren hangs around while I ring her up and pack the necklace into a little brown bag.

As soon as she's wandered out of earshot, I ask him, "Interest in ancient cultures runs in the family?"

"Oh no, that was all courtesy of Marvel comics." He grins, flashing me his perfect teeth. "How you doin', City Girl? It's been a while."

It's been a lifetime. I don't know where to start. "You know, same old, same old."

Which is the opposite of the truth. He nods and takes an

exaggerated look around the stall. "I can see that. Did you make all this?"

"No, it's K—" I hesitate, but too late.

He nods with clear understanding. "Kalin's?"

"He had to go out of town suddenly, so asked me to watch the stall as a favour."

Darren's eyes narrow, and I add quickly, "He's splitting the profits fifty-fifty. So, it's not a bad gig, really."

"Right."

An awkward silence falls between us. He covers it by examining a few of the pendants. "So Kalin makes jewellery?"

I don't like the way he says it. Like he's sneering at it. "It's only part of what he does. He's an academic too. He used to lecture."

"Used to? How old is this guy?"

"He's not that old; he's just smart."

"So, are you two officially together now?"

My stomach jumps. "No. I'm just housesitting for him."

Housesitting sounds so simple.

Living alone at the Settler's Cottage is wonderful – and it's torture. If houses have personalities, that one is a little old lady who knits, bakes cookies and has the warmest of hugs. Walking into the kitchen felt like coming back into her embrace. On the other hand, walking into Kalin's messy study felt invasive, even though his jewellery was there for me, all neatly labelled with prices and descriptions of how to lay out the stall. The study smelled like him. So did the bedroom, the duvet, and the pillow in which I buried my face. I feel like a complete creep, revelling in the ghost of his presence, and I feel pathetic for mourning his absence.

"We're just friends, that's all," I reiterate – for my own benefit, as much as Darren's.

His mouth twitches into something that's almost a smile. "Hey, I'm just asking. Because last time we spoke you seemed pretty into him."

"Did I?" I try to recall exactly what I said the day of the braai.

Did I possibly feel something for Kalin even then? Or was I just put upon and confused? "Well, as you said, it's been a while," I say to Darren.

Maybe he sees right through me; his expression is difficult to read. He sets down the pendant he was looking at. "Well, I guess I'll see you around."

"You don't have to go." Although I can understand why he wouldn't want to stay for stilted, awkward conversation, and it's not like I can offer him a cup of tea.

"Actually, I kinda do. I'm helping to set up a show at the drama department. I was just cutting through the market when I saw you."

"Oh."

"But you're here for the rest of the week, right?"

I must be more desperate for company than I realised, because my chest pulses with warmth at that, like it did when we first met.

"Yeah. Well, not the weekend."

He raises his eyebrows. Oh, right. He doesn't know about Guido's. When I explain that I'm a waitress now, he looks like he's holding back laughter. I'm not sure why he finds it amusing. He doesn't choose to share.

Whatever he thinks of my new career, he comes back the next day. And the next. The first day he brings me a wrap for lunch, and the next I buy him palak kofta – deep-fried spinach-and-cheese balls – from the Hare Krishna stand. He tells me about his work for the university, and some of the productions he's seen so far at Fest. I fill him in on the waitressing gig and regale him with stories from my nights out with the other staff. It's after one of these that he comments, "You've changed."

He's smiling broadly when he says it, and there's nothing but warmth in his eyes. Still, I'm self-conscious. I want to tell him that it's not me, it's Cindy, but I'll sound crazy. For the first time, it occurs to me that maybe Cindy is the New Lilah I was looking for. I'm not sure how I feel about that.

Chad told me about this restaurant that only opens during Fest, called the Long Table. It's set up in a church hall on High Street and, as the name would imply, there's just one long table that everyone sits at. I think the idea is that you get to meet new people and make new friends, but what I'm interested in is the fact that they serve home-cooked meals at decent prices. I never imagined I'd miss simple chicken and roast veg as much as I do.

On Thursday, when I mention to Darren that a few of us are meeting there for dinner that night, he's keen to come along.

"You're really that lonely, huh?" I say, before I think better of it.

He shrugs. "It's vac, and my family's out of town."

"What, they went on holiday without you?"

"I don't think it's a holiday. They had too many books with them." He pulls a sour face and I refrain from commenting that that seems like the ideal holiday to me.

I never pictured Darren, the boy with the easy smile who seemed to know everyone, as being lonely. But I suppose, if his friends are mostly still studying, then they would have gone home for the break.

The Long Table is loud and dim. Puddles of yellow candlelight illuminate the room in patches. My cheeks and nose burn with sudden warmth after being out in the cold. There are so many people here already, gathered in groups along the table or lining up for food that's being dished onto mismatched plates.

Someone stands on the bench and waves to me. Chad. I wave back and move towards him through the crowd while hurriedly removing my scarf and gloves. There are a bunch of Guido's waiters here, all sitting together in a tight knot. As soon as I approach, they make room for me. The girl who's currently in the middle of a story doesn't so much as pause. I know the one she's telling; I was there that night.

"Then Cindy says, 'Sorry, sir, we don't serve oysters!'" and she gestures to me.

Everyone roars with laughter and I shrug as I wriggle into my place at the table. "I thought I was very polite considering the circumstances."

"*Ja*, manners is one thing, it's the straight face that impressed me." Lani widens her eyes and nods towards Darren in a not-at-all-subtle question.

"This is my *friend*, Darren." I say, hoping she pays attention to my emphasis. She's been pointing out possible Kalin alternatives ever since I confessed my broken heart to her one night when we were out. Her favourite matches for me are straight-edged finance students who tip well, and he looks like he'd fit the bill.

Darren doesn't really get much of a word in while we eat. A few bottles of wine do the rounds, and the stories get more and more ridiculous. We talk about work a lot, because that's the thing we all have in common, but some of the waiters have even better stories from previous jobs, and some of them have known really interesting people in the past. A lull comes when a few of them go out to smoke, and I throw Darren a look to check he's okay. I find him staring at me with that same amused expression.

"Cindy?"

Oh yes, that. "Cinderella."

He doesn't need more context. He frowns.

I eat a few forkfuls of roast chicken, which is starting to get cold, and push around the cauliflower, which I've never been a fan of. He's quiet, and I sense his gaze still on me.

"Darren, a few days ago, when you said I'd changed, what did you mean?"

"Well, you know…"

I look up at him and say, in what I hope is a good-natured way, "If I knew I wouldn't have asked."

He shifts in his seat. "Okay. Well don't take this the wrong way, but when you first started here you were…" He ducks his head.

"No, it sounds too mean."

"Spit it out."

"Well, you were a bit of a dork."

Cold shoots to my core. It's not like he's telling me something I don't know. I tuck my hair behind my ear and try to think of a response.

"You're offended."

"No. I just don't think I've changed that much."

"We've seen each other every day for nearly a week, and you haven't mentioned exams once."

He's right. A few months ago, exams would have been a big event, the *biggest* event. For most of my life, being top of the class was my only goal. It was my place in the world, my contribution. I have the sudden disconcerting feeling that Lilah is slipping away, getting pushed back into my subconscious by this dominant, popular Cindy, who's taken over her body.

The part of me that is still Lilah shies from Darren's concerned look. Her fear that Darren didn't really like her that much proved founded, and she's hurt. But Cindy gives him a reassuring smile. "All right Mister Marvel Comics, you win. *I* used to be the dork."

"That's Captain Marvel to you."

"I thought Captain Marvel was a girl?"

"Not in the DC universe."

I roll my eyes at him.

Darren ends up giving me a ride home, and I appreciate his car's heater for the short time we're driving. The temperature dropped so low this week that some of the festival goers were muttering about the possibility of snow. It has not been pleasant to walk home at night. Luckily, Fatso volunteered to be my official hot water bottle, and he's usually at the door, ready to report for duty when I get back.

"So, this is where Kalin lives," Darren muses as we pull up beside the black gate. "I expected something bigger. Spiked palisades, a gargoyle or two."

"Why?" I'm genuinely curious.

"I don't know. He seems like a bit of an edgelord."

I frown. "Darren, what do you know about Kalin?"

We're in a bubble of orange light in a dark road. The windows are misted up. If there's a place for sharing secrets, this would be it.

"That's a strange question coming from someone who's lived with him."

"But you knew him before I got here, didn't you? Your mom and sister did."

"Yeah, but I never had reason to care about him before." Darren springs the door lock, a subtle sign I should get going, and he doesn't look at me.

"I think he has a secret," I say, desperately, because if Darren can give me answers, I don't want this opportunity to go to waste.

He looks at me again and his brow nudges together. "What kind of secret?"

"I was hoping you could tell me. He's been talking about this project. At first, I thought it was research. I mean, I think it probably is just research. But he's pretty dramatic about it and won't give me any details."

"Why would I know?"

"Well maybe you know his history. When Bianca—"

Darren holds up a hand to stop me. "Look, I really don't want to talk about Kalin, all right? I told you before, I don't know why my sister has a problem with him. Maybe they did the dirty back in the day, and she's still bitter. He's just a guy. A creepy guy who— Never mind."

I raise my eyebrows. "Do continue."

"I'd rather not." He sighs. "All I'm saying is I'm not the resident Kalin expert. He was just another guy before he developed this interest in you."

"He doesn't have an interest in me."

"Yeah, whatever." Darren avoids my gaze again. "You should

head inside, it's getting late."

I'm unlocking the front door by the time I realise what should have been painfully obvious.

Darren is jealous.

I play back our conversations, his looks. I remember the braai, his fingers tracing my palm. Darren likes me. Darren *still* likes me. In fact, Darren likes new me more than he liked old me. My skin tingles. I push the door open and am embraced by the smell of Kalin's space.

I hover there, even though I shouldn't be letting the heat out. Do I still like Darren? I've enjoyed spending time with him the past few days. I close my eyes and picture him smiling at me. He's gorgeous. He has a face that would be easy to love.

Lani keeps saying that the best way to get over Kalin is to move on. Maybe it wouldn't be a bad thing to pursue a relationship with Darren. Properly this time, with actual dating. My stomach flips – nerves more than desire, I think. Dates have always been a terrifying concept. But maybe, with someone who's already a friend, it wouldn't be so bad?

It's just after lunch, and I think that Darren isn't coming today, that he was even more upset by our conversation last night than he seemed. I keep watching the stall entrance, even when I have customers browsing.

Then, at about three, he sticks his head in with a tight smile. I ring up for the customer I was busy with, and the whole time my pulse is thrumming. It competes with the singing from my neighbouring stand.

When we're finally alone, Darren scratches the back of his neck. "So, uh, things got a bit tense last night, huh?"

"It's fine. You don't like Kalin, I get it."

His shoulders relax a little, and he reaches into a pocket and draws out an envelope. "You haven't had a chance to really experience the festival yet."

He passes it to me. Inside there are two tickets to the Mystery Ghost Tour. I'm thrown instantly back to that first night in Grahamstown when he tricked me with the story of the nun. I find that I'm grinning.

The tension melts from his frame at my reaction. "I seem to recall I promised I'd take you."

He didn't. At the time I was pretty sure I wouldn't be here, but he did mention the tour, and that he enjoyed it.

"You're not working tonight, are you?" he asks, suddenly worried again.

"Nope. You're in luck." I'm pretty impressed with myself for acting so cool and not even stuttering a little.

"Good. Those weren't easy to get. The tour was sold out two weeks ago."

When he leaves, it takes a while for my heart to go back to its normal rhythm. Is this a date? Surely he would have said if it was.

All the same, I stress about what to wear, and almost text Jess to ask for advice. But she'd want to know who I was seeing, and that's a can of worms I definitely don't want to open right now. So, in the end, Fatso and I agree that I'll go with comfort over style – something warm. I go for an Aran jersey I've had for years, with black slacks and flat shoes. I fiddle with my hair, try a nice updo, but it's being particularly frizzy, so I leave it loose and hope for the best. My winter jacket happens to be bright red, and it looks quite nice with the grey-and-black outfit. Jess would call it "a pop of colour". Of course, the downside is if I end up a gibbering, blushing mess, I'll look like a tomato.

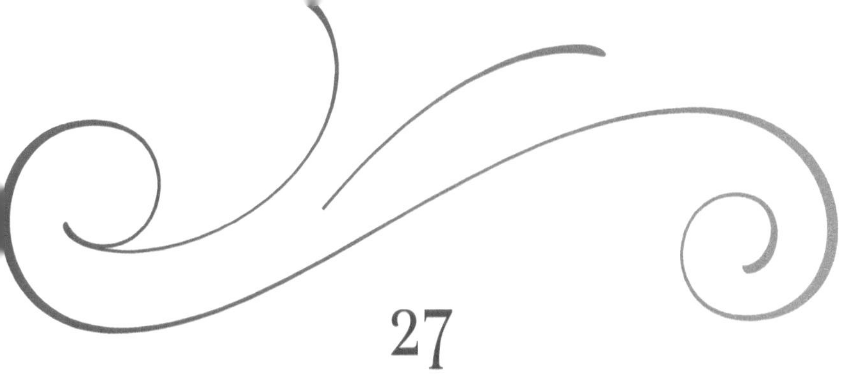

27

The tour starts at a pub called the Old Gaol. We walk through a grubby courtyard hung with lanterns into a tiny bar area where our host, in a top hat and with a cane, is busy telling ghost stories in a pompous British accent and ladling welcome drinks from a smoking *potjie* – which looks like a black cauldron. I take a tentative sip of the punch. It tastes like blackberries.

While the guide's talking, I keep stealing looks at Darren. He's clean-shaven in a collared shirt and coal-grey, double-breasted jacket. His dark hair is neat and bounces a little when he laughs at one of the ghost stories.

"And this place!" the guide says. "Well, right here, ladies and gentlemen, is where those who were sentenced to death in the old days were kept until they met the hangman's noose. Why, it is said that the gaol's final victim can still be seen in the dead of night, walking between here and the university campus."

A chill creeps down my back. That's where I was walking the night the mist came. Was the old man a ghost who'd been hanged? My pulse drums and I take a glug of the punch to try drown out the rest of the story.

We climb aboard a bus and they're playing wailing music over the speakers, and audio clips from interviews with people who've seen ghosts. I'm so tense that I jump when Darren puts his arm around me.

"Relax, City Girl. You look like you're going to faint."

Not beyond the realms of possibility.

At the front of the bus, our host speaks into a microphone. "Energy is never created, never destroyed, only transferred. This is according to a scientist named Einstein. You may have heard of him. So, what happens to the energy in our bodies when we die?"

He lets the question hang because the answer is supposed to be obvious: ghosts.

Darren whispers in my ear. "Don't worry. Our energy dissipates when we die." His breath is warm against my neck. "It goes back to the environment; it doesn't hang around without us."

"Could it be stored?" someone asks.

"That's an excellent question. Haunted objects, possession! Containers that, willing or not, store the energy of the departed!"

Darren shakes his head and smiles. Clearly, he doesn't believe in haunted objects, which is comforting.

The bus takes us to a graveyard, a few old houses and, to my dismay, several university buildings. Finally, we drive up to the monument. The whole way along the dark road, I expect to see a phantom hitchhiker. This was all a very bad idea, considering I'm currently staying alone in one of the oldest houses in this town and walking home through these supposedly haunted streets every night. I was so concerned about Darren and the possibility that this was a date, that I didn't stop to think about the spookiness. My stomach is in knots.

But when we finally turn into the monument parking lot, the lights of Grahamstown stretch out below us in a glittering carpet reflecting the starry sky and I'm at once glad I came. It's achingly beautiful. I try to track the familiar streets up to the Settler's Cottage, but there are too many lights, and I can't find it.

"Awe-inspiring, isn't it?" Darren asks. "It's one of my favourite views."

Awe, yes, and something else. A sense of scale. Every little car is at least one human, someone who has their own life, their own concerns. "There's a word for this… som—" I try to recall.

"Sonder, I think. The sudden awareness of the complexity of strangers' lives. Although someone on the internet might have come up with it."

He jabs me in the side with his elbow. "Dork."

I smile, but I'm thinking how Kalin would have appreciated that fact. And probably debated it and presented a better word as an alternative.

No, stop it. Kalin's gone. Get over it. Stop being so pathetic.

The guide leads us past the old fort to the standing stone I noticed during SciFest. He's left his cane in the bus, and he's holding what looks like two pieces of bent wire.

"Now we have a bit of audience participation!" he says. "You may have noticed we're standing in a stone circle." With a flourish, he points to another nearby rock that rises out of the ground to about my waist. Then he turns on the spot and points out three similar stones surrounding us, some of them barely visible in the bushes. There's a swell of chatter from the tour group, and he holds up his hands to quieten them. "Some say these stones are an old solar calendar, but have you ever heard of menhirs?"

"Lilah has." Darren grins at my horrified expression when everyone turns to look at me.

My face heats. *Tomato time.* I struggle to think. He must mean the standing stones in the British Isles.

"Like Stonehenge?" I suggest.

The guide snaps his fingers. "Right you are! Menhirs are most commonly found in Great Britain and Ireland. They date back to around 4000 BC. Now, we don't know much about these mysterious structures, but even scientists agree that they were likely used for ancient religious ceremonies. Something interesting about them is that they are often at the convergence of leylines. Who here knows what a leyline is?"

Darren has a sparkle in his eye and opens his mouth, but I shush him, because I actually have no idea what those are. When no one volunteers, the guide explains that leylines supposedly connect all places of great Earth energy. Supernatural events are most likely to occur on these lines, and religious buildings, and structures of great cultural significance, are most likely to be built where the lines converge.

Does Kalin know about these stones? Of course he does. He probably did a doctorate on them. Maybe they're why he's in Grahamstown in the first place, writing *What's a Celtic Menhir Doing on a Random Hill in Southern Africa? A Dissertation.*

While my mind's drifted back to Kalin, the guide has called up a volunteer to twiddle the wires. Well, that's what it looks like. Apparently, the girl is trying to sense leylines using a dowsing rod.

"Focus your intention," the guide says. But she shakes her head and hands the rods back to him.

"Would anyone else like to give it a go?"

Darren pushes me forward. "It's part of the experience," he whispers.

Before I can protest, our host's attention falls on me, and he approaches me with the rods.

They have wooden handles, and the wire is thicker than it seemed. It's only loosely attached to the handle, so it swivels with the tiniest movement. I'm hyper aware of the attention on me as he shows me how to hold them in front of my body. My breath forms rapid puffs of white in the frosty air.

"I don't think I can do this," I say to him. I mean the staring crowd more than the rods. If I start trembling, everyone will see the movement amplified by the metal.

"Nonsense. Anyone can do it. Just relax and let the energy flow through you."

He steps back. I swallow and close my eyes. If I manage to stand still for even a few seconds and nothing happens, all of this will be over.

But instead of nothing, I feel warmth flowing up through my arms. The rods tug to the right. People murmur. I open my eyes.

The rods are pointing at a specific spot. Both of them, in a neat arrow. And the air shimmers there. Mist. Mist is creeping in, tangling around our ankles. The roaring in my ears might be my pulse.

Then I hear the words.

"Overlord, show yourself!"

I drop the rods. The roaring stops. My heart is slamming painfully against my chest. *What the heck was that?* I'm pretty sure that the voice was Alayna's. Did I imagine it?

I know I didn't. Like I didn't imagine the man in the mist or the water rising at Hogsback.

Unless I'm insane.

But no one else seems to have heard it. The host laughs joyfully as he retrieves the rods and asks for more volunteers.

Darren comes up behind me, touches my arm. "Sorry, I thought you were okay with attention now."

He thinks I dropped the rod because I was embarrassed. "I guess I'm just on edge."

The bus drops us off at the Old Gaol, and Darren makes his way to the guide through the people thronging him with questions.

He greets Darren with a handshake and pat on the back. "How did you find the show this year, my boy?"

I have a vision of this man as an actor (with emphasis on the o) coming off stage, wiping the grease paint from his face and undoing a wig. But he has no makeup to remove, just his ghost guide persona.

"It was great. The steaming punch was a nice touch."

"The magic of dry ice." He gives Darren an exaggerated wink, then focuses on me. "You have quite the divining talent, my dear."

I laugh nervously. "Let me guess, magnets?"

"Oh no, that was all you, darling."

"You can't trick Lilah, Tod. She's brainy," Darren says.

"No trick. Leylines are a real phenomenon. Have you never wondered why so many important buildings are constructed in a straight line?"

"I truly haven't," I admit.

"Look at London. In fact, look at Grahamstown. You have two cathedrals, the Drostdy Arch entrance to the university, the Old Gaol, the Albany Museum, all of these buildings along two very specific lines that converge at the monument, at those stones."

Darren chuckles. "It's a nice story, but I think they call that effective town planning."

"Say what you like, Darren, but your young lady felt the energy up on the hill. I could see it." He taps his forehead. "You're a natural."

Darren drapes an arm around my shoulders. "All right, Tod. Thank you. I should be getting Lilah home."

Tod gives Darren another wink. "Very well. I look forward to seeing you next year."

As Darren leads me away, he growls low in his throat. "Some people will believe anything."

"Yeah…"

"Hey, I know I said I'd be taking you home, but it's still kinda early. You want to get something to eat?"

My stomach tumbles. The ghost bus thing was a bit ambiguous but getting something to eat is definitely entering date territory. As if his arm around me isn't indication enough.

"Ah, sure. Long Table?"

He tenses ever so slightly. "Sure."

He probably wanted something more intimate. I pretend I don't notice the reluctance in his tone. He removes his arm. We walk side by side up High Street in awkward silence.

Relief comes in the form of a man in front of the cocktail bar with a cask on his back. "Glühwein?"

Darren makes a beeline for him. "Yes, two please!"

The man might actually be the same man from the day Kalin and I were here. Darren passes him some cash and pours two cups of what looks like wine from the tap on the cask.

He passes one to me. It's warm, and it smells like cloves.

"Don't tell me it's your first time trying glühwein?" Darren asks. My expression must have said exactly what I was thinking, which is that I'm not sure about this at all.

"It's a traditional German winter drink," he explains. "Go on, try it."

"Is this going to be better than your katemba?"

He grins. "I guarantee it will."

I take a tentative sip. At first, I just taste red wine – bitter and dry. But, when I manage to swallow that down, there's the flavour of Christmas cake on my tongue – raisins, orange rind and cinnamon. It's surprisingly pleasant.

"You see?" Darren says.

"Not as bad as the katemba," I agree.

We walk a little further. The cup is comforting in my palms, and the familiar street is now festive with its bunting, banners, and twinkling fairy lights. A group passes us, laughing and talking about the show they just saw.

"I enjoy spending time with you," Darren says.

"Despite the fact that I'm such a dork?"

"I'm serious."

When I look at him, his brow is creased. He does look serious, serious enough that my insides twist.

He searches my face. "I've never met anyone quite like you."

Multicoloured lights play across his features. I bite my lip, not sure what to say. He pauses mid stride and focuses his attention on his glühwein cup.

"Look, I know I messed up before. To be honest, I didn't know you were that into me. If we'd agreed that we were exclusive, I wouldn't have kissed your friend. I wish I could take it back."

"It's not about that, Darren."

He sighs. "I know. It's about a guy who runs off and leaves you to sell all his stuff."

I push my hair away from my face. "Don't."

"I know he's done a lot for you, but guys like that— it's what they're like. You're a cause. How do you know he hasn't gone off to help some other damsel in distress?"

Tell me this is no different from any other poor, destitute creature you've brought to me.

"Helping people isn't a bad thing," I bite out.

"It is when you keep stringing them along."

"Kalin's not stringing me along. He told me plainly that he's not interested in a relationship."

Darren shakes his head, and I expect him to throw an accusation at me because the implication there is that I did want a relationship. Instead, he takes a step closer. "He's mad."

He reaches up to cup my cheek. A lump forms in my throat, but I don't pull back. Encouraged, Darren traces the pad of his thumb across my bottom lip. I feel the spark between us. That spark I felt lying in his arms under the stars. It would be so easy to kiss him now. Why don't I want to? I decided I wanted to date him, didn't I?

He waits for me to react, and when I fail to, he withdraws his hand with another heavy sigh, and he shoves that hand into a pocket. "I've liked you since the first second I saw you, Lilah. Your first day here. I keep hoping… but, perhaps I'm wasting my time."

Now I'm too hot with the warm wine and my jersey and jacket. Kalin's necklace itches against my skin.

Darren lifts his gaze to mine. "Am I?"

"Is this why you've been visiting me every day?" I ask in a much smaller voice than I mean to.

"What do you think?" The intensity in his expression provides a pretty solid answer.

He means it as a compliment. Like he's a moth and I'm the flame. And like the flame should be flattered for drawing him in so successfully. But I don't feel that at all. The back of my neck prickles as it dawns on me that perhaps every companionable, friendly moment we've had over the past week has been with an ulterior motive.

"This is a little sudden. I mean we haven't even seen each other this term."

"Well, I thought you were with someone."

I notice how he avoids saying Kalin's name. I *was* with him, just not in the way Darren means. And I think that maybe Kalin would have spent that time with me even if I'd been 'with someone' else, because he likes my company.

"I'm sorry," I say, and I shake my head. "I do enjoy spending time with you, Darren, but—"

"But not as much as you like spending time with him."

"I didn't say that."

Darren's lips form a thin line. Rejection, I imagine, is pretty new to him. "All right."

We stand face to face with the backdrop of lights and festive sounds. A cart clops by, pulled by a couple of donkeys, and the occupants whoop at us. I'm grateful for it. It gives me a little time to think.

"I feel like we rushed things before," I say carefully. "I have a lot going on right now, and I don't want to rush into anything. I like having you as a friend, I'd like things to continue as they are now when term starts. Then maybe—"

"You're telling me I'm in the friend zone."

A spike of anger threatens to make me snap something I'll regret, because if anything the opposite is the problem: we *aren't* really friends. But I bite my tongue.

"Look, Lilah, I think I'm going to take off." He gestures over his shoulder.

I nod. Dinner would be pretty uncomfortable now, even if I still had an appetite. "Thanks for the tour, and the glühwein." I tilt the cup.

"Sure."

I spend a sleepless night tossing and turning. Every time I close my eyes, I think a ghost is standing at the foot of the bed or drifting from the study. When my eyes are open, I think about Darren and second guess everything I said. And I think about Kalin.

Maybe he just wanted me as a friend; maybe I'm the moth asking too much of the flame. I turn over again. It would be so much easier to believe that if *he* hadn't been the one to kiss *me*. I can't shake the feeling that the reason he can't get involved with anyone is because of this secret project, and that it puts him in peril.

At about 4am I give up on sleep and go through to the study. It's freezing cold. The fireplace is ancient and full of ash, but there's wood beside it. After a few false starts, I eventually get the wood to take. Fatso curls up into a fluffy ball right beside the fire, and I do what I probably should have done a long time ago: invade Kalin's privacy. Somewhere, in one of these books, there's going to be an answer about his project.

I start at the top of the pile. Most of the books aren't written in English. The few that are talk about ancient rites and rituals – exactly what he said he was studying. There are a couple on gemstones mixed in with the lot, which must be research for the jewellery business.

"I'm missing the Rosetta Stone," I tell Fatso. I don't mean for translating Kalin's old texts, but for understanding all the clues that are in front of me.

Fatso ignores me.

The fire is warm, and its glow is comforting. I lean back on the settee as I page through book after book. My eyes start to grow heavy. Then…

Alayna digs through a bowl of gruel and finds a tiny roll of parchment wrapped around a lock pick. It has a message scrawled on it that's half bled away into her food.

"Midnight," it says.

She has no way to tell the time in her windowless prison, so she waits ready all night. When she hears the commotion outside, she slips the pick into the lock of her shackles. They click as her door slams open.

"Quickly, my lady. There's little time." She doesn't know the name of this agent, only that he was one of the many whom she had spying on the Overlord and that he's been posing as one of her guards for the past few weeks.

"The Keyflame?" she asks.

He shakes his head.

"Then I cannot leave."

He steps into the room. "My lady, it is unlikely we will succeed with a second attempt. Many have risked their lives…"

She shuts her eyes. Of course he's right. It would be selfish of her to stay. "I need my powers in order to defeat him." She had hoped a way to change his heart might exist, but now the day of her liberation is at hand. She's out of time.

"Perhaps we could return for the orbs," the guard suggests.

"No. As you said, too many have already risked their lives coming here." She hikes up her velvet skirt. "I will retrieve the orbs."

"There's no time," the guard insists. He has beautiful dark eyes. Right now, they're narrowed with concern for her.

"What's your name?"

"It's Liam, my lady."

"Liam, remember the words. We shall defeat him or die trying. The orbs are our best chance of defeating him. My life means little if we fail in this mission."

He hangs his head. "Then I feel I should pledge myself to this task."

"Good man. I will require someone who can cast."

Like all the Overlord's guards, Liam has magical ability. He also knows the location of the orbs. The two of them race along the quiet corridors. The castle infiltration would have been a stealthy affair — she doesn't have enough people for a full-scale invasion. They will have ensured the route out is clear, probably through the kitchens, but will *be of little help once she deviates from their course. But she and Liam make quick work of all the Overlord's people they encounter.*

At the door to the treasury, Alayna waits while Liam attempts to unravel the Overlord's protective wards. She remembers the first time she was in this corridor, dragged up from the dungeons by her ranting, paranoid father. He'd hated her, but she'd been his only heir. He was the one who'd first pursued the ancient orbs. He'd learned that the Keyflame could remove her magic. Once stripped of magic, she might make a queen. So, he'd taken her to the treasury, and he'd shown her his riches and lectured her in how to rule. As if he knew anything about ruling. He'd cut a bloody swath across the kingdom in his fevered obsession to eliminate magic. He blamed it for all the ills of the realm. Short-sighted. Foolish. Mad.

"Wait," she says suddenly. The last time she was here, there were guards. Now there are none.

But Liam's broken through the wards, and he steps into the darkened room before she can stop him.

She knows what will happen when she crosses the threshold, and yet she follows Liam in, desperately hoping she's wrong.

The Overlord stands at the far end of the room, a silhouette against two rows of bright orbs mounted on the wall. He has all of them. He's captured each of the agents she sent to search for them.

Liam is already suspended in mid-air, in that same electric spell the Overlord used on Sloane, his face frozen in an expression of agony.

"Your followers are weak. You should have chosen them more wisely," the Overlord says.

Alayna's heart is a boulder. It's difficult to breathe through her fear, her grief, but she forces herself to approach him.

"I don't choose them. They choose me."

"You remain frightened of your power."

"I do not fear it. I know better than to let it control me."

She can see the Keyflame directly behind him. It's bigger than the other orbs, and it casts a bright golden light, but it may as well be on the other side of the world, for all the chance she has of reaching it.

Still, she refuses to let him see her doubt. She stands before him with her back straight, her chin tilted defiantly.

Then she hears footsteps. Many footsteps. A rush of them.

His guards have discovered her escape. The people who came here to help her are dead. More blood on her hands.

But then, "Lady Alayna!"

"My lady!"

Not his people, hers. They flood into the treasury, as if she'd planned it like this. This must be Liam's doing. He must have managed to send a message.

The Overlord drops Liam and takes a staff from his back. "You think you can beat me at this, do you? It's been a while since I've had a good challenge. Come, let's see what your little army can do."

I wake up with a start. I'm still in the study. A book rests on my chest, the fire has died, and Fatso is curled up on my legs.

What time is it? I need to get down to the Village Green. I need to… no. It's Saturday.

Guido's. I only have to be there at twelve.

As I sit, my muscles protest and my bones click. I have new appreciation for Kalin's sacrifice, giving me the bed.

The old book I was looking at is still open. It's not written in English, but there's a drawing: six beautifully decorated circles around a central larger one. My muscles tense again. Is this what triggered the dream about the orbs? I trace the symbols in each circle, wishing I could understand them.

Dreams often tell us things that we should pay attention to, Kalin said.

Yesterday's weirdness up at the monument was an experience straight out of my strange dreams. It was Alayna's voice. She was calling to the Overlord.

I told Kalin that the dreams started after Dad was arrested, but something else changed that day. That was the day I started living with *him.* Kalin with the room full of ancient books and charms,

Kalin who I *saw* command the water to rise. Kalin who laughed at me in the lake and said, "You think you can beat me at this, do you?"

I snap the book shut. I should probably find myself a psychologist.

28

"What did I tell you about friends visiting?"

Harrold is already peeved when I walk in for my double shift. That doesn't bode well.

"Sorry," I say, because when he's in a mood like this you just apologise rather than trying to figure out what you've done wrong.

He glares at me while I unbutton my coat and hang it on the rack by the door. When it becomes clear he's not going to willingly offer up any clues, I add, "My friends know my phone number. They shouldn't come here."

"No, they shouldn't."

It must have been Darren. I can't think of anyone else who'd come looking for me at Guido's. I did tell him that I was working here today, so maybe he felt bad about how we left things last night and came to talk about it.

Harrold isn't satisfied to leave it there. "You know that festival is the busiest time of the year." This is a rant I have heard several times in the past few weeks.

"I know. I'm sorry."

"We cannot drop everything we're doing to answer questions about our staff."

I can't imagine what he was doing that was so important this morning. I open my mouth to apologise again, but he wags a finger at me. "I am the only manager. I need to be expediting when the orders are coming in that fast. I cannot be faffing around at the front of house."

Orders? Then it can't have been this morning. "When did someone come looking for me?"

"When do you think, lovey? The middle of service, that's when. Not again, you hear? Last warning."

"Yes, sorry, I understand."

If it was in the middle of service last night, it couldn't have been Darren. We were up at the monument then.

When Julie, the hostess, gets in for the evening shift, I ask her if she saw the person.

"Some guy. Harrold was pissed."

"Long hair?" Part of me hopes it was Kalin.

"No. Short and dark. You got a stalker, Cindy?"

I can't think of any guys I know who have short dark hair other than Darren. Michael would have been my only other guess – the Journ students usually stay for the vac to work at the daily Festival paper – but he's blond.

The evening passes quickly. The restaurant is packed, and there isn't time to worry about my mysterious visitor, or about anything. My favourite kind of night.

"You joining us at Jack's after, Cindy?" Chad asks while he pours out a tray of complicated drinks for one of my bigger tables. Jack's is the casino. Or, at least, it wants to be. It's more like a club that happens to have gambling machines, and I can't imagine any actors or cultured folks hanging out there. He must have picked it as a way of avoiding running into our Festival customers.

"Of course!" I would have expected the double shift to make me tired, but I'm pumped.

Lani wasn't working tonight, but she meets us at the club with a few of the other waiters who were off duty. There are no tables, so we all sit at the bar. Lani's started drinking already and is in a festive mood. She even gives me a hug.

I order myself a ginger ale (it at least looks like a proper drink), and I tell her about what happened with Darren. I get as far as telling her about the tour tickets, though, before she's oohing and aahing about how romantic it is. I dread getting to the end when a few of the other staff start listening in and making similar noises. I physically cringe when I tell them that I informed him I just wanted to be friends.

The admission is greeted with a chorus of, "*Ag nee man!*" *No, you didn't!*

Then they all exchange opinions about how nice he was when they met him at the Long Table, and how he works in IT, so he's going to earn the big bucks one day and I should lock that down. Lani doesn't have much to say, but once the others disperse, she takes my hands in hers.

"Lilah, you have to follow your heart."

I don't know whether her advice or her use of my real name is more unexpected.

"People, they will tell you to do this or do that because it seems like the right thing to them. But you have potential in life. You do not need to have a man if you don't want one."

I blink at her. Usually she's the one nudging me and telling me to "check the talent".

Before I manage a response, she pats my arm and gestures over my shoulder. A guy has caught her eye.

"*Kyk*, I'm going to go introduce myself."

She takes her drink and minces over to him.

I laugh and stifle a yawn. The busy day is starting to catch up with me. Lani escorts the guy to the dance floor. He's transfixed. She's probably going to be busy awhile. The other Guido's staff are also dancing or out smoking, so I'm alone. I check my phone for the first time today.

There's a message from Darren.

Sorry for being an ass yest. Frownyface emoji. I know ur dealing with your dad and stuff. Forgive me? Prayinghands emoji.

I stare at the screen for a good while, chewing on my lip. I start typing, take a sip of my drink, backspace everything, start typing again, put my phone back in my bag, take it out again, read the message again.

The words blur. I'm really tired. I should get home and deal with this tomorrow.

I wave goodbye to Lani as I head out.

The frigid air is almost welcome; it wakes me up a bit. Probably shouldn't have gone out after work.

I'm really tired.

Something moves on the street ahead and I jump. The festival is far behind me. This road is dark and quiet. Usually I don't encounter another soul on my walk home this way.

It's a man. He's in a black coat with the collar pulled up. As he comes up to me, he says, "I don't suppose you have the time?"

I'm not going to reach for my phone in the middle of the night in a deserted street. "Sorry, no."

My words slur. My tongue isn't cooperating. The man smiles at me and moves past. I keep walking. I pick up pace, but it's difficult because my legs are starting to feel heavy. So heavy. I'm so tired.

I hear footsteps behind me. My heart jumps. He's turned around. He's following me. I try to break into a run, but I stumble forward, and he snatches me. Cold, hard, strong fingers grip my arm, like claws. His other hand clamps over my mouth.

I scream against his palm and thrash from side to side, trying to break free, but my limbs are slow to respond. Heavy. So heavy.

I feel like I'm sinking under water.

"All right, sweetheart. You just relax," the man says against my ear.

I'm floating, limbless, nothing but a hollow chest, entirely under his control.

I've been drugged.

There's a small part of my mind that understands this, that

someone slipped something into my drink. There's the thrill of fear, like electricity beneath my skin. But it's deep, deep, deep beneath my skin. Too deep for me to reach. Too deep to give me the power to respond.

The man lifts me, and there's nothing I can do to stop him. He smells of leather and sweat.

No… no, not this.

I need to escape, I need to do something to get away, but the kick that I think I manage is no more than a twitch. My thoughts wash away, my consciousness is being dragged out to sea. I am the bay on a still, dark night. Terror is the wind across the water.

⌇

I jolt awake with the sound of a car boot slamming down inches from my face. I'm in a dark warm space, carpet pressed to my cheek. How long was I out? What happened?

The car starts. I try to shout but discover there's tape over my mouth. I can't breathe properly. I heave in air through my nose, and smell burnt rubber, fuel and exhaust. I try move my hands, but plastic ties cut into my skin. I test my feet as well. I can't move. I'm tied up. My thoughts are still sluggish, struggling to hold onto reality. This isn't like my dreams of Alayna. This is real. This is happening. My heart gallops as panic takes hold. I'm being kidnapped.

The drive goes on and on and on, and my fear doesn't dissipate. Who's taken me? What are they going to do with me?

How long will it take before anyone realises I'm gone?

I want to stay awake. I try to cling to consciousness. I don't want anything to happen to me while I'm asleep. But the drugs are more powerful than my will.

⌇

Leather and sweat. Ice cold wind. Stinging cheeks. My head is hanging upside down and pounding in time to my pulse. I can see my hair brushing concrete, then whipping up in the wind. My kidnapper's arms dig into my spine. I try to lift my head because my neck aches and all my blood is in my face, but I can't.

A large rectangle of light lies ahead. A shadowy figure stands in front of it.

"So?" He has a nasal voice.

"See for yourself," my kidnapper says.

The second man comes forward and kneels in front of my face. My stomach lurches. *I know him.* He was in BP the night I met Lani. The drunk student who tried to take her away. Now he's got me. Why? What is he going to do to me? He takes my chin roughly, looks into my eyes. I jerk my head away, and panic takes control of my limbs. I flail wildly, with everything in me. My elbow connects with something. Kidnapper drops me. I hit the concrete, roll, try to get away. *I have to get away.* I drag myself by my elbows but I'm too slow. BP grabs my legs. I kick, connect with his chin. He cries out… but a pair of shiny boots fill my vision. Kidnapper grabs me by my bound hands and pulls me up. I wriggle, yelling against the tape. His fist slams into my cheek.

Pain explodes across my face and a needle pricks against my arm. I try to pull away, but he holds me firm, and my movement makes the injection hurt. Cold liquid squirts into my veins, as cold as his fingers. Then a flood of heat like a fever. My mouth is cotton. I can't keep my head upright; I can't keep my eyes open. Everything goes black.

✦

I gasp in air. My ears are ringing. The left side of my face is numb, then it's searing hot. I choke on the air I'm trying to breathe. I'm in a chair. My arms are tied over the back and the muscles in my shoulders scream. I can only see out of my right eye and what I see makes my body flush with fresh terror. I'm in a large grey room. Very large. A warehouse or an airport hangar. Ahead of me is a giant metal door, with a smaller door cut into it, barred and locked with the biggest padlocks I've ever seen. A blue shipping crate stands off to the side and four men in dark clothes pace around it. They have guns – I don't know anything about guns, but I know those wouldn't look out of place in a war zone.

"Miss Durow, you join us again," someone says behind me. I try to turn my head, but my muscles are still uncooperative, and he shifts out of my line of sight. The movement makes me dizzy. I think it's the same man who punched me, but I can't be sure.

"I'm going to explain the rules. They're very simple. The more shit you give us, the less of a shit we give about you."

Again, I try to look at him, but he moves out of sight.

"Best case scenario, your daddy does as he's told, and you sit pretty here a few weeks."

Dad. I should have realised.

This isn't just a random attack; this is about the Dumi case. These are Dumi's people. It is exactly what Kalin feared, what I didn't take seriously.

"You're a good girl, aren't you?" the man says. "We like good girls. Good girls get fed, might even get bathroom breaks."

He moves around me then. It's the BP guy, and he has a little GoPro video camera. As I glare up at it, I see the light that indicates it's recording.

"Now, if your daddy does not do as he's told, I'm afraid we won't have the joy of each other's company for very long. The foreigners love girls like you. Silky skin, good teeth."

My heart spasms with the realisation that he's talking about selling me into slavery. He pans the camera to the blue crate.

So much fear is trapped inside my chest, beating through my veins, but I can't move to let it out. It leaks through my eyes in tears. And BP loves that. He hunkers down to my level and reaches to touch my hair. I recoil from him, and he laughs. Then he turns the camera to point at his own face. "Dumi's tired of playing games, Durow. You cut the legal crap, plead guilty on all charges, or your darling girl's going to wake up somewhere you will never find her."

This can't be real. This can't be happening. Just a few hours ago my biggest concern was what to say to Darren. I was worried about ghosts. Bitterness fills my mouth. How long have they been operating in Grahamstown? How many girls have they taken? I recall Jess telling me about some first years who disappeared. They almost took Lani.

My insides are ice. Everything I've ever worried about in my life feels stupid and juvenile compared to this horror. The man disappears behind me again. I jerk when he touches my arm with his cold fingers.

"Night-night, Miss Durow."

A needle pierces my skin again.

⚘

I do not dream of Alayna. I do not dream. Sleep is a deep dark pit, and when I claw my way up from it, I am still in the chair. My captor is nearby – I can hear him talking to someone about what he's going to do with the money Dumi's paying him. My guts churn. I move my leg tentatively. Pins and needles shoot up from my ankle, stabbing me as surely as that injection did, and I whimper involuntarily.

"She's awake," someone says.

"What, already?" A chair squeaks. "Not possible."

They both emerge from behind me. BP and Kidnapper. They're kinda soft-focused, fuzzy around the edges. BP crouches in front of me again and looks into my eyes.

A *thump* reverberates on the padlocked door. They look at each other.

Thump. Thump. Thump.

"Who saw you drive up here?" BP asks.

"Nobody."

"You're certain?"

"Of course I'm certain. You think I'm a bloody amateur?"

Thump. Thump. Thump.

"What should we do?" Kidnapper asks.

"Uh, I don't know," BP says sarcastically. "Maybe we should answer and offer whoever it is some tea?"

He stands and pulls out a pistol from his jeans. The men with the big guns are watching the doorway too. My stomach forms an even tighter knot as BP moves forward until he's standing right by the door. He levels his gun at it. Only then do I hear the voice. I can't make out words, but it's a male voice, shouting.

BP swears. "He says he wants her." He gestures to me with the gun.

Me? No one even knows I'm here.

BP stalks back towards Kidnapper. "You! You led them to us."

Kidnapper grabs me and sticks a hand into my pocket. "No. She must have a tracking device or something."

I'm still under the effect of whatever drug they gave me because my limbs are floppy, and I can't even put up a token fight.

"Tracking device? You're a pathetic excu—"

The door blasts open. Pieces of chain, padlocks and strips of steel fly away from it and clang to the concrete ground.

Kidnapper drops me and pulls out his own weapon. BP moves in front of me, blocking my view of the jagged black hole where the door was.

"No one needs to get hurt. Give me the girl, and I'll be on my way."

I know that voice, but it can't possibly be here.

"Shoot him!" BP shouts.

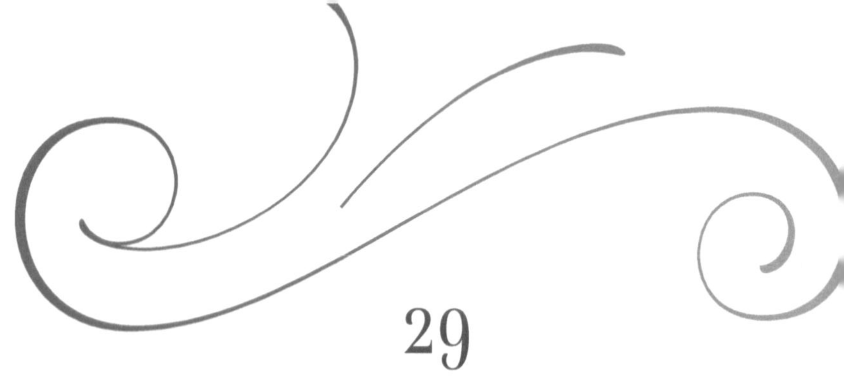

29

unfire booms, louder than I ever thought it could be. It's pounding on the inside of my skull. It echoes off the metal walls, and I scream against the tape that covers my mouth. I scream and I can't even hear myself.

No one could survive that.

A ringing silence. BP takes a breath and sticks the gun back into his jeans. He shakes his head and swears as he moves forward to examine their handiwork. And I see the shape. The man who came for me is a crumpled brown heap. My heart goes to dust.

No. It can't be Kalin. He couldn't have found me. *Please, please don't let it be him.*

BP is almost upon the heap when it moves.

"What the—"

The person gasps and pulls himself up onto his hands and knees. Honey brown hair falls over his face.

BP aims his gun straight at him.

"No!" I try to scream, but my pleas mean nothing.

The figure jerks again and again with the impact of multiple bullets but does not collapse. BP reloads and the man pushes himself to his feet.

I see his face and there can be no denying, no imagining that it's not Kalin. His jaw is set. His eyes are blazing. I've heard of adrenaline doing strange things, but this… this is something else. His shoulder is bloody, yet his hands form fists. BP aims at him again, aims at his heart where there's already a bright red patch.

Kalin brings his arms in front of his chest, then strikes outward. A whoosh of air wipes across the warehouse and the gunmen fly. One slams into the container, and another is thrown all the way to the back wall. I don't see where the others land.

BP is too far away to be affected, but he's shaking, swearing, unable to hold his pistol steady. Kalin takes a step towards him.

Someone shoots one of the big guns, but Kalin sweeps a hand through the air and there's a crash. Then silence.

What am I seeing? Am I still asleep? Is it the drugs?

"Drop your weapons. I am not here to kill you," Kalin says.

I feel cold metal against my forehead. Kidnapper. Kidnapper's gun. A new, primal fear stabs into my gut.

Kalin shakes his head. His chest is rising and falling rapidly. "Don't do that."

Kidnapper doesn't move.

Kalin closes his eyes. His hand flashes out, and a blast of cold air hits me. The chair topples over. My head cracks against the concrete floor. Black spots crowd my vision. BP shrieks, Kidnapper wails. The wind roars in my ears, or is it my own blood?

"Lilah!"

Kalin's face swims above me. He slips a hand between my head and the floor, rips the tape from my mouth.

"I'm sorry. I'm so sorry." He's scrambling to untie me.

"Kalin?" My speech is still slurred, and his gaze darts to my face. "How are you here?" I struggle to sit. "You're hurt. They… they shot you. I saw—" I can't stop staring at his chest. His white shirt is decorated with blossoms of red, like a watercolour painting.

"I'm fine." He scoops me into his arms and cradles me against his uninjured shoulder. Herbs. Camphor. Library books. And now blood. It's Kalin. He's solid and real and alive, but hurt. How is he still standing, let alone carrying me?

"Everything's going to be fine," he says.

No one tries to stop us from leaving.

The wind stings my skin as we exit the warehouse. Where are Dumi's men? What happened to them? Kalin stoops to open a car door. It bangs open with such force I fear it's going to fly off its hinges. I jerk, but Kalin doesn't react. He gently places me in the passenger seat. His car. The smell of crumbling foam and old vinyl. He clicks the seatbelt over me and hovers with his face near mine.

I can only vaguely see his eyes in the dark. He brushes my cheek, just below the place where I was punched. "I need to clean things up. I won't be long."

"No, don't leave me."

"It's all right. They're gone."

But there could be more of them hiding in the dark.

"Are you going to kill them?" My voice is tiny.

"No. Am I right in thinking they're Dumi's agents?"

I nod.

"Then I have other plans for them."

With that, he closes the door, and I'm alone in the dark car with the wind whistling all around me. My thoughts skip and jump like a worn-out CD. Nothing that's happened tonight belongs in my life. None of this makes sense. And yet it all makes sense. For the first time, Kalin makes sense.

Bianca's warning about how Kalin was only pretending to be normal; George speaking as if he and Kalin knew each other decades ago. *What do you have left to study, Kallen?* All the old things. If bullets can't kill him, is he immortal? And if so, how old is he? And there's the… It can *only* be magic. What he did to those men in there. The books filled with what must be spells. Hogsback. What I saw in Hogsback. The water rising. The sketch I drew of him the next day, in robes with a staff. In robes just like…

Kalin opens the door and I startle. He places my bag at my feet. "Rest. We'll be home soon."

I try to calm my thoughts, but suspicion fills me with bitter, horrible dread. I recall splinters of dreams that explain far too much. The drawing of the orbs in Kalin's book. *Anna.*

It can't be. It's insane. Kalin is kind and thoughtful and *good.*

But then his words in the diner… *Long ago, I did some terrible things. I was terrible.*

Just how long ago did he mean?

We're a little way down the dark road when my shivers become violent shudders, and my insides are determined to get *outside.*

"Stop the car!"

Kalin slams on brakes, and I only just manage to fling myself out of the passenger side before I start hurling. I hear Kalin's door and then his arms are around me; he's holding my hair out of my face. My guts spasm. I'm shaking so hard I can't see straight.

Kalin drapes his coat around my shoulders and pulls me against him. I'm wrapped in a tight, warm cocoon, with the wind battering at my face. I should push him away. If he is who I fear he is, I should be disgusted by him. But it's not possible. They're just dreams. *I* made up that kingdom. My lungs are uncooperative, the air is thick and impossible to breathe. What did I just witness? I desperately want a logical explanation, but I can't find one.

He rubs my back in slow, soothing circles. "You're going to be fine. It's shock and whatever's in your system. Just let it pass."

When at last I manage to get in enough air, I say, "I'm not drunk. I didn't drink. I didn't—"

"It doesn't matter." Kalin's voice is steady. "If Dumi wanted you, they would have got hold of you no matter what you did. None of this is your fault."

I close my eyes against another wave of nausea.

"How did you find me?" I ask, because my other questions are way too big.

"We can talk about it when we get home."

"Where are we?"

"Outside of Bathurst."

Bathurst sounds familiar. Of all the strange things to think of at a time like this, I remember Darren's katemba. "Pineapples."

"That's right." Kalin holds me a little tighter, and his lips brush my forehead. His arms are a life raft in the churning sea that is my body and my mind. "I should never have left you," he whispers.

We stay like that a long time, sitting quietly on the side of the dark road, in the middle of nowhere. Gradually, my trembling stops, and my lungs open. When I finally manage to climb into the car, I'm completely drained.

⁓⁓⁓

At the Settler's Cottage, I stand in the shower for ages. I stand there until the water runs cold, until my fingertips wrinkle, trying to convince myself I'm wrong.

My dreams are just dreams.

I eventually pad out of the bedroom to find Kalin on the phone.

"Yes, hello, I'd like to speak to Michael Bradach, please? Perfect."

What does he want with Michael? He's looking out of the study window, the landline pressed to his cheek. The room is still dark, and the only light illuminating his face is from the streetlight outside.

"I've been following your work reporting on the Dumi trial," he says. "If you go to this address, I think you might find something interesting… No, I'm afraid I can't give you my name. What I can give you is a head start. I will be calling the police shortly, and if you head there now, you will find an undisturbed crime scene. The culprits may have some interesting things to say. The victim was Lilah Durow— No, she's fine. It seems they intended to kidnap her to influence her father's testimony, but I'm hardly one to judge. I'll leave it to you and your journalistic expertise to decide the story."

He gives Michael the address, presses down the hook switch and starts dialling a new number. Then seems to sense me. He puts down the receiver and turns. "Feeling better?"

He's in a clean shirt now. It's beige, and looks like it's made

⁓256⁓

from some natural fibre. No sign of injury, no sign of blood, and no brown jacket. His favourite jacket will probably never be the same again.

"How did you get Michael's number?"

"Jess. *Her* number was in your mobile. I hope you don't mind?" He hands me my phone.

"Why are you giving Michael a head start? You're not trying to frame him?"

"No, of course not." Kalin's tone is bright, but there's a tightness around his eyes, and he doesn't sound like himself. "Would you like some tea?"

I nod and he moves past me into the kitchen. "I want to make sure that Dumi won't try something like that again. Plus, it could help your father's case." He pulls out a mug, fills the kettle. "If it comes to light that he did what he did to protect his daughter, then your uncle could prove duress. In which case his sentence will be significantly reduced." He pauses with a spoon in his hand, looking down at the mug. "I can't recall if you take sugar? I should give you sugar. It will help with the shock."

His hand is shaking. Shaking badly. He tries to cover it by putting down the spoon, forming a fist, and turning to look at me.

"Seems you need the sugar more than I do," I say.

"Perhaps."

I search his beautiful face. The last time we were here together, I was kissing it. Now everything's changed. A part of me screams to avoid this conversation. I can accept the tea, go to the room, and pretend it was all just a crazy dream. He didn't just use magic in front of me. He didn't just spontaneously heal.

But there's no going back. Not really. And there's no easy way to approach the subject either.

"You're the Overlord," I say.

The statement hangs between us. I wait, hope, for him to crinkle his brow, ask me if I'm concussed. I want him to deny it. I want him to tell me I've lost my mind.

Instead he takes a deep breath. "There was a point, when we were in Hogsback, when I thought you might have realised."

My heart shivers. It's true. It's really true. The subject of my nightmares is somehow standing here in the kitchen, is somehow real and living in our modern world. Is somehow my gentle Kalin.

"And Anna, who you cried out for in your sleep? She's Alayna, right? You said she was a *friend*."

Kalin's gaze drops to the floor. "She *was* a friend. Before she was my enemy. Lilah, I can only guess at what you might have seen in your dreams—"

"Are you even human?"

"No."

A wave of horror races through me. That and a deep ache, a grief for the man I'm in love with, who is not a man at all.

Kalin swallows. "My people arrived on Earth centuries – millennia – ago. We were fleeing from a world ruined by magic. Before long, we came into conflict with your people. We lost the war and your human leader offered us the underworld."

I'm trying to listen past the buzzing in my head. "Underworld? As in guarded by Hades?"

He shakes his head. "Not like in the Greek mythology. Like in the *Celtic*."

His eyes meet mine because he must know how many pieces are slotting into place then. He doesn't study the ancient Celts. He *is* one. Or… or he's one of their gods.

"This Otherworld – which is what it then was called – is what you would term a parallel universe. That's where I was born. But as punishment for my crimes, I was exiled here. Without magic." His look holds. Without magic, but he clearly has magic now. "I still don't have my own power, but I've discovered how to channel power from other sources."

"Like the wind." That thing he did to my captors.

"And water."

What I saw in Hogsback.

My knowledge of Kalin wars with what I've seen of the Overlord. "And what, you want to break into your world again, take your rightful place as leader?"

Is *that* his project?

"There was never anything rightful about my place as leader," he says bitterly. "I took power from the mad king who despised magic and who hunted down anyone unfortunate enough to be born with it. But then you know all of this already. I saw it in your drawings."

"I made it up."

"No, Lilah. You *remembered* it."

I take an involuntary step backwards. "No. I'm human. I was never in this Otherworld."

"You asked me about Anna. She was my closest friend, my greatest adversary and..." He pauses. "And she was also your ancestor."

That word thuds into me. It carries so much that I can't hope to unpack now. A reason for Kalin's friendship, a reason for Bianca's warnings. If she knows... she studies parallel universes. Is she immortal too?

Am I in danger? Is Kalin going to hurt me to reap some sort of revenge on Alayna? How does Sukwini fit into all of this? Does Sukwini know?

Sukwini knew my mother.

I need to sit down. I feel for the kitchen chair behind me and sink into it. Kalin rubs his face, presses his palms to his eyes.

"So you're what... like a, a Highlander? A vampire?"

"My people are known as the Fae."

The... he's a *fairy*? But of course he is. Those are the magical beings of Irish myth, the ones that supposedly haunt menhirs like Stonehenge.

"Are all the Fae immortal?" *Is Alayna still alive?*

"No. It's part of my curse. Part of my punishment. Immortality. I'm not permitted to die until I have served my sentence."

"And you're not twenty-three."

"I was twenty-three when I was banished."

"And how old are you now?"

He shakes his head. "You won't appreciate the answer."

"I'll appreciate you being honest with me."

He wets his lips. "*Three hundred* and twenty-three."

Three hundred? Holy hell. I can't even imagine being alive that long. Kalin was born a hundred years before the 1820 settlers even arrived here. How many things he must have seen. No wonder the university courses are no more than a passing amusement to him. And me… everything I thought I had with him feels like a cruel joke.

"I must seem so small to you."

He slides into the seat across from me. "No. No, Lilah. You're the opposite. You have the greatest mass. I mean… in the sense of a star. In space. I…" He drops his gaze again, clears his throat. "I'm trying to say… you are my centre of gravity. Everything else revolves around you."

My stomach leaps, but I know that's not true. "No, everything revolves around your secret project. I'm just a piece of debris that got caught in orbit."

"You *are* my project, Lilah."

I shake my head. Of all the unbelievable things I've heard during the past few minutes, that makes the least sense.

He reaches across the table and takes my hand. "Your necklace is a shield knot. An amulet of protection. That's why you've had the dreams. It's been warning you about me. At its base it is similar to all the charms I sell; it's infused with its own magic, and I only amplify it. It was never missing a stone, but gems and crystals hold their own power, and I knew that finding the right one—" He reaches beneath his shirt with his free hand and pulls out the pendant I saw around his neck in Hogsback. Now it's also inlaid with jet. "This is part of the same stone. It's what enabled me to find you tonight. It took me weeks to work out how to charm a stone without my own power. For a time, that was my project."

I press my palm to my chest where I can feel the necklace beneath my shirt. Kalin never believed I was safe from Dumi. He knew this was going to happen. To him it was just a matter of time.

"You knew I was in danger and you left me here?"

"I thought—"

"You thought that my security upgrades would be enough?"

"No. That's not—"

It's too much. All of this is too much. I stand and yank my hand free of his. "I… I can't. I need…"

"Lilah, wait. There's more I have to tell you."

"I can't do more. I— This is too much. It's all too much. I need to be alone."

Dawn is breaking. I can hear birdcall in the garden as I pass the front door into the bedroom, leaving Kalin, the Overlord, at the kitchen table.

⁓

I nudge Fatso over and curl up in the middle of the bed, hugging a pillow. There's still so much I don't understand. My body aches, my face is still sore from where BP hit me.

I should go to the police. I should report what happened. I should tell them about Dumi trying to bribe dad.

The man I love is an alien.

Should I call them now? What time does the station open?

An ancient alien who's fitted me with a magical tracking device.

How would I explain my escape? What is the correct procedure?

Why does Kalin want to protect me so badly? Is it because I'm what remains of her? Was there more between them?

Was the kiss meant for Alayna?

There's such a void between who she was and who I am, and it hurts like someone reaching in and squeezing my heart when I remember the way he grabbed my wrist that night and said her name.

I hear him on the phone to the police and hug the pillow tighter. Maybe my own statement can wait.

A memory returns to me of the night Kalin walked me home from the music society event. He saw the map, he asked me about it. When I told him about the evil sorcerer, he went quiet. And when he invited me to SciFest, he kept trying to ask me about the drawings. Is that *why* he invited me? And in Cape Town he saw that portrait of my mother. I realise now, she's the reason Alayna looked familiar to me. In that portrait they look almost identical.

After a long while, there's a soft rap on the door. I don't say anything, and it opens, letting in a narrow triangle of dim sunlight from the kitchen. I sense Kalin in the doorway, but I pretend to be asleep. He comes in, moving slowly and quietly, and he sits on the edge of the bed and sighs. I peek at him from beneath my eyelashes. His shoulders are hunched, and his head is bowed. Fatso scampers over to him, and Kalin reaches out a hand to pet him, but his head remains bowed.

A moment passes. He pulls off his boots. I close my eyes as he lies down next to me. My pulse kicks up. I keep my breathing regular. There's no movement for such a long time that I'm almost certain he's fallen asleep.

Then he touches my hair. He's so gentle that if I were truly asleep, he would not have woken me. He trails his fingertips across my forehead, brushing aside one of my curls. I can feel his eyes on me. The mattress shifts as he turns over.

It takes everything in me to resist the urge to reach out to him. *What would it be like to wake up in his arms?*

His three-hundred-and-twenty-three-year-old evil Overlord arms.

I lie awake long after his breath falls into the rhythm of sleep with all my emotions crashing against each other.

Somewhere in Grahamstown, Michael is probably filing his story. Lani is waking up for our shift. Harrold's already at the front desk, placing orders for fresh produce. Everyone I know is going about their lives as if nothing has changed. But for me nothing will ever be the same.

I can't stay here. It's too confusing. Everything is weird and wrong.

I can only think of one other safe place to go.

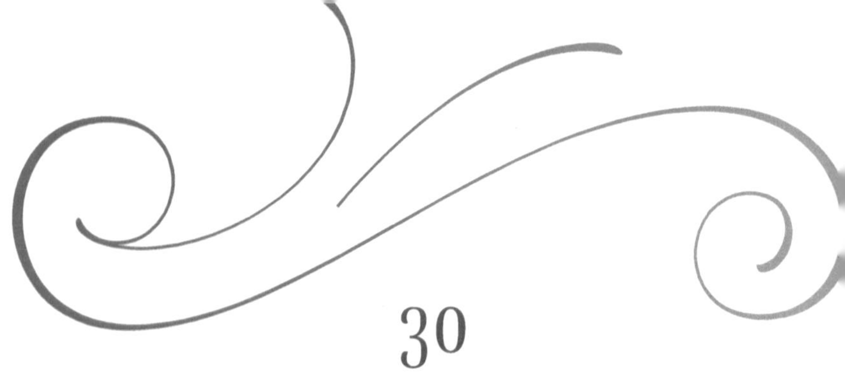

30

*D*arren stares at me. He's in a grey dressing gown, holding a mug of coffee. I'm standing on his doorstep, shivering.

"Holy shit, Lilah. What happened to your face?"

Oh. That. I didn't look in the mirror before I left. I was in too much of a hurry to go before Kalin woke, and with the throbbing pain that's been chasing through my whole body, I somehow managed to forget about the eye.

My head aches where it hit the floor, my muscles are stiff and cold, and my stomach is a black pit of discomfort. After effects of the drugs, I guess. And last night's revelations.

"It's kind of a long story. I know it's early. I just wanted to ask if your folks still had a room for me at their B&B?"

Darren's gaze moves to my hoodie, which I put on to hide my face in case there were any other thugs about, then settles on my bag, which is bulging with the clothing and toiletries I managed to shove into it.

"Did Kalin do this?"

"No! Can I come in?"

Aside from the cold, I'd rather not be in the open right now. I walked here through silent side roads, careful not to let anyone see me. And I wasn't quite stupid enough to leave the necklace with the note I wrote Kalin (*I need some time to think. Don't come after me*). Still, my heart is racing, and every movement in the complex makes my insides jump.

~264~

Darren nods and moves aside.

His house is cool and quiet. Any other Sunday and he might have been preparing for the family braai, but today it's empty. Just as I was hoping it would be. I sink onto the couch and pull out my purse.

"I can pay for the room." Tips have been good over Fest. I can afford at least a few days.

Darren locks the door. He still looks horrified. "Who did that to you?"

It's surprisingly difficult to say the words. *Human traffickers. I was nearly sold into slavery. I was kidnapped and drugged.* I feel as though I've swallowed snakes.

Darren comes closer. "Did someone break into the house? Should I call the police?"

"The police know." I fidget with my purse. I should probably go make that statement later, even though Kalin called them. I need to figure out what to tell them, and I can't even figure out what to tell Darren.

Darren sinks down onto the seat beside me, all the while focused on my black eye.

"Dumi wanted leverage against my father," I say eventually.

Darren swears. "But you managed to escape?"

"I was rescued."

The memories lash at me. *Kalin being shot in the chest, in the head, lying in a crumpled heap.*

"By the police?"

"No."

"Then by who? What happened?"

"Kalin happened." *Kalin's arms around me on the side of the road. The Overlord sending people flying across the warehouse.*

Darren says nothing, and I don't know if he's waiting for me to elaborate, or if he's quiet because of *who* we're talking about.

Here, sitting in this normal lounge with the TV and the Xbox, with this normal man who drinks wine and likes comics, the conversation last night seems even more crazy. Even Darren's jealousy is something I can understand. Kalin's passion, Kalin's shame, are as alien as Kalin himself.

"I thought he was out of town?" Darren prompts me, softly.

"Yeah… crazy story."

"Is he working for Dumi?"

"No. This is crazier than that. It's mad. It's… You wouldn't believe me if I told you."

"You'd be surprised what I'd believe about that guy."

I want to tell him; I want to get the words out so I'm not alone while reality breaks apart around me. I worry at my bottom lip. Maybe he's not the worst person to confide in. Bianca knows something. Is what she knows the truth? What if Darren knows that truth already too?

"Would you believe he's an ancient, immortal sorcerer?"

There's a long pause, and I can't read what Darren's thinking from his expression. "He's really messed with your head, hasn't he?"

So much for him knowing the truth.

"Darren, I saw it. Last night, Dumi's thugs got me. They kidnapped me. I was almost…" I still can't quite say it. "But then he saved me. He came in there and defeated them all. With magic. He raised his arms and they went flying." I'm hearing myself, and I feel the blood rush to my face. What am I doing? No sane person would say these things. "I know how it sounds."

Darren continues to stare at me, and my chest tightens.

"Well, you said you thought he had a secret," he says eventually.

"Yeah."

He gets up. "Let me call Mom and see if they have that room for you."

He goes into his bedroom to make the call, but snatches of it drift into the lounge. "He's done a number on her, all right. She's talking about him using *magic* to save her… Yeah maybe they drugged her."

They *did* drug me. Maybe this is all a dream and I'm still in the chair. I shudder. I don't want to believe that either.

"Okay… no, I'm sure that's fine… Yeah, I'll lock the door… You don't have to— Okay. Okay, sure. See you soon."

I pull out my phone and pretend to be reading something on the screen.

"There's nothing available tonight," Darren says as he comes back into the room. "You know, Fest."

Of course, they wouldn't have a room available now. I should have thought.

"But you can stay here! They're driving back tonight, then Mom's gonna try organise something. She seemed really worried about you."

"Oh. Oh, they don't have to drive back for me—"

He sits again. "She was insistent. She said you should stay here with the doors locked in the meantime. You know, just in case anyone comes looking for you." His gaze slides to focus on my bruised eye again, then he stands abruptly. "Can I get you something? I was about to make breakfast? Do you eat eggs?"

I nod. "Thank you."

"Sure. Of course. Just relax."

While Darren makes breakfast, I call Lani and ask her to cover for me at Guido's. No way I could go into work with the black eye, even if I didn't have thugs after me.

She thinks I'm hungover. "*Babalas?* That's not like you, Cindy."

I'm tempted to just leave it at that, but if Michael has written his story the truth will be all over Grahamstown soon.

"Your friend from BP got me last night," I say. "Don't worry, I'm fine."

She swears. "*Waar is jy?*" *Where are you.* "I can come by before shift. You must tell me everything. Do you want me to bring you something? Are you safe?"

Her concern is so overwhelming it almost brings me to tears. "I, yes. Yes, I'm safe. I'm with Darren."

She sighs relief into the phone. "I should not have left you alone in that place."

"It's not your fault." And I tell her about how they were tied to Dumi. I imply it was the cops who rescued me. This is all complicated enough without people at work thinking I'm crazy too. "I'm pretty sure they were also the 'friends' Harrold was yelling about."

"Mmm I'll inform him. I'll enjoy seeing his reaction." She calls him a name in Afrikaans and assures me she'll handle him and my shift.

When I hang up, I see Darren standing watching me. He doesn't comment, although I know he's probably thinking he was right about the drugs. Instead, he offers a smile. "Breakfast's ready."

I spend the day on the couch. I watch TV, and even try one of Darren's video games. It's more fun than I expected, considering most of it involves stealing cars and racing them away from cops, and considering how bad I am at it. It pulls me out of the loop of traumatic thoughts and worry, and that's just what I need.

At about three o'clock someone knocks on the door, and both of us tense. I fight the urge to hide behind the couch as Darren creeps up to the peep hole. Then he looks at me, puzzled, and opens the door.

Lani, Chad and a few of the other Guido's staff file in, and Lani has a giant sticky chocolate cake in her hands.

It turns out they were worried enough about me to scout out Darren's address, which they found in the university records under IT support. Seems it won't be a quiet Sunday for Darren after all.

At first everyone is full of questions, but Lani must sense my reluctance to talk about my kidnapping because she steers the conversation away from last night and into stories about today's customers. Before long, Darren's house is full of laughter, and he's engaged in a game of Street Fighter with Chad. There's more than enough cake to go around, and it's heavenly. If this is what Lani wants to do with her life, she has a bright future for sure.

She surprises me with a hug as she's leaving. "Just let me know if you need more cake. Chocolate makes *alles* better. *Nê?*"

Darren and Chad exchange details for future game days, and when the door closes behind them, I'm still smiling. It feels like everything that happened in the past two days was just a nightmare.

Neither of us is hungry, so Darren puts on a movie. A few minutes in, he puts his arm around me.

I keep my eyes on the screen. He put his arm around me on Friday too, and I didn't exactly tell him not to. Still, my shoulders tense, because that was before I told him that I only wanted to be friends for now. I'm watching the movie, but I can't think of anything but that arm and how close he's sitting.

He touches my hair. "I know the circumstances aren't ideal, but it's been a good day," he says in a low voice.

I tell myself to calm down as my breath hitches and my pulse starts to drum. It's Darren. I'm safe. He's not going to hurt me. But this is all wrong. This wasn't what I expected when he offered me a place to stay.

I don't want to have this conversation again. I don't want to make things awkward. It's not like I don't appreciate everything he's done for me. His fingers brush my neck.

"Darren…"

"Just relax, Lilah. You've been through hell."

What he's doing is making me anything but relaxed.

He pulls me closer. "Let me comfort you."

And he kisses me. My muscles go rigid. I'm frozen by the unwelcome attention.

"I'll make you feel better," he says against my lips.

I give his chest a hard shove. "No."

He pulls away and gawks at me, but I'm already untangling myself from his arms, getting to my feet, getting ready to run into the night.

He snags my hand. "Wait!"

I snatch it back. "I told you I didn't want this." Anger thrums in my veins. "Now I'm vulnerable, you think that's changed?"

Dad would tell me not to make a scene, but Dad also told me that I was safe when I was not.

"It was a mistake coming here." I pick up my bag, and he scrambles to his feet.

"Lilah, don't go. I'm sorry."

I round on him. "Today *was* a good day, but I suppose that was all false pretences – just like visiting me at my stall was? Do enough nice things and I'll change my mind? Is that how it works?"

It's like I'm possessed. All my bottled anger and confusion is fuelling this rage.

"I'm not like that! You're acting like I tried to force myself on you!"

"Right, I forgot how little kisses mean to you."

I can feel the impact of my words across the space between us. He wipes his face with his hand. "I *told* you, I was doing Jess a favour. It was pretend—"

"I don't mean that kiss. I mean my kiss. My *first* kiss."

His brow furrows. "*That* was your *first* kiss?" There's an edge of incredulity there that's a little nasty. Like I had no business being at university without ever having been kissed.

I nod. "I wanted nothing more, after that night, than to see you again. But I suppose I was too much of a dork for you?"

"I knew I shouldn't have said that."

"I'm still a dork, Darren. I'm still Lilah. Cindy is a mask that I use to cope, and right now I'm not. I'm not coping." My voice wobbles. "I don't need kisses. I need you to back off."

He holds up his hands. "Calm down. I'm not the threat here. I only want to help."

I try to think through the fog of anger, weigh up my options. I don't want to go outside; I don't want to walk those dark streets alone after last night. I swallow my pride and drop my gaze.

"Sorry."

"It's all right," he says stiffly. "Your emotions are clearly out of whack after everything. It's fine. It's to be expected."

I have to bite back a retort.

"Uh— I'm going to go get the spare bedding. You can take the room if you like?"

"No." Right now I have zero desire to be anywhere near his bed, but I don't say that. "Thank you. The couch is fine."

I'm so tired, but I don't want to sleep. I don't want to dream about Kalin being evil, I don't want to be unconscious and vulnerable. I switch on my phone to check the news sites. Nothing yet. There are missed calls from unfamiliar numbers, though, which might be Michael or other press looking for comment. Or perhaps something happened to him in that warehouse. What if he's hurt? What if they killed him? What if he didn't follow Kalin's tip and the story never comes out and Dumi's guys never face justice and continue to prowl Grahamstown's streets? What if they're still out there looking for me?

My chest closes. The fear tastes bitter.

You're all right. You're fine. Everything's fine. You're safe, I tell myself as I hug my knees and huddle down into the blankets. But I feel neither fine nor safe.

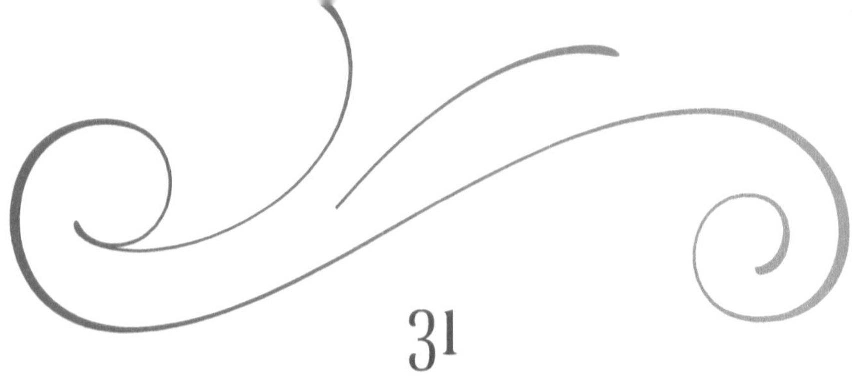

31

arren's mom, Shirley, arrives early the next morning. She sweeps into the house and takes me by the shoulders, focusing her entire attention on my black eye. "You poor dear!"

She smells like roses, and I nearly crumble, but I manage to hold it together because Darren's there, and Bianca's just come in too. Bianca is all ice and frozen rage. She hovers near the door, watching silently as Shirley takes me to the couch and sits me down.

"Tell me what happened. Darren, go make us a cup of tea."

I don't need tea. I've had three cups of coffee after a night of restless, stilted sleep and the caffeine's only served to make me more jittery. Darren has been civil, but cool and careful to keep his distance.

Now he throws a look at Bianca, then slips out of the room to do as his mother asked.

I tell her about Dumi, about how I got my black eye and about their intentions with me. My voice trembles on that part and unwelcome tears prick my eyes. I hate the way she's looking at me with such intense pity.

"I just, I'd like a place to stay until varsity starts again. If you still have a room available. I can pay."

She takes my hand and her focus doesn't waver. "Now, Lilah. Darren told me that you were rescued by that friend of yours, Kalin?"

I nod, but I'm not sure how much else I want to tell her.

"Darren mentioned you thought he used magic to save you?"

The way she says it, it's like she may have asked, "You mentioned he was wearing a blue shirt?" As if it's a totally possible and quite mundane detail.

If anyone else asked, or if she'd asked in any other way, I'd deny it outright.

How much does she already know about who Kalin is?

She studies the Celts. Bianca studies parallel worlds. They have a shared history with him. They may even know more than I do.

I lock eyes with Bianca and a shiver runs through me. The hatred is practically steaming off her.

"I thought that's what I saw, but maybe I was wrong. It happened very fast."

"What, *precisely*, happened?" Shirley prompts.

Darren comes in and places the tea on the coffee table in front of me, but doesn't so much as look at me.

"She was drugged," he says. "It was just a hallucination."

"If it was a hallucination, I'd still be in that warehouse."

"Maybe he staged the whole thing."

"That's ridiculous." I'm too tired for patience.

"Just saying, that's a pretty neat explanation for how he happened to find you."

Bianca snaps, "Shut up, Darren. Let the girl speak."

She folds her arms, and she's still standing near the door, so she looks like a bouncer.

Darren spreads his hands. "Fine. Whatever. I'll be in the study."

Shirley leans towards me. "Now pay Darren no mind. Tell me exactly what you saw, whatever you can remember."

The tension in the room now is close to unbearable.

"Kalin saved me. He bust down the door and somehow managed to knock out all the guards, even though they were shooting at him. I don't know how." I direct my gaze at Bianca again. "But maybe you do?"

She tenses. "What did *Kallen* have to say for himself?"

The difference in pronunciation is subtle, but I've heard it too many times now to call it a coincidence. She drops her arms and comes closer. "He must have offered you some explanation for what you saw?"

"No, he-he didn't." I stammer, even though my brain is screaming at me to tell them what I know because I'm certain they have answers. But whatever else he might be, might *have been*, Kalin has gone out of his way to help me.

I settle for a half-truth. "He told me a lot of things that didn't make any sense."

"Such as?"

I shrug, acting casual while my insides rattle. "He just said he's working on a project, and that he can't give me any details."

Bianca doesn't believe me. "Surely he must have said more, or you would not have run here seeking refuge with my brother?"

I think fast. "He started to say some… romantic stuff. I just got weirded out after everything."

Shirley squeezes my hand. "You've been through quite the trauma."

"It could have been worse." It nearly was.

"Bianca," Shirley says sweetly. "Call Sukwini and tell her what's happened."

My heart jerks. Bianca nods and leaves, less the daughter and more the soldier following an order.

"Why Sukwini?" I ask.

"She's your warden, I believe?"

She is, but she's out of town visiting family over Fest while res is rented out. She can't do anything for me now. I reach back in my memory for the precise words that I overheard between Kalin and Sukwini.

I will do exactly what I promised. You think I'm not ready for it? After all these years? I'm not going to back out now.

Maybe he did take a while to figure out the necklace thing, but he has at least one other secret project. Is Sukwini an alien like he is? Are they all? And whose side is Sukwini on?

Dad said I must trust her, but how much does Dad know? Does any of it connect with his secret identity?

Shirley takes me to the B&B, a little cottage with bougainvillea clawing up its whitewashed walls.

The only room available is tiny, with a single narrow bed.

"If it wasn't for Fest, I could offer you something larger," Shirley says as she opens a set of curtains and sunlight washes in, carrying with it the scent of flowers.

"This is perfect. Thank you."

She refuses to take payment for it, and even invites me to have dinner with the family later.

Before she leaves, she takes my hands in hers again. "Lilah, what you witnessed must be terribly confusing and frightening."

I nod. There's no denying that.

"The author Arthur C. Clarke had a saying. Any sufficiently advanced technology is indistinguishable from magic. There may not seem to be a logical explanation for what you saw, but Kalin is a very intelligent man. He has been engaged in some very advanced research through the university."

"He has?"

"Sometimes those of great intelligence can develop grandiose ideas about themselves. I'm glad that you came to us. You'll be safe here."

I'm grateful for the reassurance, but bitterness coats my tongue when the door shuts behind her. It might just be coffee and a lack of sleep, but it might also be that most of what she said made sense. I climb onto the bed. The white linen pillow is cool against my cheek. My limbs are heavy with fatigue. It's almost comforting to think *Kalin* might be the one losing his mind. He might not be a fairy. He might just be a delusional savant with a very scientific secret project.

But that wouldn't explain the dreams.

Even here in the quiet cottage, I fight against sleep, and the dreams that might come with it. I plug in my phone, but my eyes close of their own accord before I can even unlock the screen.

It is not the Overlord's castle that I see when I surrender to sleep.

It's his bright modern-day kitchen.

Kalin stands at the entrance to his study, holding out his hands in front of his chest. Someone else is there with him, and he's slowly backing away from them. "Let me explain."

Fatso is bathing himself on the counter, but he pauses in the middle of licking his paw to look at the person Kalin is talking to.

It's Bianca. I see the leather jacket first, then her face. She's tossing one of Kalin's books from hand to hand, advancing towards him.

"Show me." Her voice is little more than a growl.

"I am not a threat to you."

She grits her teeth. "Show me. Show me what you did last night."

"I don't know what you mean."

She gestures sharply, and he flies backwards, crashing into the bookcase with enough force to splinter the middle shelf. Fatso streaks across the room to hide under the settee. Books tumble down around Kalin. One rises into the air and slams into his face.

"Defend yourself!" Bianca yells. "I know you can!"

Blood drips from Kalin's nose. He dabs it with the back of his hand. "I wish you no ill. Some part of you must believe it, or you wouldn't have come here alone."

Another book lifts, one of his heavy history books. Bianca flings it into his stomach, and he doubles over, gasping. She strides towards him.

"So, your magic is reserved for terrorising young women?"

He struggles to breathe. "Lilah? I never intended to frighten—"

Another book torpedoes into his face, hits his left cheek and thwacks his head back against the bookcase. "Show me your power!"

"It is not my *power." Kalin pants.*

The history book lifts and rams into his stomach again.

He whimpers and sinks to his knees. "I channel the power of the earth, no more than that." He waves weakly at his workspace. "You needn't concern yourself, Guardian. I have no intention of using it on Beltane night."

Bianca's jaw works. She places her hands on her hips as she glares down at him.

"Where's Lilah?" he asks softly.

"You have some gall asking that."

He wets his lips. "You need to protect her. Her father—"

The bookcase trembles. Some more books slam down around him, and he flinches.

"Let's get something straight," Bianca says. "Lilah is out of your reach."

There's a long pause before Kalin responds. "I see. Now you have discovered the one thing I care about, you'd use her to guarantee I behave?"

Bianca doesn't answer.

"I assure you, it's unnecessary. I…" He draws a deep breath before looking up at her face. "If you protect Lilah, I will surrender myself to you that night."

Her eyes narrow. Then she turns away from him and cuts a hand through the air. His workspace explodes. Necklaces, charms, tools become shrapnel that flies towards him. He covers his face just in time. And when he looks up again, Bianca is gone.

Kalin slides down to the floor and draws his knees up to his chest. He's trembling and his breathing is ragged. A movement to his right makes him jump.

"Fatso," he whispers. "Fatso, come here. Come here, it's safe now. It's safe, boy."

The cat steps cautiously from beneath the settee, then scampers to

Kalin's side. Kalin scoops him up, checks for injuries, and hugs him.

"I'm sorry about that. I messed everything up again."

He presses his cheek to Fatso's soft fur…

…and I wake up, with my heart pounding in my eardrums and Kalin's necklace scorching my skin.

I yank it off. The metal's hot, hot enough to burn me.

It's never done that before.

I stare at it in my palm, and it slowly cools.

My mother wore a shield knot too. Kalin asked about it when he saw the graduation photo. Did he recognise it? Could it have been an heirloom passed all the way down from Alayna? Did Kalin make hers too?

Someone knocks on the door and I jump.

"It's just me." Bianca's voice.

When I open the door, she looks exactly like she did in the dream. Same outfit, same intense expression. Was she wearing that this morning?

"I just wanted to let you know that Kalin won't be bothering you again," she says. "You can rest…" Her attention strays to the necklace. "…easy."

"What did you do to him?" Though I *know*. I saw it… somehow.

She's still looking at the necklace. It's like she didn't even hear my question. I close my fist around it. "Kalin wasn't bothering me. He saved me."

Bianca has *always* been scary, but now I know just what she's capable of, she's terrifying.

Kalin called her "Guardian". What does that mean? Is she like a Fae parole officer?

She lifts her gaze to mine. "I'm sure he had his reasons." She searches my expression as if I might know what they are.

"Did you manage to get hold of my warden?" My voice only shakes a little.

"Your warden?"

Confirmation. That's not why they were contacting Sukwini. "Never mind. Thank you for the reassurance."

Her eyes narrow just like in the dream, but she nods and wishes me a pleasant day before turning to go. I watch her until she reaches the end of the corridor before I shut the door and rummage through my bag for my key to Kalin's place.

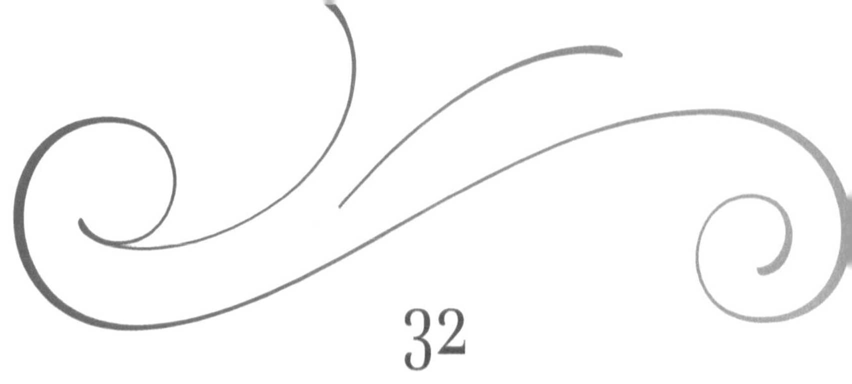

32

I didn't need the evidence, but there it is. Broken glass, paper everywhere, the remnants of pendants, beads and clasps scattered across the study. No sign of Kalin. No sign of Fatso either, even though I call for him.

The necklace works both ways.

The split jet may have told him when I was in danger, but it also signalled me when he was under attack.

What happened here is *my* fault. I went straight to his enemy. Rescuing me cost him his study, his books, his jewellery.

He's the Overlord, I try to remind myself. He's killed people before. He was a tyrant. He kept a whole kingdom under his thumb, living in fear. I shouldn't feel this bad for him.

But my mouth tastes like ash. He called me the one thing he cared about, and I betrayed him. I didn't mean to. I only wanted a little distance, somewhere safe to stay while I thought this all out. I should never have said anything to Darren. I knew how his family felt about Kalin. *That's* on me.

I do the only thing I can think to do. I start cleaning up.

Just like that day when I tried and failed to get a job, I pack away his books, I sweep the floors, I clean the counters. The scrubbing gives me an outlet for my nervous energy, but it doesn't make me feel any better.

I tense at every sound, hoping it's Kalin returning, and my heart sinks when it's not. I don't even know what I'll say to him. I want to apologise, but then what?

Eventually I set my phone on the kitchen table and put on music loud enough to drown everything else out. The light starts to fade, and still Kalin has not returned. Maybe he left town again. Maybe this time, he won't come back.

I know I should go before it gets too late. The B&B is further from here than Darren's, and I'm still frightened of walking the dark streets alone.

Plus, there was Shirley's dinner invitation. I should go, but what if I leave and Kalin returns only a few minutes later?

Night has almost completely swallowed the cottage and the little garden, when pounding on the door makes me drop my washcloth. I freeze. Who'd come see Kalin besides me?

"Lilah! Lilah are you in there? It's Darren." The glass reverberates under his fist.

Fresh guilt squeezes my insides. They must have discovered my absence and they probably think I've been kidnapped again.

I hurry to unlock the door for Darren, but before I can open my mouth to explain, he waves his phone at me. "Come, we've got to go."

"Wha—"

He snatches my arm and pulls me physically through the door. "I'll explain in the car. You're in danger."

Once I'm seated beside him in his Honda, he passes me the phone. "Press play."

It's open on a YouTube video. My blood goes cold before I even hit the white triangle. Because there I am, tied to a chair. It's the footage from BP's GoPro. Michael must have found it at the crime scene and uploaded it.

"I don't want to watch this." Wasn't living it once enough?

"Trust me," Darren says. "Skip forward if you like."

I play it at double speed with the sound down, and it's still excruciating. I look so pathetic with my droopy, drugged eyes and the red swelling that would become the black eye. When he injects me, my stomach churns at the memory. I'm about to demand Darren just tell me what's happening. Then video-me slumps and BP looks into the camera again. "No games, Durow. Or should I say *Paul Moretti*."

He laughs and the video ends. Was that just... Did he just say my father's real name? I look at Darren. He's concentrating on the road, and his mouth is a thin line. I scroll quickly to read the video description. It says that the video was retrieved at the scene where the man and his accomplices were found bound and gagged, but I am still missing. It asks people to come forward with any information about my whereabouts.

I guess that's the part that has Darren so panicked. "You're taking me to the police?"

I should have gone and made a statement. Why did I put it off? If Dad saw this and thought I was still in danger...

"You remember that article a while back? With how they couldn't find your dad registered at the university?"

"Of course I remember."

"Right, well, seems that's because he wasn't here as Derek Durow. They've been running that name all over the news after some blogger released that footage. That Paul guy *was* registered at the university though, and did get an LLB. You understand, Lilah? Your dad's got a secret identity."

Sukwini knew about Dad's false name. Does Shirley know too? It's a spider's web of lies and secrets, and I still don't know how they all connect. Shirley, Sukwini, my mother, Dad, Kalin, Kalin's project.

"You said I'm in danger."

"Yeah..."

I only realise then that we're not driving towards the B&B, or into town where Darren's parents' house or the police station would be, but out onto the highway.

"Are we leaving Grahamstown?"

"Not quite."

"What's going on, Darren? Tell me."

His jaw tenses, and he hesitates before answering. "I'm taking you somewhere nobody will find you." He glances at me. "Mom said that would be best. I guess she's worried that whoever your dad was hiding from will try find you."

More people to be frightened of? I can't keep up.

"Who are they?"

"I don't know."

"You know I'm in danger, but not from whom?"

He snorts. "Only you would use 'whom' at a time like this. Look, I'm only doing what I'm told. I'm the dumb brother; that's what I do."

There's a layer of resentment beneath those words. Does he know about Bianca's power?

He keeps his gaze locked firmly on the road, but his eye twitches. *Something's wrong.* I mean, I know something's wrong. I'm now even more of a target than I was yesterday. But I'm not sure that's it. There's something else Darren isn't telling me.

He pulls off the highway and down a dark gravel road that I can hardly see even though the moon is big and bright overhead. "Where are you taking me?"

"Grey Dam."

I've heard of it. During summer it's a popular spot for students to come braai and hang out on weekends. I suppose it would be deserted on a winter night. Still, every City Girl instinct I have is telling me this isn't right.

Darren pulls into an empty parking lot. His headlights sweep across the tree trunks and I catch a flash of the glassy lake.

We sit in the dark. He stares at the steering wheel. Eventually he says, "If I asked you to run away with me, I suppose you'd say no?"

My heart skips then pounds a staccato. When I don't answer, he turns in his seat to look at me. "I'd do it, you know? I'd take you away from Kalin, Dumi, all of them. I'd go to the highway right now and just keep on driving."

He waits for my response and, when none comes, he reaches up to cup my cheek. "I think about that night under the stars all the time. At first it was just a move, but the way your eyes lit up, the way you smiled… I got scared. I wasn't looking for anything serious. But now… couldn't you change your mind about me?"

I want to laugh. This is all just so ridiculous. "You mean right now, while there are bad guys chasing me down?"

He scowls, and I'm sure that if the moon hadn't painted everything monochrome, I might see him actually go red. Then he flicks his door lock, and all the others open with a too-loud click.

"You should go. Bianca's waiting for you by the water."

Bianca? I was expecting Shirley. I swallow down my trepidation. Bianca's a Guardian, right? That doesn't sound like a bad thing. She probably just wants to *guard* me. Kalin did try make her promise to.

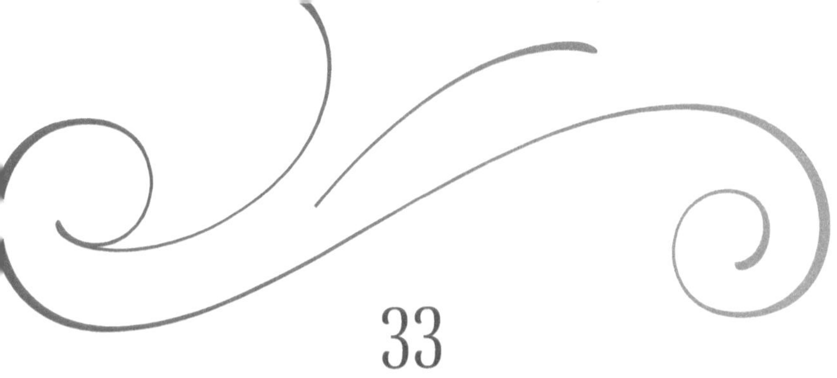

33

As the night surrounds me, unease prickles up to my neck, and Darren's offer doesn't seem quite so crazy. The only sound is my pulse. My only company is the shield knot that still sits against my skin. Kalin's with me… in a sense.

The grass is silver; the water reflects the moon. I take a deep breath, and then I hear something behind me.

I spin around as Darren's bartender friend Sibu melts from the trees. He's in a black hoodie and dark jeans, and if the moon hadn't been so bright, I wouldn't have seen him at all.

"How's it going?" he says.

"I've been better."

"Come with me."

Is he a Guardian too? I thought he was Darren's friend, but he was always around the *family*, not Darren in particular.

Our feet crunch on the dry grass as I follow him closer to the lake. A small group stands at the edge of the water, and they're all wearing hoodies or coats so that from a distance they look like they might be wearing cloaks.

I'm reminded of the lantern people in the mist. Bianca was there that night. Was she crossing between our world and the Other? She must have been, and I must have got caught in transit like that story I once read about butterflies on the Underground. I recognise Bianca immediately. She's got her hands in her pockets, and she's staring out at the opposite shore, but she turns when we approach. Shirley's there too, and her arms are folded across her chest. Unlike the others, her clothing is pale, and her hair shines bright white. There's nothing motherly about her now. She's a commander, a general. Bianca is her right hand. Now it seems so clear that I can't imagine why I didn't see it sooner.

"It's time we're honest with one another," she says by way of greeting.

"I've *been* honest with you." *Is this about Dad's name?*

"How much do you really know about *Kallen's* true nature?"

A cold wind sweeps across the water, and I hug myself, unintentionally echoing her posture. "Darren said I'm in danger. He said there were people after me."

"I'll start, shall I?" Shirley says. "Long ago an evil man rose to power in a realm parallel to this one. He had ability that had not been seen since the old days. Magic, if you will." She moves a little nearer. I back away, right into Sibu, who has taken up position behind me.

He closes a hand around my upper arm, mechanically. My pulse drums. We're in the open air but still I'm claustrophobic. The drive to run seizes me like it hasn't since that first night in Grahamstown, but I am pinned by Shirley's gaze as she draws close.

"You need to understand, Lilah. He was a cruel man, an expert at games of the mind. The histories are full of his deceptions, his advanced stratagems. He believed in magic above all else. People without it, like those who exist in this realm, were nothing but animals to him.

"Then a hero stood against him. A half-breed queen bearing the ancient blood of Nuadha. She started a rebellion that eventually closed in on him. Using ancient orbs forged in the Old World, they managed to trap him in this realm, without his power, so he could do no more harm. She might have killed him then, but instead he was cursed to live with what he had done, to live as one without magic, to bear the guilt for three hundred years. Provided a creature such as he could feel guilt at all."

I *know* Kalin feels guilt. I've seen his guilt. "Why are you telling me all this? What does it have to do with me?"

The other Guardians come closer, as if responding to some secret signal. They're standing around me, around us, in a loose circle. If I break away now, could I still escape?

"It's important you understand," Bianca says.

"I know. I already know. I know who he is." My fear is getting the better of me. Between it and the cold it's hard to think. "Please can we leave this place?"

Bianca and Shirley exchange a look, then it's Bianca who comes to stand before me. She examines my face. Her dark eyes are sorrowful.

"But do you know what *you* are?"

I jut out my chin at her with false bravado. It's the only weapon I have. "Yes. He told me. I'm Alayna Nuadha's descendant."

"Not *who* you are," Bianca's voice is gentle. "*What* you are."

The circle around us tightens. Blood roars in my ears, so loud I almost don't hear Shirley when she speaks.

"At first I thought you were just a girl. But why would Kallen be interested in just a girl?"

"Why would he shelter you; why would he protect you; why would he risk everything for you?" Bianca asks.

"They should have never brought you back here," Shirley shakes her head.

"I *am* just a girl." My voice is little more than a squeak.

Abruptly, Bianca raises her hand, like she did at Kalin. "No, you're a cage."

When her magic hits me I fly backwards, backwards into the dream.

I'm on a hill under a dark, cloudy sky. Lightning sparks in the distance, and the valley that stretches out before me is as grey as the horizon. Alayna stands here too, her heavy cloak battered by wind

I cannot feel.

"Overlord, show yourself!"

We're in the centre of the stone circle up at the monument. Those are the same words that I heard when I held the dowsing rods.

Other cloaked figures are present too, and they shift and murmur when no response comes. Lightning flashes again, closer now.

"If you are all powerful, as you claim to be, you should not fear us!" Alayna calls into the night.

Kalin materialises behind her, pale and waxy with dark, hooded eyes. The others gasp as she spins to face him.

"I do not fear you." He smirks. It's an expression I've never seen him wear before. "Though I know what you intend. The question is, are you able to use them? You see, I studied the orbs while I had them. You haven't had much time since we last saw each other. I do believe most of it was spent running." He smiles at that, the smile of a predator.

Alayna doesn't falter. She turns to look out at the valley again, at the place where Grahamstown will one day be.

"Turning your back on your enemy, are you certain that's wise?" Kalin mocks her. She closes her eyes. He lifts a staff as if to strike her, but she throws a spell into the darkness. It hits something. The something shrieks and Kalin disappears.

The cloaked figures surround the spot where her spell landed, and in the centre a man convulses, electricity running across his skin. Kalin.

"How?" he pants.

Alayna doesn't answer. She lifts her arms and starts to chant. Glowing orbs rise out of the ground in every colour of the rainbow. They spin around the stones, slowly at first, then they pick up momentum until they're spinning so fast that they form a white wall of light around us. Their power whips up hair and cloaks as if we're standing in a hurricane.

Kalin's muttering too, but his voice is sucked away as the others all join Alayna, raise their staves and chant. The words pound into him, as if they're striking him with physical force. He cries out in silenced agony.

"In the name of my people, the people you enslaved!" Alayna shouts at him. "In the name of all those who have suffered under your rule, I call upon the power of the orbs to bring justice upon you! I curse you, not with death, for death is too forgiving. I curse you, not with torture, for in torturing you, we are no better than you are. I curse you with life. By the sacred three, for this many centuries you will reflect on your crimes without the magic that has corrupted your heart."

While she's talking, Kalin struggles and he manages to get to his knees. He glares at her then, and I see the darkness of the Overlord in his eyes, and I feel the fear that she must feel, but she doesn't waver.

"By the power of the orbs, under the watch of the Guardians, it shall be done."

She draws her hands together, and as she does, the orbs circle closer and closer and closer until all the other Guardians are outside of their ring. It's just the three of us — the two of them, really — within the light. The crazy wind dies down, the orbs sink to the ground.

Then Kalin pulls his hands free.

Alayna only manages to take one startled step back before he raises a hand and cries out one final curse.

The big, golden orb — the Keyflame — responds to his command. It flies from the others and slams into Alayna's stomach. She doubles over. Her people run to her and Kalin laughs.

The scene fades away, and Bianca's face hangs directly before mine. Someone is holding me upright – probably Sibu. Bianca's fingers close around Kalin's necklace and she yanks it from my neck.

No!

I try to struggle against Sibu, but he's strong and I'm still disorientated by the dream. My limbs are cold and stiff. "I don't understand."

Bianca walks away from me. "The orb you saw him use, the Keyflame, it was what trapped his power. The original Guardians meant to destroy it as soon as the spell was done so that he could never again have access to his ability. So, with the last power available to him, he sent it into the person they all held most dear. In order to destroy his power, they'd have to destroy her."

"Sent it *into* her?"

"To put it bluntly, in that moment she *became* the Keyflame. The Guardians should have destroyed her, but they didn't. They should have destroyed the child she later carried, but they didn't. As long as the curse held, Kalin did not have access to his power no matter what form the Keyflame took. And why should they make the difficult choice, when they could let it fall to someone else instead?" Bianca's fingers flex.

Now I'm starting to understand, but I don't want to. "The child she carried?"

"The Keyflame passes down the generations."

The revelation hits me like an orb to the stomach. "You're saying *I'm* the Keyflame?"

"You're the Keyflame. I should have realised it before. He put so much effort into protecting you and keeping you safe… but we thought… we believed the Keyflame was destroyed eighteen years ago."

"Eighteen years ago? Eighteen years ago, when that car crash killed my mother."

And I died too. For a few minutes I *was* dead.

My gaze finds Shirley. She's standing with the others now. She has the decency to look remorseful, at least.

"It was reported in the papers that all three of you died. Mother, husband and baby," Shirley says. "You must understand, I took no pleasure in it. It was the price that had to be paid to ensure that he could never rise to power again. Three lives in exchange for countless others."

A wave of horror washes over me. Darren didn't lie about me being in danger now that people knew my father's real name. *These* are the people he changed his identity to escape.

Does Darren know?

"This is the year that it ends," Bianca says. "On the last day of October, it will have been three hundred years. The curse will break. And if you live, the Overlord gets his power back. I'm sorry Lilah, I truly am, but we can't let that happen. Please understand, it's important that you understand, we don't do this out of any malice, but out of necessity."

"No!" I try to struggle against Sibu, but his grip is like iron. I kick and manage to catch a shin. He stoops a little, but only holds me tighter.

Shirley gives him a barely perceptible nod, and he lets go. I try bolt for it, only to find I can't move at all. She has me in some kind of magical vice. She holds her hands out as if in supplication, but whatever she's doing makes the magic stronger.

"It will be quick." Sibu's voice is thick with regret. "And painless."

As Shirley walks forward, I'm forced to walk backwards, back towards the lake. I scream and twist and cry for help. My throat burns, my blood pumps hot. Blind panic is supposed to make me stronger, isn't it? I slide down the bank. Icy water wets the bottom of my jeans just like in Hogsback.

They all chant, like a fricken cult. In my terror, I cry out Kalin's name, even though without the necklace I know he has no way to find me. Surely it will be like in the movies – a dashing, last-minute rescue, a desperate battle? I search the dark treeline for any sign of help. The water is so cold it hurts. Shirley walks me deeper, and deeper still, until the water is splashing at my throat and around her knees. The magic lifts briefly and I have flashbacks of the bullies trying to dunk me under. I dart to the side, but instead of magic on the back of my head, a weight wraps around my whole body.

I look down to find rusted metal chains twisting around my limbs. They're slick with weeds, like some creature from the depths.

"Sibu help me, help me please. You know this isn't right. I

didn't do anything. I'm innocent. Please," I babble.

The chains tug me towards the middle of the lake. My feet lose purchase. I'm floating then I'm sinking. The last I see before I get pulled under are the figures on the shore holding hands and chanting.

Then I'm under and the water is so cold my lungs constrict, and my last breath gets pushed out in an array of tiny bubbles. I'm surrounded by darkness and cold, and the knowledge that I really am at the centre of Kalin's universe, but not for any of the reasons I could have hoped. That truth is as cold and dark as the water.

I've never been able to hold my breath very long, but I believe right up until the water floods into my nose, that someone might save me. It stings and forces me to choke, and as I choke, I suck in only water. I thrash wildly, but there's absolutely nothing I can do to save myself.

34

 right light against my eyelids. Murmuring voices. I'm so
heavy. Am I still wrapped in chains? *Am I dead?*

A hand touches my cheek. "Lilah?"

Even my eyelids feel leaden, but I know that voice, and I force them open.

Everything's so bright and out of focus, but I see Kalin's eyes, gentle and kind, with none of the darkness that was there in that dream.

And I see his smile as he says, "Thank the Greats," and brushes hair from my forehead. He *did* save me.

My chest fills with warmth, but then the memory of his true motives surges through me and I go cold.

"Move aside." Sukwini's face comes into view as Kalin obliges.

She takes my chin. "Look at me, my dear." She shines a torch into my eyes, and I jerk away. "Pupil response is normal. Do you recognise me?"

Where am I? I'm not at the lake. There's a white ceiling. A window behind them, a crocheted lampshade. This must be the Settler's Cottage and it must be daytime.

"Give her a moment to get her bearings, Nabelo," Kalin says.

He's kneeling at my side, and he's holding a… blood bag. A red tube snakes from it, twists around my arm, and ends at a needle that pierces my skin. I jolt involuntarily at the sight. I didn't bleed; why do I need blood?

293

"It's all right," Kalin says. "You're safe."

"You mean the Keyflame's safe." The words come out a broken croak. "How did you save your powers this time, Overlord?"

He starts at my use of his title.

Sukwini holds a glass to my lips and props up my head to help me sip it, but I turn my face away.

"I didn't," Kalin's voice is paper thin.

"I'm afraid the Guardians succeeded, my dear," Sukwini says.

Succeeded… but… does that mean I…? My sluggish brain grasps the concept. I died. I was dead.

"How? How am I here?" My heart feels as if it's making up for however long it wasn't beating before by beating overtime now, so hard it's like it's going to burst out of my chest.

I try to sit, but my head spins, and Sukwini eases me back down.

"Your friend, Darren," Kalin says. "He brought me your… brought you to me, here. He retrieved you from the lake, but he was too late. He thought, I suppose correctly, that I might be able to do something."

"What did you do?"

But I think I already know. I can't look away from the blood bag.

Sukwini presses a cold stethoscope to my chest. I only notice then that I'm wearing one of Kalin's shirts. It's soft, in the way that old clothes often are, but it's the bleached white of a hospital gown.

"Kalin tells me you're aware of his curse?" Sukwini asks.

"Immortality."

The last red is dripping from the bag, down the tube, into my arm.

His immortality transferred to me.

Sukwini follows my gaze. "It would not have worked on an ordinary human, but since you carry Kalin's power, and since you're part Fae—"

I glare at Sukwini. "You should have told me what I was. You should have told me what really happened to my mother."

She sets down her stethoscope and takes my hand in both of hers. "I wanted you to have a normal life."

"Normal until the Overlord takes back his powers. What happens to me when you take the Keyflame?"

I expect Kalin to offer some defence, but he just sits there.

"My dear." Sukwini pats my hand. "The ritual itself will not harm you. It should not even hurt. And once it's complete, you can continue on as if nothing—"

"Then what?" I pull my hand free. "You take over the world and rule side by side? You're one of them, right? A fairy?"

"She's a descendant," Kalin says. "Like you."

"Do you have magic?" I direct the question at Sukwini.

"She's a healer," Kalin answers.

Of course. It makes perfect sense. She healed Lani right in front of me. Although it's not exactly what I would have expected from someone bent on world domination. She gives Kalin a meaningful look. Something silent passes between them.

"What?" I say, hotly, because I've had enough of their secrets.

"Energy cannot be destroyed." Sukwini watches Kalin while she speaks. "But it can dissipate if what contains it is no more."

Like ghost guide Tod said. I'm not sure what she's getting at.

She leans forward a little. "His magic is dangerous. No one should have that level of power. Since it passes down the generations—"

"Nabelo, don't," Kalin urges.

She ignores him. "The only way to be rid of his power, for it to be destroyed for certain, is if that which carries it is destroyed."

"Me."

"The other Guardians believe that, yes. However, there is another way. On Halloween night, Kalin will become mortal once more. His powers will be restored to *him* then."

I'm about to tell her that I know this, when I suddenly understand.

I look to Kalin for confirmation, but his head is bowed.

Only one of us can live. That's what she's saying. One of us has to take his power to the grave. I can't draw breath; there's a bubble pushing against the inside of my chest, like I'm drowning again.

"No." I shake my head. "No, that can't be the only way. Transfer it into an orb again, a jar, something that isn't him."

"I'm afraid that's not possible," Kalin says.

Maybe it's a trick. He's just pretending to go along with this so he can get his power back. I almost want him to be evil, so I know he's not going to die so soon.

But nothing about the way he's hanging his head says scheming Overlord. "What you witnessed between us in Nabelo's lodgings that day wasn't an argument," he says quietly. "I was reassuring her that just because I… just because…"

"I'm assuming nothing has changed?" Sukwini echoes his words from that day.

He stares down at the bed. "Nothing's changed." He wets his lips. "Nabelo, would you mind giving us a moment alone? I owe Lilah some answers."

"I'll go make us some tea."

Kalin doesn't speak until she's out of the room, and when he does, he delivers his words to the bed covers and not to me. There are dark marks beneath his eyes and his hair is clumped and dirty, although the sunlight behind him makes it look like spun gold.

"Eighteen years ago, I was told the Keyflame had been destroyed. It was almost a relief. When my sentence was done, I would be mortal and remain free of my power. The Guardians would likely end my life anyway, as a precaution, and I planned to succumb to them willingly. I was enjoying my final year, filling it with lectures and concerts and reading. Then I read something I shouldn't have." He glances up at me. "Your notebook."

He returns his gaze to the ugly quilt. "I saw my life reflected in your drawings. Still, I wasn't certain. So many stories have been based around the myth of my people. But when I saw your mother, when I saw the shield knot around her neck, and that face… and when you told me about the accident, I knew. I went to see Nabelo at the crack of dawn that first morning, and she confessed the truth. She was there the night the Guardians killed your mother, intending to kill you. She was the young nurse at the scene who saved the baby, her friend's child. And she hid you. I was never supposed to know. We were never supposed to meet. My power would be returned, and I would die before I knew I had it. That was the promise, Lilah. The one you asked about, that I made to Nabelo that morning. My promise was to die."

The whole time I listen to him, I hear at the back of my mind, like the beating of giant wings, *he's going to die, he's going to die, he's going to die*, but still the last sentence thunders through me.

"You asked how I knew Nabelo. As a Guardian, her role was to watch me. When she saw that I was trying to help, trying to atone, she offered me her assistance, as a healer."

I recall her words: *Tell me this is no different from any other poor, destitute creature you've brought to me in the time we've known each other.*

Kalin sets down the empty blood bag. "From the time I knew who you were, all I wanted was to protect you from the other Guardians. I didn't intend for— I don't want my powers back, although you have no reason to trust me now." He starts to peel away the tape that's holding the needle in place. I grimace, expecting a sting, but he's so gentle that I hardly feel it.

"I deserved to know all of this," I say.

"You're right." He still can't meet my eyes. He eases the needle out and presses a cotton ball to the place where it was. His hands are warm and steady, even if his voice is not.

"The truth is, I was a coward. So many times, I wanted to tell you everything, but I…" He sighs. "Do you know how I spent my 323rd birthday? My final birthday?"

I shake my head again.

"In the study, next to you, working on jewellery and talking about books. I couldn't imagine anything better. I was selfish. I thought that if I told you that I was going to die— if I told you that I was the monster who'd haunted your dreams— I'd lose you. And my selfishness put you in danger. I'm so sorry. If this hadn't worked… If this hadn't…"

Even with everything that's happened, I can't bear to see him hurting.

"It did work. I'm fine."

His gaze flicks to mine. I see a look of desperate hope there. Hope that I could forgive him, perhaps.

Bianca said he was good at this – lying, mind games, seeming like something he's not. He's had three hundred years to plan everything, to practise that expression. Wouldn't this be the perfect strategy? The *really* long game. Send the Keyflame into his enemy and wait. Wait three hundred years to make her descendant fall in love with him, so they're determined to follow him to the end, to surrender the power. And when everyone expects him to die, he rises again.

Maniacal laughter and all.

But why try so hard to do good? He was a regular at the soup kitchen long before we met. He never misses a weekly visit with George. He could have killed Dumi's men, but he didn't, and he didn't hurt Bianca when she attacked him, even though he could have.

He shies from me again and busies himself straightening out creases in the bedclothes. "I've done everything wrong. If I hadn't spent so much time with you, the Guardians would never have grown suspicious. When they asked me about you, I tried to lead them away. I thought if I couldn't be with you, at least I could protect you. But all I did was leave you vulnerable. And when I managed to save you from those thugs, I sent the journalist there. I didn't know there was a tape, I didn't check. And your father's name— it wouldn't have been revealed if I hadn't… and they wouldn't have had that final piece of confirmation. The magic only worked as long as they didn't have the name."

"What magic?"

"Nabelo's spell. To hide your father from us, from the Fae. I knew his face, but couldn't place it. You recall? Initially I thought it was because of his celebrity. They would have all thought the same. Until they had the *name*. The name that I gave them through that tape."

Dad's jet-faced watch pops into my head. Dahlia said jet was good for hiding from the "evil-eye" and Kalin asked for it specifically when he was building his Lilah-defence necklace. Maybe it was part of the spell. Now I'm questioning everything. Is anything in my life untouched by this conspiracy?

"If I had handled things differently, you wouldn't have run to them." Kalin's voice goes thick. "I never meant to frighten you. That is the very last thing I would want."

The emotions that chase across his features are raw and painful to watch. They can't be a lie.

"You didn't give them the name. Dumi did," I say.

His Adam's apple bobs. "Even now, when you should hate me most, you're trying to reassure me."

The door opens and Sukwini comes in with a tray of tea.

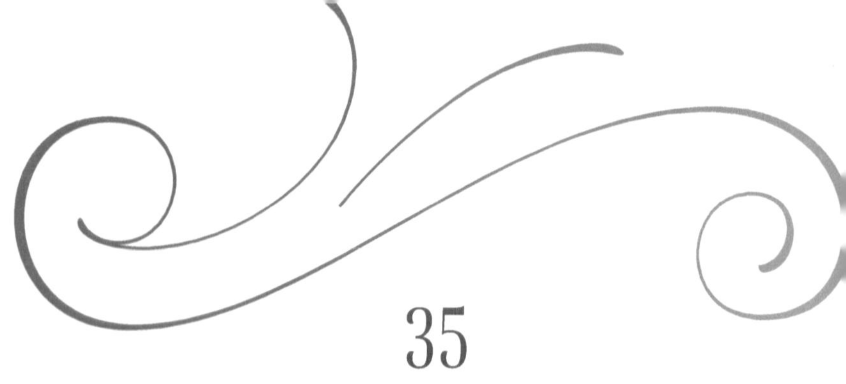

35

I sip a strong cup of rooibos while we discuss my death. Sukwini wants to make sure the Guardians continue to believe I'm dead. She will arrange for a body, like she did the first time I died. Someone will be dredged up from the lake and, with the bloating, only DNA – which she'll switch – will confirm it to be me.

"And I change my name like Dad did, start life somewhere else?"

"You stay here," Kalin says. He hasn't touched his own tea. "After Halloween – you'll be safe and may return to your old life."

"And you'll be dead."

He nods. How can he not know how he *is* my old life? Or at least a large part of it. I felt his absence keenly while he was away. A lump forms in my throat when I try to imagine that feeling, but knowing for certain that he's not okay and he'll *never* come back.

"Lilah, at first your father's legal troubles were an ill-timed frustration, but perhaps we can tie your murder to Dumi," Sukwini said, yanking my attention back to the subject at hand. "Following from that video, it shouldn't be too difficult to convince a judge."

My stomach sinks because I hoped that maybe this whole Dumi thing was tied to the Guardians, and that would also melt away on Halloween night.

Sukwini is looking at me expectantly, but it's Kalin who replies. "No, I won't frame someone innocent."

"They're hardly innocent."

"They didn't murder her. Besides, how is she to return to her life after the ritual if we do this?"

The two of them continue this back and forth over the logistics of my demise. I should be invested in this conversation, I should care, but I feel oddly detached.

Kalin huddles in a patch of sunlight, switching his gaze between his mug, the bed, and my mother's childhood friend, but never me. What's the date? How many weeks do we have until Halloween? How many days? How many hours?

"What's the date?" I ask, startling them both.

After a beat, Sukwini offers a small smile. "You were only gone for a few hours."

That doesn't help. That's not why I want to know. "It's July." The last shift I was supposed to work was Sunday, the 9th. "That's less than four months. That's…" I do quick calculations. "That's a hundred and fourteen days."

"Lilah…" Kalin tries for soothing.

"A hundred and twelve." It's Tuesday. "What's the time?"

I cast around for my phone before remembering that it's probably at the bottom of a lake. Sukwini has a wristwatch; I make a grab for it. The large, old-fashioned face shows it's nearly ten thirty.

"What time's the ritual?"

Kalin stands and paces away. Is he going to leave the room? At the door he pauses with his fists in his hair. "You shouldn't have told her," he growls.

"Yes, *you* should have." I try to swing my legs off the side of the bed, but Sukwini catches me. "A hundred and twelve times twenty-four. That's… two thousand and—"

"Shhh…" Sukwini takes my mug and tries to wrap me in a blanket, but I fight her.

"Seven hundred and—"

Kalin doesn't move. My head starts to throb. There's a burning behind my eyes like I'm going to cry. "Two thousand seven hundred and twelve." That's how many hours he has left. "You can't die. You can't surrender to them." My murderers.

"Lilah, my dear, it has to be this way." Sukwini wraps me in her arms. Warmth floods through me. Her magic? It's like a sedative, stroking my senses, coiling around my aching heart. "It has to be this way; the power is too dangerous."

"You should have left me. You should have left me dead." I don't mean it. I don't want to be dead. But Kalin's head snaps up then, and he finally looks at me. Really looks at me, as if I've cursed him.

Sukwini's magic is like the drug the kidnapper gave me. It makes me heavy. I never ever wanted to feel this way again and I fight, I fight so hard to stay awake, and the whole time, Kalin stares at me like I just slapped him.

﹌

I wake in the middle of the night, twisted in sodden bedclothes. My muscles ache, and my skin is cold with sweat. In my dream, the duvet was the chain and it was pulling me down, through the icy water, into hell.

The cottage is cold and dark, but the air around me is packed close and shimmers with hidden life. Ghosts, fairies, the shadow-fingers of the tree outside. My head pounds.

"Kalin?"

I can't make my voice loud enough to call him. I try to get up, but my limbs won't obey; they only tremble.

"Kalin?" I whimper again.

The walls loom at me, at Escher-esque angles. Something brushes past my arm and I shriek before I realise that it's Fatso. His eyes flash in the dark as he runs to the window and hops onto the ledge. Even he is running from whatever's in this room.

I was meant to die. I am unnatural. I don't belong here.

Hell is coming to claim me.

Tentacles of fear reach up from my gut, closing my throat. I am alone, I am entirely alone, and I can't do anything. I'm going to die here, and no one can save me.

The door bangs open, and I scream again. Then Kalin is there, on his knees at my side and he's wrapping my shaking body in his arms.

He feels my forehead and curses. "I was afraid of this."

Kalin frees me of the bedclothes, and I cling to him in terror. "Am I dying again?" It's all I can do to force the words out.

"You have a fever. Sometimes this happens after blood transfusions when the blood is incompatible."

It's not what I thought, but it might be just as bad. "My blood's attacking your blood."

"Yes. Your immune system is feisty."

He tries to stand, but I don't let him.

"I'm going to call Nabelo."

The breath exits my lungs in a rush. She's a healer. She can help. I let Kalin go.

The room pinwheels, and I rest my head back on the pillow. When I wake again, Kalin is leaning over me with a glass of water. "I can't get hold of her. She's on duty at the hospital. Here, take this."

Two ordinary tablets sit in the palm of his hand. I recognise them as Panado. Paracetamol. The thing you take when you have a mild headache. How are they supposed to help?

I don't have the strength to argue, so I swallow the pills and drink the water. Kalin presses a cool cloth to my head, and it feels amazing. In the silence of the room, I can hear him breathing. I can feel his fear as if it's flowing down his arm, through the compress, into my skin.

"Talk to me," I plead.

"What would you like me to say?"

Anything to chase away that awful silence, that sense of impending doom – a doom solid with the knowledge that one of us is going to die soon. "Three hundred years, you must have some stories to tell."

"You may have to narrow it down for me."

"When did you decide to stop being evil?"

He strokes my hair back. "I don't know that I decided to stop being evil... The 1930s changed me, I think. They changed everyone alive to see them."

"Were you here?"

"No, I was in the States."

"Fitzgerald?" I say weakly, which is my way of asking whether he was there to enjoy the roaring '20s featured in *The Great Gatsby*. Books make good short code between the two of us.

He smiles faintly down at me. "Yes. Fitzgerald. Then Steinbeck."

The Grapes of Wrath. A novel about the horrors of the Great Depression. I imagine an immortal, travelling the dust bowl, nothing but bones, but unable to die. I reach for his hand and squeeze it in my clammy palm.

"Don't pity me, Lilah. Of the people I met during that time, I am the least deserving of your sympathy. I have seen people with nothing give everything for each other. I have witnessed hundreds, thousands of deaths that were undeserved. Yet mine, that was most deserved, was denied."

His low voice washes over me, as dark as the room around us. I'm eager to move onto happier memories.

"What happened after the Depression?"

"You know your history; you know what happened after the Depression."

World War II. So much for cheerful. "Did you fight?"

He shakes his head. "I made a vow to never take another life. I was a medic."

My fever presents me with images of Kalin running across a beach, while bullets rain down, to drag a prone soldier to safety. I see him holding a different blood bag, his cool hand pressing against a different forehead. My chest warms. Of course he'd be a medic. The Kalin I know would be a medic.

"You could be making this up," I mumble, giving voice to thoughts as they come into my head. "'Cause I'm the Keyflame, and you want me to trust you."

"I could be," he confirms.

I slip into dreams again. Instead of metal chains and hellfire, there's dust and landmines.

Kalin wakes me with another glass of cold water. "I still can't get hold of Nabelo. Lilah, you have to fight this."

I'm in the dust bowl, the sun is too bright and my head aches. "I don't know how," I tell him.

My blood *is* fighting. That's the problem. An army of sand rises in my mind. His curse is going to kill me after all.

Icy water against my face shocks me out of my vision. He's pressing a fresh, dripping towel to my head. "Lilah, listen to me. I don't know… I don't know that we can rely on Nabelo to get here in time. You're burning up. You need to fight."

He lifts my hand to his lips and kisses it. Then he whispers something against it. Is he *praying?*

Kalin is scared. He's really scared. I thought he was frightened before, but my condition must have worsened.

I'm sinking into sand again, then I'm back on the beach with the mines. All is still – there's no sand army. The waves are frozen in the act of hitting the shore and the sunlight glints off them bright white, stinging my eyes. I lift a hand to block out the light, but it does nothing.

It's not the sun. It's a glowing orb.

It's the Keyflame, hovering there across the water, large enough to obscure my view of the opposite shore. It pulses with a heartbeat. The beat becomes the ticking of a clock. Like a great grandfather clock. Like a mine. I should be terrified of it, but it's so beautiful, and the way that it feels on my skin is the way that I feel when I'm with Kalin.

A voice talks to me, but I can't make out words. It's the wind brushing against my eardrums, but some desperate, vulnerable part of me imagines it's my mother's voice.

"The choice is yours," the whisper seems to say. "Yours. Yours."

I don't know what she means, but I want to follow her across the sand, I want to see her.

The sand is hot as needles. I race across the beach in the direction I think the voice is coming from, but it stays as distant.

Another voice sounds from far away. Kalin. He's pleading with me to fight. Fight what?

The choice is yours.

I don't understand, but I know I don't want to die. I look down and find that I'm now knee-deep in the burning sand. I need to do something. If this is a dream, maybe I can imagine some sort of weapon, some way out of the sand.

I picture Alayna. Strong, beautiful, powerful. I roll my shoulders back and raise my arms, imagining I have her ability. Sand swarms around me, bright and hot as fire. I imagine power, and beams of white light rush at me from the Keyflame. They flicker through the spectrum and settle on what I know, more than see, to be ultraviolet. There's so much of it, so much power. I gather it around my arms in spindles like cotton candy.

It awaits my instruction, a whisper of a word. But what do I tell it? The heat is unbearable and the only enemy I have is my own damn body.

In response to that thought, a figure rises out of the sand. I think it's the sand army I saw before, but it's not. It's me. She's wide-eyed and she hugs a book to her chest.

It's strange to see me like this again. This was the girl who arrived in Grahamstown, whose greatest fear was not fitting in. I hated her for being weak and innocent. I pushed those parts of her away and buried them here.

"Lilah, you need to let Kalin's blood do its thing. It's unfamiliar and scary, but it's going to help," I tell the vision of me. And even though I'm in the middle of a fever dream, I feel silly saying it.

She surprises me by responding. "It's not your magic. It doesn't belong here."

"Yes, it does." Am I really trying to argue with my immune system? "We're going to die if you keep fighting it."

Lilah reaches out a hand to touch the magic, like a curious child reaching to pet a dog for the first time. The magic rises at this, and it reaches towards her. A tendril of power twists around her outstretched hand as if to say, "How do you do?"

She takes a step backward. I see the fear in her. I recognise it. "No! Don't run!"

Her eyes dart from side to side. She's caged by my request. Then she stares straight at me, and sand shoots from the ground to either side of me. It forms itself into big heavy chains. Chains made of stone. And they twist around me, just like the chains in the lake.

Again, the magic tries to go to her, but this time I sense it wants to fight. I hold it back. I don't know what will happen if I let the magic attack me, but I'm not going to find out. My throat blazes, and it feels as though those big stone chains are slamming into my skull. The temperature rises further.

"What are you doing!" I demand of myself.

"What if he's evil? What if this is all part of his plan?"

I can still kind of hear Kalin's voice coming from far away, pleading with me to fight. And almost as if it's in response to him, the echo of that other voice. *The choice is yours.*

"You don't know what will happen if the magic takes control!" Lilah shouts at me, with her fists bunched up. "The magic doesn't belong here."

Lilah is too frightened to listen. This is the fear that plagued everything I did for years, and now it's made manifest. Again, I have to hold the magic back as the chains tighten around me. I can't breathe. The light across the water is shining brighter.

I'm going to be killed by my own hallucination. *My* hallucination. This is *my* dream.

I try to think of something comforting. My room back home –
Dad sitting on the bed teaching me to read. My favourite teacher's
classroom, where she let me hide from the bullies under the guise
of helping her with admin. A stuffed animal I had when I was six.
Tammy telling me about *The Lord of the Rings* and us playing Kiss,
Marry, Kill and shrieking with laughter. None of these things ease
the tightness around my chest or the aching in my muscles. None
of them stop the chains from pulling me down. Too much has
happened since then. That reality is too far away.

So, I think of the cottage, the warm kitchen, Fatso sitting on
the counter. I think of a pile of books, thoughtfully chosen for my
enjoyment.

Frightened Lilah hugs herself and slides down onto the sand.

I think about the way it felt when Kalin hugged me, and how
he smiles when I understand one of his literary references.

"The world is frightening and unpredictable," I tell myself, and
I don't want to sound like a trite Facebook meme, so I search for
something I can say to reach her specifically. "It's like the night
before a big exam, when you want to throw up because you're so
scared you won't know the answers. But somehow, we always make
it through, right? We've gotta sit this test."

I let the magic go to her. It unwinds itself from my arms and
flows in rainbow shimmers towards her. At the last second, she
stretches out her arms and accepts it.

The sand starts to crumble away from my legs. The tide draws
out. Kalin's voice grows louder. I open my eyes, and he's still
holding my hand to his lips whispering, "Please don't die."

"I won't," I tell him.

Then I sleep deeply and dreamlessly.

36

I don't know how long the darkness has me, only that I wake to the sound of rain pouring down outside and raised voices in the kitchen.

My stomach clenches with dread, although I can't make out who's arguing.

After a few false starts I manage to get to my feet. I lean against the door to steady myself, and when I press my head to the wood, I can hear words.

"Please don't kill her." Is that… Darren?

"If she knew what was good for her, she'd run." Kalin's voice is dark enough to send a chill right through me.

"I don't understand why she did what she did." Darren's pitch ramps up. "I don't understand any of this. She's not a bad person."

"You claimed to love Lilah when she was lying dead in your arms, and yet here you beg for her murderer's life."

I feel like I'm still dreaming. Darren talking of love? Kalin plotting revenge? I can picture him on the other side of that door in the same cloak he wore when he was interrogating Alayna.

"She's my sister."

"Mmm." Kalin's voice moves further away, towards the study. "I knew another of your blood once. A coward who turned on his queen the instant his own life was in peril. You should consider yourself fortunate I didn't take *your* life when you first arrived here." Each word is heavy with barely contained rage. "If you wish her to live, I'd suggest you keep that woman from this place. Need I remind you: she is mortal and I am not?"

I need to go in there, I need to see this man speaking with the Overlord's tongue, I need to see Kalin in the act of his alter ego so that I can believe it in my heart.

"I can't. She—" Darren's strangled words are cut off by knocking on the kitchen door. My every muscle tenses.

The sound of keys in a lock, a pause, and then Bianca's voice. "I thought I'd do you the courtesy, Overlord."

"What's this?" Kalin's voice.

The sound of a paper packet crumpling.

Silence.

I so desperately want to know what's happening that I stoop to the keyhole, like some kid in a spy story. Through the small gap, I can see Kalin holding a chain. He's perfectly still.

It's my necklace. My shield knot.

"Darren?" Bianca is still in the doorway. "What are you doing here?"

Darren must be near the fridge. "I was looking for Lilah."

Kalin doesn't move.

"Well I'm afraid there's been an accident," Bianca says.

It's no courtesy. She's here to gloat. *Your power's gone, Overlord.*

Kalin lashes out and grabs her by the neck, so suddenly that she doesn't have the chance to cast a spell to protect herself.

"Stop!" Darren launches himself into my field of vision, but before he reaches them, Bianca kicks Kalin in the stomach and a burst of magic sends him skidding backwards out of view.

The lights flicker. Water splashes across the floor. The cutlery drawer flies out of its place and crashes against something, or someone, I can't see. Probably Kalin. The water is flooding the kitchen, leaking under the bedroom door. Where's it coming from?

"What do you mean to do, Kallen? Drown me?" Bianca calls.

Darren slips and slides across the floor towards his sister, through water that's now ankle-deep. It's too deep to have come from the taps so quickly. Kalin must have used magic to bring in rain from outside.

"Stop this!" Darren shouts. "Whatever you're doing, stop it!"

Knives rise into the air. The lights flicker again.

Oh no. That's what Kalin intends. He's harnessing the electricity like he harnessed the water. He's going to electrocute them. He's going to kill them both.

I fumble for the door handle as the knives fly. If Bianca knows I'm alive she'll kill me again. There's another mighty *wham!* as Bianca levitates something into the wall.

"You can't win!" Kalin cries. "Do your worst, Guardian. Do your absolute worst."

He marches into view again. No black cloak, no magical staff, yet a hundred percent Overlord. "You will die for what you've done!"

He raises his arms, the way he did in the warehouse. I can almost see the raw power surge into him, ripple along his frame. Behind him, Darren pulls his body weight back then surges forward, aiming for Kalin's middle. Darren doesn't stand a chance.

"No!" I slam my hands against the door at the same instant as the electricity snaps from Kalin with a crack so loud it drowns out my voice. Bianca lifts into the air, Darren too, and something invisible barrels into Kalin, collides with his chest and knocks him down. He lands hard on the kitchen floor in a giant splash. The electricity flashes across his skin and dissipates.

He stares at me, his chest heaving.

Bianca and Darren still haven't landed. Darren is also looking right at me, frozen like a cartoon ghost and just as pale. But Bianca's eyes are closed, her face peaceful as if in sleep or worse.

Kalin staggers up.

I open my mouth, but he shakes his head wildly and makes a cutting motion in the air. He steps forward and I scuttle back.

A crease forms on his brow. Then he comes towards me again, in two large strides. I'm still too weak to struggle as he scoops me into his arms and carries me back to the bed.

My heart is thundering. I push him away. Even that feels like so much effort. Fatigue claws at my mind.

"Let them go," Kalin says softly. "I'll deal with them."

"No. You can't. You can't kill—"

"I won't. I promise I won't." He touches my cheek. "You're going to exhaust yourself. You need to let them go."

"Let them go?" What does he mean? I'm not doing anything.

"The water isn't charged. You can set them down safely."

Set them down? I breathe out, and I hear the smack of bodies hitting the floor. Kalin nods, then sweeps out and shuts the door behind him.

What just happened? Did I… did I do magic?

I hear Bianca's heated voice, but Kalin's is low and calm. I hear him apologising, I hear Bianca kicking the water. Darren says nothing. Kalin asks Bianca to leave, so he can grieve in peace. At first plaintively, then a little firmer, and she finally goes.

"You managed—" Darren says a moment later.

"Not now. Go with your sister before I lose my temper again."

I hear splashing as Darren follows. The door is closed and locked behind them.

Then Kalin comes into the room again.

We watch each other. I breathe in and out, in and out.

Eventually, he says, "You're feeling better?

"You were going to kill them."

He sits down beside me, looking directly ahead of him. "I wasn't." He shuts his eyes. "It wasn't enough to kill them. I wanted to ensure that they thought my grief genuine."

"All I have is your word."

"And, evidently, my power."

A jolt runs through me, as truly as if he'd shocked me. Somehow, I lifted them into the air and held them there, out of the water. Somehow, I accessed the power stored inside the Keyflame.

"Because of your blood?" I guess.

He inclines his head. "I'd imagine so."
"This has been one hell of a week."
His expression doesn't alter. "That it has."

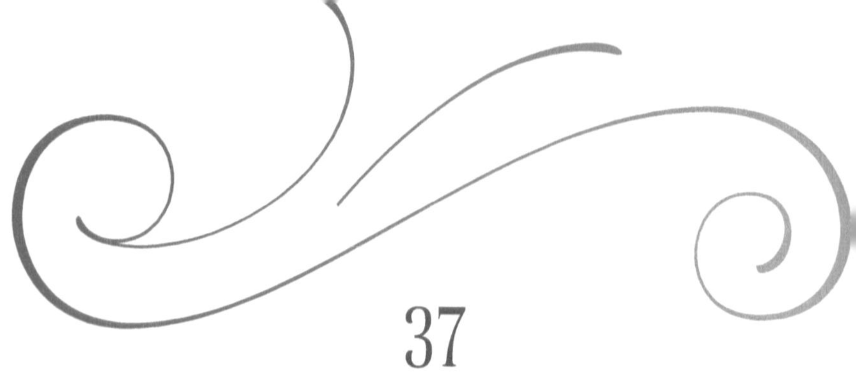

37

$\mathcal{K}$alin dials Sukwini from the phone in the study, and I fetch a bunch of towels from the bathroom. When I return to the kitchen, he's saying, "No, I don't think he'll tell them anything… I understand, but he brought Lilah here to be resuscitated. Presumably he won't wish for her to die again."

They must be discussing the risk of Darren knowing I'm alive. I throw down the towels and swish them around in the icy water. They don't make much of a difference. Kalin managed to draw a lot of rain in here.

"I know. It was a calculated— Yes, but she was already aware of what little I'm able to do… I'm not sure, I suppose Lilah told her."

My insides squirm. Sukwini must be lecturing him about using magic in front of Bianca.

"Nabelo… Nabelo, listen, it's the end game. The time for secrecy has passed. Now we need only wait… All right. All right, I'll check… Yes, I'll let you know… All right, stay safe."

Kalin sighs as he sets down the receiver.

"You didn't tell her about me having your power."

"No, I didn't."

So much for *the time for secrecy has passed.* "Why?"

He leans against the doorframe, watching my half-hearted attempts with the flood. Cutlery is still strewn everywhere, and the drawer is shattered near the fridge.

"It seems I made a mess of the place again, and after you went to all that trouble cleaning it for me."

He's avoiding my question. His gaze slides away from mine. A gash below his cheek leaks crimson and there's a matching red slash across his bicep that makes my heart squeeze. Bianca's knife work, no doubt. He touches his arm gingerly.

"Does it hurt?"

He nods. "But not for long. Let me help."

He closes the distance between us and takes my right hand. Then he steps behind me, exactly like when he was teaching me to cast the fishing line. His arms encompass me and his stubble presses against my cheek as he positions his mouth near my ear.

"Visualise the water being pulled into the centre of the kitchen." His breath brushes my skin. "Imagine it being sucked there by a vortex."

I can't visualise anything but him. His body is so warm. My pulse skitters. I still want him. And I still trust him. No part of me here, now, can believe he's evil.

"You didn't answer my question," I croak. "About Sukwini."

He turns my hand. "Pull the water with your mind."

"Kalin."

"Nabelo's a Guardian. It's her duty to destroy my power. When it was dormant in you that was one thing… but now…"

"Now you think she might hurt me?"

"Now I think I've already come too close to losing you, too many times, to take a risk like that."

The air leaves my lungs.

Before I can formulate a response, he prompts, "Focus on the water."

"I can't cast magic. I'm not a fairy."

"You already have, and you are. Although, we don't use that term. Close your eyes."

I do, then I'm only more aware of him. I smell his herbal scent, feel the shape of him pressed against me.

He chuckles low in my ear. "Your magic is curious."

"What does that mean?"

His grip on my hand tightens. "It means focus on the water. Reach towards it with your mind."

I picture the magic like it was in the dream, an invisible tendril extending to brush along the surface. It seems so crazy. Like someone's going to jump out of one of the rooms with a hidden camera. Then I feel an icy splash against my calf and my eyes shoot open.

The water is moving where I imagine touching it.

I blink, look at Kalin. *Did he see that too?* His face is so very close to mine. He gives me that half-smile. "See, you're a natural. Now, try bring it to the centre."

I imagine arms opening wide, wide enough to encircle the whole room. Then I pull them inward, and the water moves, just as Kalin said, into the middle of the kitchen. It's exactly what I saw him do at Hogsback and it's *easy.*

"Good," he murmurs. "Now, siphon it up into the sink."

"Siphon?"

He lifts my hand and the water rises too. "Not all of it. You're still weak," he cautions. "A little. Show it where you want it to go. Make the rest follow."

I suppose he means like a tap flowing backwards, but how do I hold liquid with my mind? He adjusts his grip on my hand, and I falter. Some of the water splashes out of my control. Kalin folds my fingers into a loose fist. "I always found that it helped to form the hand into the shape you intend. Alayna called it a nervous habit. Here. Pretend you're holding the water in your grip, lift it up."

The first time I try, nothing happens because I'm blinded by ridiculous jealousy directed at my great-great-great-great… great-great? Grandmother. Instead of picturing myself holding the water, I'm picturing her standing in his arms like this, but I control myself, and the next time I try, I pull a stream of water up towards the sink.

"It's a little bit like using a mouse," I say, more to myself than to him.

"Mouse?"

"Computer mouse. Control by proxy."

"Ah. I'll take your word for it."

"You've never used a computer?" I know he doesn't like modern things, but how has he managed to submit assignments?

"I have, but not by choice, and I've certainly never felt the same level of control."

"Luddite."

He snorts.

I concentrate on guiding the water up to the sink. Getting it into the sink is a little trickier. I pause, try tip it. Some of it falls into the plug hole, but I'm still holding most of it. Kalin takes my other hand, opens my palm and guides it upwards. It's like I'm a conductor.

"I'm sure this was a scene in *Fantasia*," I say, but he doesn't respond. His lips brush against my neck and heat shoots to my core. All thoughts of water fly from my mind and the whole lot of it crashes down and splashes up to my bare knees, but I hardly care because Kalin turns me in his arms. For a dizzying moment I think he's going to kiss me again. Then he ducks his head and draws a shaky breath. Neither of us moves for a long while.

Then, at length, he says, "Nabelo asked me to find out how much you told the other Guardians."

My heart contracts. "I didn't mean to tell them anything. I only wanted a place to… I thought I was losing my mind and maybe they could confirm I wasn't. I told them I thought you used magic to save me. That's all. I'm so sorry."

He shakes his head. "The fault is mine. I should have warned you about them as a matter of priority. You'd learned I was the evil immortal being you've been having nightmares about your entire life; I can't blame you for seeking refuge with my enemies."

"She came here, and she hurt you, because of me."

"I was never in danger."

"She broke your workspace, your books, your—"

"Merely things."

"You were frightened."

To that he offers no response.

"I'm sorry," I repeat.

"I will accept your apology if it will ease your conscience, but it's unnecessary." His gaze drops to the floor again and he steps away from me. "You should rest. I'll clean this up."

I am tired, but there's no way I could sleep now. "No, I can do it."

He scans my face. Then he smiles. "Of course you can. Together then?"

Without waiting for my answer, he goes to the other side of the room. He does a complicated movement with his hands. Water starts to pool around him, like at Hogsback. He lifts his arms, and the water rises with them. His eyes are closed and his brow furrows with strain. I mimic him. Now that I know what to do, the water comes rushing to me. It lifts when I imagine it lifting, it pours when I imagine it pouring. My water is already draining away while Kalin struggles to reach the sink.

I stare at my hands.

I did that. I did magic. "How long will these powers last?"

Kalin finally manages to tip his water down the plug hole and he wipes sweat from his brow with a sleeve. "I'm afraid this is new territory for us both, but I imagine… a hundred and twelve days."

The bottom drops out from my stomach.

My elation dissolves completely. He's referring to the date of his death that I calculated. The date that his power returns to him. I rub up and down my arms. I'm still wearing his shirt and it only comes down to mid-thigh. Now the adrenaline has worn off and he's no longer lending me his body heat, I'm freezing. "I have access to your power now. The Keyflame was an orb, there must be some way I can make it go back to being an inanimate object we can destroy?"

"I'm sorry. I've looked. I've been looking." He waves towards his study.

Was that what all the research was about? All the hours he spent holed up in there, the strange illustrations in his books? *You are my project, Lilah.*

"The orbs were forged on another world," he says. "They were brought here by the ancient king. They are relics made from materials we don't have here, using magic we've long forgotten. No doubt Alayna, with an entire kingdom at her disposal, tried and failed. And every Keyflame, every Guardian, since... There is only one solution here."

It hurts. It hurts so bad. I hug myself, but it does nothing to ease the ache.

"I brought this fate upon myself, Lilah." He's read my expression. "I am the one who created this curse. It is right that I am the one to end it."

I recall his laugh when he threw that spell at Alayna. "Why did you do it?"

"The curse?" He frowns. "I wish I could tell you it was part of some great stratagem, but the truth is shamefully petty. She had defeated me. I couldn't save myself, but I could give her an impossible choice. Either her line became custodian of my power, or her line would have to die."

"You had no guarantee she'd have children."

He inclines his head. "But I knew it was likely. She was the only descendent of the great Nuadha. Bloodlines are important to my people. It would be no easy thing for her to intentionally end that line."

My line. I'm the descendant of some fairy hero. "And who are you descended from?"

"A blacksmith." I wait for him to elaborate, but he leaves it there.

"So where did your power come from?"

He sighs. "The Overlord would have told you it was fate."

As he says that, I see it in my mind. A dark throne room, crows nesting above. The Overlord stands upon a dais, lecturing his generals, and his prisoners, about how his rise was inevitable.

Memory or imagination? I shiver.

"You're cold. Come, I'll light a fire."

He takes me through to the study and wraps me in the brown blanket. The blanket smells like him from all the nights he's slept here. I huddle into it while he orders pizza.

An hour later, I'm curled up next to a roaring fire with a full stomach and two empty pizza boxes. Kalin must have known how ravenous I'd be, because he ordered extra.

He pulled the chairs from the kitchen into the study so we could sit opposite each other, using the one chair as a table. It's far from a sophisticated dining arrangement, but it's cosy and he's close enough that our knees would knock if mine weren't tucked under the blanket.

He appraises me, and I'm not sure what he could be thinking until he says, "It's the magic. It's hungry."

"You make magic sound like a living thing."

He shrugs. "It's not, but… you'll see what I mean."

"That's ominous."

"It's meant to be." He shifts position and focuses on his plate. "I never guessed this could happen. It is something of a relief, knowing you can defend yourself if required. At the same time, magic is like…" He pauses to search for the right analogy.

"An extra limb?" I offer. An invisible limb that can do stuff, sometimes on instinct, the way you might reach out to stop a fall. Sometimes with intention, like lifting the water.

"A parasite."

I raise my eyebrows.

"You take psychology. Consider the subconscious. How much goes on in your body that you're unaware of? You don't think about breathing, you don't think about the movements your fingers make when you're nervous. I believe you're even unaware of the way you brush your hair from your face when you focus."

I pause with my hand on its way to do just that and I bunch it into a fist instead.

"Magic has access to your darkest places, all your secret desires. You may think you have control, but it's never complete."

I recall the violet magic wrapped around my dream arms. *You don't know what will happen if the magic takes control.* A chill travels down my spine. "You're saying your magic made you evil?"

He stares into the flames. "It made me capable of things most people would have only fantasised about. I had no fear; my magic could protect me from anything. The ordinary, everyday, concerns of others had no effect on me. I was above them all. At the height of my power, I didn't even need to focus a clear thought on enacting my will. It would just happen."

"Background tasks."

At his curious look, I say somewhat sheepishly, "Sorry, analogy from this century again."

"You're starting to make me think a robot uprising is imminent."

"Oh, it is." I shift closer. "Is that what you meant about my magic being curious? It was reaching out without my knowledge?"

His expression transforms into one of amusement. "The experience was not unpleasant."

"What did it do?"

"I... probably shouldn't say."

Heat flushes up my neck, and I must go bright red, because Kalin laughs.

"Not that."

It's good to hear him laugh after all the recent tension, but I'm still mortified.

He leans forward and turns my arm so that the wrist is facing upward. With his gaze on mine, he trails his index finger down the centre, from elbow to palm. I shut my eyes. The sensation is intense. Goosebumps prickle across my flesh, and my breath catches. He does it again, and warmth blossoms in the pit of my stomach.

"That." His voice is low. "But all over."

I swear. He laughs again, because I don't think he's ever heard me curse. He repeats the action, tortuously slowly. I know he's toying with me, but I don't want him to stop.

I reach out with the imaginary hand, with my magic, and touch his hair. I trail my attention down his jaw line, caress his neck. He sucks in a breath and I know he's feeling these things as if I really was doing them.

"Two can play at this," I say.

"You have an unfair advantage." There's a huskiness to his voice I haven't heard before.

The magic is fun, but I can't feel his skin, and I want to. I want my real fingers to slide beneath his collar, I want my real lips to taste him.

He gasps and his hand closes over my wrist. "Lilah, stop."

I open my eyes to find his cheeks flushed. The power withdraws. "Did I do something wrong?"

"No. I just… I don't know that this is a good idea."

"You think using the magic will corrupt me?"

"No. Not that." He lets go and moves his chair back. "Things are complicated enough. I… I'm going to take a shower."

The phone rings while he's away, and I know better than to answer. When he comes in again, he checks the number and returns the call without saying anything to me.

I gather from his side of the conversation that it's Sukwini with an update on the state of my death. Kalin nods along and makes affirmative noises.

We're back to him looking everywhere but at me.

"Yes, I spoke to her," he says eventually. "Only what she saw in the warehouse." He glances at me as he says this, but only briefly. A pause. "Yes, I think she'd like that, but give it a little time."

When he hangs up, I ask what it is he thinks I'll like.

"Nabelo will bring your things. Whatever you had stored at your residence."

I have at least three boxes of clothing and books that went into the storeroom when they rented our rooms out to Festival attendees.

"When is she coming?"

"She thought after the memorial service would be best. So probably after term starts. Do you have enough here to get by until then?"

Memorial service. The rollercoaster that is this day plunges downwards again. My friends will all think I'm dead. They'll mourn for me. And Dad... I feel like I'm suffocating. Kalin goes out of focus, and when I don't answer, he goes to the other room.

I don't expect him to come back, but he returns barely a moment later.

"This might cheer you up."

He's holding... *that looks like my phone.* He passes it to me. It *is* my phone. The last thing that Dad gave me before we were separated. "How do you have this?"

"It was on the table when I came home."

The battery's dead, but it's *here.* I was so swept up in Darren's panic, I didn't even realise I left it. Like me, it's been granted a reprieve. I can message Lani and Jess and Tammy. I can let them know I'm okay, I'm just lying low.

"Please don't," Kalin asks.

My head snaps up. Did my magic do something to Kalin while I was distracted?

He looks at me imploringly. "I know you wish to spare them pain, but it's safer for everyone if no one else knows you're alive."

"So, you can read minds?" Nothing would surprise me now.

He sits beside me. "No, but I can read your expression."

I turn the phone over in my hands. "When will they find out I'm dead?"

"The authorities will get a call about a body in the lake tomorrow, but it usually takes time to get an ID. They'll inform next of kin first. So possibly a few days."

I laugh hollowly. "You sound like you've faked a lot of deaths."

"I have."

I look at him so fast my head spins.

"My own?" He says it as if it's the most obvious thing in the world. I suppose it should be. I mean, no one's supposed to live as long as he has. Certainly not without ageing. How many names has he gone by? How many identities has he assumed?

"Is your name really Kalin?"

He inclines his head.

"But the Guardians call you Kallen."

"Yes. Kallen is the original pronunciation. As you might imagine, I'm no longer fond of it."

"George still uses it."

"Mmm," Kalin confirms. "You try explaining correct pronunciation to a linguistics professor." A ghost of a smile lights his lips, and he shakes his head. "It means Mighty Warrior. He said it suited me better. If only he knew…"

"How much *does* he know?"

"Oh, I've told him all of it. But what he chooses to believe… that's another story."

The one friend he didn't lie to. If I wasn't the Keyflame, if my life hadn't been in danger, would he have told me anything at all?

I return my attention to my phone. "If you were worried about me messaging my friends, why didn't you just hide it?"

"I wouldn't do that. You have little enough agency in this situation as is."

He's leaving it up to me. He's trusting me to do the wise thing.

Somehow that's worse than if I didn't have a choice at all, because I don't want to prove that trust ill-founded. But I don't want my friends to go through that grief either.

I turn my phone over and over. "Don't worry. It needs a charge before I can do anything with it, and my charger's a prisoner of war."

"There's a store in High Street that sells them. I'll get you one tomorrow."

"You don't have to do that."

"Wouldn't want that brain chip to explode."

I appreciate the attempt at humour, but I can't find it in me to smile.

"Besides, there is one person you could still communicate with."

"I don't know that I have that much to say to Miss Sukwini."

"I mean Darren. You'd need to be careful, but since he knows you're alive, I don't see any reason you shouldn't speak to him. I'm sure he's anxious to hear you're well again."

I'm not quite as sure. Darren took me to that place. Darren knew something was wrong or he wouldn't have suggested we run away together.

"Darren doesn't have magic, does he?" I ask.

"No."

I turn the phone over again. "But his mother and sister do. Isn't that strange?"

"Magical blood is complex and the power was dying out even in my time."

I imagine what it must be like, to be surrounded by people more powerful than you, and I do feel a little bad for him. Maybe he didn't even know before the dam. How difficult it must have been to find my body in the dark, how cold the water, how heavy the chains without any powers to help him lift them.

He was courageous, if too late. Maybe I do owe him my gratitude.

38

Kalin called the magic a parasite, but during those first days of my incarceration in the Settler's Cottage, I come to think of it more like a pet – well, not like a goldfish or kitten. Like a Rottweiler. Most of the time, it lies dormant at my feet or is happy to fetch apples for me from across the room. Then there are the times I'm anxious or startled, and it tugs at its leash, ready to rise to my defence. Like when the police come to question Kalin about my death and I have to use magic to hide myself, while simultaneously stopping it from attacking the detectives when they make accusations. Even then, the magic doesn't feel particularly alien or malevolent. It's familiar, like it's always been there.

Kalin, on the other hand, feels increasingly distant. He withdraws into himself. He doesn't offer any more guided lessons. He doesn't so much as touch me. It's a mission to get more than two words out of him, and it hurts. I try to distract myself.

I research fairies. How many of our human myths are true? Difficult to determine when Kalin refuses to answer questions.

I know he can lie because he lied to me about everything for months. I know that he has no aversion to iron. He said his father was a blacksmith so that rules that out. I suspect that there is some truth to the thing about electromagnetic interference though. You'd be hard pressed to find Kalin near a radio wave. Exhibit A: That tape deck in his car. Exhibit B: The landline telephone. Exhibit C: No TV.

Then again, that could just be Kalin being Kalin.

The garden is walled on all sides, so it's safe for me to go and dig in the dirt, to pull weeds and try to discover the hidden flower beds. It's the closest I can get to leaving the house. I draw, I get through my to-be-read pile for the first time in years, and I teach myself to bake.

But none of it eases the chill around my heart when I try to engage Kalin in conversation and fail. He's not unkind. It would almost be easier if he was. He makes sure I have everything I can think to ask for, even extravagant baking supplies that I only realise are expensive once I see the price stickers. I ask him if it's because of his approaching death, but he just shakes his head and changes the subject.

He spends most days out of the house, most nights in the study. And in the absence of his company, my thoughts dwell in dark places. I worry about Dad. I imagine all the worst ways he could have found out about my death. I worry about my friends too; I think about the Guido's staff trying to smile at customers while grieving. I ache for them when conscious, my gut heavy with guilt, and toss and turn with memories of chains when sleep overwhelms me.

During the second week, Sukwini comes by to drop off my things. The house is full of fragrant haze from the oven when I sense her coming up the path. I flick on the kettle and get the nicest teacups out – they're mismatched, but at least they aren't chipped.

I'm so relieved to see another person I almost hug her.

Instead I say, "I made cake, and scones, and biscuits," as I show her in. "And please take some with you. Kalin doesn't really eat, and I'll never finish them before they go stale."

Her eyebrows rise as she takes in how every surface is covered in food. "Keeping yourself entertained, I see?"

I plop down opposite her. "Trying my best. You haven't seen the study."

"What's in the study?" she asks cautiously.

"Drawings, mostly. I found some YouTube channels on mapmaking, but I ran out of paper. Kalin said he'd get me more, but I think he forgot."

We talk a bit about the past few weeks. Well, I talk. She seems concerned when I mention Kalin hasn't been around much and asks me questions I can't answer about his whereabouts. "He's probably feeding puppies or something."

I manage to keep up the bright, cheerful front for a good while, but Sukwini's large, sorrowful eyes are a constant reminder that everything is not all right, and eventually I know I have to broach the subject I've wanted to discuss with her.

"I've been thinking… Well, you know how much time I have for thinking," I say, as I pour her a second cup of tea. "About Dad. I know that you can't tell him I'm alive because the prison calls are always monitored, but you helped him fake his own death before, right? So, I've been thinking, maybe you can drop a hint—"

"My dear—"

"No, wait. You say something that only he understands. Nothing direct, but he's very intelligent and you could—"

"Lilah, I'm afraid that's—"

"If you could just let me finish." I pull the piece of paper where I scribbled ideas out of my pocket and spread it flat on the table.

She grabs my wrist. "No, Lilah."

My magic rises, ready to come to my defence, but I keep it down. "Just give him a little hope. See here," I point to one of my suggestions. "You could reference the spell you did, or you could say something about the watch—"

"I said, no."

Her magic beats against my skin, and it takes all my control to stop mine from responding. I bite down hard on my bottom lip.

"I'm sorry, my dear. We cannot afford any additional risks at this time."

"If you don't do something, *he* might do something stupid. I'm all he has!"

"I'm aware of that." She's still holding my wrist.

Of course she's aware. It's all her fault he's alone. "Why didn't you warn her?" *My mother.* "You must have known what they planned. You must have known they were going to kill me. Was it *too risky* to warn her?"

My words hit home. Sukwini sits ramrod straight. "I *did* warn her," she says. "And it was my warning that led to her death. She attempted to run, with you."

I stare at her.

"Your mother was protected by ancient charms woven by generations of my family. I was raised to guard her *always*. She was the one fated to carry the Keyflame to the end, to face Kallen in that final moment." Sukwini stands and glares down at me, and for the first time I understand her true power. She is a healer, yes, but something else too. A warrior. "She was destined for that purpose. She was never meant to *breed*."

I see the daughter of the MK spy in her hardened gaze. My stomach is a knot, I can hardly breathe, and I'm holding my power so tightly to me, because I know, *I know*, that Kalin was right. What will she do if she sees it?

"My mother was supposed to kill Kalin?" I squeak.

Sukwini closes her eyes. "There is magic at work here that even I do not fully comprehend. You come from a very long, very powerful line. The only way to preserve it was for the Keyflame to be protected, despite the danger, and for the bearer to face Kallen the night of reckoning. In the moment he became mortal once more, in the moment before he could use his power, she was to kill him. She was raised to do it, and I was raised to protect her until that day. And I failed."

Does Kalin know this? Or does he think, as I did, that Sukwini was a Guardian like the others who went rogue when she learned the Keyflame was her friend?

She sags back into her seat. "That night, the night everything changed, I realised that I had two choices. I could take you and raise you and train you as your mother had been. But you would likely never have enough power to defeat Kallen, as the blood – after so many generations – had now mixed with a human."

The way she says *human*… Have all my ancestors on my mother's side been Fae? If so, I'm not just part Fae, I'm *half*-Fae. What does that even mean? I can't think about it now.

"But you didn't choose that," I say carefully to Sukwini. "You cast a spell on Dad and hoped for the best."

She lowers her chin. "I would reveal you on the night of the ritual, and the element of surprise would allow us to defeat Kallen."

"What did you tell Dad about all this? Does he know about the ritual?"

She nods, and her hands wrap around her teacup. "He knows that the ritual is the only way to ensure your continued safety, and that in being there that night you will prevent a great evil from rising, and that you will not be in danger. All of this is true."

I try fight back the betrayal that fills my chest. Dad knew. He knew he was bringing me into Grahamstown to face this. My whole life, he's known. Pushing me to get good grades so I'd be enrolled a year early, lecturing me about keeping myself safe, turning me away from my fantasy drawings. He forced me down this path and never once considered telling me why.

I tighten my fists. "No, it's *not* true. Kalin isn't evil."

"The power must be destroyed," Sukwini says.

"It will be destroyed when he dies. Regardless of when. What's wrong with letting him reach old age?"

"It's too much of a risk."

"Kalin's a good man now. He can control it." *If I can control it, he certainly can.* A reckless energy races through me, in defiance of my grief. "I know he can, I know because—"

The study door swings open. "Nabelo, thank you for stopping by," Kalin says.

Sukwini spins around to face him, nearly toppling her chair.

I didn't even know he was here. I thought he left before I woke. I feel the blood draining from my face, and I don't make eye contact with him as he comes into the room and says to Sukwini, "Please take some of these pastries home with you."

Sukwini stares at him. No doubt she's going through everything she said that she might not have wished for him to hear. Then she seems to get a hold of herself. She waves a hand in the air, and my boxes from res come floating up the garden path to set themselves neatly in the doorway.

"This is a difficult time for all of us." She gets to her feet and addresses me with a parting comment, "I believe it's best if you don't do too much thinking."

It's a warning, and it sends a shiver right through me. "Yeah, I'll stick to cakes."

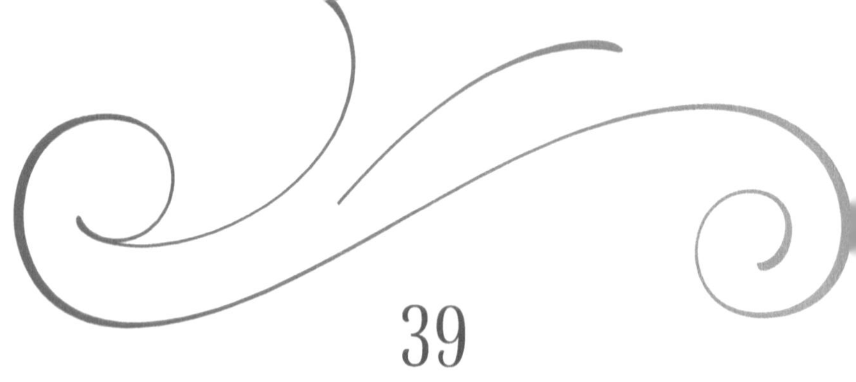

39

As soon as Sukwini's gone and we're alone in the kitchen, Kalin says, "What do you think you're doing?"

So, he *was* listening in, and he did interrupt specifically to stop me from revealing my – his – power. *Nice to be trusted.* I square my shoulders. "You heard her. She's sworn to protect me. She won't hurt me."

"You don't know that."

"She needs to understand the power's not going to make you the Overlord again."

"You don't know that either. You're stating a lot of supposition as fact."

"It hasn't corrupted me."

"You've had it for a matter of days!"

"And I'm eighteen. I know nothing of magic or control. You've got three hundred years of penance behind you."

He runs his fingers through his hair, which is hanging loose at his shoulders, and I fall silent even though I have more to say on the subject. Not for the first time, I find it difficult to imagine him so much older than me. He's gathered years to his name but hasn't matured. He's still a young man, with a young man's mind, and a young man's moods – he's just lived a very long time as a young man.

I bite my lip and dare to ask, "Did you know? About my mom being bred to kill you?"

He takes one of the scones and stares at it. "No. Although it does make sense."

"I'm glad that Sukwini didn't raise me to be your assassin."

His eyes meet mine for barely a moment before they go back to the scone. "How's Darren?"

"What?"

"Never mind." He turns, no doubt to return to his cave for the rest of the day.

"Why do you want to know about Darren?"

"I don't particularly. It was a clumsy attempt to change the subject."

"I don't know how Darren is."

Kalin pauses. "You haven't spoken to him?"

"Turns out it's hard to put, 'You got me killed but thanks for retrieving my corpse' into a message without sounding a little passive aggressive."

The scone becomes incredibly interesting again. "You should speak to him."

"Why? Have you seen him?"

"No."

A one-word answer. What a surprise.

"You mean like ask him to be a spy?"

"No." He takes another step towards the study.

"Kalin! If you want me to understand what you mean, you're going to need to use words."

"I'm trying to think ahead. November first. You're going to be pretty much alone. Might be nice to have someone to comfort you, that's all."

A little *oh* sound leaves my throat. It feels like I just fell into a pit full of snow. "You're playing matchmaker?"

"It's hardly matchmaking. I'm the one who walked you home, you recall, that night in February."

When I was bawling over Darren. My ears go hot at the memory. "A lot has happened since February."

"I'm well aware." He sighs, then says to the scone. "How is it that two weeks can be harder than all three hundred years that went before?"

A void fills my chest. "Tell me what I'm doing to make things so hard and I'll stop."

"You're not doing anything, Lilah."

"Is it the magic?" The last time we were close was in his study when I teased him with it, when he told me how hungry it was. He hates his magic, and now it's a part of me.

He appraises me, his expression inscrutable. He's finally looking at me, and now I wish he wasn't. I fold my arms to ready myself for his response. I don't know what I'll do if he voices my fears, that he can't stand to be near me now this power thrums through my veins, that I repulse him.

"It's not the magic," he says at last, setting down the scone, but the way he says it is hardly a relief. It's something else, then. Maybe he's just had too much of me. For all my waitress training, I'm still awkward, I'm still a dork. And he's stuck with me. The last few months of his life, and he's trapped with some annoying teenager who keeps making heart eyes at him.

He starts towards the study again, but my magic jerks out and slams the door. He stares at it a moment before slowly turning back to me. *Did I do that intentionally?* I think I did. I need answers, no matter how hard they are to deal with. I can't bear another hour with this rift between us, let alone several weeks.

Outside, the garden is alive with birdsong. Sunlight streaks through the space between us in wide beams, caught in the flour from my culinary escapades.

Kalin stands there like a golden statue.

"Tell me. Tell me what changed between us?" I fail to hide the anguish in my voice.

That breaks the spell. He comes alive, marches towards me. I flinch, but he pauses a few feet away, his gaze travelling over my face.

"Kalin?"

He reaches out a hand and touches my nose. I can't breathe. *What is he doing?*

I recall that night, the one he just mentioned, the look that passed across his features as he guided my own finger to my nose. He has a similar look now, brow slightly furrowed, as he gently… *dusts it off.*

There's flour on my face.

How ridiculous I must look. It must have been there the whole time I was talking to Sukwini and now while trying to have this serious conversation.

He smiles. His cheeks dimple and he ducks his chin and laughs.

The sound flushes through me like hot chocolate. It's light glinting off water, a forest pool. It's the sound of me losing my heart.

And I'm two seconds from reaching for the open packet of self-raising and smearing it all over in a desperate attempt to prolong the sound.

"I heard what you said to Sukwini." Kalin's solemn voice brings me back to myself. "About me being good." His chin is still ducked as he asks, "Do you… is that something you truly believe?"

I nod.

"I wish I could believe it too." He's close enough that his presence prickles against my senses. His aura, I suppose Dahlia would say.

"What's stopping you?"

"I am the Overlord."

"Were. You *were* the Overlord."

"I know what I am capable of."

"*Used to be* capable of."

He shuts his eyes. "Lilah…"

He draws a deep breath. I wait. His aura shifts and brushes against mine. I feel more than see how it glisters dull silver; how it's weak and depleted and tired, so tired. The touch of his energy washes over me like static electricity, and mine responds, rising to caress it, to comfort it. My magic and his magic. My will and his. They twist around each other; they vibrate against my skin – our skin – like a thousand soft feathers.

Kalin pulls his back. "Nothing changed." His hands curl tight around his palms, as if they hurt. "I told Nabelo it wouldn't affect me." He's speaking through gritted teeth. "I told her I'd still sacrifice myself to the Guardians, that I was still willing to die, that nothing had changed. I thought I could control it, like I thought I could control my magic." Then, in a much weaker voice, "I don't want to fail again." And his whole body slumps.

"Kalin, what are you talking about?" I touch his shoulder and he stiffens beneath my hand.

"Isn't it obvious?"

"If it was obvious, we wouldn't be having this conversation."

He lifts his gaze, so that our eyes meet, and the pain I see there knocks the air out of me a moment before he says, "I love you."

The three words I never imagined, never dared hope I'd hear him say. They fill the kitchen and hang in the air with the sunbeams. I gape at him.

"I'm in love with you," he states, as if I didn't hear it the first time. Or maybe he sees my astonishment and knows the words aren't registering. "I'm in *love* with you, Lilah, and that love is like a quagmire. Every moment I spend with you, I get sucked deeper. I thought it was bad when you first lived here. Then I had to go and kiss you, and since then every time I look at you, that's all I want."

He turns from me again, claws at his hair. "I know it's wrong. You don't have to tell me. I'm older than you, not human, not at all like… and besides, the small detail: everything horrible that's ever happened to you is my fault. I have no right to feel the way I do. It should be enough for me that you live. It will be enough. I just need… I need space."

He takes one step towards the study. That's all that he manages before I grab his arm, swing him around and press a kiss to his lips.

He reacts with a startled "Mmph!" Then his arms are around me and a wave of magic thrills through my body, setting every one of my nerves alight. My head fills with music and the taste of his lips. His hand slides to the nape of my neck and I pull him closer even though we're already pressed together, closer so that our bodies are practically fused, so I can feel the heat of him against me through our clothes, so our magic mixes and swirls around us.

When our lips part, he's panting, and he's staring down at me like he's not sure what just happened.

"I love you too," I whisper.

I've known it for a long time, but his body jerks, and he looks at me with such intensity… and confusion.

"It can't be that surprising." I smooth out the creases around a button on his shirt, suddenly self-conscious. "I mean, we did kiss before."

"That… that was before you knew." He caresses my cheek and I look up into his amber eyes. "When Darren brought you to me, he said… I thought that the two of you… he implied…" It's not like Kalin to struggle for words. Finally he settles on, "You went to him, when you learned what I was."

Oh, Kalin. "I went to him because Shirley owns a bed and breakfast."

Someday I'll tell him about Fest and the ghost tour, but not right now. This is too precious, having Kalin in my arms. It's only a matter of time before he pushes me away again, starts listing reasons why this is a terrible idea. I stand on my toes to nuzzle his neck, to breathe him in.

"This isn't fair." His voice is hoarse against my ear. "How am I supposed to resist this?"

He turns his face to catch my lips in another dizzying kiss. It's slow and deep and I melt against him. My universe is that kiss and the steady thrum of my pulse in my ears, until his hands slide down to my hips.

Then a new need sparks within me, molten and undeniable.

"You're not. You're not supposed to resist it," I say, short of breath. "Screw the Guardians. And Sukwini, if she wants you to die. We can fight them together. You can live."

Kalin makes a sound low in his throat. "Don't. Don't say that. Don't offer me this."

"Why?"

"All I've ever wanted. To be whole again, to grow old, to have you." He shakes his head. "I don't deserve it."

I cut him off with another kiss and I curl my fingers into his shirt, keeping him close. If only he could see himself as I do, see the difference between what he was in the days I dreamed about and what he is now. His hands drag up my sides, lifting my blouse. The cool air is a delicious contrast to his warm touch. My magic is impatient, and it sweeps over him, touching areas he may not want it to. He whimpers as I pull it back.

Something shifts between us. I meet his blazing gaze. One heartbeat. Two. Then his lips find mine again, and his kisses are frantic. I was the instigator, but I'm no longer leading this dance. He washes over me. His scent – herbs and now musk; his taste – like sunshine and magic; and his energy – drowning out everything that's not him. I don't realise he's backing me towards the bedroom until I'm pressed up against the door. He lifts me, so I'm pinned between it and his body. One particular part of his body makes itself known. Heat floods up to my cheeks.

"Lilah, I want you," his voice is raw with need. "But we don't have to, if you don't… we can wait."

His breath puffs against my throat, then his lips brush against my neck, sending a fresh thrill down my spine.

"No." Waiting is the very last thing I want to do. Each day we've already waited feels wasted. My nerves are a tight bundle in my stomach, but they're over-ridden and over-ruled by all the other sensations crashing through me. I want more. I want everything. I reach for the door handle.

I wake to a dark room and the memory of being curled up against Kalin's body, floating weightless.

Something's missing.

I reach for Kalin, but my fingers only brush empty sheets.

He's missing.

Fuzzy with sleep, I wrap myself in the quilt and pad through to the kitchen. It's dark and cold, but there's a light shining from under the study door.

I nudge it open. "Kalin?"

He's lit the fire, and he's seated in front of it with his back to me. His shoulders are still bare, and he doesn't turn to look at me. Instead, he lifts a hand. One of his largest tomes rises off a shelf and shoots across the room into his palm.

My stomach flips.

"Kallen," he corrects me. He stands, completely naked. The firelight plays over his skin, and it glows bright as if there's a halo of magic around him so strong that I can see it with my bare eyes. "That name would likely be more appropriate."

He stretches out his other arm, and curls the fingers of his empty hand. Every book, every piece of paper in his whole study, lifts into the air. His muscles don't even strain.

I reach for my magic automatically. It's not there.

My magic *is missing.*

I grasp for it, scramble for it, and I back away from the man before the fire who I know then has stolen it. No, *claimed* it. Claimed it and claimed me.

The Overlord has his power back.

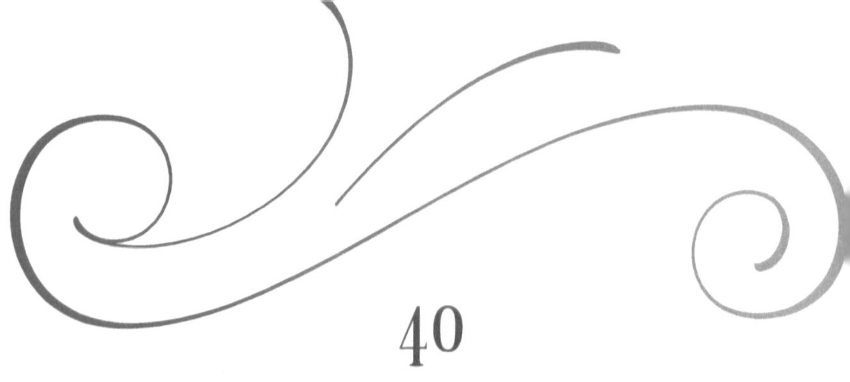

40

The Overlord turns his head to me. His expression is blank. "It seems we performed a spell."

My mouth is dry, and my heart slams in my chest. The books are still hovering. Is he going to throw them at me, like Bianca threw them at him? But even she couldn't lift them all, all at once. He could kill me. I should run, but I'm frozen. I can't even make my tongue move.

His eyebrows draw together. "Or did you?"

I can do nothing but stare at him, my beautiful Kalin, coursing with power. His eyes are dark with it, his pendant glints in the firelight, and though I know he is no taller than he was before, he seems to dominate the entire space.

"Did you tell the magic to do this?" he asks.

"Do what?" I manage to say, and my voice shakes.

"This!" He slams down all the books, and I squeak. He moves towards me. "Lilah, answer me. Did you do this? Was this some misguided attempt to cajole me into fighting for my life? Because if you did this, you *must* undo it."

I hear the words, but they fly about my brain, unable to attach themselves to one another.

He's inches from me. "Lilah, did you command the power to return to me?"

I shake my head.

"Are you certain?"

I nod.

He slumps. "Perhaps you did it subconsciously? Perhaps you were thinking about protecting me?"

That doesn't sound like the Overlord. "Kalin?"

He closes his eyes. "It's not your fault. I didn't mean to frighten you. No, that's untrue, I *did* mean to frighten you, but it was wrong of me. You wouldn't do this intentionally."

It *is* Kalin. The relief that floods through me is so potent that my knees go weak, and emotion wells up into my throat.

"You have your powers back?" I whisper, even though the answer is obvious.

"It would appear so."

"Does that mean… Is the curse broken?"

"No." He flicks a finger towards his work counter, and a knife rises a little. It's slick with blood, and my heart gives a thud that feels just as hard as all those books landing. He must have cut himself to see if he'd heal. "No, it's worse than that. It's far worse than that."

He turns away from me and paces back to the fireplace. "When I was the evil sorcerer who ruled over your Kingdom of Night," he refers to the Otherworld by the name I had written on the map in my res room, "I may have had spies everywhere, I may have controlled the trading ports, I may have had power beyond that of any other living person, but one thing I did not have was immortality."

Now he does.

"If I do not go up to the gateway on Beltane, if I am not present for the ritual before the orbs, the curse will never break."

My stomach twists at his words. Before I can think of what to say in response, he turns to me. "I stand before you a man who is capable of absolutely anything. Including living forever." His voice goes dark again. "You should run. You should flee. If I wanted to, I could wipe you across the room with a thought. If I wanted to, I could remove your free will, keep you as a pet until the day of your death, and then use my blood to bring you back, again and again and again."

I hug myself, reacting more to his tone than his words. "Do you want to?" I swallow. "Do you want to do those things?"

His look softens, as does his voice. "Of course not. But if I did—"

"But you don't." I reach towards him and I stop just short of touching him. I can't sense it anymore, but I'm touching his magic. In my mind I see that silver aura, now brilliant with strength and vitality. "Maybe you can control it this time."

"*Maybe*? You'd rest the fate of the entire world – multiple worlds, perhaps – on a maybe?"

I force myself to meet his eyes, now a deep chocolate brown rather than the warm amber they were before. "You became the Overlord out of anger, didn't you? You sought revenge for the razing of your village, for the grave injustices committed by Alayna's father?"

He inclines his head without breaking my gaze.

"You said before that the magic responds to your subconscious desires. Things are different now. *You're* different now. Maybe your subconscious is also just hungry for scones?"

He doesn't smile, but he sighs and draws me into his arms, which I take as a victory. He still feels the same as he holds me, and I imagine that I do sense the brush of his magic, wrapping me in a safe cocoon.

"You've had a shock," I say in my most soothing voice. "Come to bed, things will seem better in the morning."

Maybe when he wakes, he'll realise this isn't a bad thing. Now he has a chance to prove to the Guardians that he's not evil. Now he can survive past the ritual that will make him mortal again. Now we can be together for longer than three months.

He presses a kiss to my forehead, and instead of going through to the bedroom, he guides me down onto the settee where he holds me until I fall asleep.

I turn over and my hand lands with a thump on the floor, jerking me awake.

"Kalin?"

The light through the study window carries the blue tinge of dawn, and embers still glow in the hearth. I run a hand through my knotted hair, and the movement dislodges something that was lying next to my head. A piece of paper floats down to the ground.

I recognise Kalin's handwriting before I manage to get it close enough to my sleepy eyes to read.

Dear Lilah,

Please forgive me. I remain a coward.

Ice flushes through me and I fly into a sitting position.

"Kalin!" I call, hoping that I'm wrong about the rest of the letter. But there's no answer, and as my eyes slide down the page, I feel increasingly sick.

You deserve better than this, but if I'd waited for you to wake, I know I would have lost my resolve. My small life is not worth risking the world. It's not worth risking you. I need to be somewhere where I cannot hurt anyone and will not be tempted to give in to this affliction.

Know that I have had a long life, and that for one night it was a good life. Thank you for giving me everything. I'm sorry I could not be more.

I scramble up and nearly trip over the blanket that's twisted around me. I'm naked, but that doesn't stop me from rushing to the door. It's still early. I might be able to stop him.

But the kitchen is dark, the garden is empty, and I can see through the gate that there's no car parked in the driveway. He's gone.

My hands shake as I force myself to read the rest of the letter.

The spell on the house will break at the completion of the ritual. The cupboards will remain well stocked and the rent is paid up until the end of the year. I do not own much, but what I do is now yours.

Love,
Kalin.

I sink down into the dewy grass. It's freezing out, but I stare at the note until it blurs.

When self-preservation eventually drives me inside, I bundle up in my warmest clothes and sit on the kitchen counter, eating pastry and watching the front gate. I stay there for ages, blinking back tears, waiting for Kalin to realise he's stupid and come back. My body thaws, but inside I'm still ice cold. How did everything get so awful so quickly? My breath shakes as I breathe out. *Come back, please come back…*

An hour later, maybe two, Fatso waltzes into the kitchen from the bedroom. He must have come in through the window. He chirrups in greeting and looks up at me expectantly.

"You weren't his cat, and you're certainly not mine," I say, and my eyes well up again because he *was* Kalin's cat, by choice if not officially. And we've both been abandoned, even if he doesn't know it yet.

I slip down and pick him up. He's so warm, and he nuzzles against my neck and starts purring when I head for the fridge. I pull out the milk carton.

Another appears in its place. I blink.

I made a comment the first day I was here. *If you plan to keep pets, you should keep something edible in the cupboard.* Was Kalin thinking of that when he cast this spell? It breaks everything I thought I knew about magic. Novels usually place some limit on it – you can't make gold, you can't produce food, you can't create something from nothing, you can't cast a spell unless you're physically there. But in reality, I suppose there are no such rules. I thought I understood the magic when I had it, but I only scratched the surface of what it could do. I'm ridiculously naïve, and that's probably what Kalin was thinking the whole time I was trying to convince him he could control his power.

Fatso laps up his milk happily, then jumps up on the counter and out the window.

"Ungrateful bastard," I say under my breath.

I watch him traipse across the garden and duck under the gate.

And then he runs in from the bedroom again. He sits down in the middle of the floor, looks around, looks at me, meows indignantly, and jumps up onto the counter and out the window again.

What the…?

Again, Fatso appears in the bedroom. This time he plonks himself down and starts washing his face. The slow cogs of my brain start to turn. I take out the note again. *The spell on the house will break at the completion of the ritual.*

I thought he meant the thing with the food in the cupboards, but he dedicated a separate sentence to that. I go to the gate myself. Fatso trots after me. I reach out tentatively to open it, expecting to hit a barrier.

I don't. Of course, I don't. That would be ridiculous overkill. I know he doesn't want me to leave and announce to the world that I'm really alive, but he wouldn't physically trap me here. I laugh at my overactive imagination as I push the gate open and step out.

The sun hits my eyes and all I see is white. Then I'm standing in the bedroom.

I turn around just in time to see Fatso emerging from the wall. He stops, halfway through, so that he's half a cat. Then he backs away and disappears again. I dash to the kitchen to see him reappear at the gate.

No! Not only has Kalin left me, but he's *caged* me. Three rooms for three months completely alone. I pace across the kitchen. My breath comes in short, sharp gasps. And as I ask myself why he would do this, I know. Oh, I know. He did this because he knew I wouldn't just sit here and let him die. My safety be damned. He knew that I would find a way to come after him.

And that's exactly what I'll do.

He made a mistake trying to trap me. If he hadn't done this, my grief would have kept me bundled up and useless for at least another few days. He would have had a head start. But now he's granted me rage. And I will use this rage to get out of here.

41

I spend that first day trying to outsmart his spell. I climb over the garden wall (and end up in the study), I manage to get onto the roof and walk along it to the back of the cottage. While I can see the street, as soon as I scramble down, I land on my ass in the kitchen. When night comes, I'm exhausted and stiff. I light a fire. The wood helpfully replenishes itself too.

I can't face sleeping in the bed. So, I curl up in the study with Kalin's mysterious books and a translation app – only to discover that I have no signal. Whatever Kalin's done, he's completely cut off my access to the outside world. I can't go on social media, I can't text, I can't even phone anyone. I eye the fire. Might not be the best idea considering the circumstances. I quickly douse the flames.

The next day I do it all over again. And the next day. And the next.

I toss stones over the wall to see if I can find any weakness in the barrier. I stack furniture and climb up to try get over it. I even hack through some of the overgrown bushes at the edge of the garden to try crawl under them. But when I shimmy beneath the fence, I bump my head on the bed.

By the end of that week I have no answers, only a house full of stones, a body full of bruises and the knowledge that Kalin is getting further and further from me.

It takes another few days of repeating things I've already tried before I finally admit defeat and climb up to the roof with a bottle of wine I found at the back of a cupboard.

I try to yank out the cork with my teeth, because that seems like the thing to do, but I can't even manage that and end up digging it out with a knife. It's an acerbic red and, from the dust on the bottle, I'd guess that Kalin was given it as a gift many years ago. It's probably really fancy, but I can't appreciate it. It fills my mouth with the taste of metal, and it's all I can do to force myself to swallow it. I take a large swig and yell expletives at a neighbourhood that probably can't even hear me.

It's a quiet road, and no cars or people pass in the entire time I'm sitting there. The sky fades from blue to yellow to indigo. The air smells of rain and woodsmoke and when the stars come out, I think of Hogsback, and of Kalin, and of how I had that happy smiling Kalin in my arms. And now I'm never going to see him again, never going to touch him again, never going to feel the brush of his magic. I've held off grief, because I've held off accepting that there's no way to get to him. I've tried so hard to be brave through everything. Dad, the kidnapping, my own death, the guilt at lying to all my friends. But now, staring up at the vast sky, getting quietly drunk, I feel so incredibly small and alone that tears roll down my cheeks.

As if in sympathy, clouds roll across the moon and the sky starts to cry too. Rain patters onto the leaves of the jacaranda and I huddle into my coat, awaiting the cold splash of it on my skin. But I remain completely dry. I get shakily to my feet and peer out at my surroundings. The rain is nothing but a vague shimmer in the dark, lit only by streetlights, but I can see the colour of the pavement change, and *not* change on my side of the barrier. I pull my phone out of my pocket and switch on the torch. As I shine it around me, I can clearly see exactly where the rain stops.

I can see the bars of my cage.

A single corner of the roof is dark and rain-slicked. Kalin was in a rush, and he did a clumsy job. I kneel right up against that corner and reach out a hand, just like when I was trying to sense Kalin's aura. I close my eyes, breathe deeply and move my hand forward.

It might just be my imagination (or the wine), but I think static brushes against my palm.

Focus on the water. Reach towards it.

I reach towards the rain as if Kalin was ordering me to do that now and it wasn't just a memory. My head swims. I'm drunk, and this is stupid. I can't use magic anymore. I'm not a fairy.

You already have, and you are. Kalin's words echo back at me.

"Stop it!" I tell him. Even hearing his memory voice hurts because of how badly I want to hear his real voice.

Yet Sukwini said something about that too. *You would likely never have enough power to defeat Kallen, as the blood – after so many generations – had now mixed with a human.*

She didn't say I wouldn't have power, just that I wouldn't have *enough* to defeat him. I recall the way Kalin's magic felt before he got his power back, that dull, depleted aura. And yet even dull and depleted he managed to defend me from Dumi's men and he challenged Bianca.

"I am Lilah Nuadha," I whisper. It sounds better than Durow, the name that I thought was mine for so long. "I am Lilah Nuadha, and I may not be the Overlord, but I have power."

This would be so lame if I was sober, but even though the words slur on my tongue now, I get a thrill from them. I'm not little frightened Lilah. I am not Lilah's Cindy mask. I am Lilah, of an ancient powerful bloodline.

I remember the sensation of reaching forward with Kalin's magic, and I picture doing the same, even though I can't feel anything respond.

"I am Lilah Nuadha. I have magic. I command you to let me through."

I repeat it over and over with my eyes pressed closed until I'm almost certain that what I feel against my palm is not sweat, but rain.

Let me through. Let me through. I command you to let me through.

There it is. It's really there. Rain pattering onto my arm. I dare to look, dare to hope that it's not in my head and my arm isn't just poking through the wall in the kitchen. I'm prepared to see half an arm. What I'm not prepared to see is the air glowing. It's like there's a giant soap bubble in front of me. The colours slide between silver, and pink, and blue, and gold.

I can see Kalin's barrier. And I can break it.

⁓⁓⁓

First, there's the problem of finding Kalin.

I manage to get down from the roof without falling on my drunken face and retreat to the study, where I pace. It's a small wonder that we haven't worn tracks in the floor of this room between the two of us.

My head is swimming. Would Kalin have told George where he was going? I wonder vaguely if his car has one of those trackers and then remember this is Kalin we're talking about. Of course it won't. Maybe if I reported the car as stolen…

No.

No, there's a much better way. I dig through his jewellery.

He wouldn't have thrown it away. I know he wouldn't have. It must be here. It must—

There, in a box all its own, is my pendant. I grin when I see it.

He managed to find me using this thing when I was kidnapped, which means I can find him the same way. I'm not really sure how it works, but that's Future Lilah's problem.

My more immediate problem is how I'm going to reach him.

Uber would be the obvious solution, but it doesn't operate out here. Even if I decided to go all grand theft auto, I never did get those driving lessons.

Would Darren help me?

Hah! He'd probably be relieved to hear that Kalin's going to die.

I hug myself and sink down onto the settee, trying desperately to think through the brain fog. The brain fog wins. I flop back. The room spins around me, like the night Kalin walked me home from the music gig.

I close my eyes, seeing that night all over again. As I drift off, the beginnings of a plan take shape.

I know how I'll go after him.

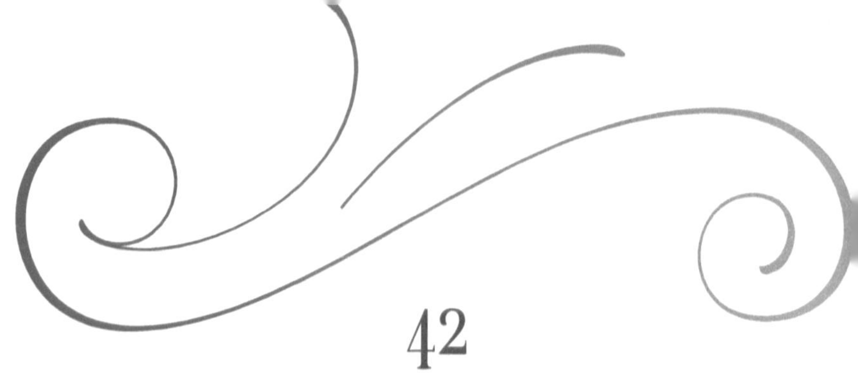

42

I think I might faint. My stomach is a mess and my head feels like it's being squeezed by a giant pair of pliers. Probably should have had more water and less wine last night.

Probably I'm still drunk, because I'm on campus.

I have a hat, hoodie and dark glasses, and I've been very careful not to let anyone see me.

Still, I'm in enemy territory. What would Sukwini do if she discovered me?

I try not to think of that. I focus on my pulse and on my backpack cutting into my shoulders. The entire time I'm walking down the narrow corridor, I pray silently that no one comes out of their rooms.

Finally, I reach the door I want. My insides somersault. There's music coming from inside. *It's not too late to give up and go back to the cottage, to safety,* a small voice inside me says.

It's a very small voice. The rest of me knows I have no choice. Kalin's life is on the line.

I knock. The music pauses. I'm going to be sick. The door opens.

"Yes?" Jess snaps.

"I need your help."

Her eyes stretch and her mouth drops open. It moves, but no sound comes out.

"Who's there, babe?" someone asks from within the room. *Oh crap.* Bed springs move and I throw myself flat against the wall and hold my breath.

Jess doesn't speak, and my heart rate climbs. Sweat prickles on the back of my neck, because I know that voice. Michael – Michael the journalist, i.e. the worst person (next to the Guardians) who could discover supposedly-dead Lilah hale and hearty.

His footsteps approach the door.

"Uh…" Jess says. "Uh, nobody. I mean, it was just Lindsay. She, uh, just wanted my help with something quick. I'll be right back."

Oh, thank the Greats.

Jess closes the door behind her and faces me. "Lilah?" Her voice is so high, I'm pretty sure it would scare dogs away. "But— You— But— You're—"

I shake my head and press a finger to my lips. The corridor is not the place to talk. I grab her wrist and pull her towards the laundry room at the end of the passage.

The machines are whirring. They're all well into their cycles, so we should be alone for a bit. I pull her in and close the door behind us. The room is warm, and it smells like soap.

She leans against a drier with a hand on her heart, heaving in the humid air. "You're dead. This can't be real. This is a dream."

"I'm not dead. I had to fake my death."

She stares at me. "Fake… fake your death?"

"Yeah. It's a long story."

Her huge eyes shine with tears. Then she launches herself at me and wraps her arms tightly around my neck and sobs.

"Lilah! I thought you were dead," she says between gasps. "They found your body. There was a memorial."

I hug her while guilt chills my belly. "I wanted to tell you."

I can't believe I'm about to ask something of her after putting her through this. I gently extricate myself from her arms.

"Jess, listen. You remember Kalin?"

She's still pale with shock. "Who?"

"My friend. The, uh, one you said looked at me like I was a Gucci bag on sale."

"Oh. Yeah?"

"He's in trouble. Big trouble. He's going to die if I don't help him, but I can't help him without—"

Dammit Lilah, what are you doing? You let this girl believe you were dead and now you're going to demand she be your chauffeur?

Jess's stricken features contort into a frown. "Without what?"

"I can't help him alone," I say. "Look, I understand if you don't want to help. I haven't exactly been a good friend, even before the whole being dead thing. But I don't trust anyone else." That much is definitely true. "And I don't know exactly where he is, but I know he's not in Grahamstown."

"What do you mean?"

I draw a deep breath. "He ran away and—"

Jess takes my hand. "Not that. I mean about not being a good friend. Lilah, you're like the only reason I passed the first semester. And you always listen to me and—"

I don't hear the rest because she wraps her arms around me again, and her words are muffled by her tears and my mass of hair, although I think I do hear her wail something about *and I kissed your boyfriend.* I pat her back and have to shut my eyes to stop myself from crying. I didn't think I meant that much to Jess. I knew we were friends, but I thought since she was so superficial about so much else that she'd get over me as quickly as she got over Philip. I'm embarrassed at myself, at this whole situation, at daring to be alive. My temples are still aching, and it's only the thought of Kalin dying that keeps me from breaking down myself.

Jess eventually recovers and dabs her face with her sleeve. "You said I could help? How can I help?"

Getting into the little pink mini without being seen is a pretty challenging feat in and of itself. It's parked in the front lot right outside Sukwini's window, and since I have no way of knowing if she's home – or when she'll come home – I ask Jess to pick me up round the corner instead. I hide in the bushes and only tumble into the back seat once I'm certain no cars are going past.

Jess eyes me in the rear-view mirror. "Where to?"

I wriggle out of my backpack and get the pendant from the front pocket. "Just head to the highway for now."

"I've… I've never driven on a highway before." She chews on her bottom lip and nods to herself. "But I can do it. I mean, it's the road to Grahamstown, right? It won't be busy?"

She starts the car. I close my eyes and try to focus on the jet. It is a little warm, but that could just be from being inside my bag. Or it could be because Kalin's going to die. So far, not very helpful.

"What are you doing?" Jess asks.

"Uh… getting directions?"

Maybe it has to be against my chest. Bianca broke the clasp, but I stick it under my shirt and hold it to my skin. It's definitely warm. I lie flat on the back seat and will a vision to come to me. Nothing does.

"We're on the highway!" Jess reports after a few minutes. "What lane should I be in?"

"The slow one."

"Which one is that?"

As far as rescue efforts go, we're less like Charlie's Angels and more like something Rowan Atkinson would star in. Someone hoots and speeds around us.

"The other one," I suggest.

Jess indicates and changes lanes with a little yelp.

Is it my imagination, or is the pendant growing hotter? I peek over the front seat to look at the road ahead of us. "Which way are we heading?"

"I don't know!"

The pendant *is* growing hotter. It's starting to hurt my fingers. "Turn around."

"What?"

"I think we're going the wrong way. Turn around."

Jess does a U-turn in the middle of the highway, and swings into oncoming traffic. She screams and slams on brakes as a tour bus roars past and I'm flung into the back of the seat. "I didn't mean right now!"

"I told you I haven't ever driven on a highway before!"

A man leans out of his cattle carrier to swear at us as he passes. Jess starts the car with shaking hands.

The pendant is still warm when we go back past Grahamstown. The monument now looks even more ominous than it did that very first day, but once we're heading in the other direction away from town, the pendant starts to cool.

Are you kidding me? Kalin managed to find me through a game of reverse Hot and Cold? I somehow assumed he'd had something a little more… nuanced.

The road narrows down to one lane, much to Jess's relief, and there's nothing but farmland to either side of us.

"So… you want to tell me more about this danger?" Jess asks.

"It's complicated."

"Is it to do with why you had to fake your death?" She gasps. "Is it to do with the mob?"

"Ah…" It would be easy to just say yes and pretend it's Dumi who's after Kalin, but I don't want to lie to her. "Kalin thinks he has to die to save me, but he doesn't. We're kinda saving him from himself."

"Oh! I saw this in a movie once! The mob kidnapped you and said they'd free you if he turned himself in? Is he like an undercover cop?"

That's not the worst thing for her to believe. "Well, I *was* kidnapped. Michael wrote about that, didn't he?"

"Yeah. Everyone thinks they're the ones who came back and

drowned you."

I see an opportunity to distract her from the subject of Kalin. "So, you and Michael?"

Jess looks at her hands on the wheel – in the perfect nine-and-three position straight out of the learner's manual – and, to my surprise, blushes. "Yeah. After the memorial, he was really there for me, you know?"

Michael moves fast. "He always was crazy about you."

"You think? I think he was mostly crazy *at* me. But we're getting there. You know what they say, you don't know what you've got till it's—"

"Turn left."

Jess spins the wheel and careens into the slipway to the left. I have no idea why I said that. None of the signs look familiar. The best way I could describe it is literal gut instinct. But when I have nothing else, I have to trust that.

There's nothing to distinguish the landscape. It's all green and grassy, aside from the vague smudge of mountains in the distance. But the pendant turns cooler still as we continue along that road and I know I must have made the right choice.

"Lilah, how are you navigating?" Jess asks at length.

"You wouldn't believe me if I told you."

"Tell me and we'll see."

I'm a little worried she'll turn around and take me back to Grahamstown if I do. "Well, here's the thing. I'm, uh, a wizard."

Wizard sounds better than fairy.

Jess shakes her head. "You know, if you don't want to tell me that's fine, but you don't have to make fun of me."

At least she doesn't turn the car around.

We drive a long time. I focus on the road ahead, waiting for clues; gut clues or pendant clues, I'll take anything. Still nothing. The most exciting thing that happens is the road takes us over a little river, but we can't see it because it's super overgrown. The blurry mountains draw closer and maybe I've been staring at them too long, but there's one poking out behind the others that has a sort of familiar shape.

Wait! I sit forward and squint at it.

My heart rate climbs. I know what it is. I didn't need the stupid pendant. I didn't need Hot and Cold. I should have known immediately where Kalin would go.

That's the hog's back. It's the name of that sort of geological formation, Kalin told me the last time I saw it.

The last time he was there was so he could use his powers, now it's so that he *doesn't*. It's far enough out of the way that he's not a threat, and close enough that he can get back to Grahamstown for the ritual.

"Head towards that mountain," I say.

Jess frowns and hands me her phone with the Maps app open.

⁂

We stop in the little Hogsback deli for food, and I swing by Dahlia's shop to ask if she's seen Kalin.

"Not since you were here, darling." She raises her eyebrows. "Well, isn't that interesting."

I'm almost afraid to ask. "What?"

She comes out from behind the desk and walks around me, just as she did that first time. "Your aura's changed, love. Your crown chakra is wide open."

"Oh, um, maybe you can read Jess's aura. I'm sure she'd be interested in hearing about hers," I suggest. Jess is looking at some jewellery nearby, and it takes me a beat to realise it's what's left of Kalin's stock he delivered last time.

Dahlia acts as if I didn't say anything. "Your third eye is awake. Is this Kalin's doing?"

"It must be."

Dahlia touches my arm, I feel the brush of warm static that I've started to associate with magic, and I see a flash of clear sky blue. "Yes, purple," she says. "A little dark, perhaps, but heading in the right direction."

I manage to convince Jess to leave without buying anything – I have no idea what spells are on that stuff, and the last thing we need is her purchasing a have-a-baby-with-Michael charm because it looks pretty. It's more of a struggle to convince Jess to walk up to the campsite after I find no sign of Kalin's car in the village.

"I am *not* wearing the shoes for this," she complains.

Then, a few minutes later, "Have you been to Joburg? This is *not* my natural habitat. We don't *do* mountains."

I offer to take her back to the car to wait, but she pouts and falls silent.

The campsite is deserted, and there's no sign that anyone has been here recently. I fight back the disappointment that threatens to overwhelm me. It's getting late, and I haven't brought any kind of camping equipment.

But Kalin's *here*. I know he's somewhere here. I won't give up now.

I head for the path that I followed last time. It's different now from how it looked in autumn, but I recognise the route because I committed it to memory through sketches. Up we go, past the familiar rocks and fallen tree trunks, up and up, both of us calling Kalin's name.

"You can go back to the car if you want," I suggest again, because I feel bad for dragging Jess out here and she looks so very uncomfortable in her pink skirt and pumps.

But she shakes her head. "I didn't drive all the way here, *on the highway*, to let you be the hero."

I know from her expression that that's not it. She doesn't want to leave me alone in this forest. I definitely never gave Jess enough credit.

Eventually, we come to the precipice where I first saw Kalin doing magic. I only realise when I'm standing on the cliff that I was expecting to see him at it again, somewhere down there. But even though we're above the canopy, the trees are packed together too tight and the river is empty.

"Kalin!" I call out to the forest below. There is no answer.

"We should probably head down. It's starting to get dark," Jess says.

She's right. Above the trees there's still plenty of light, but when we head back along the path, in the shade of the leaves, it's going to get dangerous.

I hold the pendant in my fist. The temperature hasn't changed since we arrived here. It's just normal cool metal now. Useless.

Unless…

An idea occurs to me, and it's the absolute worst idea. I dismiss it immediately, but it comes bounding back straight away. It's an awful, horrible idea. But it could work.

"Push me off this cliff," I tell Jess.

"Ha-ha, very funny."

"I'm serious."

She frowns and folds her arms. "Lilah, that's like the most dramatic thing I've ever heard."

If Kalin senses a threat to me, and he's close, I know he'll come. But it can't just be a pretend threat. It has to be real.

I step carefully towards the edge. I can feel my rapid pulse in my throat and my stomach sinks right down to my ankles. Gravity claws at me. A gust of icy wind stings my face.

"You need to trust me," I say to Jess.

"You're insane. I'm not going to kill you."

I take another step forward. "I'm not going to die." Kalin's blood worked once. It will work again. Won't it?

Well, maybe I'll get a terrible fever again. But I fought that off once, didn't I?

Anyway, he's so super powerful, I'm sure he can heal me. If he can cast that spell on the house that makes food from nowhere, surely he'll be able to heal me?

My legs tremble. It's going to hurt. Really hurt. I'm going to break a lot of bones. I'm trying to imagine the pain, but maybe I shouldn't. Maybe I should just do it. Would that work? Would me being a threat to myself work?

"I told you, I'm a wizard," I say.

"You're crazy, that's what you are. Come away from there!"

Another step forward. *Oh, Greats.* I'm not sure if I can do this. Every instinct in me is shouting for me to back away.

"Lilah, please, please stop." Jess's voice hitches up in pitch.

I can do it. Alayna would be able to do this. Just close my eyes and—

"Lilah!" Kalin's voice shouts.

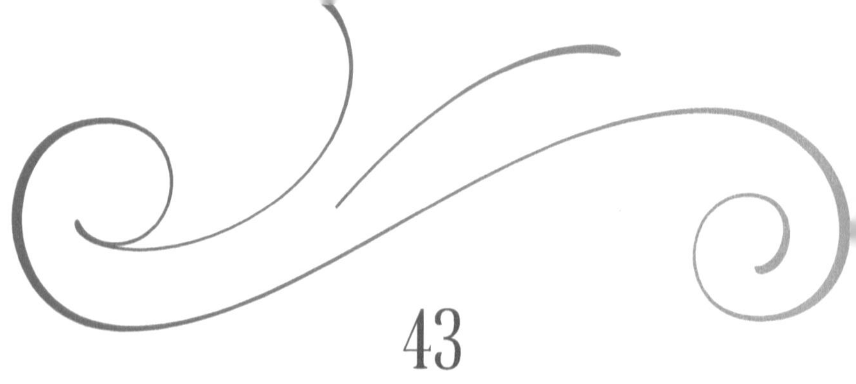

43

I spin and almost lose my balance. Kalin's at the edge of the trees, only a few metres away. His hair is loose and he's wearing a different brown jacket – one made of leather, lined with fur. He's holding a stick that could be a spear and could be a staff. It could also just be a walking stick. He looks so wild, yet so elegant. I'm completely paralysed. I can't speak, I can't breathe. And it's nothing to do with his magic and all to do with the pure emotional impact of seeing him again.

He takes long strides towards me. "What in Boann's name are you doing here? You *can't* be here." He pulls up short when he notices Jess. "No. You… It was foolish enough to come here, but to involve someone else? I would never have expected this of you."

I don't know what reunion I had in mind, but it wasn't this. My relief is wiped away and replaced with the churning rage I felt when I first realised he'd trapped me.

"Well, I wouldn't have expected you to lock me in a cage, but here we are!" I shoot back at him. "And I'm here to rescue you, by the way. Because if you think I would ever just sit back and watch you die—"

"It wasn't a cage! You were *safe!*" He rounds on Jess. "Who saw you leave?"

"No one," she squeaks.

"To—" I reach for some kind of Irish mythological figure, but only come up with, "To the Guardians with being safe! You abandoned me, you didn't even bother to say goodbye, after-after—" I splutter, because I'm all too aware of Jess's keen attention. "You *are* a coward."

"I know that!" He waves his arms, and the air shimmers around them. "But I was trying to do what was *right*. Could you not permit me to do one thing right in the entirety of my existence? One thing!"

Jess is gaping at him. She must also see the air shimmering.

"This is *not* the right thing!"

"You profess to know what's right?" He takes another step forward. "Remind me how long you've lived, Lilah?" Darkness leaks into his voice. "Remind me how much experience you have in determining right from wrong?" Another step. The air is positively swelling around him, like a mirage. "You know nothing of the cosmic scales. You know nothing of magic. What arrogance makes you think you know what's right?"

He's like a forest demon, and I probably should be frightened of him. "I know *you*."

"You do *not* know me." He chops a hand through the air, and the ground beneath me gives way.

There's a desperate moment when my feet have no grip at all, and I'm plunging towards the canopy, then Kalin's got me by the upper arm and he's hauling me up to solid ground again. He's panting and he hugs me to his chest and makes a small, desperate sound.

"Did you— Did he just?" Jess asks.

Kalin speaks against my ear. "You see. You see now. My magic. I can't... It can't..."

"It's okay," I say. "It's okay. I'm okay."

"This time." Kalin pulls away abruptly and turns from me. "We need to leave here. By now Nabelo will have figured out something's not right." He starts on the path down, and I follow him. "When you were locked in the pocket universe it didn't matter because she couldn't get to you, but now— And you must have gone to your residence to request Jess's aid, correct?"

"Yes, but she didn't see me."

"Someone might have."

"I was careful."

"If you were careful, you wouldn't be here now. We'll leave the car you came in. Jess will have to accompany us."

"Wait, what?" Jess calls behind us.

"If the Guardians kill me, you can fix me," I proclaim with bravado I certainly don't feel, while skidding down a particularly steep incline. Kalin's long legs are carrying him down at such a pace I'm struggling to keep up.

"Nabelo knows that. If they get hold of you, they certainly won't make that mistake again."

"But Sukwini's on our side."

"Miss Sukwini?" Jess asks. "What's going on?"

"Wrong." Kalin doesn't even pause to look at me. "She stopped being on our side the second the power returned to me. She is no doubt already searching for me, and you may have led her straight here."

I roll my eyes. "You've been gone a few days. She probably just thinks we're shacked up together."

"Wrong again." Kalin stabs the ground with his stick to stop himself sliding. "Jess, how was Intervarsity?" He raises his voice to address her.

"Uh…" Jess stumbles forward and makes a grab for a tree branch. "Why are you asking me?"

"I assume you attended?"

Intervarsity is an annual sporting event between the Eastern Cape universities. Darren mentioned it, and he made it sound like a big deal. Apparently, some people go as far as dyeing their hair in the university colours. I don't know much about it. It happens some time in third term, but I've had bigger things to worry about.

"It was fine."

Wait, was?

Kalin asks, "And I assume you went home for the spring vac?"

"Well, yeah."

I leap over a log and manage to grab his arm. "What are you saying? What's the date?"

He calls to Jess, "What is the date?"

And he looks me right in the eye as she answers.

"October 15th."

A hollow pit opens in my stomach. It feels like a terrible nightmare.

"You cheated me." I thought we had three months. Three months left for me to convince him to live, or at the very least three months together before he decided to die.

"I wouldn't have made you stay in that house alone for months, Lilah." Kalin says softly, and the first sign of tenderness crosses his features. "I took it out of space *and* out of time. Every one of your days was a week out here."

If I had been any slower to escape, he'd already be dead.

"Can someone tell me what's going on?" Jess asks.

"What's going on is there are dangerous people looking for me," Kalin provides, still focused on me. "And they will hurt Lilah if they have to. We need to get her somewhere safe."

He takes off down the hill, and I follow numbly.

Kalin's camp is further downriver this time, and I can tell, even in the half light of dusk, that he's lived here a while. He's got a larger tent, a tripod with a cook kettle over the fire, and a whole rack of fish ready to fry. He grabs a bag from inside the tent then continues onwards, leaving the camp exactly as it was.

A little way down the mountain, he asks for my phone.

The first call he makes is to Dahlia. He wants to borrow her car. The next is more cryptic.

"Queen to F8," he says without preamble.

The person on the other end says something in response and Kalin nods. "Thank you."

He ends the call and pockets the phone.

"What was that about?"

"George. He has a place where we can lie low."

The headlights illuminate grey patches of road ahead of us, and the rest of the world is dark. A tense silence fills the car. I can feel Kalin's anger, but he doesn't say anything, so neither do I. My own frustration and hurt simmer as I gaze out at nothing.

Jess gives up protesting, and asking where we're going, and demanding her phone back (Kalin confiscated both of ours) and eventually falls asleep in the back seat. Then we are serenaded by her snores – a persistent grating sound that echoes my emotional state.

Every so often I steal a glance at Kalin. The dashboard lights cast strange shadows on his profile, but it's still him. We're sharing a space again. This is what I wanted, isn't it? But for me it's been just over a week since we last saw each other. For him, it's been months. Long enough to dull all desire, and all regret.

Eventually he asks, quiet and stiff, "How did you escape?"

"I got drunk and nearly fell off the roof."

He doesn't smile. I fold my arms and lean against the window. I think I can see lights way off in the distance, but it might just be a reflection. "I got drunk enough to believe I could."

"You found your magic."

He says it as if he always knew that I had my own power, and that annoys me. More secrets. "Yeah."

Silence.

"Fatso's pissed at you, by the way. You caught him there too."

"I know."

At my look, he elaborates. "I didn't want to leave you alone."

"Well, you did. He's a cat. Not like he's going to discuss Dickens with me."

"No," Kalin agrees.

I freed Fatso before I left. It will be a wonder if he returns to the cottage after that ordeal. Then again, it will be a wonder if any of us do. I don't think I could bear to go back there without Kalin.

I want to say more, but I can't find the words to give shape to my feelings, and when I try, my eyes sting. So, in the end, I just stare into the darkness.

Eventually we pull onto a long dirt road. The house at the end is a solitary building, crowded by milkwood trees. When we get out of the car, I smell the roaring ocean.

Kalin opens the front door without a key, then punches in a security code he must have got from George. When he switches on the lights, they reveal an exquisitely decorated beach house with a vaulted ceiling. The whole back wall is made of glass, with a sliding door onto a porch. The main room is as big as Kalin's cottage. Everything's covered in white sheets, but I can make out a large sofa, a flat-screen TV and a dining room table. Up a couple of steps to our right are Japanese-style shōji sliding doors with leaping fish painted on them that must lead to the main bedroom. There are four doors to the left, and through the one that's hanging open I see a kid's bedroom.

"Dibs," Jess says, brushing past me. "You lovebirds can have the big room."

I know she's angry with me too. She was all for helping, but no one told her it would mean being practically kidnapped. The door bangs shut behind her.

Hopefully one of the other rooms is a spare bedroom.

"What is this place?" I ask Kalin. Dad and I didn't exactly struggle for money, but this is something else.

"A vacation home belonging to George's children."

He waves a hand, and the white sheets lift off the furniture, into the air. "They live in Australia now, and only visit every few years. Always in the summer, of course. So, we're in luck."

"They just keep this whole house here to visit every few years? That's crazy."

"Mmm." With a flick of his wrist, the sheets fold themselves and float into a neat pile in a corner.

"Why doesn't George live with them there?" I ask.

"He's too old to emigrate, so they put him in the home."

"Oh." Poor George. I always just assumed he was a bachelor, but how sad to have had a family, grandchildren even, and to only see them every few years. That must be why Kalin makes such an effort to keep him company. Now Kalin might not see him again either.

If he hadn't gotten his power back, if he hadn't run, then he'd still have many chess matches to look forward to. Does he blame me? The air between us crackles.

"I couldn't just let you die," I say in a tiny, strangled voice.

"Yes, you could." He strides across the room and opens the sliding door onto the porch. The smell of the sea fills the house. We must be right on the beach.

Music blares from the kid's room; Jess has clearly found a way to entertain herself.

I follow Kalin outside. Our footsteps crunch onto sand. It's completely dark, but Kalin casts a ball of light into his palm and the beach glitters white in a small circle around him.

"What are you doing?"

"Our closest neighbours are two kilometres away on the other side of the lagoon, but we should still be careful."

It must be overcast because there're no stars, no moon, just Kalin by his sorcerer's light as he walks along the sand with his back straight and the fur curling around his neck so that he looks enchanted and regal.

He pauses at the very edge of the water, where the sand looks like glass and the incoming tide reflects his magic in strange, otherworldly patterns. "I'm going to put a spell of isolation around the house, so that it looks empty to the rest of the world." He bends to pick up a piece of driftwood.

"Is that what you did to the cottage?"

"No. It's far less complicated."

A reckless thought grabs me. "Show me how."

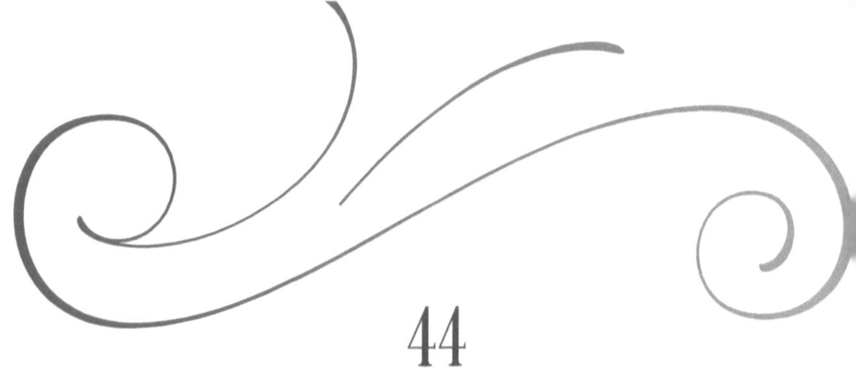

44

Kalin narrows his eyes.

"You said it yourself. I've found my magic. I want to know how to use it," I say.

"It's likely that my blood only awakened the echo of magic in you, and it will fade in time."

"Maybe," I acknowledge. "But maybe it's more than that. Sukwini said my mother was bred to fight you."

Kalin cocks his head. I expect him to argue further, but he scratches a symbol into the sand at his feet. "Copy this."

"What does it do?"

"It will help us define the perimeter."

It's a complicated Celtic knot and it takes me a few tries to get it right. Even when I do, Kalin frowns at it and commands me to draw it again.

After about fifteen repeats, he grabs my wrist to stop me. A pulse of unbidden desire races up my arm at the touch of his skin.

"No. I said *copy* it. All of it."

All of—? Oh.

Magic. It's got magic in it; I'm just not seeing it. I tug my wrist back and try again. How can I put magic *into* a thing? I haven't tried that yet. Is that what Kalin did to the jewellery he made?

I reach inside, grasping for something, anything, that will confirm the magic is really there. I still feel the same as I did before Kalin's power. I'm just Lilah.

Kalin pinches the bridge of his nose. "The magic will fade as my red blood cells die off. Perhaps what you tapped into yesterday is no longer there."

He watches me as I stab at the sand pitifully.

"Go inside, Lilah. I'll finish up here."

He's so dismissive and it hurts. "Look, you're super powerful, so you can *tell* whether I have magic. I know you can, because I could when I had your power. So, if there isn't any, you don't have to go through this whole thing to make it worse."

He paces around me, "Oh, I can sense many things about you, Lilah. But I'm afraid if magic is one of them, I need to see *evidence*."

I turn to face him, but he keeps moving so I have to keep turning. "Will you stop that! I know it matches your whole dramatic…" I gesture with my hands. "Your whole new *thing*, but I'm getting dizzy."

"All right." He stops and I'm a little pleased to see the corner of his mouth twitch. "Let me put it plainly. This is a test. If you pass, I will train you to use your power."

A shiver travels down to the tips of my fingers, but before I can be too happy about the offer, he adds, "At least, as much as is possible in the time available."

Right, in the time available before he dies.

"And if I fail?"

"I seem to recall there's a library."

"So, then I spend the next two weeks reading."

"Torture, I know."

I square my shoulders and return to the business of drawing out that symbol. Infuriatingly, Kalin doesn't keep quiet and let me concentrate.

"There's no shame in being unable to," he says. "I won't judge you for it. Your whole life, you believed magic was nothing but a dream, and you could go back to that. After the ritual, you could return to who you were before. There's no harm in giving up."

I shove the stick into the ground after that one. "Would it kill you to have a little faith in me?"

He actually laughs. "Well, considering the circumstances…"

"Were you this annoying before you got your powers back? I can't recall."

"Oh, yes. An arrogant know-it-all, I believe it was. Should we go inside? I'll fix us a drink."

I pick up the stick and begin deliberately tracing the lines again. "I'd like to see you drunk."

"Intoxication with these powers? I think not."

Why did he mention alcohol? Is it supposed to be a jab about walking me home in February? That's not when I called him an arrogant know-it-all, but it was the same day so perhaps he's mixing it up.

No. No, it's a reminder of how I accessed my powers last time. I pause in my drawing to look up at him. His expression offers no acknowledgement, but I think his eyes sparkle. Yes, they're crinkled at the edges as if he's teasing me. A dead giveaway.

I just need to find some of that determination again. This isn't going to work if I'm half-assed about it. It needs all my willpower.

I try recall the feeling when I broke through the barrier. The name – Nuadha – is only part of it. The name represents… purpose. The whole time I was growing up, my identity had a missing piece. Now I've found it. Now I think I understand who my mother was. She was a rebel; she believed that love was worth the risk. Yes, she made mistakes, but she studied journalism because she wanted to make the world a better place. She believed she had a life, a reason for being, beyond the machinations of the Guardians. Without even knowing her, I realise I am like her. I am more like her than I am like Dad. And *we* are like Alayna. *The choice is yours.*

In my mind the stick glows and the power pours down it, a vivid purple just the way that Dahlia described it.

"Good," Kalin says. I don't see his expression, because my eyes are still closed. "Now we can start working."

We walk the whole beach laying down symbols, and I have to keep my eyes closed because that's the only way I can see the power. Each symbol is connected to the next, in a giant loop. When we're done with the beach, we go up into the dunes around the side of the house, push through tangled milkwoods until we come around the front, then continue on the other side, where we finally connect the line to the first symbol. My arms are aching and shake with the strain. We do not talk other than Kalin offering advice. He draws an outer ring of way more complicated symbols and when he connects those, I feel a buzz as the spell activates.

"When you become more adept, you'll be able to draw the symbols in your mind and you won't have to lay them down physically," Kalin explains.

"Why did *you* need to lay them down physically?"

"I didn't need to." And he sets off towards the house without another word.

⁂

Kalin conjures up some pizza, and Jess comes out of her room when she smells it. I stuff slice after slice into my mouth.

Magic is hungry.

I catch Jess appraising me, but she's too polite to say anything. When Kalin goes out of the room to throw away the boxes, she leans in and says, "So, he *is* your boyfriend now, right?"

Nothing like the hint of romance to put Jess in a better mood.

"It's complicated."

"Well uncomplicate it, girl. He was hot before. Now? He's got that whole dark vibe going on. Hot AF. *Hot AF.*"

She's not wrong about the vibe. I'm about to tell her she doesn't understand, but I remember how angry she was when I wasn't straight with her before and, after driving me all the way to Hogsback and getting stuck here with us, she deserves to know why. Besides, I wasn't exactly thrilled about being kept ignorant.

It's not fair for me to do the same to her.

"He's kinda out of my league and the situation—"

She holds up a hand there to halt me. "He's not out of your league. You're like the smartest person I know. He's totally into that."

"He's also totally a super powerful immortal sorcerer."

Jess laughs and covers her face. "You're weird, you know that?"

"Yeah. But it's also the truth."

She peers at me from between her fingers. "Just how gullible do you think I am?"

"Well, regardless of whether you believe me or not, that's the case. And he's supposed to throw himself on his sword at the end of the month. Okay, well, given how fantastical this all sounds, I should probably clarify that there isn't an actual sword. At least I don't think there's an actual sword." I *can* picture Bianca using a sword. "Point is, he's supposed to die, and the people who are chasing us want to ensure that happens. So, yeah, complicated situation."

Jess doesn't say anything for a long moment. Then she shakes her head and gets up and goes to her room. The resounding bang of the door slamming behind her confirms: she didn't believe a word.

"Good talk?" Kalin asks from the doorway.

"You might have come in earlier and showed her some magic."

He sits down opposite me. "I could rip space time open right in front of her and I doubt she'd believe it. Humans are very good at not believing in magic."

"*Will* there be swords?"

His expression clouds. "Unlikely. Although Bianca has shown a fondness for blades."

"Yeah." Even trying to picture his death in a theoretical sense makes me ill.

I kick the floor, and stare at the tabletop. The sea breathes between us. "Kalin, when you were, I mean, when I was locked in the cottage… Did you hear anything about my dad?"

"I'm sorry, no."

I assumed as much. He was out in the middle of nowhere.

I pick at a flaw in the wood, then stop myself. This table is probably worth a month of Guido's tips.

"Lilah…" I look up, hoping that he'll offer me reassurance, but he's focused on his lap and he clears his throat. "I'd feel better if you slept with me tonight."

"Slept with you!"

He half rises out of his chair and holds up his hands defensively. "*Beside* me. I— I meant in the same room. I don't want to risk…"

He trails off because what is there really to risk? He must realise he's being irrational. He's hidden the house, and no one even knows we're here. I almost say no, just to spite him, but then I picture sleeping with his body next to mine. Even though I'm still mad at him, I nod.

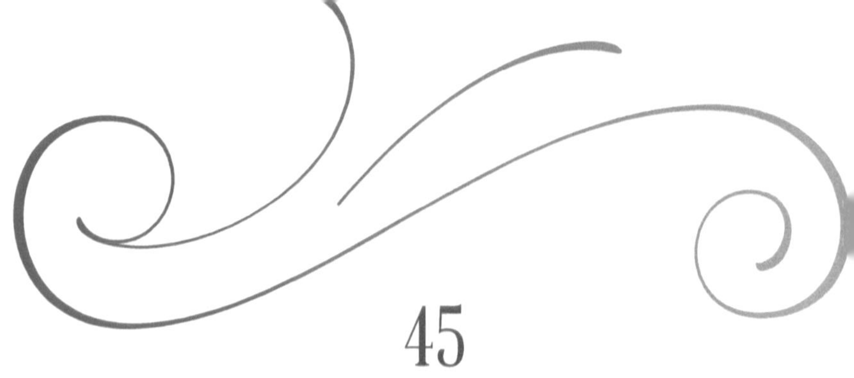

45

espite the excitement of the day, I can't sleep. Kalin is heavy beside me. He's lying on his side facing away, fully clothed. His body shifts as he breathes, and I long for its warmth, but I don't dare touch him. I'm stiff and cold, inside and out.

I managed to escape his spell, I risked everything, I brought Jess into this, and for what? Kalin is determined to die anyway. I pull my knees up to my chest and try to swallow down the rising emotion. Now I'm still, now everything's quiet, there's nothing standing between me and overwhelming despair. In the months since he trapped me, he's gotten over me. Clearly. I wish I could be over him too. Instead, memories from our night together haunt me.

I slide my hands under his shirt. The room is cool, but he's a furnace. His muscles are taut, and I remember how they looked in the water at Hogsback. Understated but beautiful, like the rest of him.

I roll over and stare up at the naked wooden beams high above me.

"It's been a long time since I've done this," he whispers.

"How long?"

He runs his fingers up my bare back. "Very."

I try to focus on the roaring of the waves outside, pushing away the memory of his touch. But he's too close. I can smell his hair.

His hair in a curtain over us, his stubble against my cheek, his lips along my jaw.

"We don't have to do this now." Hot, breathless words.

My mind is blank, my blood is flame. "I want to."

"You're certain?"

He brushes his hand down my side and I arch towards his touch. "Yes!"

"There's something we should do first." He takes my hand and guides it across my belly, whispering instructions while tracing symbols. A spell to prevent conception.

That was the last time I used his power. Now, so close to his death, my mind wanders. What would have happened if we hadn't performed that spell?

A part of him might have lived.

Sure, and I could have raised his kid on a waitress's salary. How romantic.

I huddle down into the blankets and give in to silent tears.

ತ್ಲ

Gauzy fabric flutters across my face, and it takes me a minute to remember where I am: the beach house's main bedroom, facing a window that looks out onto the ocean. Everything is white – the delicate curtains, the sand, the overcast sky, the reflection off the ocean, the wood panelling, floorboards and bedcovers. The other side of the bed is empty. I stretch and wince when stiff muscles complain. I don't remember dreaming, but I feel like I've spent the night in a cold stone building.

I haven't dreamed about Alayna since I died, and now I wish I would. There's so much I want to know about her, and about Kalin's past, but my subconscious offers nothing but an aching sense of loss.

There are voices coming from one of the other rooms and I trace them to the kitchen, where I find Jess sitting at a granite counter and Kalin – with a cloth over his shoulder – frying eggs.

"Lilah, pleased you could join us. I thought you might sleep the day away," he says.

I run a hand through my sleep-mussed hair. "What time is it?"

"After eleven," Jess provides.

I pull myself up onto one of the stools beside her. Kalin sets a plate of scrambled eggs down in front of me, and I recall the last time he tried to cook me breakfast and Fatso tripped him up. He still remembers how I like my eggs.

Jess has hers sunny side up, and she almost chokes on a forkful when I say, "Guess the magic wore me out."

I think I see the corner of Kalin's mouth lift. That's the only warning I get before he says, in a silky voice, "If that's what you'd like to call it."

Luckily, I'm not eating when he says that or I would have likely spat all over the counter. Jess's head snaps to look at me.

Oh, that's not fair. That's not fair at all. He doesn't get to be all flirty. He doesn't get to make my insides do *that* when he's been so cold since we found him.

He passes me a glass of orange juice that I know he must have conjured from nothing, then has the gall to comment, "You've gone bright red."

He's also struck me mute. I can't think of a single witty thing to say in response.

"If you like, you can take it out on me on the beach later."

"Should I leave you two alone?" Jess asks.

***

Kalin's idea of me taking my annoyance out on him on the beach, turns out to be him beating me up with magic.

He seems to be trying his utmost to make me regret asking for lessons. I didn't realise how much I'd need to rely on my physical body to use magic. But, as Kalin said during that very first lesson in the flooded kitchen, stances do help me visualise the power. To the outside observer, the drills we do up and down the beach would probably look like Tai Chi, but in my head, I'm hearing way less wind chimes and way more 1980s training montage.

"We're going to concentrate on defence," Kalin says. "You won't be able to take on a Guardian yourself, but you may be able to buy me time to get to you if it comes to that."

He then makes me practise casting what I suppose can be called shields, but are really just *whumps* of energy that push out from my body, deflecting anything coming towards it. The first few couldn't even protect me from a grain of sand, but when I get the hang of it, Kalin starts casting real spells at me. After the first one pounds into my rib cage, I don't have to dig down far for the willpower to stop him.

When we eventually break for a drink of water and are sitting side-by-side on the beach, I venture, "Do you really think the Guardians will come after me?"

"Most certainly." I notice for the first time that Kalin's got a tan. It must be from living in Hogsback. It suits him.

"Why?" I doodle absently in the sand. "I mean, you said yourself that they wouldn't try killing me again."

"They won't. Killing you would achieve little, considering the power is in me now."

"Exactly."

He's staring out at the grey ocean and his jaw twitches while his mind works. Eventually, he says, "Lilah, you remain the key to my power."

"This just keeps getting more complicated. How? The Keyflame's like tethered to the power until the ritual or something?"

"No. Far more mundane reasons."

"Such as?"

"Such as, they know that I would rather die than see you hurt."

My stomach drops and my blood rushes cold. For the second time today, Kalin has me speechless.

He stands and dusts sand from his legs. "As you're aware, I fully intend to die. That may be all they require of me to keep you safe. But…" He turns back towards the rolling waves. "If they are more ambitious, they'll realise that all they need to control me, is you. My power is not insignificant, as I'm sure you've noticed. There are many things I could do to this world, given enough incentive."

"So, they would torture me to make you do stuff?"

"Correct."

Kalin offers me a hand and helps me to my feet. My insides are all shivery while my thoughts teem with assassinations, floods and all manner of other havoc Kalin could be driven to wreak.

When he does speak again, it's in a whisper like the tide. "Leaving you was not a choice I made lightly."

"But you've had time to come to terms with it."

"Yes."

Somewhere overhead, gulls cry. I bite my bottom lip. "I can't say I'm sorry for coming after you, because I'm not."

He inclines his head in acknowledgement of my non-apology. "Likewise, I can't apologise for trying to keep you safe."

46

The next few days start the same. We eat, we train. And every day ends the same. Kalin and I share a bed, but never touch. In between there's Jess. At first, she's freaked out at the idea of being unable to leave and asks me loads of questions about just who's after Kalin. I don't want to upset her, so I tell her what I can without mentioning magic: that he did some bad things years ago, that now some people want revenge. I assure her multiple times that we're safe here, that Kalin can protect us and I hint that he's working on a plan that will allow us to return home soon.

On the third day of training with Kalin, the sun breaks through the clouds and Jess makes an appearance on the beach. She watches us while she tans in a bathing suit that Kalin claimed belonged to the house's occupants, but I know he probably pulled from thin air.

That night I expect questions about what we were doing, but instead she tells me a long story about a guy she dated who was into martial arts.

"And he made me watch these Japanese cartoons about it. That's what you two look like. You look like cartoons. I'm surprised his hair hasn't gone all stand-uppy," she holds her hands over her head to indicate a super-saiyan hairdo.

"My hair is stand-uppy enough for the both of us." The sea breeze has not been kind to it.

"Well if you'd told me we were going on a beach holiday, I'd have brought the ghd."

It's probably a good sign that she's referring to this as a holiday and not as an abduction. "If I'd known we were going on a beach holiday, I would have packed some books."

She points to the library, which is a small whitewashed room between the kid's room and the toilet.

"*My* books," I clarify. "Most of those are travel journals and coffee table memoirs of celebrities."

"Which celebrities?"

I never thought I'd see the day she was more interested in books than I was. The next time I come in from training, she has her nose buried in Joan Rivers' *Diary of a Mad Diva*.

⚬⚬⚬

The wind picks up and it sweeps a cold front towards us. Perhaps it's the speed at which the clouds move, or it's the ceaseless whining gale, but I'm more aware than ever of the dwindling time left before the ritual.

I become decent at shields, and I beg Kalin to show me more, more, more. I learn to push things and to pull things, I even manage to levitate things a little, but it's not enough. I want more.

When he finally relents and agrees to show me how to conjure flame, he stands behind me and says, in a way that sends a shiver down my spine, "It's addictive, isn't it?"

He reaches around to position my arm, in a way that I've now grown accustomed to. I treasure these moments when he's close, but they never last.

"What?"

"The power." His warm breath brushes my ear. "Perhaps now you can understand. It's never enough. I teach you one spell, and before you even master it, you're hungry for more. Do you not see how dangerous that hunger is?"

"It's not hunger that drives me."

"Be honest with yourself, Lilah. There is no shame in it. It is the nature of things—"

"No, it's not." I turn in his arms.

He looks down at me but doesn't move away. "It's in *your* nature. The academic, who devours knowledge, who yearns to know more, to be better. There is no end to it. The more I teach you, the more you'll desire."

Could that be true? That is how I feel about knowledge, but I've never felt that way about anything physical. I've never wanted to be an Olympic gold medallist, I've never wanted to run a marathon. What I crave isn't to *be* great.

"I don't have that kind of ambition," I say.

"Don't lie to yourself. I know those lies. I've *told* those lies." He steps away. "I cannot in good conscience continue to teach you until you admit to the hunger. In order to control it, you need to acknowledge it."

Says the man who'd rather die than try to control it. I don't want to lie, but I refuse to lose this precious time with him. So I nod and swallow my own doubts. "All right. I'm hungry for the knowledge."

"And the power."

"And the power, I guess. Will you still show me how to summon flame?"

Summoning flame is so much harder than any of the other lessons so far, and I just can't seem to get the hang of it. A part of me wants to believe that Kalin's intentionally withholding some vital part of the spell to prevent me from becoming addicted to my power, but I know the more likely reason is I'm just not good at this. It's not an academic sort of knowledge. It involves my mind, yes, but also my spirit and my body. It's less like taking a test and more like learning to drive.

That evening the promised storm finally breaks over the little house and knocks out the electricity. Kalin disappears into the library, mumbling something about entertainment, leaving Jess and I at the dining room table.

I try (unsuccessfully) to light some candles with magic while Jess chatters. Thunder rolls overhead and she jumps at the crack of lightning.

"Aren't you supposed to be used to storms?" I comment, because electric storms are an almost daily occurrence in Johannesburg.

I can hardly see her face in the growing shadows. Instead of answering me, she asks, "You're sure we can trust him, right?"

"Who, Kalin?"

"No, the fricken president. Yes, Kalin." She leans closer to whisper, "You said he was working on a plan, but I've been watching him and all he does is karate or whatever and read."

He is working on his plan. His plan is waiting for death day. I hate thinking about it, and I really don't want to talk about it.

"I trust him," I say a moment before he walks in with a pile of boardgames.

Kalin, of course, has no issue lighting the candles. And Jess isn't paying enough attention to realise he doesn't use matches.

"Can't you just fix the electricity while you're at it?" I ask.

"Once I know where the problem is, yes. Although probably an exercise in futility until the storm clears. You're not afraid of the dark are you?"

"I'd be less afraid if I could cast fireballs from my palms like some people."

George's family must really like boardgames because there's a whole load that I've never seen before. We forgo the classic Monopoly and Risk in favour of a spooky game called Betrayal at House on the Hill. The haunted house theme is perfect for the weather, and the flickering shadows of the candles. A little too perfect. The beach house creaks and groans with the wind and this time I'm the one who jumps at lightning flashes against the sky – much to Kalin's amusement.

We're about twenty minutes in when there's a new sound: a strange rapping noise. I think Kalin's doing it to scare me, but he looks just as alarmed.

"Could it be a branch on the roof?" I ask.

"The trees aren't tall enough."

Jess shrinks back in her chair.

Kalin realises what it is an instant before we do, and he shoots to his feet. "It's the front door."

He approaches the door slowly, with one hand held up as if to caution us to be quiet. I know that the real reason is because he has a spell ready to fling at whoever is there. Jess sinks down until she's almost hiding under the table. I duck too.

There's no peephole, and Kalin's brow furrows as he tries to sense whatever's on the other side of the door. It remains furrowed as he unlocks the door. He opens it only an inch.

"I'm warning you," a shaky voice says. "I've told people where I am. If I disappear, they'll come looking for me."

"Understood," Kalin says. "Can I help you?"

"I'm looking for a girl." Thunder rumbles. "Her name is Jessica—"

Jess squeals and knocks over the board in her haste to get to the door. Kalin barely has time to get out of the way before Jess flings herself out and into Michael's arms.

"You came looking for me!"

"Of course I did. Are you okay? Why are you here? I've been trying to call you. I thought you'd been kidnapped or—"

I crane my neck to try see him, but Jess blocks him completely. "How did you find me?"

"Yes," Kalin says, nonplussed. "How *did* you find her?"

"Ah—" I see a hand emerge above Jess's head, waving a phone. "Find My iPhone."

"Find my what?" Kalin asks.

Laughter bursts out of me, raw and overwhelming. I double over and can't get in enough air to explain to Kalin. With all this magic, all his paranoia, Michael found us with an app.

"Is that—" Michael steps into the room. "Is that Lilah Durow?"

I try to control myself, given the severity of the situation. I point to the phone Michael's holding and open my mouth to explain, but it's no use.

"Yeah, it's Lilah," Jess says, taking over when it becomes apparent that I am unable to get a grip. "The mob's after us."

"Not technically the mob," Kalin says.

"Is she okay?" Michael asks.

"Find My iPhone!" I declare to the room and start laughing afresh.

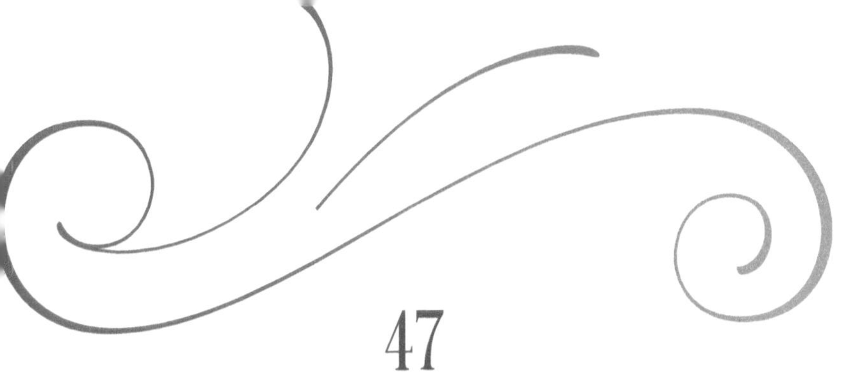

47

Michael is only one more person, but now the house feels full. He admits that he was lying about people knowing where he was, and he shows Kalin how to disable the app on our phones. I think that's when Kalin realises why I was laughing so hard, because he looks up and catches my eye. If he wasn't such a technophobe, he could have saved himself a lot of amulet-making time.

Well, Shirley did say that advanced tech and magic were similar.

We tell Michael that we only have to stay here for another week and a bit, then the threat will have passed, and we can go home. Michael, journalist that he is, wants to know all the details. Why did I fake my death? Is Dumi involved? What did Kalin do to get us into this mess? I give him vague answers when I have to, but mostly I leave the non-answers to Kalin; he's good at those.

The one thing Michael can offer, however, is news about Dad.

He's surprised when I ask. "Of course, you wouldn't know."

We're all sitting together in the lounge. Jess, Michael and I are on the sand-coloured sofas. Kalin is at the table, packing away the board game.

My heart stumbles. "Is he okay?"

"Yeah, better than okay. I mean, well, aside from what happened to you, but when he hears you're fine, he'll be okay."

I resist the urge to shake him. "What happened?"

"Your dad turned witness. When you were… well, he figured he had nothing to lose, right?"

This doesn't cheer me up the way Michael seems to expect it to. "So, he *was* guilty then."

All this time I'd held onto hope that it was a misunderstanding, that it was maybe even tied to the Guardians. I can feel Kalin's eyes on me, but he doesn't say anything. Probably thinking, "I told you so."

Michael leans forward. "It was duress. They offered him money first, but he refused. This was years ago, and it wasn't anything as serious as human trafficking. Just stepping down from a much smaller case against one of Dumi's goons and letting a less-qualified prosecutor take it. He didn't accept the money, didn't step down. Then apparently, they learned he had a daughter. The next time Dumi asked him to do something, they threatened you. And he said it started small – small things that didn't seem so bad. Then when Dumi himself was finally brought up on charges, he arranged for your father to be the prosecutor. He thought that meant he was safe, but your father was secretly working against him. When Dumi discovered the truth, well, that's when the Hawks showed up at your house."

Michael is sounding far too enthusiastic about all this, like it's a movie to him, but it makes my stomach twist. "And he couldn't just run away with me, because I had to be here for the ritual. And Dumi knew his name, which would put me in danger from the Guardians, no matter how far we went."

Michael looks at me strangely, but I'm beyond caring.

"Where's Dad now?"

"He's in witness protection."

That's better than jail, I guess.

"I'm sorry," Kalin whispers.

Kalin's general mood sours as the days progress. He's short with me when we're training and hardly speaks to the others. To make matters worse, Jess and Michael are super lovey-dovey. They just snuggle the whole time and call each other awful pet names.

And it's not like I can even complain. I'm responsible for them both being here.

One night, when I'm sitting in bed feeling miserable, I try the fire spell again and it *works*.

At the glimmer of a spark in my palm, I give a whoop that makes the snoozing Kalin jerk upright. His magic swoops around us like a valkyrie, rattling the door and tearing at the curtains, before he realises there's no threat.

He glares at me. The moonlight catches his cheekbones and lends his expression an extra dose of severity. I meekly hold out my hand, with the tiny little flame dancing in it.

It's a real, physical manifestation of my power and he looks as dubious about it as I am thrilled.

Sure, it's not the biggest flame, but it's mine and I refuse to be ashamed of it.

Kalin's eyes go unfocused. "That's the first spell I ever cast."

"The *first*?" It's taken me days to get it right.

"Yes, unintentionally. I was still a child." He reaches for my hand and my pulse quickens. He doesn't say anything for a long time as he holds it in his and absently traces the skin around the flame. It's taking a lot of energy to keep it alight, but I'll keep it burning as long as I can, just to maintain that contact.

Then he says, "She used to call me Ember."

I don't need to ask who *she* is. I pull my hand away and extinguish the flame.

"You loved her." It's not a question. I know the answer.

"Yes."

No surprise, yet my heart still sinks. I know I'm the facsimile, the echo. Alayna was a warrior queen and I'm an anxious teenager.

I shouldn't have woken him, and I shouldn't have asked.

"She was my first friend, and the first person I met who was like me. She encouraged me to accept myself and my power. She was naïve enough to believe in me."

Kalin's watching me now, the far-off look gone.

"How long were you together?" Why am I asking these things? I must be a masochist to want to know more about the tragic love story in his past.

"Together?" His brow knits. Of course he'd make this even harder.

I wave a hand in the air vaguely and fix my gaze on the duvet. "Together. In love. Before the soldiers came."

Kalin smirks. "Well, considering Alayna was nine and I was eleven…"

I blink.

"We were children. Playmates. You thought otherwise?"

"I… you just said you *loved* her."

"I also just said she was my first *friend*."

All my wild imaginings struggle to reframe themselves: The close contact while learning spells, the name called in the night, every sordid detail I created in my mind. They were kids. Magical kids playing with spells.

There's a teasing note in Kalin's voice when he says, "So, if I understand correctly, you were under the impression that I courted both you and your ancestor?"

I jab at the bedclothes, embarrassed. "No. I was never under the impression that you *courted* me. More like tried to avoid courting me."

"And failed spectacularly."

I don't answer and I sense his attention still on me. At length, he says, "Goodnight, Lilah. Please don't set the curtains on fire."

⚜

Rain lashes at the shore, and I'm forced to sit indoors and sketch while Michael and Jess canoodle. Maybe I should have just stayed locked in Kalin's cottage. At least then I wouldn't have had to suffer through this. Every time their hands touch, every tender look, every whispered exchange is a punch to the gut.

During one particularly amorous session that involves at least four ridiculous pet names, my pencil snaps and I go into the library to get a new one.

Kalin is, as Kalin always is lately, in a chair reading. He doesn't even acknowledge me when I come in.

"Surely you've read all these books before?" I comment.

"No." He flips a page. The cover is a watercolour of a man in a floppy hat with lures dangling from it.

I give up my quest for a pencil. I can't bear to be in this house anymore. "I'm going outside."

"Wait!"

I don't. I head out into the rain. It's the horrible, icy-cold type that stings my skin, and the wind drags my hair into my face. I run down the beach to where we practised and begin doing my shield drills. It's kind of satisfying how they push away the rain, and the wind provides enough resistance to make it a challenge, but it's freezing, and my clothes are wet through in seconds. I grit my teeth and persevere.

"Lilah!" Kalin jogs towards me.

He casts something over my head, and the rain stops. I look up to see it hitting an invisible barrier and sliding away. "Teach me how to do that?"

"Come inside."

"No, I'd rather be out here." I step away from his magical umbrella.

He grabs my arm. "This is going too far. You need to stop."

He believes I ran out here to get my magic fix? I fling a shield spell at him that sends him skidding across the sand away from me. I think it impresses us both.

He strides back. His hair sticks to his face and his coat is slick. "Lilah, I can't leave you with this addiction."

"So, don't leave me then."

He growls. "We've discussed this."

I cast another shield at him, but he's ready for it this time and blocks it easily. "No. We never discussed anything."

"Why are you acting like this?"

My wet hair slaps against my cheeks. "How should I act, Kalin? How should I be acting? Stuck in there with them like that and knowing that every hour brings me closer to the time you die? Maybe you can sit and read and ignore it, but I—"

"Reading is an escape," he says, almost too softly to be heard over the wind. "You should know that."

"Well maybe you shouldn't be escaping into books, maybe you should be escaping from the Guardians." I shoot out another shield.

"And what, use my power and my immortality to take over the world? You would like that, wouldn't you? Now you have a taste for it?"

I grab at the roots of my hair. "Stop it."

Does he honestly think so little of me? He comes nearer.

"What's the plan, Lilah? Should we start by taking out Dumi? Freeing your father?"

The possibility hadn't even occurred to me. This is what he thinks? That I've been plotting? It's a physical pain in my chest. I stare at him. The rains washes over me.

He comes closer still. "Then I suppose we fix the South African government? And after that, maybe we can try North Korea? Where do you want to live, Lilah? Where should we build our *palace*?"

"Stop it." I intend to respond with anger, but my voice breaks.

It must give Kalin pause, because he stays where he is.

I shake my head. "I don't want any of that."

"Lilah…"

"Go away! Leave me alone!" My jaw aches from the cold and from yelling.

"I can't do that!"

"That's exactly what you're doing! You're going to go and die!" I ball my fists. The gale whips away some of my words. It feels good to shout, to let go of the pent-up rage. "I spent days breaking through your spell to come after you. I thought, after all the times you rescued me, I could save you. I thought I could make you see sense. But I was wrong about you. You can't be saved. You're too stubborn. Too arrogant. Too much of a coward. You'd rather believe that I've gone evil—"

"I didn't say you were—"

"Addicted then! A magical junkie who dreams of world domination. You think casting spells in the rain is so fricken appealing that I can't help myself? I'd freeze for that little hit of power? You think I want to learn spells so I can be the next Overlord? You've lived for three hundred and twenty-three years and that's what your experience tells you?"

I blink back hot tears. "You'd rather believe that, because otherwise you have to face up to the fact that your power isn't to blame for the choices *you* made all those years ago. You'd have to face up to the fact that they were *choices*, not compulsions. But no, that's too much to ask. So now I'm trapped here, watching you die." The tears spill onto my cheeks and I heave in air.

Kalin offers no response. The rain pours down around him.

"I don't give a damn about magic." There's a sob building in my chest. I lift a handful of wet sand with my mind and throw it at him. It scatters in the wind long before it reaches him. "You think you know everything. But you're an idiot and you're cruel. You're so cruel sometimes, without even knowing it."

His face falls. He *does* know it. If there's one thing that Kalin is hyper aware of, it's his guilt.

"How can you not understand? I don't want power. I don't want magic. I want..." I suck in a breath. "Everything you teach me… it's a piece of *you* I get to keep after… I don't want any of that, Kalin, I just want you."

He closes the distance between us and takes me into his arms. Even in the rain, he's so warm. He still smells the same, feels the same.

"I'm sorry," he says. "You're right. You're right about everything."

He presses my head to his chest. His heart is racing and his breath is unsteady. I shouldn't have said those things, no matter how true they are. What good could come from hurting him?

I could stand in the rain like this forever. I would, gladly. It's better than every other alternative I can think of for passing the time between now and our final goodbye. But Kalin takes my hand and guides me into a stance, and teaches me how to cast my own umbrella, just as I requested.

It's late when we return to the house, wet and numb from cold. Jess and Michael are curled up together on the couch, so I go straight to the bedroom to dry my hair. I'm about to flick the drier on, when Kalin comes up behind me and silently removes it from my hand. He sits down beside me on the bed, and runs his own fingers through my hair. They're warm – unnaturally warm – and I smell the steam as he strokes his magic through my wet tresses, slowly, and with so much care that it doesn't even pull when he encounters a knot.

It feels amazing. I'm about to ask him to teach me *this*, when he dips his head and kisses my neck. My body locks up as hope and desire whirl through me. We're fighting, aren't we? I shouldn't want this so badly, but I do. My every nerve waits for the next kiss. *Will there be a next kiss?*

I turn my head. Our eyes meet. Then our lips meet.

Both times we've kissed before, it's been a reckless act of passion. Now there's all the more reason to be desperate, but instead the kiss is slow and tender. His magic curls around me. I can feel it holding me protectively.

His eyelashes flutter against my cheek when he pulls away.

"What was that for?" I ask. He's been so cold. Why the change of heart? Is it pity?

He swallows, then says softly, "I want you too. I want a life with you, more than anything."

My heart stops, then restarts itself. "You don't have to say that. I lost my temper out there. I'll be fine." A lie. I'm sure he can hear it's a lie. There's no way I'll be fine when he dies.

"You called me on my crap." He offers the ghost of a smile and reaches up to caress my cheek. "I have been cruel to you. Unforgivably so."

I sigh. "Not everything is unforgivable."

"I've done enough unforgivable things. And you're right, of course, it was me and not the magic." He shuts his eyes. "I'm so sorry. I was projecting my own weakness onto you. You didn't deserve that. You don't deserve the way I've been treating you. You don't deserve any of this."

It's like the layer of ice around him has shattered and I'm talking to *my* Kalin again. The cold hard thing in my chest unfurls, like a leaf seeking light. "So you don't believe I've gone all power crazy?"

"No. You had my power for weeks and did nothing untoward with it. That should be proof enough."

I offer him what I hope is a playful smile. "I seduced you." I want to lift the mood a little, before we both suffocate under the weight of his guilt.

"You never needed magic to do that."

I look up into his dark, Overlord eyes. But even now they're brown instead of gold, they're filled with that same gentle affection that I've seen there so often. This moment feels delicate, like any minute and he'll go back to being grumpy and cold.

He wraps his arms around me and pulls me close. Our clothing steams as his magic dries it. We stay like that a while, until he whispers, "In three hundred years, I've never felt the way I feel about you. I've been keeping you at a distance, trying to make this easier. It hasn't worked. Nothing will make it easier. And in the process, I've hurt you."

"Kalin—"

"I don't want to leave you again." His voice cracks and he buries his head against my neck. "I don't want to die."

I hold him to me, this all-powerful sorcerer capable of bringing nations to their knees. I hold him and I stroke his hair, soothing him as best I can. Which is worse? Cold Kalin, or broken, hurting Kalin? I search for something to say, some way I can comfort him.

"If me having power for weeks and doing nothing bad with it is proof enough that I'm not power hungry…"

He starts to speak.

"Shhh, hear me out. I'm not talking about the past couple of months when you were running from your power. I mean before. You've been channelling earth magic for how long? Years?"

"It's not the same," he murmurs.

"It *is* the same. How many opportunities have you had to hurt people? How many times have you *wanted* to hurt people, and you haven't? When you saved me from Dumi, you even told *those* guys you didn't want to hurt them. And you didn't defend yourself from Bianca, even when she threw all those heavy books at your head. Even though you could have killed her and eliminated a bunch of problems. The magic isn't a parasite, Kalin, it's a part of you. You're not who you were when you were the Overlord. I've seen the Overlord. I wouldn't have come after you, I wouldn't be here, if there was any doubt in my mind that you're not the same person. You've changed. Your magic has too."

His grip around me tightens. "I deserve to die."

"You *will* die. Whether it's next week, or in sixty years. Either way, I will be there with you and you won't die alone."

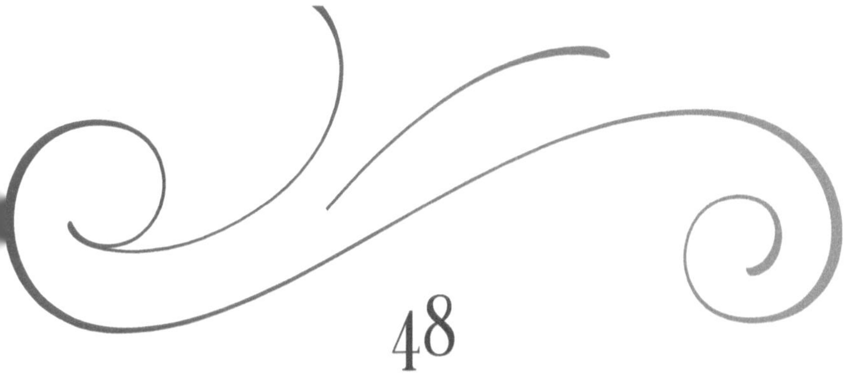

48

In many ways, this day is like the others. We all eat breakfast together in the kitchen and avoid Michael's questions about where the groceries come from. Then Kalin and I go out onto the beach to train.

But in other ways, it's entirely different. The way Kalin catches my eye when he ducks and dives the questions, the way Kalin and I walk hand-in-hand along the shoreline, looking at the shells and driftwood that the storm brought in rather than casting spells.

He points to an anemone in a rock pool, then says, "I may need to start teaching you some more offensive spells."

I follow his gaze, but the anemone waves its tendrils benignly. "Because I've perfected all the defensive ones?" I tease. I know I haven't.

He turns me to face him and tucks a curl behind my ear. His expression darkens. "Because I may need to ask you to fight."

I try to read his expression, the tilt of his mouth. "Why?"

"I don't know what will happen in the moment the curse breaks. I know that I'll be made mortal. What I don't know is just how *compos mentis* I'll be. You may need to hold the line for a minute, maybe more. It will be dangerous."

My stomach lurches. "Kalin, what are you saying?"

"I'm saying you may need to fight the Guardians."

I shake my head. "No, I got that." I search his face for confirmation. "Does this mean… what does this mean?"

He cups my cheek and rests his forehead against mine. "It means I'm either finally courageous enough to face my own power… or I'm too much of a coward to leave you. I haven't decided which."

"You're going to live?"

"I'm going to *try*. That's all I can promise."

If anyone was watching, they'd probably think we just got engaged, the way I squeal and wrap my arms around his neck and kiss him. I think he even spins me around. It's hard to tell through the wild elation that's rushing through me.

"It's not going to be easy," he cautions as he sets me down. "They've had years of training, and we've had days. Lilah, we might both end up dead. This is probably a terrible idea—"

I press my finger to his lips. "Don't talk yourself out of it. Show me what to do."

⚶

Another thing that's different about this day, is Jess is sitting alone when I return to the house after training.

"You're back early," she says, lowering her book.

Turns out offensive spells take way more energy than defensive ones. I flop down next to her. "Where's Michael?"

She stiffens and hesitates.

"You didn't have a fight, did you?" That would be awkward for all of us in such a confined space, judging by how they acted last time they had a falling out.

"No…" Her gaze darts towards the library. "Ah, where's Kalin? He's still going to be out there a while, right?"

My neck prickles. "He's checking the perimeter. He'll be back soon." It's been his habit to do this every day since Michael joined us. "Jess, where's Michael?"

"I think he's just reading or something. Mich—" she starts to call him, but I fling a shield at her. It hits her in the stomach, and she doubles over, gasping as I scramble off the couch and fly for the closed library door. I hurl it open, hoping, praying, he's not doing what I think he is.

He's sitting at the little desk by the window, and he's talking on the phone. He jumps when he hears the door and immediately ends the call.

"Who was that? Who were you talking to?"

His eyes go wide, and he looks beyond me as Jess runs up, still gasping for breath. "Don't overreact, Lilah. It's not a big deal. They said they won't run the story until we're safe."

"What story?" I growl at Michael. It's taking everything in me to not throw one of the offensive spells I just learned at him. "Who were you talking to?"

He holds up his hands in a gesture of innocence, although he's still got the incriminating phone in the one hand. "You can't blame me. I'm the Durow guy. I mean, I've been covering this thing since the beginning. The fact that you're alive— it's going to make headlines all over."

"*Bylines*, you mean." I snatch the phone from him. "How long? How many calls? What have you told them?"

He takes my shoulders. "Lilah, you need to calm down. I know you're in love with the guy, but listen, do you even know that the mob is really after you? I spoke to the cops; they have Dumi in custody, and his thugs wouldn't have come near you after I ran the story on how they kidnapped you. It was too incriminating. Plus, they all believe you're dead. You're hiding out here, but maybe you don't need to. Maybe this is all just in *his* head."

I round on Jess. "I told you why we're hiding."

"Yeah, you're a wizard and he's an immortal sorcerer. I got it. Do you even know how crazy that sounds?" She's holding her side, but speaking as if I didn't just cause that pain with magic.

"We're going to get you out of here," Michael assures me. "I wasn't going to say anything because I know your head's still all twisted up, but we've been planning it for a while."

All those whispering sessions. I wriggle out of his grasp. "*Who* did you call?"

"I spoke to the lawyer at the paper. He said that since your father's out of the picture, your guardian at the moment would be your warden."

No. Blood roars in my ears. He's called Sukwini. He's gone and called Sukwini. "You've killed him. You've killed him and you've killed me. You have no idea what she's involved in, no idea what's really going on." I want to strangle him, and with my magic I could, but I resist the urge and make for the door.

He grabs my arm. "She's on her way; she's bringing the cops. I can't let you go, Lilah. Jess, shut the door!"

I take a breath to call for Kalin, but Michael clamps his palm over my mouth. Michael is much stronger than I am, and his arms hold me perfectly still, but what he doesn't bargain on, is magic.

I pull a Bianca. I grab hold of the nearest book with my mind, and I hurl it at his face.

I think it's more surprise than pain that loosens his grip as it clocks him in the jaw. I shove my elbows out, and my magic too. He crashes backwards, right into the desk, and I make a break for it.

Jess looks like a deer in the headlights. She doesn't even try to stop me. I think I hear her say, "You *are* a wizard," as I pass.

The car keys are on a little silver tray by the door. I snatch them with magic and bolt out onto the beach.

"Kalin!" No sign of him. He must be round the other side of the house.

Michael has the gall to chase after me. "Lilah, wait!"

I run up onto the dunes. The small milkwood branches batter my face and arms. "Kalin!"

Michael follows. "Lilah, stop! No one wants to hurt you! We're not the enemy!

My heart batters against my rib cage. *Yes, you are.* I turn to face him. The sand rises around me, just like in my dream. He skids to a halt and stares at it.

"I don't want to fight you, but I will."

"What the hell?" I can see that he's trying to find a logical explanation for this, but there isn't one.

I'm ready to lob the sand at him if he makes another move, but then magic whispers behind me and I whirl around because I'm so scared it's Sukwini.

It's Kalin.

"What's going on?" he asks.

I press the keys into his hand. "We have to go. Sukwini's on her way."

I feel the snap of his rage as he glares at Michael and says, "Ever the journalist?" in that deep, Overlord voice.

Michael takes a step back.

"Kalin." I grab his wrist. "Kalin, there's no time. We've got to go."

He nods and we sprint for the car.

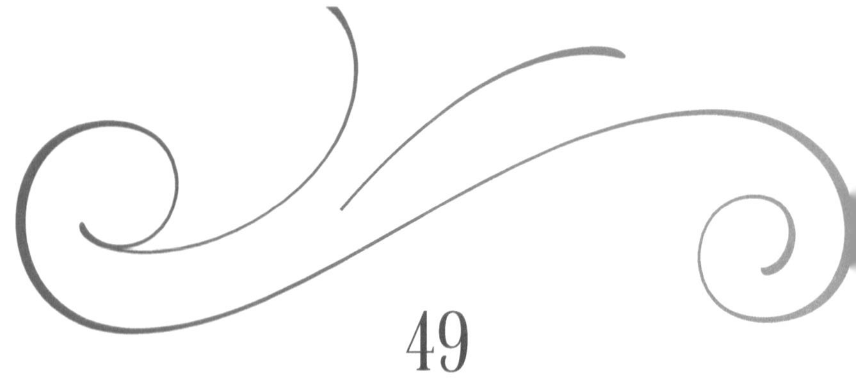

49

We hurtle up the long dirt road in Dahlia's rust bucket. My pulse is still racing, and I can't stop trembling. All I can think is how much power I felt from Sukwini that day in the kitchen, and how strong the Guardians' chains were. I thought I'd have more time to prepare, I thought we'd face them on our terms, and I thought I wouldn't be so tired and worn out after a day of training. The few spells it took to escape Michael drained what was left of my energy.

"Breathe," Kalin says. "Breathe and tell me exactly what happened."

As I do, his knuckles go white on the steering wheel. We reach the top of the road and swing onto tar again.

"Where are we going?" I ask.

"I don't know. Away."

Kalin's rattled and as the speedometer creeps over 120 kilometres per hour, the car starts to rattle too. The road runs long and straight through grassland. It's bordered by tangled shrubs and small trees. We're going fast enough that they blur. We streak past a sign that says we're heading towards Port Elizabeth.

"Maybe we should go to the city. More people, more space to hide," I suggest.

Kalin nods. "All right. It's the best idea we have."

The road takes us over a river mouth and past a tiny holiday town. I sink back in my seat. *Get to the city, lie low, we might be fine.*

For a while there are buildings to either side of us, then they drop away, and we're back to flat fields.

"Lilah, how long has that car been behind us?"

I turn in my seat and there, near the horizon, on this long straight road, is another vehicle. The only other vehicle. My heart jerks.

"Probably a holidaymaker."

Kalin puts his foot down and the car vibrates, the windows shake, the little dream catcher hanging from the mirror lashes from side to side. He eases up. The other car is still gaining and there's nowhere for him to go. No side streets, no turn offs. Kalin swears.

"I'm sure other people use this road. It's probably someone from that village going to PE to do shopping." But even as I speak, unease snakes up my spine. Whoever they are, they're going really fast. It's that feeling I've only had in dreams before, when the monster's coming and my legs won't work.

"Can't you do something magical to make us go faster?" I ask.

Kalin glances at me. "I am. I'm holding this machine together. It certainly wasn't built for this."

I can see the strain in his muscles, which I mistook for stress.

"Well, can't you just conjure a better car?" Like he could do with pizza and orange juice.

"That's not how it works."

The other car draws closer, and closer still. My mouth goes dry. At the same moment that it's near enough for me to make out it's a police car, magic slides over my skin. One of the occupants is casting a spell.

The tyres screech. It's like we're in a motorised toy, and someone has their thumb on it, so we can't move forward. I smell burning rubber, then a *whump* of magic passes over my skin and my ears pop. I recognise it as the shield spell, but it's far more powerful than anything I could cast. The pressure on the car eases, and I dare not check to see how close they are now.

Kalin yanks the wheel to the left and we lurch off road. He can't mean to go cross-country in this thing! My teeth slam together, and the rust bucket shakes so much I don't know how Kalin is possibly holding it in one piece. We crash into something – a fence maybe – and it scrapes along the side of the car. Kalin sends out another shield, then some other spell that I don't see but feel in my bones and at the back of my jaw.

We thump onto a parallel road, going in the opposite direction. Alarmed sheep stare at us as we pass. Kalin's panting and sweat glistens on his forehead. I should be able to help. With all the magic he's taught me, I should be able to *do* something.

"Tell me what to do!"

He looks over his shoulder to cast another spell, and at that moment a little boy runs out into the middle of the road. Kalin reacts on instinct. He swerves away from the child. Dahlia's car can't take the sudden change in direction. For an instant, we're skidding on two wheels, then the car smacks over onto its side, and everything's tumbling past. Light, dark, light, dark. Then there's only dark.

❧

My ears are ringing and my face stings. There's a deep ache in my abdomen. I open my eyes and can't understand what I'm seeing. Broken glass stained red. Brown grass, pressed to the floor. No, to the windscreen. I'm hanging upside down.

"Kalin?"

My confusion lifts a little, and I remember the chase.

"Kalin!"

He's dangling next to me and he's bleeding from the head. I know he's not dead. He can't be dead because he's immortal, but that doesn't stop the terror that pierces my gut. He's unconscious, and his neck is at an odd angle.

"Kalin!"

My door opens and hands reach in to drag me out. I'm too dazed to cast magic at them, I'm too disorientated to think of anything but Kalin. He needs to heal. He needs to respond. I keep shouting his name and wriggling and kicking.

"Is she alive?" someone asks.

"Very much so," Sibu answers. It's his arms that are holding me. Him and someone I don't recognise, someone in a police uniform.

The other car is parked at the side of the road, and Sukwini stands in front of it. Her colourful dress flutters in the wind as she moves towards me. "Lilah, dear, let me see your injuries. Let me get a look at you."

She doesn't seem like the enemy. She doesn't seem like someone who'd want to torture me. Maybe Kalin's wrong. Maybe she is still on our side.

Then the front door of the police car opens and Shirley steps out. Bianca follows, from the passenger side. Magic crackles from her. "Come on. We don't have much time before he wakes up."

"No!" They won't trap me this time. They won't *kill* me this time. I draw on my terror, draw on the pain in my stomach and push out the best shield I can manage. This time Sibu *will* let go. He does, and he goes flying backwards to land hard on the tar. The cop does too.

I clench my fists. If they want me this time, I'm not going to go quietly.

"Lilah, listen to me," Sukwini says. "This is all a big misunderstanding."

"No. You're working with them. They murdered me. They murdered my mother. There is nothing to misunderstand."

Bianca whips the air with her arm, and I throw out my energy. Whatever spell she flung at me, hits my shield.

"Well isn't this interesting?" Shirley says. "He's *trained* her. I told you, Sukwini. It's just as well you came to us when you did."

They're all watching me. I look around for the child. But of course there was no child all alone out in the middle of nowhere. It was an illusion, a trap.

Shirley holds out a hand towards me, and slowly beckons. The air between us pulls taut, there's a tug in my navel, and then my feet are skidding, sliding on the tar towards her as if there was a rope around me. I try to fight it. I kick the ground and writhe against it, but there is absolutely nothing I can do to escape. In a last-ditch effort, I try casting a shield, but she just laughs.

"This will all be over soon," Sukwini says.

"Mom!" As Bianca shouts the warning, I feel the snap of magic behind me. Then I'm yanked free of Shirley and fly backwards into Kalin's arms. They close around me, possessively.

"So, it's true." Shirley must mean about him having his power back. Is there a hint of fear in her voice?

"It's true," Kalin confirms. "If you want me, fight me. Lilah has no part in this anymore."

"That's where you're wrong, Kallen. She has always had a part to play. It is her destiny to stop you. Bianca?"

Bianca reaches to her side and draws a sword. A freakin' sword. *I knew it!*

This is not an ordinary sword. It looks like something King Arthur would carry, and it radiates magic.

Kalin ducks his head to whisper in my ear, "Remember what I taught you." And he shoves me aside.

Bianca rushes at him with the sword held high. Shirley casts. Not at Kalin, but at me. I dive out of the way of her spell and land hard on the road. I roll clumsily to my feet – one of the many things that we practised on the beach. Sibu makes another grab for me, but I cut an arm through the air and push him over with another spell. Kalin dodges and dives around Bianca, while casting wildly at Shirley. I throw out a shield, just as she sends another spell my way. But I'm not fast enough to block Sibu again, and he grabs me around my middle and wrestles me to the ground. He pins my hands above my head.

I recall the fire spell, and it takes a few tries, but I manage to make my hands burn hot. He hisses and lets go. I grab a fistful of sand and throw it in his face. When he jerks away, cursing and blinking, I wriggle out from under him.

A bolt of electricity lands right next to me. It thunders through me, and the ground trembles. Another lands on my other side. I look up to find Shirley with her arms stretched wide, and power I can actually see travelling along her arms to her hands. The light reflects in her eyes. I block another bolt, but the sheer force of it knocks me back. Then, butterflies. Not in the cartoon knocked-unconscious sense. In the very real sense. A swarm of yellow butterflies obscures my vision. I can't see anything but wings. Panic seizes me. I throw out shield after shield in every direction.

Get control of yourself, Lilah. You don't need to see!

Like the night we set the perimeter spell across the beach, I close my eyes and feel the scene with my *mind*.

There's someone right in front of me, someone whose magic I don't recognise, but it feels yellow like the butterflies. I slam my energy out towards it, and it goes sprawling. I'm panting and my sides ache. I can't keep this up. Sibu comes at me again. Red aura. His magic meets mine. Our powers war, pushing against each other, kicking, biting. When our bodies come together, it's with my elbow in his jaw, his fist in my stomach. I fall, unable to breathe, but my magic is only aggravated. It shoots out at his knees; he repels it and launches himself at me. I twist his weight off me, scratch at his cheeks, and my magic takes him by the throat.

I open my eyes. His face is very near. He stares at me, gaping. I could kill him. My power is greater than his. He's lost focus. His fingers flex in desperation for air.

I knee him in the groin then let him go.

My limbs tremble with strain as I climb to my feet, just in time to witness Bianca slicing through Kalin's shoulder.

Time slows. Kalin flings back his head and cries out as his arm – his whole left arm – just falls. My body goes cold with horror. This is how they plan to defeat him. How many pieces do they mean to cut him into before they take me away? I can't see the blood because that side of him is facing the other way, but my stomach roils, and bile rises to my throat.

"Kalin!"

The arm will grow back, but he's still in agony. He falls to his knees, overwhelmed by it. Bianca backs away from him, sword lowered, sheet-white.

"Continue!" Shirley orders.

Bianca lifts the sword again, but she can't seem to bring herself to strike.

Kalin's head is bowed, and his shoulders move with the deep, agonised breaths he's sucking in.

"Leave him! I'll come with you," I call.

Kalin's head snaps up. Even his lips are pale. He shakes his head, mouths the word "No".

I step towards Shirley on shaking legs. Miss Sukwini comes out from behind the car and holds out a hand to me. "Come, my dear. Come."

But I hear the creak of metal behind me and turn to see the wreckage of Dahlia's car lifting into the air.

"You will *not* take her," Kalin says. His eyes flash bright and he throws the car right at Shirley.

She casts a shield. The wreck shatters against it. I cover my face, but metal does not rain down around me. There's no sound at all. I look up. The parts are hovering in the air over us. Kalin has his remaining hand stretched towards them. Shirley lifts her own arms, slowly, as if with great effort, and all the parts float towards each other.

It's Overlord versus Guardian General. Her power is electric blue. His melts the air and makes my skin hum. No one else moves. Kalin staggers to his feet, but he wobbles. Even the Overlord can only suffer so much blood loss before he grows weak.

Metal collides overhead, sparks, crumples. Kalin would be more powerful than her, if he wasn't nearly unconscious. I can see his strength failing. I want to help, but I don't even know what he's casting. I could levitate maybe one of those pieces, but that's not enough.

Then Bianca comes unfrozen. She moves so fast that I have no hope of shielding Kalin before she drives the sword into his chest.

The wreckage flies at them both. I dive forward and cast. Not a shield, but a wall of hardened air over them. An umbrella. The metal hits it, and I feel the ricochet of energy as my barrier smashes. I bought just enough time for Bianca to dive clear, but Kalin...

My chin slams into the ground, I taste blood, then there's a sickening crack and pain radiates up my body. A chunk of Dahlia's chassis has landed on me – a door, I think. My head is swimming in pain. Is my leg broken? I try to see Kalin. I can't, but I can hear him cry out as bits of car thud into him over and over and over again, I can feel his energy gutter as he's buried in metal.

A shadow falls over me. Bianca's boots fill my vision. I scream at her – words I've never said before, words I think I might have made up. The metal lifts off my body and someone moves me. I am blinded by fresh agony, but I know the red aura as Sibu carries me towards their cop car.

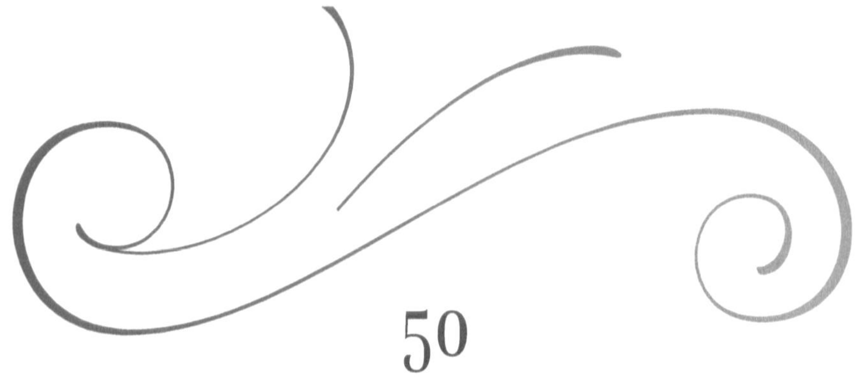

50

I'm in a dark, cold room that smells like damp and feels like concrete. I'm chained.

My body doesn't hurt anymore. Sukwini healed my leg, my abdomen, my chin and even my bitten tongue. But she could not heal the ache in my chest. In the absolute darkness of this cell, I see Kalin's arm falling again and again, as if it's burned into my retinas. Where is he now? Is he still buried, alone, in pain?

I curl into a tight, shivering ball.

I have no idea where I am. Sukwini sedated me, probably for some peace and quiet. My throat still feels raw from screaming. Is there any way Kalin will survive this? I picture him under that pile of debris. He agreed to try to live. But now I'm captured.

We can still fight.

I can't lose him.

My thoughts run around in desperate circles for time I cannot measure, until the door cracks open. A triangle of light illuminates whitewashed walls around me, which are brighter than I thought, and as my visitor steps into that light I see his face.

"Darren!" I try to stand, but the chain around my arm is too short. "Thank the Greats. You have to help me."

He flinches and thrusts a brown paper packet towards me. "I came to bring you food."

"I don't want food," I lie. I'm starving, but that doesn't matter. I need to find Kalin. I need to make sure he's okay. "Help me. You can get me out of here."

"I can't." He drops the packet and starts to shut the door again.

"Darren, please, don't just leave me here!"

The door closes.

⁓

The food they give me must be drugged because I'm constantly groggy, and each time I surface from sleep, I feel as if I've been unconscious for days.

The first time I'm escorted from my cell to use the bathroom, I expect to be led into a dank corridor. Instead, the monument stands before me, blazing with reflected light, its masts reaching up into low-hanging cloud.

I'm within the stone walls of the old fort, no more than a few feet from the menhir circle where the ritual will take place, no more than a few kilometres from the Settler's Cottage, where I should be now, at Kalin's side.

The bathroom stands separate from my squat, square prison room. Two people I don't recognise guard the door. I can sense vaguely that they, unlike Darren, have magic. And I can sense far less vaguely, by the way they watch me, that they have orders to kill, or at least hurt me a lot, if I try anything.

I entertain two fantasies during my imprisonment. The first is that one day, when I'm led out to relieve myself, I'll catch a group of students traipsing up to the monument, or someone walking their dog, and I'll call for help and they'll get the police to come save me. The other is that Kalin will be the one to save me – that he'll just appear one day, like he did when Dumi's thugs had me, and he'll use his amazing powers to whisk me away.

But for all I know, the Guardians have put me into a little pocket universe and as the days stretch onwards, I take comfort in that suspicion. The alternative is that Kalin is too weak or injured to rescue me.

Every time I see Darren, I beg for help, and every time

⁓411⁓

he denies it.

"They're going to kill me like they did before. Don't you care?" I demand of him.

"Of course I care. And they're not going to kill you. This is just temporary."

It doesn't feel temporary. It feels eternal.

One day I wake to Bianca standing in the doorway, with a white dress draped over her arm.

I fling a spell at her that she sweeps aside as if it's nothing. "Where's Kalin?"

She comes further into the room. "I imagine he's somewhere in town preparing for tonight."

My veins flood with ice. *Tonight.*

"You left him there. Buried—"

"He's the Overlord. He no doubt recovered within the hour." She holds up the dress. It's long and plain except for a gold ribbon along the neckline.

I glare at it.

"We all have our roles to play in this." Her voice is strained.

"No. We don't. You can stop all of it. He doesn't need to die. He already has his power. He isn't evil."

She rubs her temples. "You believe yourself the expert, after knowing him for less than a year. Lilah, I have studied him my entire life. I have trained for this day since I was old enough to stand. This is what I was born to—"

Raw rage uncoils in my chest. "You were born to be a *murderer?*" My anger isn't only for Kalin, but for my mother, for Dad, and for everyone who suffered because of what was deigned necessary hundreds of years ago.

"I'm not a puppet! I'm not going to perform this dance just because some dead people said so."

There's a glint of cold flame in her gaze when she responds. "This isn't a dance, Lilah. This is damage control. The original Guardians meant to destroy the orb. *He* was the one who cursed your line. You see him as a man, but he's not. He's something ancient, twisted and cruel. Our saving grace is that he does not have the full extent of his abilities back, that he still needs to come here—"

"He *does* have his powers back. I told you."

She chuckles mirthlessly. "Believe me, if he was at full power, there is no possible way I could have bested him in battle."

I consider the possibility for a mere moment, then I remember finding him in the study – the look on his face, the fear. There has to be another reason he was holding back during that fight. Maybe he was tired. Or…

"Maybe he didn't want to hurt you."

As I say it, I know that's the case. No matter what Bianca's done to him, to us. No matter what rage burned within, or how desperate he was to keep me from her grasp, he couldn't have killed her. She isn't only a Guardian. She's a person, with a life, a family, a career. She's so much more than this role she's determined to play.

"He's done with using magic that way. He's not evil."

I think I see Bianca's expression flicker, but it happens so fast I can't read her.

She holds out the dress.

⁕

I don't want to wear the dress, but they refuse to give me food or let me go to the bathroom until I change. So, in the end, I do, because it's a small price to pay for those comforts. Bianca returns for me just before sunset, dressed in dark green robes with a high collar. As she leads me from the fort, others step in to follow us. My guards, Sibu, the police guy, some more people I don't know who were probably at the lake, and Darren. It's kind of like a wedding procession. I wish it was that, and not the opposite. They're leading me to witness the man I love's death.

Shirley is waiting for us at the stones, dressed in golden robes with draped sleeves. Sukwini is with her, in green like Bianca, but she can't seem to meet my gaze. Shirley does a complicated hand gesture, and something happens to the air. It goes… weird. As with all things magic, I feel it more than see it. It feels like those curtains over the bedroom window at the beach house. Gauzy.

It's a clear day, and quite warm, but with another movement of Shirley's fingers, the mist rolls in, and it rises just like that night I was walking back from the library. Now past my ankles, now past my knees, now over my face. But instead of the blind whiteness of that night, the mist ripples and shapes emerge from it. Here a standing stone, there a Guardian.

The mist lifts.

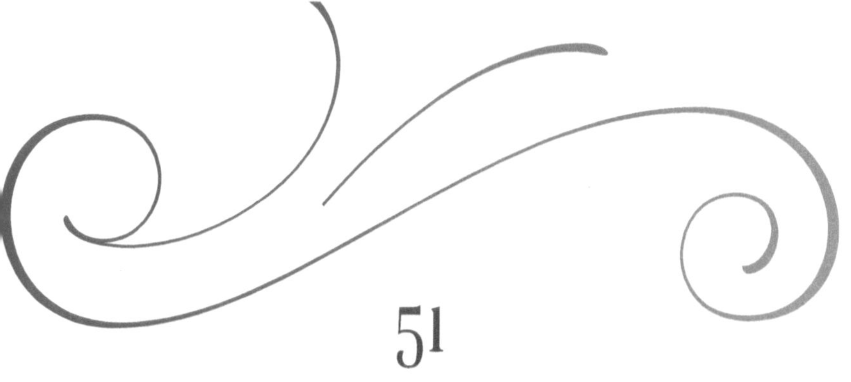

51

There's no 1820 Settlers Monument. Instead, the stone circle sits in the palm of a huge hand, connected to a giant arm, reaching out from a stone woman at least as large as the Statue of Liberty. She's holding us in her one hand, and an orb in the other. The sky blazes red behind her.

It's Alayna.

Even with chiselled features, I recognise her. I stand on my toes to peek over the edge of her hand. There's a crowd below us, waving little lights like during a sappy song at a concert.

Kalin called the stones a *gateway*. I must be in the Otherworld. In the fairy realm. The people below us are *fairies*. It's difficult to make out details from so high up, but I'm pretty sure none of them have wings.

Shirley stands in the centre of Alayna's palm, with her hands raised, and she speaks in a strange language that I shouldn't understand, but I do.

"The hour is at hand. The Overlord will finally face the justice we have sought for generations. Today, you will at last see him meet his end."

Her voice echoes out, louder than it should be. Bianca grips my upper arm.

"He approaches!" Shirley declares.

The crowd swells. My stomach flips over. I'm not ready for this. I can't do this.

"Don't move," Bianca murmurs, as if sensing my instinct to run, though I'm not sure where she thinks I could go.

Shirley steps aside, and we all watch the centre of the stones. For a long time, there's nothing there, and I don't breathe. I dare to hope that Kalin has given in to his cowardice and fled, chosen to live forever rather than come here to die.

But then the mist rolls in, and his outline shimmers before me, as if carried here by the mist itself. He materialises facing away from me. My heart surges. The Fae react with a tumult of sound. I try to imagine what it must be like for them, seeing this legend in the flesh, but one thought blots out all others: *two arms.*

He's thin and ragged, in a dirty henley shirt with a missing sleeve. He turns on the spot, taking in the scene. His skin has a grey tinge and his stubble only partly hides the hollows of his cheeks. He looks like he's already dead. When his gaze falls on me, Bianca draws her sword and holds it to my throat.

The crowd vibrates with whispers. How much of what's happening so high above them can they even see?

Kalin's eyes roam over me, no doubt searching for injuries. Then, without any prompting, he sinks to his knees.

"No!" I pull against Bianca's grip, instinct overriding common sense. She has to move the sword a little so I don't slice my own throat. "No! Kalin! You said you'd try!"

He looks up at me, and his expression is so soft, so tender. "Let me do this one thing right."

"No!" I throw a shield at Bianca's arm, and the sword jerks away enough that I can pull myself free. I'm aware of noise, of the crowd reacting, of Shirley shouting as I fly into Kalin's arms. He holds me and tucks his head against mine. I bury my face in his shirt. I feel his heartbeat, his power that he's keeping close and not using. He needs to use it. Why isn't he using it?

Rough hands pull me away from him. I try to hold on, but he lets me go.

Now it's not just Bianca who holds me, with her magic sword, but some other Guardians too. Shirley steps towards Kalin, and a wind sweeps over the stones. It's cold and smells of smoke. The remaining Guardians arrange themselves in a circle around him. Just like in the dream. Just like when they first took his power. And they start chanting.

I can't see Kalin anymore, but I hear his scream. I picture the last time, how electricity chased over his skin, how they tortured him to keep him powerless. But they don't need to do that now. He's submitting to them of his own will.

"Kalin!"

Bianca's grip is even tighter than before.

"Stop! Stop hurting him!"

Kalin howls in agony, and something in me breaks. I see red. I see flames. I kick wildly, and each kick lands – on shins, on knees, on anything I can reach. I'm less a person and more a collection of flailing limbs, and my magic, that Rottweiler that I've kept on a leash, pulls against its restraints.

I let it loose.

I'm not sure exactly what happens, only that Guardians shriek and wheel away from me. I run forward.

"Lilah! Stop!" Bianca shouts. "I can't let you ruin this!"

She flings her sword at me. It flies straight and true, aided by magic.

"No!" Something slams into my side, and I'm pushed clear.

The sword sings through the something instead.

Darren. He staggers and collapses, with a sword sticking out of his middle.

I back away. My lungs stop working. I know what I'm seeing and yet there must be some mistake. This must be a trick, an illusion. Darren wouldn't do that, couldn't do that.

"No!" Bianca falls to her knees beside him. I can't move. He's bleeding, his mouth open, his eyes staring.

I don't understand. Why would he do that? My ears roar and my knees are numb. He wouldn't even help me escape before.

Bianca leans over him, checking for a pulse. She's distracted. I should take advantage, but I can't move.

The ground shakes violently, and I'm thrown from my feet, sprawling. My teeth slam together, and something *roars*. *What the hell is it?* Did Darren trigger it? Is it a spell to trap me? A result of the chanting? It gets louder and louder, and the statue shakes harder and harder, like a plane caught in turbulence. Surely Alayna's arm will break? I blink grit from my eyes, and when my vision clears, I see only Bianca shielding Darren with her body.

Then, abruptly, the shaking stops. My ears ring. I'm still on my hands and knees, deciding whether it's safe to stand, when a blinding light flies out of the stone in front of my face. It stops about a meter up and hangs there.

It's an orb. A green orb. And there are five others. They hover in a circle around the Guardians. Then, as I climb to my feet to stand on shaky legs, they start to rotate.

No one's moved to stop me yet, and I have a moment to wonder why before I see it. I'm *glowing*. My stomach is *shining*.

I'm literally the Keyflame.

Light bursts from the centre of the chanting circle too. Golden, like an echo of the orb inside me. It must be Kalin. The orbs spin faster, and faster still. Their colours blur together as they kick up a hot wind that batters my skin. *Foop-foop-foop*. I need to get through them, but they're going too fast.

Then Kalin screams again and I'm galvanised. I dive forward.

Everything goes white, like crossing the barrier around the cottage, except instead of stepping into one of the rooms, I step onto a beach.

The waves are frozen in the act of hitting the shore and the sunlight glints off them bright white, stinging my eyes. I lift a hand to block out the light, but it does nothing.

It's not the sun. It's a glowing orb. It's the Keyflame, hovering there across the water, large enough to obscure my view of the opposite shore.

It no longer pulses. It no longer ticks.

I've been here before. I'm standing inside my subconscious.

Am I dead? Did I just kill myself?

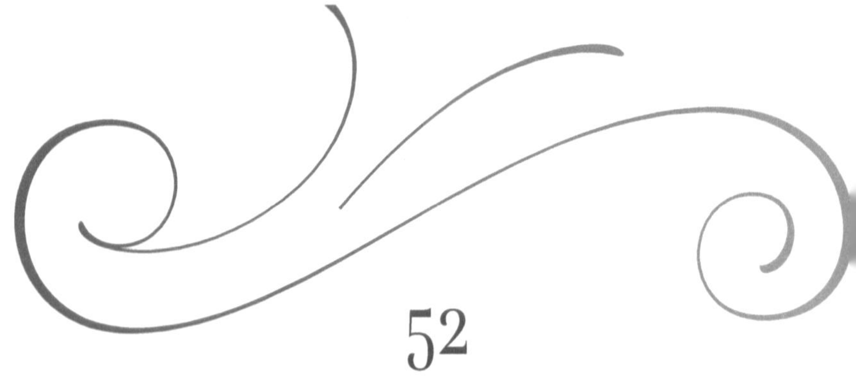

52

I look around. "Hello?"

"Hello," a musical female voice answers.

"Mom?" I ask hesitantly.

A figure appears before me. Not my mother. Alayna. She's every bit as beautiful as she was in my dreams, but now she wears the green velvet dress of a queen, and there's a majesty about her that was never there before.

"What is your judgment?" she asks.

Judgment? "I don't understand."

"It is your duty as the bearer." She holds out her palm and a bubble of magic forms. She's in the exact same pose as her statue. In the bubble, images play.

Alayna doubles over. Kalin's just cast the orb into her. Liam, the rebel with the beautiful eyes, is the first at her side. She feels fine. She doesn't understand. Kalin laughs...

Alayna is pregnant. She's staring out of a window at a snowy landscape. Liam strides into the room behind her.

"Did he speak?" she asks.

"Eventually."

She cringes but listens as her husband tells her of how the Keyflame will pass down through the generations, unless they stop it. Kalin's powers will return to him unless the Nuadha line dies.

"Was he well?" Alayna asks when Liam's done.

"He's a street rat, a drunk. Without his power, he is nothing..."

A baby lies on a velvet cushion. Powerful sorcerers gather around it. Alayna paces.

"What do you mean you can't remove it?" Liam demands.

"She is the Keyflame, Your Royal Highness. The only way to destroy it, would be to destroy her."

"And you all agree with this assessment, do you?" Liam buries his head in his hands. "We will need to find someone else. There must be someone who can help."

"It doesn't seem to be hurting the princess. You could leave it. Perhaps future generations will find a solution?"

"No," Liam says. "The further we grow from the Old World, the more our magic fades. We must do something now."

Alayna moves to the window. Spring has blanketed her kingdom with flowers. She knows what she must do...

A darkened room and the baby in her arms. Magic twisting through the air like silk. Old magic, half-forgotten magic. She cannot remove the Keyflame, but she can alter it...

Now Alayna looks at me and says, "They wished for me to kill him that night, the night we brought him to heel. Instead I cursed him with *life*. Kallen always had a goodness in him. It was my heart's hope that in his time without magic, he would find that goodness again. We need him. We know, even now, that our magic is fading with every generation born to this land. By your time, most of us will be without it. Kallen could do magnificent things for our people with his power, but the decision falls to you. He cannot be permitted to return to what he was, and if he needs to die this day, then so be it.

"I have trusted only a most treasured friend with what I have done here. Her children and her children's children will protect my line, despite those who wish us dead. And if I am talking to you, my descendant, we have succeeded. The time has come to pass judgment. The choice is yours."

The choice is yours. The words from the fever dream. That's what they meant? Sukwini's family protected the line, not so that we'd *kill* Kalin but so we could *save* him. Even in this wasteland inside my head, I'm giddy with realisation, with hope.

Alayna gave me the memories so that I would have the knowledge to decide. They were always there, lurking within me, presenting themselves in the form of sketches and maps, waiting for the day I met the Overlord. Kalin thought the dreams came from the necklace, but I think he was wrong.

"You're a better puppet master than I gave you credit for," I whisper.

She looks at me blankly. She's a memory too, tucked away somewhere inside me. There's no way to interact with her, even if I wish I could. She starts to fade.

"No, wait!" The sand fades too. I'm regaining consciousness. *Too soon.* "*How* do I pass judgment?"

I crash into the circle of Guardians and go down in a tangle of limbs. The chanting stops, but the orbs are still spinning, providing a curtain of light between us and our audience as I scramble to my feet. Kalin is before me, trapped in a cage of energy with his limbs splayed outward and his head flung back in a silent scream.

Shirley steps out of the circle and raises a hand as if she's going to cast at me. "Don't move!"

I can't fight her. She's too powerful. And even if I could, there's no way I could fight all of them.

"I am Lilah Nuadha," I say in a voice so small I can hardly hear it over my own heartbeat. They're the words that helped me before – maybe they can help now. I have nothing else. I roll my shoulders and repeat, louder this time, "I am Lilah Nuadha! I am the Keyflame, and I am here to pass judgment!"

I feel the colour rising to my face, because I'm aware of how ridiculous I sound. I'm a small nobody and she's a mighty general. My words are big, but they're all I have. I've seen a lot of pretty impossible things over the past months, but nothing quite so impossible that it gives me faith simply uttering my judgment will change anything.

Lines of bright gold spread along Kalin's cage, like fault lines. His transformation back to mortal must be nearing completion. I'm running out of time.

"Judgment?" Shirley's eyes pierce into me. "Judgment has been passed. The Overlord is to be no more."

I ball my hands into fists, squeezing so hard that my nails cut into my palms. "The choice is not yours to make! It is *my* birthright. I am the Keyflame, I am Alayna's heir."

She steps closer. "Heir? You weren't even meant to be born. You're a curse."

She waves a hand, and her magic sends me flying across the circle. I hit the ground so hard that the impact vibrates from my hip all the way up to my shoulders.

"You're wrong!" I shout.

Kalin howls. His cage splinters, and I'm still drawing breath to shout a desperate pardon when it shatters and Kalin tumbles to the ground in a heap. The orbs stop spinning and stay suspended in the air, like paper lanterns.

I was too late. I failed.

"Let this whole business be done with." Shirley strides towards Kalin. I try cast a shield over him, but she bounces the spell back with a shield of her own. "Bianca!"

My heart stutters. She doesn't know. Shirley doesn't know what happened to Darren.

She calls her daughter's name again, her voice clipped with annoyance. She's no doubt expecting the warrior to emerge from the gathered Guardians, sword in hand.

Instead, the response is a strangled cry. "Mom?" It almost doesn't sound like Bianca at all.

The first hint of uncertainty puckers Shirley's brow.

"Mom, help. Help, please."

The circle of Guardians disintegrates as some turn to see what's happened, as the ones closest to the grisly scene react.

Shirley remains perfectly still. "What trick is this?"

Kalin groans and this draws Shirley's ire. "What have you done?"

The Guardians part. Sibu comes forward, carrying Darren. Limp and lifeless, he looks smaller, younger. I flush cold.

Shirley staggers backwards, and the colour drains from her face. Sukwini rushes between her and Darren, holds a hand in front of his mouth, feels his pulse points.

Is he dead? I don't want to believe it, but he looks so very dead, and Sukwini offers no reassurance.

Shirley rounds on Kalin. "*You* did this!"

I don't even think he's conscious. He makes no move to defend himself as she throws a spell at him. But this time, she's too unfocused to stop my shield.

I manage to cast just in time to protect Kalin. "No, *you* did this! He was hurt protecting me. Protecting me from your fanaticism, your hate."

My words have the desired effect. She leaves Kalin and turns on me. I manage to shield myself from the first bolt of electricity, but the second catches me in the ribs, and my vision blanks as the pain sears my insides. I choke, struggling to suck in air.

Shirley isn't capable of reason now. She's a force of blind grief, and around us everything descends into chaos. The Fae below are shouting, the Guardians are a mess of confusion. I can't pay attention to any of it because Shirley is relentless. Her magic cracks against another shield, throwing me off balance. I let instinct take hold, and fall into a roll. Another bolt of electricity hits the place where I landed.

Then the ground disappears beneath me. I fling out a hand and manage to snatch the edge of the platform. My shoulder jerks painfully. There's nothing but air for at least fifty feet below my dangling legs. I try to pull myself up, but I'm not strong enough.

Shirley stands over me, panting, eyes wild. She raises her arms and, like when she fought Kalin, I *see* the power travelling across her skin. I am terror. Nothing I can cast will withstand that. My bowels turn to water. This is how I die. Once and for all.

She flings her spell and I recoil, but nothing hits me.

Someone cast a shield.

"Do we really need more bloodshed this day?" Sukwini appears above me, and she offers me a hand.

My heart and lungs come alive again. I reach for it.

"This is not the place for a pacifist," Shirley says and her magic snaps out at me again.

It cracks into my skin and it *burns*. Agony sears up my arm. A scream rips from my throat as my body spasms against the pain. My fingers fail to keep their grip. I'm falling, grabbing at air.

Then something snags me.

Magic.

Kalin?

I'm lifted back to the platform. Sukwini hauls me up and hugs me to her.

Bianca is behind her mother. Her hands and sleeves are red and she lowers them. It was *her* magic. The magic she used to smash Kalin's workspace, to hit him with books, to throw knives at him, is the magic that levitated *me*.

"What are you doing?" Shirley demands of her. Bianca doesn't answer. She stares straight ahead, at nothing.

Sukwini holds me tightly. "What are *you* doing? This is an eighteen-year-old girl."

"A girl who should not exist! Move aside, Sukwini."

"I will not."

Shirley bellows her rage and sends a wave of magic at us that's so large, so hot, that it scalds my skin before it even hits. But it doesn't hit. Sukwini waves it away like Bianca waved aside my measly spell in the cell.

Being thwarted stokes Shirley's anger even more. She yells and rushes at us. Sukwini pivots and throws me aside. Shirley slams into her and they both nearly topple over the edge.

In books, magic battles are always described as beautiful things full of colour and light, but there is nothing pretty about this. It's a brawl. Shirley presses a hand to Sukwini's face and red welts rise. Sukwini cries out in pain. Then Shirley is flung back by a blast of air and Sukwini sends a punch of magic at her stomach, yelling at her to calm down.

I cradle my burnt hand to my chest and shimmy backwards, away from the fighting. Everyone is distracted. I can help Kalin. I climb to my knees, turn towards him.

He's gone.

Has someone taken him? Hurt him? Has he managed to escape? I can't see through the press of bodies, and my already racing heart kicks into full panic, like hummingbird wings in my chest.

Sukwini cries out something in Xhosa and Shirley rises into the air. Sukwini holds her there with one hand, but her shoulders are heaving with the effort.

With Kalin's power it was easy. With Kalin's power, I did it without even knowing.

Where is he?

"Traitor!" Shirley calls. "And on this day of all days. On this day when we're to fulfil our purpose. Now you show your true nature! Viper!"

"It is not my purpose to kill children."

I'm not a child, but I'm not going to protest the point. Then I realise the word choice was deliberate. She's talking about Darren.

"Lilah did not kill your son," Sukwini says. And it may as well have been a curse for how it strikes Bianca. She crumples inwards.

Shirley struggles against Sukwini's magic. Bianca makes no move to help her and neither do the other Guardians.

"I will not let you harm Lilah." Sukwini has to hold Shirley with two arms now. "I protected her eighteen years ago. I protected her four months ago. I will protect her now."

A murmur travels through the Guardians, but it doesn't seem to be in reaction to her words. It spreads towards us from the other side of the stone circle and heads turn away from Shirley and Sukwini. I catch the word, "Overlord", and scramble to my feet, but I can't see anything.

What has he done? What's happened to him?

Even Sukwini looks to the source of the disturbance.

I push through the crowd, heedless of the danger.

"Where am I?" someone asks.

That was Darren's voice, I'm almost sure of it. I wedge myself between two Guardians, realising belatedly that one of them is Sibu. He doesn't seem to notice me. He's staring at the strange tableaux on the ground. Kalin's got Darren's head in his lap. Darren is looking up at him with his brow furrowed. Kalin's still pale, slouched and breathing heavily. His hands are on Darren's chest and they're glowing.

Kalin performed a miracle.

Everyone here wanted him dead, and he just came on over to the injured guy and healed him. I don't know if he senses me, but something makes him raise his head. His tired eyes meet mine, but only briefly, just long enough for me to see that they're bloodshot and lined with exhaustion. Then Bianca pushes through the crowd. She comes up short when she sees Darren.

"What's going on?" he asks her.

Her hands fly to her mouth and she lets out a sob.

Kalin passes her the sword.

They share a look. I ready a shield. I will not let her stab him again. But Bianca drops the sword and her head.

I step forward, into the small open space around Darren, and I turn to face the crowd. I am acutely aware of every eye focusing on me, but there's no time for doubt. I can't afford to be timid Lilah. There are no masks now.

I dig deep into Alayna's memories to find the language that the Fae will understand, and I speak in their language, hoping that my words will travel the way Shirley's did.

"We are here today to determine the fate of the Overlord. Alayna Nuadha knew this day would come. She ensured that her descendant would carry the Keyflame. She entrusted that descendant with the power to decide his fate. That descendant is me."

The Guardians don't move to stop me. Well, that's something.

I raise my voice and manage to keep it steady, even though I'm trembling. "You were told that today you would witness the Overlord die. You have arrived a century too late. The Overlord died a slow death over the years he suffered in my realm. He is no more. This man's name is Kalin, and he is no longer the same person. If what you have seen here has not convinced you, then know this. He has had the Overlord's full ability for over three months, and during that time he has hurt no one."

That draws a reaction. I guess Shirley never made it common knowledge. I have to wait until the hubbub dies down before I can continue speaking. And while I wait, while I pause and absorb the impact of my own words, I realise something, and a shiver races through me.

The choice is yours.

Did you do this? he asked. I denied it. I was wrong.

I *did* give him that power. It *was* me. A memory comes to me, clear and bright. His arms around me, his lips on mine, a swell of emotion, of absolute trust. Knowing, for certain, that he is not evil and wanting, more than anything, for him to live, and praying to anyone who would listen to *let him live.*

Something listened. The Keyflame listened.

I passed him back his power.

It was my judgment. It has already been made.

And knowing that, I know exactly what I need to do.

I hold out my hand and will the Keyflame to appear there, because I understand now. That's what Alayna altered. She gave the bearer the ability to control the Keyflame. I'm not a vessel, I'm not a key. I'm the one in charge.

Before everyone, the golden orb that was somehow a part of me manifests in my palm. In my dirty white dress, with my mess of dark hair, I'm a mirror image of the statue. "Kalin will atone, not through his death, but through helping you," I continue, in this strange and powerful language. "Alayna wanted his power to be a beacon, to reignite the magic of your kind – *our* kind. He is here now, not as a cruel dictator, but as a teacher and as a servant to the Fae. The Overlord is dead, but Kalin will live!"

The Keyflame rises into the air with the other orbs. They glow brighter and brighter. I try to watch them, but the light becomes too much, and I have to close my eyes. When I open them again, the orbs are gone. I'm still blinking away their afterimage when I feel Shirley's aura approach.

I turn towards her and hold out my hands to cast if necessary. She walks straight past me to Darren, sinks to her knees beside him and gathers him into her arms. Sukwini emerges from the crowd behind her. She and Kalin share one of their intense unspoken exchanges.

He rises slowly. Is she going to attack him? Would he even defend himself?

"Nabelo, I'm going to take Lilah home. Will you stand in my way?" He speaks quietly, but the Guardians probably hear him all the same. There's no other sound.

"You heard the promise she made," Sukwini says.

"I did."

"The prince will want to see you."

"It's a prince now, is it? Last I heard there was a king."

"What's going on?" I interrupt them. Even the Fae crowd below is silent and when I look, I find them *kneeling*. Why?

Kalin's hand slips into mine. "I told you your bloodline was special."

"They're bowing to *me*?"

"Yes, Lilah Nuadha, they're bowing to you." He smiles at me. "How does it feel to be a celebrity?"

It feels *bizarre* and I'm not sure I like it. I'm starting to understand that as much knowledge as I gained from Alayna's memories, it wasn't even nearly enough to fully understand what I've fallen into.

"Can we leave?" I ask Kalin.

He nods and waves a hand. The mist rises, blotting out Sukwini, Shirley, Bianca, Darren and all the others.

Epilogue

Fatso greets us at the cottage door, much as he did the first time we arrived here together. He meows at Kalin, then runs to me and twists between my legs.

"Seems I've been ousted as the favourite," Kalin comments.

I scoop Fatso up and bury my face in his fur. "You're lucky he's still speaking to you at all."

The kitchen is warm and streaked with sunlight. It smells like home. I set Fatso down on the counter and go fetch him some milk. Which is perfectly fresh thanks to Kalin's pocket universe spell.

"What did Sukwini mean about the prince?"

"A problem for another day."

"Kalin…"

He leans against the counter with his hands in his pockets. "You promised I'd help the Fae."

His sentencing. "I… it's what Alayna wanted. She hid memories in the Keyflame. She spoke to me. She told me their magic is dying, and she wanted you to live so you could help."

His eyebrows shoot up. I've seldom seen Kalin genuinely surprised and the effect is almost comical.

"Seems she never lost that 'naïve' faith in you after all."

He doesn't return my smile and his brow creases.

"Did I make a mistake? Was that a bad decision?" What have I condemned him to?

He shakes his head. "No, it was fitting. And you know I am willing to help, to atone, in any way I can. I only wonder at what our future might hold. I will need to travel there to be of use and I doubt they'll let their rediscovered Nuadha disappear into obscurity."

"You're saying we're both going to have to move to fairyland?"

He comes a little closer and reaches to tuck a lock of hair behind my ear. "Possibly. Eventually."

There's a lot I need to do first. I need to find Dad. I need to let the world know I'm still alive. I need to pass first year.

Kalin leans close and whispers, "However, I could lock this cottage outside of the normal flow of time a while."

I grin. "You'd better let Fatso out first."

"He'd miss us too much."

Kalin kisses me. I want a hot shower, and twenty hours of sleep in a warm bed. I want food that doesn't come out of a brown paper packet. But most of all, I want this. Kalin, alive. The two of us alone in the cottage with our cat who isn't really our cat but definitely is.

Fatso bumps against my elbow and I give him a scratch behind his ear.

"That sounds perfect," I say. And it really, truly, does.

Thank you for reading Keyflame.

For more Keyflame content and to be alerted of future books by the author, you can subscribe to her newsletter at tallulahlucy.com/newsletter.

ACKNOWLEDGEMENTS

I was lucky to work with the most amazing team imaginable for this book. My editor, Nerine Dorman, is also the founder of the authors' co-op, Skolion, that made this book possible. Nerine's wisdom and advice has helped shape the writer I am today. Masha du Toit, who was one of my most valued beta readers, had endless patience for me when I popped into her inbox to ask her about both the book and its design. Yolandie Horak, my copy editor, is superwoman (don't tell her I revealed her secret identity). She edited the whole novel in under two weeks. She's also been my constant cheerleader throughout this project. My proofreader, Laurie Janey's, eye for detail is unparalleled and her understanding of story enabled her to go above and beyond with polishing up this book. Special thanks also to Abigail Holden, who donated her valuable time to doing final checks.

I had a wonderful beta team who read the chapters as I revised them. Thank you to Cathrine Rose, Niki Cilliers, Shantell Lucas for giving thoughtful feedback on every chapter and to Jenny Rainville, Monika Dresen and Stacey Riek for all of your input. Additional thanks to Crystal Warren and Jessica Aberdein for assisting with research. Lastly thank you to Mom and Dad for always encouraging me, to my sister Jodi for being my first reader, to the friends who helped with the very first draft (Natalie Morley, Ashley-Kate Davidson) and most of all to my husband, Graham van der Made, for giving me the space, time and endless encouragement to finally get this novel out into the world.

ABOUT THE AUTHOR

Tallulah studied journalism at Rhodes University in Grahamstown and has recurring dreams of returning to that strange and magical place.

While working as a technology journalist in Johannesburg, she met a man at a gaming convention and followed him home to Cape Town, where they now live in a small apartment that's completely overrun with books.

If Tallulah ever retired from her career as a social media manager, she would spend her days going to art classes and taking online courses in rare and specific skills so she could bore more people at parties.

Twitter: www.twitter.com/tallulahlucy
Facebook: www.facebook.com/tallulahlucy
Instagram: www.instagram.com/tallulahlucy

GLOSSARY
OF SOUTH AFRICAN TERMS

Ag nee man – Oh no (said in pity)

Alles – All

Babalas – Hangover

Boerewors – Literally translates to "farmer's sausage" in Afrikaans. Made from minced beef, pork and spices.

Braai – An open flame barbecue.

Broer – Brother

Ek – I/me

Ja – Yeah

Jou bliksem – You bastard

Komaan – Come on

Kots – Puke

Kyk – Look

Moenie worry nie – Don't worry

Nê – Hey? / Don't you think?

Potjie – Literally translates to "little pot" in Afrikaans. A round, cast iron, three-legged pot used for cooking stew outdoors.

Rooibos – A local type of tea. Translates to "red bush".

Shebeen – Township pub, originally run as an alternative to bars that people of colour were banned from during Apartheid.